BELOW

BELOW

RYAN LOCKWOOD

PINNACLE BOOKS
Kensington Publishing Corp.
www.kensingtonbooks.com

PINNACLE BOOKS are published by

Kensington Publishing Corp.
119 West 40th Street
New York, NY 10018

All Kensington titles, imprints, and distributed lines are available at special quantity discounts for bulk purchases for sales promotions, premiums, fund-raising, educational, or institutional use.
Special book excerpts or customized printings can also be created to fit specific needs. For details, write or phone the office of the Kensington special sales manager: Kensington Publishing Corp., 119 West 40th Street, New York, NY 10018, attn: Special Sales Department; phone 1-800-221-2647.

ISBN-13: 978-0-7860-3287-7
ISBN-10: 0-7860-3287-1

First printing: July 2013

10 9 8 7 6 5 4

Printed in the United States of America

First electronic edition: July 2013

ISBN-13: 978-0-7860-3288-4
ISBN-10: 0-7860-3288-X

For April, who always believed in my potential.
Thanks for making me buy that book in Seattle.

PART I
IMMIGRATION

CHAPTER 1

The water was deep.

Miguel couldn't see the ocean around him in the moonless night. But he knew it was very deep underneath the boat. The lights of shore had vanished behind them many hours ago.

The long, narrow *panga* rode over the dark swells faster than a man could sprint. Seeing anything in the water would be impossible, even in the daylight. Yet Miguel again peered over the side of the boat. He was certain that beneath the frothy chop dancing on the dark surface were thousands of feet of nothingness.

He turned away to avoid the cold spray that rhythmically slapped the hull and slid back down out of the wind. Huddled against his brother in the bottom of the weathered *panga,* he tried to make out the faces of the fifteen or so other men in the darkness. All were older than him. He could only see their silhouettes, crammed together and rocking with the swells as the boat rose and fell. Like him, these men headed to an uncertain future wearing cheap T-shirts, Windbreakers, faded jeans. Like him, they carried all their money inside plastic bags zipped into pockets or stuffed into small daypacks containing the few other prized possessions they owned. Almost everyone wore a crucifix around his neck.

Each of them also carried one other item: a small, waterproof flashlight. Miguel felt in his pocket to make sure his was still there.

A man jumped up and hurried past Miguel, kicking his bent legs as he passed before vomiting over the stern. Miguel looked away and tried unsuccessfully to make out the expressions of the other passengers on the far side of the crowded boat. He hoped they couldn't see his face, either—the young, smooth face of a frightened boy. He wondered if these men were like the dark water around them, if even in the daylight he would be unable to see what was going on beneath their expressions. Miguel was grateful for the darkness. He was scared, and knew his own eyes would show it.

His older brother leaned against him, wrapping a strong arm around his shoulders. It was cold being on the water, especially with the constant headwind as the boat pushed northward. But Miguel knew his brother wasn't trying to warm him. Elías simply wanted to comfort his teenage brother, even though he must be worried, too. That was how Elías was. He was a good older brother.

Miguel wasn't sure how they had paid the coyote who now stood at the helm. They had almost run out of money since leaving Honduras a week ago. Then this morning they had met the young, skinny smuggler in the crowded streets of Ensenada.

The coyote's gaunt face suddenly appeared in the darkness above Miguel, discernible in the faint light cast by a cell phone. He looked anxious as he briefly toyed with the phone; then his face disappeared in the darkness. Miguel remembered that the man was wearing a black cap with an American football logo. He wanted to turn on his flashlight so he could see better, but this coyote had warned them all to leave their lights off. He had assured the brothers he had done this before many times, that they needed to relax. Miguel didn't trust him.

The loud drone of the engine dropped off as the coyote eased down on the accelerator, causing the bow to dip as the boat slowed rapidly. A minute later, the sound dropped again, to an idle, and the boat leveled off as its own wake caught up to it and nudged it forward. The *coyote* cut the engine, and suddenly it was as quiet as it was dark. All Miguel could hear now were the small waves smacking against the metal hull of the boat.

He grabbed the curved side and rose, looking out over the night water. There was only darkness. *No, wait.* There was one small, distant light on the water. Off the bow, he noticed what appeared to be another boat. Was it the one they were looking for? He watched it, wondering if it was headed in their direction yet. He looked at the driver and saw that he, too, was aware of the boat.

The distant light went black, then reappeared again. It blinked on and off repeatedly in a one-two-three pattern, then disappeared. Miguel realized it was probably some sort of signal. The other boat must have been sending it blindly for some time, since the unlit *panga* Miguel rode in had to be invisible. The coyote reached under the helm and retrieved a small spotlight, which he directed at the other boat. He turned the beam on and off several times. Then, stowing the light, he turned away from the helm in the darkness and spoke in an urgent, hushed voice to the men in the boat.

"*Oye. Este es el lugar.*" A few men stood, but most just looked at the coyote. Miguel knew then he was not the only one who was afraid. It was one of the older men who spoke first.

"*Señor,* are you sure we will be okay? We are far from shore. How do we know the other boat will find us?"

"Your lights, *viejo*. Remember to leave them off until the boat is almost to you, though."

The old man nodded, but looked uncertain as the coyote continued.

"You will probably feel cold after being in the water for a while. Don't worry. The other boat will be here quickly, before you become numb. The water is very warm tonight. You can all swim, *verdad*?"

Everybody was silent. Miguel realized he was nodding in the darkness.

"*Bueno.* It will be less than a half hour before you are picked up. Pay the other man the rest that you owe. And remember, everyone must hold on to the others. The currents can separate you if you let go of each other. Nobody will come looking for you if you leave the group."

It was time, but nobody moved to leave the safety of the boat. Miguel glanced at his brother, who now looked worried.

"Okay. *Vámonos!* In the water, now. Everyone, into the water!"

CHAPTER 2

Hunger drove them.

Despite their considerable size, they glided in close unison through the deep, unlit water. As a school of small fish or flock of blackbirds moves together, they behaved not as a collection of individuals, but as one large organism. A shoal.

There were more than a thousand of them.

Their collective movements were always executed with grace and fluidity. Their actions were quick but unhurried, their forms powerful, but not bulky. Millions of years of evolution had perfected their form and honed their function. The effortless beauty of their movements concealed their primary purpose, their reason for being.

They were predators.

Beneath their smooth exteriors were hidden the sharp, dangerous tools of the hunter. Tools that seized, tore, maimed, and killed.

The open water around them had remained seemingly the same as they moved in darkness with the cool currents. They were accustomed to this cold, dark, featureless world. To endless expanses of open ocean. Yet these were unfamiliar waters.

The shoal had been migrating for weeks now, always in the same general direction. It was not the first shoal to make this migration, but few had gone before it, and none of this size. The shoal was not aware that others like it had ventured to these waters before, would continue to come this way after they were gone. Its members merely followed the impulses that guided them.

Their world was perpetually dark. Would always be dark.

They cooperated perfectly, operated in coordinated unity. More efficient than any army, they relied upon instinct instead of training to guide their graceful movements and deadly actions. Yet they shared no camaraderie, no loyalty. They were indifferent to one another, with no feelings or concern for the others that moved with them. They needed each other, and simply used each other for survival.

They needed each other now. For days, they had continued in the same direction, encountering no resistance but finding less and less sustenance. The prey they were accustomed to eating had dwindled in these waters, and their hunger had grown.

Following their daily rhythm, they had risen hours ago. The ocean had yielded little to slake their ceaseless hunger.

Now they desperately needed to feed.

CHAPTER 3

The boat was gone. The group waited helplessly on the dark ocean, bobbing on the surface in the dim starlight.

Miguel noticed that several of the men had already turned on their flashlights underwater. Feet and legs, treading the water slowly, were faintly visible now. A few of the men, most of whom weren't much older than his brother, were murmuring to one another. The rest were silent.

The ocean had felt very cold at first when it flooded through Miguel's clothing as he had entered the water. Even in July, the waters off Southern California were cool. By the time the last person had entered the water, and the coyote had started up the *panga* and sped off to the south, the water felt warmer against his skin. The boat had vanished quickly into the darkness, its drone fading into the lapping sounds of the ocean.

Staying afloat was fairly easy, since the ocean was so saline and Miguel was comfortable in the water. But he was scared of the dark, the cold, the uncertainty. He knew the water would soon feel much colder, if the other boat didn't arrive on time. And something else had been bothering him since they had plunged from the boat into the dark ocean.

"*Mano*, what happens next?" Miguel looked at his brother. "Who is picking us up? Where are we going?"

"*Está bien, manito.* Soon we will be safe in America. Everything will be okay." Elías reached over and squeezed his arm, white teeth flashing in the faint light. But the smile disappeared, and his brother looked away.

Miguel floated next to Elías, each grasping the other's shoulders. He looked around and realized that none of the other men were holding on to one another as they had been instructed to do. Self-conscious, he let go of his brother and treaded water several feet away from him. It was a calm sea. There was no need to hold on to anyone.

He looked down into the water at the flashlight in his hand. Why should he leave his light off? Besides, nobody would be able to see it underwater. He turned it on and directed it downward. In the bright beam, he could see his legs and feet clearly, but the dark ocean was hungry for the light and quickly absorbed it.

"Turn it off, *manito*. You don't want to get caught, do you? Besides, you're wasting the batteries."

"In a minute." Miguel knew his brother was right, but he was anxious.

Below the beam of the flashlight, in the depths beneath him, he saw nothing but immeasurable blackness. He looked at the undersides of the other men's faces, illuminated eerily by the artificial light refracted through the waves. His gaze returned to his own feet again, and the blackness below them. He watched thousands of minute particles, white in the bright light, floating around his legs above the black, bottomless void.

He wondered what was down there.

The shoal abruptly slowed, in unison. There had been a new stimulus.

Light.

Not the familiar, expansive light from above, but small, moving lights. Possibly the lights of prey. Many large, black eyes near the front of the shoal sensed this. The lights had disappeared, but the stimulated individuals propelled themselves more rapidly upward, toward where the lights had been, followed closely by the rest of the immense gathering.

The shoal ascended quickly. It slowed after a short time, its members sensing that they were now close to where the lights had been. Above them, a single light reappeared. They were very close now.

They approached from below. The enormous mass of predators moved silently, invisibly through the ink-black water, slowly observing the light above. They rose and banked slowly around the light, assessing. There was movement in the light. The eyes in the shoal detected large objects in the weak illumination. Unfamiliar objects. This was not the small prey that glowed, and it was too close to the surface. Yet it was similar; it was living.

It might be prey.

As the light went out, the shoal began to change color, unnoticed even by its own members' powerful eyes in the darkness. Several of them began emitting

faint pulses of light from their bodies. Rapidly the
shoal communicated. Many fins fluttered in the dark.
The enormous mass of the shoal changed shape. For-
merly packed into a huge ball, its members now slowly
spread to form a massive circle around the extinguished
light.

　　And moved toward it.

CHAPTER 4

Travis Roche was thinking about the money.

He was floating far offshore in *Sea Plus*, his father's thirty-five-foot fishing boat. He sat in the stern, alone in the dark, and sipped a bottle of Mexican beer as the salty breeze played through his unwashed sandy-blond hair.

Tonight's gig sure paid well, and was less risky than when he had smuggled weed. Another midnight run to deliver a batch of wetbacks into SoCal. Last time, the grateful immigrants had paid him without protest, then hustled away in pairs once they had gotten to the dock, just like he had asked them to. Easy money.

That was it—all he had to do. When he reached the marina, his work ended. Hector had said the money would be even better this time, since there were supposed to be like fifteen guys. Travis didn't care. There was plenty of room in the boat.

And what did it matter anyway? So many immigrants were crossing the border nowadays that a few more wouldn't make much of a difference. But helping these ones would sure as hell pay for a sweet month in Baja this fall. Great surf and no crowds.

This far off the coast, Southern California was a different place. Slower, quieter, more relaxed. Travis sipped his beer and sent a stream through the gap in his front teeth, over the side of the boat. It was too humid to make out anything in the distance—even the lights of shore. He was thinking about how long he could surf in Baja with this cash when his cell phone began to chime on the dash.

Hector.

Travis stood, walked barefoot over to check the new text message on the display. He touched a button and read the new message on the backlit screen:

15. 11S 466580 3612210.

The number of immigrants, and the UTM coordinates. A few minutes later, after he entered the GPS numbers into the boat's Garmin, he flashed his spotlight to the south. Moments later, he noticed a distant light on the ocean, responding from some distance. He watched the light as it flashed four times again in rapid succession. It was definitely Hector.

He was about to make the drop, at the north Coronados location, just as they had planned on Travis's last trip to Baja. This sort of open-ocean transfer, far from the coast and requiring immigrants to actually enter the water, was a pain in the ass. But they had to smuggle the immigrants this way so the Border Patrol wouldn't ever be able to use its new toy—an unmanned Predator drone with cameras and infrared sensors. The drone could detect the meeting of two vessels offshore, close to the Mexican border, and a bunch of warm bodies moving from one boat to the other. It couldn't detect body heat radiating through cold seawater, though, and this way would never record two vessels coming together.

With international terrorism a serious concern, the government was intensifying its security at the Mexican border, and offshore smuggling in particular. Illegal aliens were as desperate as ever to cross the border, and they were trying all kinds of methods to enter the States—tunneling into San Diego to emerge under old houses, navigating the desert on foot, stowing away in semi-trailer loads. And some tried to take boats to California. All the unimaginative boat runners moving immigrants into Southern California were getting nailed.

Not Travis and Hector. This would be their second successful operation. And as long as they didn't attempt it too often, Travis figured he had found a way to pay for some mad surf trips to Central America. Maybe even Hawaii. Besides, Travis liked Mexicans. They just wanted a better life and all, right?

Travis drained the rest of the beer and tossed the bottle overboard as he moved toward the helm. He didn't have time to screw around once the drop had been made, and knew he had to hurry. Even summer waters got cold if you spent too long out there, and currents could move a floating group far and fast. If he hurried, Travis could simply cruise over to the coordinates using the GPS and the previous visual cue from Hector. He would slow when he neared and look for flashlights, which Hector would have given to the men in the water. That was it. Piece of cake.

The operation was really quite simple, as long as the

weather was good. They would have called it off otherwise.

Travis found the ignition and turned the key.

The boat didn't start.

"Shit!" He turned the key again, but there was no response from the motor.

"Calm down, bro. You can figure this out." Travis talked himself through the problem. He knew it wasn't the battery, because the lights worked and he didn't hear a clicking sound when he turned the key. Maybe the engine wouldn't start if the prop was raised. He wasn't sure, because he wasn't much of a mechanic. He checked the prop, but it was down in the water. Swearing again, he walked back to the helm.

After several minutes, Travis laughed when he saw the problem. He had shut the boat off while still in gear, and left the throttle out of position. He popped the throttle back into neutral and turned the key. Relief washed through him when the motor immediately rumbled to life.

He would have to hurry now. That had cost him precious minutes. He eased the Boston Whaler forward until it pointed south, then gunned it. As the boat cut through the dark swells at more than twenty knots, rapidly closing the distance to his destination, Travis felt better. It was only two miles or so. Probably would take only five minutes or something. Travis liked the rush he got from doing this, the chance he could get caught. Kind of like riding a mondo wave.

Besides, he had to pay for his surfing somehow.

CHAPTER 5

It was very still. The swells, small and gentle, made faint lapping sounds as they found the exposed shoulders of the men around Miguel. The water smelled of salt. He normally liked that smell, when he got to see the ocean. Now it only seemed foreign. He looked up at the stars. They were bright, but cold and distant. He shivered.

They had been floating in the darkness for what seemed a long time. The *panga* must have left them ten minutes ago. Or maybe twenty. He was sure the other boat should have already come. Was it coming at all?

Everyone in the group had grown quiet. A few men floating together nearby were saying something about the boat not coming, discussing what to do if it didn't show soon. Miguel looked around, in every direction. He couldn't see the lights of shore.

He looked down into the water again, wondering how far away the bottom was. His brother would be mad if he kept turning on the flashlight, but not being able to see anything was making him scared.

Miguel suddenly remembered his wristwatch, which

his uncle had brought to him as a gift when he had visited from America. He pressed the button on its side and the face lit up, a bright green circle. It cast very little light in the water around him, but he could at least read the hands. He would watch the time, which would give him something to do. The light went out after several seconds, and he counted to thirty.

He lit up his watch again. Only twenty-two seconds had actually passed. In the greenish underwater glow, he could see small particles, green in the chemical light, floating around his jeans-clad legs and pale feet. Below that, nothing but blackness.

Just as the watch light went out, he thought he noticed something far below him.

Another faint light. No, not a light—a glow. A momentary, greenish glow, kind of like his watch, but coming from below him. Miguel's heart jumped, and he felt a surge of adrenaline course through his body, accelerating his heartbeat. Had somebody dropped his flashlight? He became transfixed on the deep water, staring down past his feet to try and see the glow. He turned on his flashlight and shined it downward for a minute, then switched it off and stared down into the dark again as his eyes adjusted. A minute passed.

There, again!

He was sure he saw it this time—a widespread, pale glow, faint but distinct. Down below him. Below all of them.

The other men began to whisper. Maybe they had seen it, too. Much of the water below and to his left had glowed faintly, but not all at once. The glow had rippled through the deep water, like firecrackers going off.

"*Mano*, did you see that? The light below us. *Qué es?*"

Miguel looked toward his brother, and realized he had drifted away from him in the past few minutes. Miguel was maybe twenty feet from the others now. He shouted at Elías again, and then raised his hand out of the water, pointing down with his flashlight so his brother could see. But the larger glow, coming from underneath them, was gone again.

"Turn off your fucking light, *manito*! Seriously. You want to get caught?"

"But did you see it?"

"I saw nothing. Only your fucking flashlight. Don't worry. The boat will be here soon and we will be safe. *Oye!* You are too far away. Swim back to me."

"But *mano*, there were lights under the water!"

His brother didn't respond. Miguel looked down again, but only saw blackness. He strained to see the glow again. The brief pulse of glowing, greenish light had rippled widely, but had come from many different sources. It reminded him of a gathering of fireflies he had once seen when visiting his cousins in Mexico, but instead of yellow winking lights, these were pale, greenish glows.

Miguel's heart pounded. He would use his watch to see. It was much dimmer. He turned his watch light on and directed the face underneath him, back and forth, trying to see something in the soft light it cast. But it was far too weak, and he saw nothing except for his slowly moving feet.

* * *

They were close now.

The lights had reappeared momentarily, inviting the attention of the gathered host. The shoal began to circle where the lights had been. Spiraling closer, shallower.

The sensitive eyes in the shoal no longer needed the lights to see the shapes that had emitted them. They could now clearly see the larger objects revealed in the dim starlight from above the ocean. The objects moved slowly, drifting, but the shoal sensed that they were living. Unfamiliar, but nonthreatening. Ripples of color moved through the shoal, as messages were sent. The mob swirled slowly closer, now very near the floating objects. It slowed, hung motionless in the ocean, each member emitting gentle pulses of water.

Another faint glow rippled through several members of the shoal. One of the largest individuals, a female with only one eye, was drawn to a specific floating object. A small glowing light flashed on this object.

The light of prey.

The large female watched as the glowing light moved rapidly; first it shot upward, disappeared, then reappeared again, darting side to side. Moving evasively, like prey. This excited her, and the shoal around her sensed her excitement.

And her aggression.

The shoal rippled with expectation, as though a shock wave had coursed through it. Slowly, the massive assemblage changed shape as aggressive, excited members surged toward the source of the light, forming a large finger protruding from the group. At the tip of the finger, the one-eyed female emitted several more rapid bursts of light. The eager members stretched out from the main body.

The small green light winked on, very close now. The large female moved toward the light that had drawn her focus. The moving light.

Tentatively, she touched it.

Something brushed Miguel's wrist.

He quickly pulled his arm back, against his ribs, and watched in horror as some *thing* withdrew in the light of his watch. The light went out again.

Instantly Miguel was alert, his heart drumming in his chest. The thing that had touched him had been smooth, but firm. It had touched him gently, the way his grandmother rubbed his head. But it had not been human.

In the green wristwatch light, the thing had looked like some gigantic outstretched hand. A grotesque hand with impossibly huge, thick fingers wriggling away from the glowing watch face. Miguel began to breathe even faster as his adrenaline surged, and his heart pounded blood through his ears. He turned on his flashlight and swung it around beneath him, but saw nothing.

"Something touched me, *mano*!" He wanted to shout but could only muster a loud whisper. "It touched my skin."

His brother looked at him in alarm. "What touched you, *manito*?"

"There!" Miguel shouted, drawing everyone's attention.

"*Tiburón*!" The men began shouting at one man's mention of a shark.

Something moved again at the edge of the flashlight beam, but it dodged the direct shaft of light so he couldn't get a good look. It wasn't a shark. No, not a shark or any other fish, even though Miguel thought he saw a fin.

It was big, like the sharks he'd seen dead on the beach, but it moved in an unfamiliar way. No, not it. *They.* As he redirected his flashlight, he saw more than one large shape moving at the outer limit cast by the artificial light. The shapes advanced, withdrew again. For several long moments, he stared down, not wanting to see anything, but even more afraid now that he couldn't see anything in the beam.

The flashlight went out.

Miguel shook it, but it remained off. He pressed the button on the side of his watch and directed it toward his legs again. Nothing.

Just before the watch light went off, something darted toward him.

Pain shot up his arm as the thing gripped his wrist and released it, and he knew he was bleeding.

And then panic seized him.

She gripped the object and tugged, tiny teeth cutting into soft flesh as she squeezed and pulled. Then, abruptly, she released the object, assessing. Fat. Blood. Flesh. This was food.

The painfully brighter light that had appeared on the object moments ago had frightened her away briefly, but had now attracted the focused attention of many more in the shoal. Now the light had gone out, replaced again by the light of prey.

As the hungry one-eyed female eagerly moved to grip the fleshy body again, the others in the shoal sensed her excitement, were stirred by the thrashing prey, the blood now entering the water.

She advanced with the shoal and lashed out again, seizing the object, pulling it down. Two others quickly joined her, grasping and hooking the object, overwhelming it. With powerful thrusts, the hungry mass of writhing beasts began to pull the prey downward in the darkness.

For a split second, Miguel saw a large, pale shape glowing in the darkened water below him as he turned to swim away. As he kicked frantically toward his brother, the thing seized his foot.

This time, it did not let go.

He realized he was being dragged under when his screams were drowned by the water flooding his mouth. As his head went beneath the surface, he felt a powerful grasping on his legs, his arms. Grasping everywhere. Something sharp cut through his clothing and into his skin. He struggled to free himself, but had the terrible realization that he was being overwhelmed.

Miguel looked up in desperation and watched as several lights turned on above him. He was being pulled deeper. The lights rapidly dimmed as, impossibly fast, he was dragged down. More shapes rocketed toward him, clung to him, dug into him, covering his body. His ears protested loudly, painfully, as his eardrums ruptured suddenly in the mounting water pressure. The tiny flashlights had vanished far above him. Despite his pain and confusion, all he could think about was swimming up for air.

He was aware of something large and meaty wrapping around the side of his face, biting deeply into his neck.

Eating him.

A greenish light flashed near his face, and in the brief glow he saw a large, lidless eye. Then the thing on his face wrapped cold flesh around his head, enveloping it, mercifully covering his eyes.

He was still descending when everything went black.

CHAPTER 6

The small pop-up window on the marine GPS appeared with a beep, displaying a familiar message: *Arriving at destination*. Travis eased back on the throttle to slow the sleek inboard and scanned the water. The sea was fairly calm, so he shouldn't have trouble finding the group. He didn't want to run over any of them accidentally, so he slowed to a few knots and watched the waves ahead for lights on the water.

Ahead, he saw one light appear, maybe a hundred and fifty yards off the bow. But that was it. Maybe one guy was signaling for the whole group. Then he saw another light, farther away, way off to his right. *Too* far to his right. Something was wrong here. He waited to see other lights appear, but only a few more appeared between the first two lights, and none of them were directed at him. They seemed to be pointed in all directions.

Travis noticed another light now, much closer and directly in front of him. He eased the Whaler toward the light, steering so that he would pass just to the right of the person in the water. As he neared it, Travis stepped over to the port side for a better look. He realized the light wasn't held above the water, as it should be. It was bobbing on the surface.

Something was definitely wrong.

The boat drifted past the floating light, just missing it, when something else bumped gently against the hull. Travis looked toward the bow and, for a moment, he saw what appeared to be a person floating in the dark water next to the boat, being pulled beneath it as it drifted past.

Someone was going under the boat.

Travis dashed back to the driver's seat and yanked the throttle into neutral. He leapt to the stern, grabbing a life preserver, looking for the person to pop up. There. He saw the man again. He was still floating face-up in the water, drifting down the side of the boat. Bobbing like the flashlight. Travis squatted on the transom for a better look, and realized why. He stopped breathing.

This man wasn't moving. Even in the dim light, Travis could see that the man's dark T-shirt was torn, as was his stomach. *Fuck, this dude's dead.* The boat's momentum continued to carry it past the man, preventing Travis from getting a clear look at him.

Travis tried to assimilate what he was seeing, not wanting to believe he may have just seen a dead body. He needed to turn the boat around and check. But where the fuck was everyone else? There was a noise.

A cough.

The dead man had coughed as the boat moved away from him. He was alive?

Travis spoke. "Hey, amigo . . . can you hear me?"

The man remained silent as the boat drifted farther

away. Travis put the boat in reverse and let it idle once again as he neared the motionless figure on the water.

Travis reached out with a long-handled fishing net and placed it over the man's head, since it was the only part of the man he could reach. As he dragged the man closer, the net forced his head underwater. The inert man came to life, sputtering as he inhaled water, then coughed as he weakly fought at the net with his hands.

"*Tranquilo*, bro!" Travis forgot his Spanish. "I'm trying to help!"

Travis somehow managed to move the struggling man next to the swim platform on the stern. As he drew the man closer to the lights on the transom, Travis could see that he was seriously injured. He was moaning. Even in the dim red stern light, holes and tears were visible on his clothing, his torso.

Travis reached down to grab the injured man. Maybe he could slide him onto the boat. The man's body felt like it weighed a thousand pounds. As Travis tried for a better grip, his hand entered a warm, wet hole in the man's thigh and he felt his fingers brush against something smooth and solid.

Bone.

He recoiled, realizing that he had just touched the man's exposed femur. He regained himself, and grabbed onto the man's wet shirt and dragged him onto the transom with the help of a small wave.

He could now see that the man was bleeding badly, the dark fluid spreading in swirls before seawater washed over the white transom. Travis didn't want to pull a bleeding, dying man into his dad's boat.

Travis looked at the apparently unconscious man illuminated by the red navigation light on the stern. Blood poured from a gaping hole in his right thigh. There were a few smaller holes lower on the leg. And the foot was missing on that leg. No right foot at all, just empty space below the shin. Surprisingly little blood was draining from the stump. What the hell had happened? This couldn't have been the other boat, could it? A shark?

"Tiburón? Fue un tiburón?"

He asked the question several times, but the man just lay supine with his eyes shut. His body was splayed out near the back of the boat, as far up as Travis had been able to drag him. Travis managed to form a crude tourniquet around the mangled leg using a length of rope from the boat's bumper, but he could tell it might be too late. Blood had spread across the bottom of the boat and was slowly draining down the stern. Travis stood and looked around the dark ocean for the others. A few flashlights were visible nearby, bobbing on the waves. Travis shouted several times, but nobody answered.

They were all gone.

Travis really wanted a joint. He was torn between starting the boat and getting the hell out of there, or staying in the hopes that there might be a few other men in the water. Hector had said there were fifteen of them.

Fifteen.

But there was only one now. It didn't matter. Sharks or something had killed them all. Travis was suddenly overwhelmed with the urge to flee. He'd already been there too long. But what the hell was he going to do with the guy in the stern?

He made up his mind, knew what he was going to do. He took two quick strides toward the man's body. He would check for a pulse, then he was going to dump the body and get the hell out of here if he was dead.

Travis paused over the bloody man splayed out in the stern.

"Wake up, goddammit. Tell me what's going on, man, or I'll leave your ass out here!"

The man didn't answer. His breathing was very quiet.

As Travis leaned down to grab his shirt, the man's eyes began to slowly open, staring empty at the moonless sky, unblinking in the bright white cabin. He was older than Travis, probably in his thirties, with a weathered face and wet, black locks clinging to his forehead. Travis realized he was watching the man slip away and started to cry.

"Come on, man, don't die. What the hell am I supposed to do with you? What the fuck happened here?"

Travis grabbed the man's head and shook it. Suddenly, the man lashed out and grabbed Travis's wrist, their eyes locking. Travis yelled out. The man spoke.

"*Los diablos.*"

"What? What did you say? What do you mean, *los diablos*?"

The man's grip weakened, and he began to relax again, his eyes glazing over. He took a slow, shallow breath, met Travis's eyes, and whispered the words a final time.

"*Los diablos. Los diablos rojos.*"

CHAPTER 7

The diver descended the anchor chain into blackness. Every few feet farther from the surface, he felt the water pressure building in his ears, forcing him to equalize the pressure by pinching his nose and blowing into his sinuses. Hand over hand, he gripped the heavy, algae-coated chain to keep his bearings in the cold, dimly lit water and prevent the current from sweeping him away from his destination on the bottom a hundred and twenty feet down—a sunken Canadian destroyer.

The only sounds Will Sturman could hear were the hiss of air flowing through the diaphragm of his regulator as he inhaled, followed by the loud burst of bubbles rushing past his ears as he exhaled in the deep.

He glanced at his digital depth gauge as the readout reached ninety feet. Looking off into the gloom, he began to notice the pale, hulking shape of the destroyer emerge from his otherwise uniform field of view.

Sturman felt something bump into his scuba tank.

He paused with one hand on the anchor chain, then rolled over in the water to face upward, shining his dive light up toward the surface. In the beam of light, di-

rectly behind him, was one of the ...
brought down. A middle-aged woma...
through drifting organic particles, he counte...
of the divers by their lights. Four. Everyone was ...
behind him, all within thirty feet or so. They were almost to their destination, a silent mass of rusting steel
that never saw daylight.

The *HMCS Redemption* lay upright on the sandy
bottom, just as she had gone down. Intentionally sunk
to form an artificial reef, it was regardless a stroke of
luck that she had come to rest upright, just as she had
plied the surface. Many a planned and purposefully
sunken ship accidentally ended up on its side, despite
the best efforts of those sinking it. All that was visible
to Sturman in the darkness a hundred feet down was
the span of the ship from bridge to prow; blackness
consumed the rest of the three-hundred-and-seventy-
foot leviathan.

This was the first of two dives today, so he would
bring the group down deeper and let them explore inside the hull if they wanted. On the later dive, nobody
would be allowed as deep or permitted to stay under as
long. The demolition crew that had sunken the *Redemption* had removed her doors, cut holes in the side
of the hull, and had otherwise made her diver-friendly
before setting off the charges to sink her, so it was easy
to navigate by wreck-diving standards. He would still
need to keep a close eye on these folks, though; they
were relatively experienced divers, but if they got
turned around in the darkness of the hull he wouldn't
have much time to find them before they ran out of air.
At this depth, many divers burned through their air
supply in less than twenty minutes.

As Sturman reached the bottom of the anchor chain, ally a permanent mooring line fixed to a buoy at the surface, the current began to weaken. He noticed a lingcod as big as his leg below him, resting on the deck where the chain was bolted to the wreck. That lingcod was always here. The fish looked as though she might be dead and never even twitched in his presence, but he knew she was just conserving energy. The mooring chain next to her was affixed on the foredeck of the destroyer. Divers usually started here and followed the length of the ship and explored as time permitted in the lighter currents near the vessel.

Sturman let go of the chain and passed the lingcod, and began to move over the deck with smooth strokes of his swim fins. He took deep, slow breaths to minimize his air consumption, and looked over the ship in reverence. He had seen this vessel in its final resting place hundreds of times, but he never grew tired of looking at it. He liked being down here. In the darkness.

Sturman glanced at his air gauge. Twelve hundred psi of air remained in the tank—maybe eight minutes of bottom time, if he wanted to be really conservative. Sturman was rarely conservative with his own air, but he never put his clients at risk. The divers he had in tow would almost certainly run out of air sooner. He had let the foursome leave in pairs ten minutes ago, and had been studying a patch of giant white-plumed anemones sprouting from the deck like oversized cauliflower. The Metridiums fluttering in the current were each over a foot tall and practically as wide.

Sturman looked at his watch. It was time to round everyone up and return to the surface. Two of the divers had returned ahead of schedule and rested on the deck beside him near the base of the anchor chain. In another minute, he would need to go looking for the other two, but he could wait a little longer. He preferred to keep the whole group together as a dive wound down and air ran low. Just then he noticed a faint light in the distance, moving toward them down the hull.

As the light approached, Sturman realized something wasn't right. There was only one beam pointed toward him, closing on him fast. Every diver had brought down a dive light, and they had been instructed to stay in pairs.

Sturman made eye contact with the pair next to him and signaled for them to ascend to the safety stop near the surface. The divers gave him an "okay" signal with thumb and forefinger, the universal scuba message indicating they were all right and understood. The two divers began to kick upward as Sturman finned toward the lone diver approaching along the foredeck.

Looking into the diver's mask, Sturman could see by the man's expression that he was terrified. *Jack,* Sturman remembered. *His name is Jack.* Jack was trying to pantomime something to him, but since he was unable to speak underwater, it wasn't clear what he was trying to get across. And their air was running out.

Sturman held up his hand in the other diver's face, palm outward: *Stop.* He then looked the panicked man in the eyes and gave a large, exaggerated shrug: *Where is she? Where is your dive buddy?*

The diver looked back at Sturman for a moment, exhaling a burst of bubbles through his regulator, then shook his head and shrugged back. Either this guy didn't understand the question or didn't have the answer. Sturman squeezed the man's shoulder and pointed to the mooring line, then gave a thumbs-up: *Ascend the chain now.* The man shook his head no—understandable, since it was his wife he had left behind. Will squeezed the man's shoulder again, harder this time, and locked eyes with the man, repeating the command to ascend.

One thousand psi. Sturman was beginning to worry. He had made sure the reluctant diver had begun his ascent up the mooring line and then, with a series of powerful kicks, had set off alone down the length of the sunken destroyer. Past huge double guns, each large enough to shove a soccer ball into the barrel, past a metal bridge rising several stories off the deck. He had covered almost the full length of the wreck, but hadn't seen any sign of the missing woman.

His mind went through scenarios as he weighed the possibilities and his options. He had about six minutes before he would have to ascend. The woman probably had simply been separated from her husband, and would head up soon on her own. She had logged a lot of previous dives, and Sturman had taken this group out before without incident. But there was another possibility. She could be trapped somewhere, or lost within the ship. Not likely, though. No. She had simply become separated from her dive buddy, so he hadn't been able to help her.

Eight hundred psi. Sturman had reached a large opening amidships and headed down into the darkness of the hull. Now he was moving along the upper interior deck, passing through hatches that mercifully had had their doors removed. If it had been dim in the water outside the ship, in here it was truly black. The little bit of sunlight that filtered down through over a hundred feet of particle-laden water was unable to penetrate the intermittent openings in the ship to offer any illumination in its belly. The waters of Southern California were not the clear waters of the Caribbean.

Sturman's whole world had become the single cone of light emitted by his powerful dive light, which reached through a dozen or so feet of black water swirling with detritus before being absorbed by the darkness.

Six hundred psi. Sturman swam through an opening in the deck, down into the next lowest level. Looking up into the light streaming down from a hatch through particles in the water above him, he thought, not for the first time, that being inside this ship was almost like being in an underwater cathedral.

He wondered how quickly he would be able to get out of here when it was time to scramble for the surface. He needed five hundred psi for an adequate safety stop. Damn lady must be crazy. What the hell was she up to? *Stay calm, Will.* He took a slow, deep breath. If she was here, he would find her.

*   *   *

Four hundred and fifty psi. The ship was a labyrinth. It all looked the same. In his light, Sturman saw only empty spaces and small, square rooms no matter where he was in the innards of the wreck. Walls and hatches crusted over with barnacles. An occasional fish darting through the beam of light. It was past time to head for the surface.

Fairly certain he had thoroughly searched the upper level, Sturman reached another hole in the floor, a stairwell leading into the next level down. Two levels under the main deck, he reminded himself. He figured he was somewhere near the stern of the boat now, but everything looked the same. He had been inside this boat many times, but never in a hurry. He had always planned on where he would go, followed a predetermined route. He forced himself to think about the locations of emergency escapes on each level.

Three hundred psi. A few minutes of air left. Sturman could only hope the diver had gotten to the surface on her own. Maybe she had ascended while he was in here searching, but he had no way of knowing. He glanced again at his gauges. Now three levels down into the ship, he was somewhere near the outer hull and a hundred and twenty feet down. He was going through his air so fast now that he could have watched it drop on the gauge as he took each breath. *One more hatch*, he thought, *then I need to surface.*

The seriousness of it hit him. *Jesus, don't let her be trapped down here.*

No more time. He had to ascend—now. He reached

the next room, and finning through it, he saw a faint light maybe thirty feet ahead and to the left. One of the holes cut into the hull before the boat had been sunk. Essentially an emergency exit. He headed toward it as he sensed his air supply dwindling, moving impossibly slow in the water, as if the ship wasn't going to let him leave. He entered the next chamber and something glinted in the beam of his dive light.

He'd found her.

Two hundred psi.

Like an animal caught in a trap, the woman was thrashing in the beam of light, kicking up sediment and clouding the dark water. No bubbles rose from her mouthpiece. She may have just now run out of the last breath of air and was in a state of desperate panic to free herself. Sturman kicked toward her, pulling his regulator out of his mouth. He spun her around forcefully as he reached her, holding the mouthpiece in front of her foggy mask. She spit out her own mouthpiece, snatching his and forcing it between her lips.

She drew a huge breath, exhaling an explosion of bubbles around his face. Sturman reached back and grabbed the Spare Air canister attached to his buoyancy control vest. There was no way this lady was going to relinquish his mouthpiece and share it so they could buddy breathe together, and there wasn't enough air in his main tank for both of them anyway, so using his octopus was out of the question.

The Spare Air tank, a tiny canister he carried for emergencies and had used only once before, would give him several minutes of air to surface if he controlled his breathing. He placed the mouthpiece of the tiny tank in his mouth and took a cautious first breath. It still worked.

Sturman gave her a reassuring look: *Everything's all right now.* She didn't seem to see him. She was still panicked.

He looked behind her and quickly realized why she was still down here. The primary regulator at the top of her scuba tank, which connected her air hoses to the tank, was somehow jammed into a hole adjacent to a hatchway, perhaps where hinges had been torn free. Sturman grabbed her tank and regulator, twisting with all his strength in each direction, wrenching the woman back and sideways. The tank popped free.

Grabbing the woman's vest and pulling, Sturman shoved off the wall with his free arm, kicked hard, and accelerated toward the distant opening in the hull.

Fifty psi.

Sturman looked at his air gauge as he and the other diver reached the exterior of the ship, not slowing as they passed through the opening in the side of the hull and began to arc up toward the surface. Sturman maintained his grip on the woman's BC vest, since she was still breathing from his air tank. This was going to be a real balancing act, he realized. They needed to surface quickly, but too fast and they would certainly get a bad case of the bends. As it was, they were certain to suffer some ill effects. There wasn't enough air for a safety stop at fifteen feet.

Far from the anchor line, they began to drift in the current as they ascended in open water. Sturman continued to look at his depth gauge, dumping air from his vest to control the ascent. Ninety feet. Eighty feet. Seventy feet. They were surfacing too fast. He grimaced. This wasn't going to be good.

He needed to slow them down, since they probably still had two or three minutes of air in his emergency tank—at least at the low pressure of shallow water, where air lasted much longer than at depth. Before they surfaced, they could share the Spare Air as they let the nitrogen that had built up in their bodies escape when they exhaled in the reduced pressure of shallower water. Hell, he thought, they might get out of this unscathed after all.

Without warning, the woman spit out her regulator and kicked for the surface.

Sturman suddenly realized that the air in his main tank, which the woman had been breathing, must have just hit zero psi.

She was out of air.

The woman clawed for the emergency tank suspended just below Sturman's mouth, ripping it free of his bite. She tried to put in the mouthpiece, but was clearly in a state of panic now. After a moment of fumbling with the miniature tank, she let go of it and kicked upward. Sturman tried to hold on to her with one hand and caught the sinking emergency tank with the other. He couldn't let her just pop up from sixty feet. The risk was much too great.

Sturman heard a faint metallic clink and felt the woman begin to rise. *Shit.* Her weight belt. She had released her weight belt, and was attempting an emergency ascent.

He glanced down and watched as her thick, nylon

belt, laden with twenty pounds of lead weights, slipped past her long blue fins and plummeted toward the wreck below. He quickly dumped the remaining air out of his buoyancy control vest and tried to hold the woman down, but knew they were rising fast as he felt the air in his sinuses and rib cage rapidly expand. They were in for a ride.

Sturman knew he had two choices: try to slow their ascent and put himself at greater risk, or let her go and ascend more gradually himself.

For Will Sturman, there was really no choice.

He squeezed the woman's vest tighter and raised the Spare Air tank in front of the woman's face so she could see it, but she was wriggling like a speared fish and her mask was fogged completely over because of her rapid breathing. Her flailing arms hit the small tank away again, and Sturman realized this woman was going to drown if she didn't get her head above water immediately.

As they accelerated upward over the last forty feet to the surface, escorted by a host of their own expanding air bubbles, Sturman exhaled continuously, calmly, and wondered why in the hell he still chose to be a divemaster.

CHAPTER 8

With his arms outstretched, Sturman could have easily touched both sides of the large, horizontal cylinder.

Even though he was tall, about six-two, with a wide arm span, any space he could reach across with his arms and couldn't stand up in was much too small for comfort. Semi-claustrophobic, Sturman had first taken a scuba class right after high school to help him conquer his avoidance of confined spaces. It had worked. Well, that and his general fearlessness. He didn't worry much about dying, never had. Seventeen years later, he could remain relaxed while breathing compressed air through a hose, a hundred feet underwater, at intense water pressure, while swimming through narrow openings in a sunken vessel. But he still didn't enjoy being confined.

The rapid ascent from the *HMCS Redemption* this morning had ended with them breaching halfway out of the water with the momentum of their ascent. Sturman had looked over at the female diver to see bloody froth coming out of her mouth and bubbling out of her nose into her mask. That had frightened the hell out of him, but the woman had stayed conscious and wide-eyed as he towed her back to his boat. Sturman had realized she must have held her breath on the way up and damaged her lungs.

Besides her lung injury, they had both almost immediately started to feel the first effects of the bends. Sturman had gotten a headache moments after surfacing, and by the time they reached the boat two hundred feet away his face had begun to itch and his shoulders and elbows were tingling.

On his marine radio he had called for an ambulance to meet them at the dock. To prevent serious injury and lessen the pain of the decompression, they had been rushed to the hyperbaric chamber at the hospital in La Mesa. When they had reached the hospital an hour later, Sturman, although primarily concerned with the injured woman, had felt intense pain in his upper joints as the nitrogen gas bubbling up in his tissues wreaked havoc on his nerves. The woman, in greater pain and still bleeding some from her mouth, hadn't even been able to talk at that point. She had been confused and delirious, and when she had been able to speak through the pain and bloody froth, all she had kept asking was where they were and what was happening.

Now she was unconscious on the floor of the chamber, underneath a light blue hospital blanket. A nurse sat beside her, monitoring her vitals.

"You are suffering from decompression sickness."

Sturman turned to see the doctor, a middle-aged Indian man, looking at him through one of the five small, circular windows in the chamber. His voice had emanated from a small speaker inside the chamber. On his white coat was a metallic nametag: DR. PESHWAR.

Sturman walked over to the porthole and saw a button labeled TALK next to a small speaker. He pushed it.

"Thanks for the diagnosis, doc. I thought I was in here for the view," Will replied. As a divemaster, he already knew all about the bends.

The doctor scowled at him and shook his head. "Do you think this is funny, sir? That woman nearly died."

"I've got a helluva headache," Sturman said. "Say what you've gotta say."

"Your bodies absorbed a lot of nitrogen when you were underwater, and when you surfaced too quickly, the nitrogen didn't have time to leave your body," the doctor explained over the small speaker. The chamber walls were too thick to speak to each other directly. "What you are experiencing is the bubbling up of nitrogen in a gaseous form in your blood and tissues, particularly in your joints. Mrs. Buckner also has suffered trauma from an air embolism. Apparently she held her breath on your ascent and ruptured her lung."

He paused, fixing Sturman with an accusing stare. "She's lucky to be alive, Mr. Sturman."

Sturman's face flushed. "And you think it's my fault, right?" The doctor didn't reply. Sturman looked down for a moment, then back at the doctor. "Will there be any permanent damage?"

"It's hard to say right now. You should be all right, since you made it here so quickly. It's likely you'll make a full recovery. As for Mrs. Buckner, we'll need to keep a closer eye on her. And run more tests once she's finished in the chamber."

"So how long 'til we can get out of this contraption?" Sturman asked.

"You'll need to be in the recompression chamber for twelve hours to be safe. If the symptoms return later, we'll need to have you come back."

Sturman watched the doctor leave the room, then sat back down on one of the benches running alongside the chamber. He sighed. The dive charter business had been bad enough lately, because of the lousy economy and the lack of disposable income. And Sturman was getting tired of babysitting people who took too many chances underwater, putting his business at risk.

Maybe it was time to find something new. But diving was all he had.

CHAPTER 9

The Lighthouse, a brick-walled pub on a side street two blocks up from the Capistrano Bay harbor, was a favorite haunt of the men who worked on the water. The Lighthouse drew fishermen, sailors, beachside vendors, and divers, who could all be found playing darts, shooting pool, or drinking too much inside the low-ceilinged one-story hangout. Tourists who walked in usually turned around and walked right back out.

This evening it was fairly slow as usual. Sturman was sitting inside the joint on a wooden bar stool, brooding over a beer. He listened to Jimmy Buffett singing "Come Monday" over the speakers on the walls and watched Jill move around behind the bar, halfheartedly focusing on her long, tanned legs and bare midriff.

Jill noticed him looking and smiled. "What you looking at, cowboy?"

Sturman looked away. He knew Jill was interested in him, but he liked things how they were. He didn't want to complicate his life.

The Lighthouse was the one place besides his boat

where he spent a lot of his free time. Too much of his free time, he knew. But what the hell.

He peeled at the wet label on the beer bottle as he thought about the accident that morning and the long day at the hospital. That woman had really screwed up wandering off and leaving her dive buddy like that. She could have gotten herself killed. But Sturman couldn't let it go; after all, she was the one unconscious, spitting up blood in the hospital.

"She's lucky to be alive," the doctor had said.

Sturman set down his beer and covered his face with his hands, rubbing the stubble on his chin, then took off his well-worn cowboy hat and ran his hand back over the matching stubble on his closely shaved head.

Sturman and the sick woman had spent ten full hours in the recompression chamber together, her mostly sleeping off painkillers and sedatives. She had awoken briefly once, asked where she was, then drifted back to sleep. Sturman had stayed awake, fighting off guilt. He knew he'd let her wander too far off in the wreck; he'd given the divers too much freedom to explore. He knew better. When you bring out divers you don't know well, you always keep them on a short leash. Now he was drinking off some of the guilt, when he knew he should have been headed home for a good night's sleep.

"Hey, buddy. How you feeling?" A handsome Latino with a dark goatee had just come through the heavy wooden front door and was approaching Sturman, smiling broadly. Joe Montoya wasn't in uniform, so Sturman knew he was off duty as a sergeant for the county sheriff.

Sturman smiled weakly back at Joe and, replacing the hat on his head, tipped it to his friend. Joe sat down on the stool next to Sturman and spun on it to face him.

Sturman sipped his beer and didn't answer Joe's question right away, pausing for effect. "One time right after I moved here we drove down to Tijuana, stayed up all night drinking cheap tequila, and then you took a beatin' in an alley outside that bar when you tried to leave with some guy's girlfriend. Remember that?"

Joe nodded and laughed, a loud, contagious laugh. "Yeah, man. You saved my ass."

"Remember how we felt on the drive home up the Five the next morning?"

Joe smiled.

"Well, that's about how I'm feeling," Sturman said. "Hey, amigo, thanks for bringing her back, and for taking care of the dog."

Wincing, he raised his arm to shake Joe's hand. His buddy had been there to take care of his two most prized possessions—his boat and his dog. Joe had a family and long hours with the sheriff's department, but Sturman could always count on his help when he needed him. Joe shook his head. "Man, so you're really all messed up? You don't look any shittier than normal. Is that lady gonna be okay?"

"I don't know. Her husband will probably sue me, even though he's the one who lost her."

"No shit. You should've just left her ass down there." Joe raised his hand to the bartender, pointing at himself. "I'll have what our cowboy's having."

"Put everything on my tab, Jill."

Joe was always making fun of Sturman's cowboy hat

and slight country-boy drawl. Sturman didn't wear boots much anymore, but he would always be a cowboy.

Joe tried to get the story out of his friend. Sturman knew Joe wanted more details, but he wasn't much of a talker. When Sturman explained how he had freed the woman from the ship hatchway, Joe said, "Too bad you can't talk underwater. You could've gotten that chick to agree to anything for an escort to the surface."

"Hell. I'da been happy to just get a tip."

As was his way, Joe kept up the bad jokes. Beginning to feel the effects of the alcohol, Sturman laughed despite himself. That was Joe Montoya. When he wasn't working, the man was never serious. Sturman had always figured that was a cop's way of dealing with seeing gang-war victims and four-year-olds dismembered along highways.

After another round of Dos Equis, the conversation died off. On the other side of the pub, someone struck a cue ball and the racked billiard balls separated with a loud smack a moment later.

"Hey, man, you've dove and fished in this area for a long time. You know anything about a big fish called 'the devil' or a devil fish or something?"

Sturman was silent for a moment. "What the hell are you talking about?"

"Some guy got attacked by a shark or something a few days ago, and the kid we're holding now claims the guy said something about the devil before he died. Looks like a shark laid into him."

Sturman sipped his beer. "Some people call mantas 'devils' because of the shape of their head. I've never heard of a 'devil fish,' though."

"Mantas don't attack people, right?"

Sturman grinned. "You sure don't know shit for a cop with a boat. Mantas are sure as hell big enough, but they don't even have any teeth."

"Huh. Anyway, this was another one of them coyotes smuggling immigrants by boat. The kid we arrested says he was supposed to pick up a bunch of them and shuttle them back. Can you believe that shit? Some Mexican just dumped them in the ocean, and this other guy was supposed to pick them up."

"You fuckin' Mexicans."

"Fuck you, Sturman. Anyway, kid says only this one dying guy was there when he showed up. Coast Guard went out, but never found anyone else."

"Not many shark attacks around here. Not many dangerous sharks."

"True, but not many people float around in the ocean offshore at night. I don't know. I figure the kid's probably full of shit anyway."

A man across the room began shouting at Sturman. "Hey! Hey, shithead! Yeah, I'm talking to you. Fuckin' cowboy in here again?"

The men looked to the back of the bar at a group playing pool. The tallest of them, a shaggy-haired older man in a muscle shirt, was leaning on his pool cue and staring at Sturman.

"You hear me, shithead? I'll bet you my left nut I can take you in the next game." The shouting man grinned, revealing yellowed teeth and a golden-capped canine.

Joe shook his head. "You still hanging out with that lowlife?"

Sturman couldn't hold it against his friend for not liking Steve Black. He fell into a mother's category of people you should stay away from. "Steve's a dirty old man, but he's been a pretty good friend."

"He's a fucking racist, Sturman."

"Well, nobody's perfect." Sturman turned and shouted back at Black. "I'll take your bet, you dumbshit. But you still owe me from the last time I mopped up this place with your ass."

Black smiled at Sturman, a cigarette dangling from his mouth.

Jill jumped in. "Watch your language in here, assholes." The room erupted in laughter.

Sturman slid off his stool and made his way toward the pool tables, with Joe reluctantly in tow. He had always thought Steve looked just like an old pirate, minus an eye patch and a parrot. Black was another local divemaster, and had been friends with Sturman for almost eight years. He was a tall, wiry man, with unkempt gray hair and wrinkles creasing a sun-bronzed face. His stained Carlos 'n Charlie's tank top left his deeply tanned, tattooed arms fully visible, as well as a few prominent scars. He wore three gold chains around his neck and had on worn leather sandals and cargo shorts.

Steve raised an arm to block a mock punch from Sturman, then shook his hand.

"Hola, amigos. Sturman, I didn't know you were still hanging out with Mexi-melters."

"Anytime, old man." Joe looked calm enough as he delivered the invitation, but Sturman saw that his fists were clenched.

"I'm not fuckin' with the police. I'm not stupid."

"That's enough. Keep it nice." Sturman shot them both a hard look. "You wanna play, Montoya?"

"No. I gotta get going. Girls are home tonight. Sturman, I already fed Bud dinner for you. See you soon."

After Joe walked away, Steve shook his head. "Why you hang out with that cop?"

"He's better looking than you."

"Seriously, son. Last thing we need is Mexican cops here in California."

"Drop the racist shit, Steve. You got a smoke, you bum?"

Sturman's body had taken a lot of abuse already today, and he was trying not to smoke as much, but after a few beers a cigarette sounded pretty good.

Sturman realized he must have smoked at least five or six cigarettes as he lit a final one and stumbled out of the bar after midnight. He'd played a lot of cutthroat with Steve and his biker friends, who were talking more game than they brought. Their usual night at the bar, with Sturman playing well until the liquor convinced him to focus on other things.

After drinking too much beer to win any more games of pool and almost giving in to Jill's attempts to take advantage of him, Sturman called it a night when he felt the darkness creeping into his head. He left and headed down the dark, empty street to the harbor. As he staggered along the floating dock toward his boat, he could hear Bud barking inside the cabin. His mutt always knew when his master was approaching by the sound of his footsteps, be they sober and measured or drunken and lurching.

Sturman fumbled to get the key in the lock and then let Bud explode out of the cabin. He smiled as the muscular dog, a tan Lab-pit-whatever mix, ran in impossibly small circles on the slippery floor of the boat, slamming into Sturman and sliding into the sides of the boat.

"Hey, buddy. You've probably gotta piss worse than I do." Sturman took the dog for a short walk up the docks, to the grassy area on shore. Then they returned to the boat and he fed Bud and cooked two packs of ramen noodles in the tiny kitchen. Living on a thirty-six-foot dive boat with a full-grown dog was tight, but when the economy had taken a nosedive, Sturman had left his apartment to keep his business and boat. He would never sell the boat.

When his belly was full and he could no longer keep his eyes open, Sturman lay down on his bed in the forward cabin, still fully clothed. Before he passed out, lying alone in the dark, he thought of her. Somehow, he always thought of her.

If he drank enough beer he found that he could sometimes get past it. Tonight the booze did its job, and with Bud curled up next to him, Sturman fell asleep to the gentle rocking of the boat. The last thing he heard as he drifted off was the soft ringing of metal rigging as it clanged against the aluminum masts of sailboats in the harbor.

CHAPTER 10

Joe Montoya awoke feeling exhausted. He'd slept badly again—the nightmares of a police officer with a lot of years on the job. He rolled over, away from the light coming through the bedroom window. He kept his eyes shut as he listened to his wife moving around the room, getting ready for work. He could hear his teenage daughters arguing downstairs.

After a few minutes, he began to think about the day ahead. He knew he needed to get out of bed. He sat up with a moan and swung his legs over the side of the king bed.

"Nice of you to join us this morning, sleepyhead," his wife said. "You still smell like a bar." He knew she was just testing him—he'd only had a couple of beers. She was always worrying about his health.

Elena was dressed professionally in a beige silk blouse and gray skirt. She was a legal assistant at a local law office, and kept more regular hours than her husband. As a sergeant for the county sheriff, Joe often worked late and weekend hours. He wondered for a moment why she always looked her best when headed to work, instead of when spending time with him.

"I'm fine, baby. Will needed someone to talk to last night, that's all."

"Already in a bar after his accident yesterday? Is he all right?"

"Yeah, he's okay. He's really sore though."

"Was he upset about Maria again? You can't keep staying out late drinking with that man because he's still upset about his ex-wife. He drinks too much, and you drink too much when you're with him. Did you smoke last night?"

"Maria was never his ex-wife. She was his *wife*. And he's my friend."

"So you did smoke?"

"I didn't stay out late, I didn't drink too much, and I didn't smoke. You done interrogating me?"

Joe shook his head and looked away from his wife. Elena walked over to her husband, pulled his head against her breasts, and hugged him. "I'm sorry. I know, baby. You're a good friend to him. Just try not to get caught up in his lifestyle, okay?"

Joe became focused on the feel of his wife's firm, slender waist under his hands and the smell of perfume in her long hair. He felt a tingling in his groin. At thirty-eight, she still turned heads, with her high cheekbones, smooth skin and dark, liquid eyes. Joe ran his hand through her silky black hair.

"How much time do you have before work, mama?"

"No, baby. Not today. I have an important meeting and I can't be late. Besides, the girls are still here."

Joe sighed. He knew better than to waste his time

once his wife had made up her mind. As stubborn as her mother.

He dressed and went down to the kitchen. He said good morning to his girls and poured himself a mug of black coffee, then joined his daughters at the oak breakfast table.

"What are you two arguing about now?" he asked.

His youngest, a slightly plump girl with shoulder-length hair, spoke first. "Alicia won't let me use the car, Dad."

"She's lying," Alicia replied. "I said she could use it, but not tonight. I'm taking out Tiff and Stacy." Alicia was eighteen, three years older than her sister, Gabriella, and the prettier of the two. She was taller and slimmer, and drew much more attention from boys.

"Gabby, you're not old enough to drive alone anyway," Joe said.

"But Dad, I thought you or Mom could ride with me and I could take Rachael to the mall!"

Joe shut his eyes and rubbed his temples. "Stop whining, *mija*. I'm not in the mood. We can go tomorrow, okay? Your mom will be off work. Let your sister use the car tonight." He raised the mug to his lips and took a long pull of hot coffee.

"Alicia is having sex with Corey," Gabriella blurted. Joe nearly sprayed the table with a mouthful. "Rachael's sister said that . . ."

"Gabriella, that's enough!" Joe glared at her. She looked away and crossed her arms. Just like her grandmother, Joe thought. At least she wouldn't put up with shit from the boys like her sister. He turned from her to Alicia. Her lack of protest was enough, but when she broke eye contact and looked down at the floor, he felt his face flush. After an awkward silence, he decided to change the subject.

"You working today?" Alicia had taken a summer job at a teenage clothing store. The Rage, or something like that. She was headed off to USC in the fall, which wasn't going to be cheap. He was paying for her school, but couldn't afford to buy her the clothes and shoes she brought home every week.

"Duh, Dad. I work every Friday. You getting Alzheimer's or something?" Like some of the guilty perps he questioned, now she was trying to play it cool.

"Right. So will you be home for dinner?"

"But I just told you I'm taking out my friends. Are you okay, Dad?"

"Yeah, *mija*. I was just hoping you might eat with us before you head out."

The room got quiet again. When Gabby retreated to the downstairs couch to watch MTV, Joe took the opportunity to get up from the table. He heard Alicia leave the kitchen behind him.

Joe stood at the kitchen window, staring out at the warm, overcast morning. His thoughts shifted from his daughter's romantic life to the immigrants who had died at sea. He had dreamed a lot about them. He pictured them all being killed by a school of sharks, like those sailors who died when their battleship went down in World War II.

And he kept thinking of the dead man's torn body. He still had a lot of questions for that kid about what had happened.

CHAPTER 11

They sensed the ocean floor somewhere beneath them and the surface not far above, and instinctively pressed away from both into the bustle of hundreds of their kind moving through the dark water.

The water here was not deep enough for the entire shoal. Like giant undersea wasps swarming within a congested hive, the immense assemblage of organisms had become densely packed as each member of the shoal sought to avoid the sloping bottom, while also seeking deeper water away from the bright light filtering down from above. Although the murky North Pacific hundreds of feet down would be absolutely black to most creatures, to their kind these shallower near-shore depths were brightly lit.

Most in the shoal rarely brushed or bumped against any of the largest females in the group. They were avoided out of self-preservation, since they were much more powerful and aggressive. Several were three times the weight and nearly twice the length of the others, despite the shoal being a fairly uniform group of mature adults. Their size served as a warning to the others not to aggravate them.

The members of the shoal did not consider their location as they hovered in the dark water. If they had, they would know they were not supposed to be here, that these waters for millennia had been too cold, too full of predators and competitors to allow their presence. Although they had never been able to survive here before, they were here now simply because nothing was preventing their intrusion.

While their migration, the expansion of their species, was new to them, they had continued to follow the same daily cycle their kind had followed for thousands of years. During the daytime, they retreated a thousand or more feet beneath the surface to suppress each member's metabolism, hidden from the sunlight, the heat, the activity of the surface.

At night, they rose to feed.

The higher oxygen levels and warmth of shallower waters enabled them to increase their metabolisms, intensifying speed and strength and reaction time. Their enhanced abilities allowed them to overtake prey easily in the dark water using their powerful eyes and deadly appendages.

But the water here was too shallow. The shoal had been unable to retreat to a comfortable depth, and most of the massive horde had grown agitated. They were accustomed to the nearly bottomless depths of the deep ocean. Yet the shoal had ventured into shallower and shallower water in recent weeks, following its collective instincts.

And its hunger.

For days, those assembled in the shoal had found little to satiate their unmatched desire to feed. They had happened upon some of the smaller deepwater prey on which they normally fed—anchovies nearer the surface and lanternfishes farther down—but the schools had been small and many in the group needed much more sustenance to survive.

Always the water temperature had remained relatively constant and the directional currents had facilitated the shoal's migration. Each evening, the shoal had risen with the upwelling of cool waters to feed closer to shore. Each morning, the shoal had retreated to the depths farther offshore, following a sinking eddy current of cold water making its way back toward the abyss. Always the shoal pushed itself in the same direction. As it searched for food, rising and descending in its never-ending cycle, still it continued purposefully in a single lateral direction, drawn away from the place where it had originated.

The members of the shoal gradually calmed when the day began to wane and the bright sunlight from above faded toward black, as another daily cycle progressed into night. The twilit water above was becoming much darker and more familiar, and no longer pained their eyes. They began slowly rising along the steep slope of the bottom, toward shore, to feed.

The largest females moved near the head of the fleet. They would be the first to feed when prey was discovered.

These females had lived longer than most in the shoal. They had attained their great body size by managing to stay alive longer than the others around them, and by being more aggressive than the others at taking prey. This fearless aggression had yielded them more food, which had turned into greater body mass. But it had come at a cost.

The largest of these females had only one eye. A scar of wrinkled flesh covered the place where the other had once been, between the smooth length of her body and her set of appendages. Evidence of past battles for survival blemished her otherwise smooth skin.

One of her sisters, nearly her own size, moved through the water alongside her. Bearing even more scars than the one-eyed female, she had lost the tip of one of her two broad fins when a shark or swordfish had nipped it off when she had been younger and smaller. She bore countless scars along her body, and when she grasped at her prey, she did so without one of her limbs. It was a useless stump of flesh, far shorter than the others since one of her own kind had torn it off.

As the dominant females coursed through the mass of their peers, moving slowly toward the front, their wide, unblinking eyes caught a flash of silver in the darkness above them. Then another.

Prey.

In an instant they changed their body shapes and colors, no longer smooth, pale torpedoes meant for travel but instead fierce red blossoms that opened to expose not petals, but tools meant for violence. They uncoiled their weapons and thrust their bodies upward toward the prey, single-minded of focus.

They intended to kill.

A member near the front emitted an excited series of brief flashes of light, which appeared green in the nutrient-rich water. The light blinded its silvery prey as it lashed out and ensnared the fish before the others could reach it. The one-eyed female arrived at the stricken prey an instant later, thrusting her own weapons through the water and digging their small teeth into the fish as it thrashed in the dark water. Dim light from the distant surface glinted off silver scales as it desperately attempted to free itself.

The fish struggled as the large female drew it toward her powerful maw and violently gnashed into its side, removing a tremendous hunk of flesh. The thin bones in the fish easily snapped inside the great beak, and blood poured from the gaping wound as the fish's life slipped away.

Around the members of the shoal, thick, silvery fishes with vivid yellow tails and white underbellies were clearly visible to their large eyes. The pulses of light generated by the shoal confused the school of fast, powerful prey as they overtook it.

The aggressors rapidly changed colors as they attacked, their skin turning bright reds and purples instead of their usual pale white. Frequently, they emitted the green-cast bursts of bioluminescent light when they were most excited, for the fish they attacked now were not the smaller fish they had been feeding upon for days, but instead a larger, more dangerous prey that could sustain the shoal with the nourishment it needed to survive and grow. But to attack these fish was to do battle.

Larger than the quarry and greatly outnumbering it, the shoal quickly began to overtake the prey. The shoal attacked in squads, surrounding the school of broad, silvery fish and engulfing its terrified members. Soon all that remained in the black water were the drifting, inedible remains of the fish.

Yet there was not enough food.

The largest females had eaten much of the meaty fish, but had lost some of the flesh to other ravenous members of the shoal. Their hunger remained. As they propelled themselves slowly through the bloodied water, they searched for something larger than the floating bits of tissue around them. The shoal parted in front of them momentarily, and ahead they saw something else. Something that excited them, caused them to again become aggressive and single-minded of purpose.

Ahead of them was a small, glowing object.

This was like the bioluminescent light of the lanternfishes on which they had always preyed. The one-eyed female moved toward the glowing green object, and saw as she approached that there was not just one, but several glowing objects near her in the water. All were moving erratically, as if wounded. She began to pivot in the water to direct her weaponry toward the prey. The small glowing lights had immediately attracted the attention of most of the shoal and now, as she spun her great bulk to overtake the prey, a smaller, faster member of the shoal hurtled past her toward one of the glowing objects. In an instant, the prey began rising rapidly toward the surface, meaning to escape her smaller sister's grasp. It could not. Her sister lashed out and seized the glowing object, drawing it in.

Then her sister began to struggle.

The smaller object was somehow drawing her up with it, toward the surface, and she was now desperately emitting powerful jets of water, struggling to free herself.

The larger, one-eyed female no longer focused on

the glowing object. She now began to focus on her struggling sister.

The large female sensed that her sister was incapable of escaping the object she had seized. She was defenseless, with the dangerous parts of her body still wrapped tightly around her prize, and the soft, unprotected flesh covering the rest of her body exposed.

Focusing on her sister's flanks with her one remaining dark eye, the enormous female rushed forward and clasped her vulnerable sister in a tight embrace.

And bit into her.

CHAPTER 12

"I've got one, Dad!"

John Whittaker's twelve-year-old niece leaned back, bracing her hip against the gunwale and pulling hard on the fishing pole. Something had just taken her line. From the looks of it, something big.

"All right, Megan!" John shouted. He watched as Megan's dad, his older brother, put his own rod in a holder on the side and rushed over to help her. Megan was struggling to control the powerful fish that had just struck her jig. John's niece was a tomboy, and strong for her age, but out here there were some really big fish. If she had hooked a bluefin or albacore instead of a yellowtail, she might easily have a fifty-pounder on the line.

The yellowtail had been arriving off Southern California for a week now, in their seasonal northern migration as the local waters warmed to around seventy degrees. Every summer for the past four years, John had brought his niece and older brother, Daryl, out with him to fish the yellowtail runs and hope for an occasional hefty tuna—both were fish species that lingered off the Southern California coast for a few months each year. Yellowtail amberjacks were John and Daryl's favorite game fish—they put up a real fight and later yielded a decent homemade sushi. Besides, fishing for yellowtails was probably Megan's favorite thing to do, and John loved the chance to make his niece smile.

The trio had been out all afternoon, plying the waters about five miles off La Jolla in John's sturdy boat. He had focused on the area where the continental shelf abruptly ended and the bottom plunged dramatically to the abyssal plain thousands of feet down. Until fifteen minutes ago, they hadn't had a bite. All John had seen on the depth finder had been smaller fish, and nothing had struck the trolling lines.

Then their luck had finally changed.

Just as the sun was setting over the ocean and John was about to turn the twenty-three-foot vessel for the harbor, he had located a large school of fish below them, maybe a hundred and thirty feet down. Based on the size of the sonar readings, John knew they could be over a school of yellowtails. They had removed the trolling lures and dropped John's new jigs over the side, letting the line spool out over a hundred feet. Almost immediately, Daryl had hooked a yellowtail and handed the pole to his daughter to reel in. Megan's excitement as she hauled in the fish had been contagious, and they were all laughing and hooting as they landed three more yellowtail as twilight darkened the sky around them.

John had tried many lures and baits to catch yellowtail over the years, including live anchovies, frozen market squid, and chum, but this time he had brought out his new candy-bar-sized glow-in-the-dark lures.

Each hollow lure had three sets of treble hooks and housed a glow-in-the-dark insert that a friend had told him drove the fish crazy. His buddy had been right.

Now Megan and her father were struggling with something else on her line, something much larger than the fifteen- to twenty-pound yellowtails now thrashing inside the bait cooler at the stern as they fought off death. John suspected they had just hooked an albacore—that would be a real treat.

"You guys think you can handle that?" John asked.

"I've got a really big one, Uncle John! I can't reel him in!"

Megan's straight brown hair hung in her face as she strained to control her fishing rod, despite the fact that her father was leaning over her and grasping the pole with his hand as well.

"She's not kidding, John. This one's a real monster!" Daryl looked as enthusiastic as his daughter. John knew the feeling. The great thing about deep-sea fishing was that you never knew what you had on the other end of the line.

Suddenly, the pole jerked downward with such force that it slammed Megan's hands into the gunwale.

"Shit! My fingers!" Megan cried out and let go with one hand, but her dad maintained his grip on the pole. She held her hand against her thigh and grimaced.

"Watch your language, honey," Daryl said. "Here, hand me the pole."

He took the fishing rod firmly in both hands and pulled up on it in an effort to create enough slack to reel the fish in. The pole jerked violently downward again, pulling Daryl's portly two-hundred-pound frame into the side of the boat, then popped up again so rapidly that he staggered back into the boat and nearly fell over backward.

"Christ, it broke the line!" Daryl shouted.

"That's fifty-pound test. Are you sure?"

"There's nothing on here, John." He reeled in the slack line.

John slid his own rod into a holder on the stern, then tossed his baseball cap onto the dash and plopped down in the driver's seat to look at the depth finder. He saw vague, unfamiliar shapes on the display that hadn't been there before, mostly around a hundred and fifty feet down, with a bottom depth of two hundred and twenty-three feet. He realized they were into something new.

"Looks like we might have a school of albacore or bluefin under us, guys. Holy shit, that's one big school of fish. Keep an eye on that other pole, Megan!"

"You really think an albacore could have broken that line, John?" Daryl frowned, but his bearded face was still flushed with excitement.

"I don't know. Maybe a shark's in the mix." A mako shark's teeth could easily have severed the line.

John picked up his rod again, lowered the jig until his pole tip hit the surface of the water, then jerked it several times up and down. Next he would reel it quickly toward the surface to see if anything gave chase. On his fourth and final upward jig, just as he planned to start reeling, his rod was nearly wrenched from his hands as he hooked something heavy.

"Got one!" John tightened his grip as the fish made a powerful run. "Guys, this thing is huge!"

He pulled back on the rod, lifting the tip up, then reeled line in quickly as he lowered the tip, before tension could build on the line. He repeated the process a few times, marveling at the resistance on the other end of the line, as he fought the fish toward the surface.

"Whoa! We've got another!" Daryl rushed toward the other rod on the port side, still braced in its holder. "Megan, you better let me get this one."

John continued reeling in his catch, periodically letting the fish strip out line as it fought to head into deeper water. Gradually the quarry tired, and after several minutes it no longer made powerful runs on the line. John looked over at his niece, who stood beside her father, staring down into the dark water.

"Megan, this is a big one, but it's tiring. I think you can handle it now." John looked at the hand she had smacked against the boat, still clutched at her side. "How's your hand?"

"It's okay. Can I reel it in? You don't mind, really?"

"I've caught plenty of these before. You ready?"

Megan smiled and nodded. John muscled the tip of the rod high in the air, gaining a moment of slack, then quickly handed the rod down to his niece. Megan grabbed the pole in a white-knuckled grip and started reeling, but almost immediately was stopped as the fish went on another run.

"I don't know if I'm strong enough!"

"You'll be all right, sweetie. I'm right here if you need help."

John watched for five more minutes as his niece fought to draw the fish in closer to the boat. When he figured their catch was nearing the boat, he stepped to the far side of the boat and reached into an open side compartment, pulling out a sharp gaff with a long, wooden handle.

"Uncle John, what was that?" Megan's expression had changed. She looked frightened.

"What was what? What did you see?"

"There was a glow in the water. The water under the boat lit up."

John stepped near her and looked over the side of the boat, down the taut line, squinting his eyes.

"I don't see anything, hon. You're just tired. Don't worry—you've almost got this sucker landed. Just a few more minutes."

John looked over at his brother, who was still fighting to land his own fish. John peered down into the water again, searching for Megan's jig. It should be close now. There. The glowing, fluorescent jig appeared, maybe ten or fifteen feet down. Something big was hooked to it, but it was hard to see in the evening light.

"Okay, Megan, there he is. Try to lift your pole tip."

"What is it?"

"I don't know yet."

John leaned forward, out over the side of the boat, lowering the fist-sized hook at the end of the gaff into the water, as Megan strained against the line, lifting the tip and grunting.

The glowing lure drew closer. John grasped the chrome boat rail in his left hand and dipped the gaff as deep into the water as he could. The lure moved a few feet closer. Something was *squirming* around it. The writhing thing in the water was not a tuna.

"What the hell . . . ?" John flinched away from the water, yanking his arm back toward the boat. In the faint glow near the jig, something twisted and turned itself around the line. Something soft. Pulpy.

"What is it, Uncle John?" Megan was breathing hard.

"I don't know. Let me pull it closer."

John grasped a fistful of the line with his free hand and pulled the jig toward the boat. He didn't want to gaff this thing and bring it on board until he knew what it was. As the creature reached the surface, several snakelike arms broke through the waves around the lure. Above the arms appeared a large, black eye, staring up at them. As John looked into the eye, a powerful jet of cold water struck him full in the face, entering his eyes and open mouth. He jerked his head away and closed his eyes.

"Fuck!" John spat out the seawater, which had a funny taste. He kept his eyes shut—he didn't want his contact lenses to pop out. As he wiped at his eyes with his sleeve, they started to burn.

"It's pulling me!" Megan yelled. "I can't hold on!"

"Just drop the pole, honey!"

John rubbed his eyes, trying to clear the burning water out of them.

"Uncle John! Dad, help!" Megan shrieked. "My sleeve is caught!"

John managed to open his burning eyes a slit. Megan was leaning far over the side of the boat, bent double toward the water. He could see that her Windbreaker was stuck to the pole or line somehow. As he lunged toward her, her left arm was wrenched downward. Her feet lifted off the wet surface of the boat and she went over the side and into the water with a loud splash.

"Megan!" Her father looked over his shoulder, still struggling with his line. "John, get her back in the boat!"

"I'm trying, goddammit!" John fell forward in the boat, still wiping at his eyes with his sleeve as he searched for the life preserver. He managed to get his eyes open and saw that his arm was covered in a black, inky liquid. He grabbed the life ring from its hook and stepped toward the stern. The black fluid was all over the bottom of the boat. Smeared footprints still showed where Megan had stood.

John looked over the side of the boat. He saw only dark waves rolling into the side of the boat. It was nearly night, and the light was very dim, but the waves were small. Why couldn't he see her? He felt a surge of panic.

"Megan! Megan!"

Daryl shouted, "John, where the hell is Megan?" He stopped reeling and looked anxiously at John.

"Jesus Christ! She was somehow caught in her line. . . ." John was rooted in place, unable to move as he realized his niece was right then being dragged under by the thing at the end of her line. He couldn't think. In the water under the boat, out of nowhere appeared a brief glow, then another momentary flash of light. Then he heard a splash.

"Megan!" Daryl had dropped his rod into the water. He crashed against John, shoving his brother to the side. For a second, maybe two, he looked down into the water for his daughter. He yelled her name again, then took a quick step up onto the gunwale and dove into the dark water.

From above them, the large females in the shoal felt the vibration pass through their soft bodies as a substantial object hit the surface of the water.

After starting to feed on her living sister, the dominant one-eyed female had become hooked to the glowing green prey in her sister's arms and had released her meal before her brethren could overtake her in a similar fashion. She struggled to free herself from the unexpected upward pull of the object. With a sudden burst of power, she fought against it, then immediately stopped moving upward, the glowing thing becoming immobile in her grasp. Furiously she crushed it in her beak, spilling only a bitter fluid, then released the inedible object and swam back toward her wounded sister.

Many more in the shoal had already descended upon the dying female and had managed to tear away much of her flesh. The one-eyed female turned to pursue another group that had detached from the shoal and was headed rapidly to the surface, following another glowing object.

As she neared the surface, something large that had entered the water was dragged down past her, obscured by a writhing huddle of her brethren. Prey. But her attention quickly was diverted by another large, heavy object that created a sharp vibration as it entered the water a moment later.

She moved upward toward the source of the vibration. She immediately sensed that the object was prey, familiar prey, something she had fed on before. Her instincts told her that this creature and the other that had just been swarmed by the mass of her kin were food.

She turned her body slightly to fix her single eye on the prey and assess its defenses. Through the darting members of the shoal, she sensed that the large creature swimming down toward her in the darkening water was nearly her size and weight, but moved clumsily, slowly in the water. It must be dead or dying, and was therefore likely incapable of defending itself. As she closed to within a body length of the prey, she saw its two eyes fixed on her own.

Suddenly the prey moved faster than it had before, thrusting its head toward the surface and thrashing its lower half, its two legs propelling its thick body toward the surface.

The large female felt her nerves tingle as her senses heightened and her muscular body tightened, her flesh changing from a mottled pink to crimson red in the dark water. She twisted her body to direct her weaponry toward the fleeing prey and darted upward, lashing out with two longer tentacles to ensnare it.

But she was not the first to attack. Another large female—the badly scarred sister she recognized by the missing fin tip—rushed ahead of her and caught the slow creature as its head broke the surface of the water.

They rapidly towed the quarry back under, then pulled it tightly into them, engulfing it in their many powerful arms. The two sisters gripped its body tightly, dragging and pulling with powerful bursts of water from their siphons. They moved away from the surface, toward the deep. The prey was thrashing violently, jabbing and striking at them, but they sensed no injury or pain.

Together they pulled the creature farther down. Others from the shoal approached and latched on to its thrashing body; several gripped its leg, another its torso next to the one-eyed female, yet another affixing itself to its face. Drawing the prey tightly against her as she held her position on her own patch of flesh, the large female dug her sharp beak into the creature's side through its loose outer skin. Underneath the sheath of fibrous, inedible fabric her beak met with warm, bloody flesh, rich with fat, and she bit further into its belly.

With a few powerful spasms, the prey finally gave up its fight and yielded to the shoal. The hungry mob, gathered tightly into an enormous ball around the dying animal, drifted slowly down into the blackness as it fed.

CHAPTER 13

Sturman pressed his thighs against the handrail to maintain balance in the slow Pacific swells, then groaned with satisfaction as he sent an arc of piss off the bow of his boat. As the stream entered the water, the ocean magically lit up around it in a swirling, turquoise glow.

"Let there be light." Sturman let out a loud, drunken belch. "Hey, Pop, check this out."

Steve Black walked over, beer in hand. "Fuck me! Glowing shrimp! Why don't you go swimming with 'em, Sturman?"

He shoved Sturman in the back, nearly pushing him over the rail. Sturman managed to keep his balance and turned to face Steve, unsmiling, his face flushed. Steve laughed and slapped him on the back.

Sturman's expression slowly melted into a grin. "Watch it, old man."

"Just fuckin' with you, son."

Sturman's old drinking buddy was one of the few people he couldn't stay mad at. "Try that again and I'm gonna turn around and water down your feet, asshole."

"Go ahead. It's your boat."

"By the way, they're plankton, you dumbass pirate."

"What the hell are you talking about?"

"They're not shrimp. They're plankton . . . little crustaceans that light up when you *piss* 'em off." He had once spent a lot of free time learning about marine biology. There was a time when he thought he would get a degree and study the ocean. But that was long ago.

"I'll be damned. You're smarter than you look."

"I've never lit 'em up with my piss before."

"Where the hell you learn this stuff, son?"

"You should try reading sometime. If you know how."

Sturman finished and watched the glowing plume quickly vanish from the water. "Where you goin', guys?" Sturman considered for a moment. "You know what, boys? I think I'll take a swim."

"You're crazy, son. That water's fuckin' cold."

"Suit yourself."

Sturman zipped up his fly, tossed his straw cowboy hat at Steve, then executed a less-than-perfect dive over the rail, directly into the water where he had just urinated. Bud probably wouldn't follow him in. The dog had gotten bored with the men after they started getting drunk, and was now sleeping in the stern of the boat.

As Sturman entered the cool water, he opened his eyes and saw that the tiny bubble trail he had just created was aglow. He watched the glowing tracers follow his hands as he waved them through the water. He flapped a hand up and down in front of his eyes, striving to see one of the miniature creatures in the ghostly underwater light, but realized in a sober part of his mind that even with a dive mask on he wouldn't be able to see the individual critters—they were too small.

After half a minute, when Sturman felt his lungs burning for air, he kicked for the surface. Floating on the dark ocean next to his boat, he looked toward the bright, artificial lights from shore. How utterly different the harsh white and yellow lights of shore looked in comparison to the soft, supernatural bioluminescence he had just witnessed.

They were only a mile or so off the coast of Capistrano Bay. The moon was nearly full, the winds were light, and the sea was mostly calm. He savored the moment, knowing it was fleeting. It wasn't often he was happy to be alive. Now, though, he was drunk. He usually felt better when he was drunk, because it made him forget, and the water was his favorite place.

That morning, Sturman hadn't been in such a cheerful mood. He had been restless all week, following the doctor's orders to stay out of the water for several days following his accident. Nothing a six-pack couldn't fix, though. He and Steve had begun the evening by wandering over to one of the tourist-friendly bars to knock a few back. While Steve had tried his luck with two younger cougars visiting San Diego for the weekend, Sturman had been his usual brooding self, to the disappointment of the two brunettes. Things had been going remarkably well for Steve. The women were intrigued by his pirate charm until he had gotten buzzed and started talking about the size of his penis, scaring them both away.

Only very adventurous or unintelligent women attracted to the criminal type could stomach Steve's crude attitude and rough appearance. Steve really wasn't a bad guy at heart. Just really rough around the edges. It probably didn't matter anyway—those cougars had been looking for super-virile surfer dudes or soldiers in their early twenties. The old pirate never had a chance.

Steve had been unaffected by the rejection. He had bought Sturman a few more beers before wandering off to hit on some younger tourists. Left to brood on his own, Sturman had started to think about Maria. He told himself that he was saving his friend from being shot down again when he suggested that if they hurried, they could get in a few hours of fishing.

They'd left the bar, grabbed some fried chicken and beer at the store, and walked to the harbor and Sturman's floating refuge. He didn't like being around other people when his mood grew sour, especially women, and the boat that served as his home and office was where he went to think. And get drunk.

Sturman dove down several more times and played with the shrimp, but the water was less than seventy degrees and he quickly cooled. He swam around to the stern of the boat and climbed the swim ladder, then stood dripping on the transom, goose bumps covering his wet skin. As he wrung the seawater out of his T-shirt in the moonlight, Steve Black looked down at him from the flying bridge. He was reclined in the padded swivel chair, his long gray hair pulled back into a ponytail, listening to music softly playing over the boat's built-in speakers.

Sturman listened with him for a moment and began to feel a familiar lump creep into his throat. Brooks and Dunn's rendition of "My Maria" was wafting into the cool night air.

"Mind changing the station, Pop?"

Steve reached to turn the radio dial to a local classic rock station. "Sorry, Will."

"It's all right."

Growing up landlocked, Sturman had always wanted a boat. He had once pictured himself traveling the Caribbean and Mexico in a boat like this one. He had modified the thirty-six-foot fishing boat into a bachelor pad and home business, designed for diving. He had affixed tank holders in the stern and removed the dining table just inside the cabin to offer paying divers plenty of room to sit on the bench seats as he shuttled them to and from dive sites. *Maria* was a great vessel for a small dive operation that catered to groups of four or five divers, but she wasn't big enough to live on comfortably. Sure, she had a galley, a head, and decent sleeping quarters in the bow, but she was a lady designed only to spend a weekend with, not for the commitment of moving in together.

Sturman's needs were simple. He ate out often and worked as much as possible. He could always be seen wearing his old cowboy hat, cargo shorts or old jeans, and a worn T-shirt. Off the boat, when he had to wear shoes, he opted for flip-flops or an old pair of shitkickers.

Sturman looked up at Steve. His friend was out cold.

"We better head in, Pop. I'm not lonely enough yet to sleep with you."

As Sturman dried off, his friend began to snore, but "My Maria" kept playing in his head and soon he was again melancholy. He climbed the ladder to the flying bridge, now feeling thoroughly chilled and a little more sober in the ocean breeze. As they motored slowly back toward the harbor, he allowed himself to think about her.

When he neared the no-wake zone of the harbor, Sturman eased back on the throttle and climbed down the ladder. He stepped around Steve, who had moved down to the stern and curled up near Bud, out of the wind, and headed into the cabin to find his bottle of rum.

CHAPTER 14

Two Presumed Dead After Fishing Trip
OCEAN "GLOWING" WHERE FATHER, DAUGHTER VANISHED

It was a smaller headline, tucked away in the local section of the Sunday edition of the San Diego daily paper. Slouched on his brown leather couch, Joe sat up as he reread the subhead, focusing on one word in particular:

Glowing.

The kid running immigrants had said something about the water glowing for a moment near his boat, but Joe and the other interrogators had laughed it off. The kid had been drinking, and was probably a liar. They figured he had simply seen the glow of the floating flashlights he said were on the water. Joe read the rest of the brief article.

LA JOLLA, CALIF.—A Claremont Realtor and his 12-year-old daughter were reported missing Saturday night, following an afternoon fishing trip on which they went into the water. Both are presumed dead, although no bodies have been recovered.

Daryl Whittaker and his daughter, Megan, were

last seen by family members when they left to go deep-sea fishing with Whittaker's brother. Police say the brother, John Whittaker, told them in a statement that his brother and niece both fell off his boat while the trio fished for yellowtail. According to the statement, both simply vanished under the surface despite calm conditions. The National Oceanic and Atmospheric Administration reported one-to-two-foot swells and fair weather in the area on Saturday.

"According to Mr. Whittaker, his niece fell into the water while fishing off La Jolla, and her father dove in after her," said La Jolla Police spokesperson Janet Sharp. "Mr. Whittaker has stated that neither his niece nor brother ever resurfaced, and that the water underneath the vessel was glowing when the pair vanished."

During the summer months, glowing lights in the Pacific Ocean off Southern California are often reported. The glow is generally seen in the wake of boats at night, due to the presence of bioluminescent plankton that produce light when disturbed.

No charges have yet been filed in the case, but foul play has not been ruled out. Sharp says the Coast Guard and La Jolla Police Department are looking into Whittaker's story and plan to have boats out today on a search for the missing pair.

Whittaker could not be reached for comment.

Joe lowered the paper onto his lap and leaned his head back into the couch, shutting his eyes. A glow. Could there be any connection here?

Two thoughts occurred to him. First, that the loss of the immigrants last week might not have been an isolated incident. Second, he was starting to realize he should be doing something about this, but it was his day off. He felt the first pang of guilt and threw the paper across the room. This was crazy. His wife was right when she said he tried to bear the weight of the world. What the hell was he supposed to do here?

"What's the matter, baby?" Elena was in their open kitchen preparing breakfast.

"Nothing, hon." He forced a smile. "Padres lost again."

Elena was beating eggs in a large metal bowl. "Why do you care so much? It's only one game."

"Only one game? You know how much I love baseball. Better be careful what you say before my morning coffee, lady. Unless you want to be spanked."

Joe looked back to the article. *A little girl.* The article said a twelve-year-old girl had gone missing. Joe looked over at Gabby. His daughter was lying on the floor, playing a video game. She wasn't much older than that. He slid off the couch and crawled up next to her, nudging his shoulder against hers.

"Stop it, Dad!"

"You winning, *mija*?"

"You don't win this game, Dad. I'm building my army."

"Why play if you can't win?"

"You win later. I need to build my army first."

"Of course you do."

The thought of losing Gabby kept forcing its way into Joe's mind. He couldn't even begin to think about what it would be like. He put his arm around his baby girl.

"Get off me, Dad! You just made me go in the wrong door. . . . Now I've got to go all the way back around again. Thanks a lot."

"Anytime, baby."

Joe thought for a moment about the case with the missing immigrants. He could leave that for now; he would look into the fishing accident first.

CHAPTER 15

The next time Sturman got drunk, he wouldn't do it the night before a rough day at sea. Although it was a beautiful Sunday morning, the heaving Pacific swells were much larger than they had been recently. Some storm in the southern hemisphere had sent them up overnight. Well, at least the surfers would be happy.

Sturman made the promise to himself—a promise he had broken many times before—as he gripped the helm of his boat to keep his balance. He swallowed hard, forcing back the bitter bile rising in his throat.

Maria was out in the open ocean, idling over a small area. The boat bobbed up and down, her flying bridge swaying from side to side as Sturman followed his search route. The bright sunlight glinting off the waves made scanning the water very difficult, and amplified his headache and nausea.

Sturman sometimes volunteered with the county sheriff's office on their large-scale marine search-and-rescue operations. One drawback was the lack of early notification. The night before, he had polished off most of a bottle of rum and passed out on his flying bridge.

At dawn, his cell's ringtone had woken him with a request from Joe Montoya to join the search this morning. His head pounding and his mouth dry and tasting of stale alcohol, he had called Joe back and reluctantly agreed to help.

He wasn't very optimistic about today's search, and wished he had asked for more information before he agreed to assist. This looked like it was going to be more of a search for bodies than a rescue. Probably a homicide, based on the witness's story. During the briefing, Sturman had learned that this guy had claimed his brother and niece had fallen off his boat last night. The man had said both of them had gone under, although the sea had been much calmer yesterday.

Not a very good story. Sturman figured if you were going to kill someone, you should probably use a little more imagination.

He felt another wave of nausea as the boat pitched to one side. He looked at the Asian man sitting next to him in the flying bridge, a small, animated guy about Sturman's age who had been talking for the past several minutes. Sturman wished he could get some solitude today.

When you went out with the county on SAR operations, you never went alone. Today, he had been forced to take Mike Phan on board. Mike, another volunteer, was an amicable guy and normally good company. He wasn't the best passenger when you didn't feel like conversation, though. The guy never quit talking.

". . . her swimsuit bottom on the sand, and then I look up and realize she's standing right there. Bucknaked! Holy shit, man, it was funny. Sturman? Hey, man? Are you hearing anything I'm saying?"

"What's that?"

"You're not hearing a word out of my mouth, you big prick."

"Watch it, you little bastard. For a minute, I thought I saw something over there."

"Nothing?"

"Guess not."

"This is what you get for getting smashed again."

"Are you my mother, you little Oriental bastard?"

"Asian, not Oriental, you fuckin' redneck. Seriously, Sturman. You need to slow down on that shit."

"Mike, watch our heading for a minute." Sturman moved past the small Vietnamese man to the ladder, then hustled down and made for the stern. He reached it just in time to lean out and vomit into the churning wake of his boat. He finished with a few dry heaves, wiped his mouth with the back of his hand, and stood up and tipped his cowboy hat at Mike. He felt better.

Mike was at the helm of Sturman's boat in the flying bridge. He shook his head. "Joe know you're still drunk when you head out on these searches?"

Mike was usually assigned to Sturman's boat when they went out on SAR operations. He didn't have his own boat, but he was a certified rescue diver like Sturman, could drive a boat pretty well, and was happy to have an excuse for a free day at sea. He managed a call center in La Mesa, and Sturman knew he didn't get to spend a lot of time on the water.

The pair had been out for several hours now, cruising in their designated search pattern off the coast of La Jolla. Sturman didn't think they'd find anything. If the uncle had dumped his victims in the ocean, he probably wouldn't hand over the exact coordinates to the search team. The SAR team had estimated the ocean's currents at the location the uncle had given, then sent the volunteers off to search different areas based on predicted drift patterns. Volunteers were assigned to the perimeter of the larger search area, with Coast Guard and other official vessels nearer the center. The operation was focusing on a patch of open water northeast of the location where the two had gone into the ocean, much closer to shore, though still well off the coast. The ocean had been relatively empty all morning, save for the other rescue boats nearby and a few weekend fishing vessels visible from the tops of each swell.

Sturman stood at the bottom of the boat, facing south. Down here, closer to the water, the boat rocked less violently. He looked at the surface of the ocean, trying to see past the sunlight glinting off the millions of angles on the waves, thankful for his polarized aviator sunglasses. Searching right now was probably a waste of time. The sun was almost to its zenith, and it was practically impossible to spot anything on the glinting surface. He turned away from the sun and looked toward the northern horizon, focusing where there was slightly less sun glare. He was looking into the waves and thinking about sleep when something nearby caught his eye.

Something orange.

He was sure he had seen a small flash of orange at the crest of the wave, but moments later it had disappeared. Not much out here was that color. Unless a dead garibaldi had floated up, he had seen a man-made object. Possibly a life vest.

Hunters, road crews, and rescue teams wore fluorescent orange or green for a reason: they were the most visible colors to the human eye. They also stood out in dim light, unlike the color red. Sturman, once a hunter and aspiring fireman, knew this was the reason many fire trucks and hunting vests had decades ago been switched from red to fluorescent green and bright orange.

"Hey, Mike, slow up a minute."

"You see something, man?"

"Maybe. Off our port side, maybe fifty yards. Something orange."

Mike slowed the boat, turning the helm to the left. Both men stared off to where Sturman had seen the flash of color. For thirty seconds, both men were quiet, focusing on the waves.

"I don't see anything. Where did you see it again?"

"There! We just passed it." Sturman was pointing aft of the boat, over the port side. "I'll keep my eye on it, Mike. Bring the boat around."

"Got it."

As Mike steered the Wellcraft toward the floating object, Sturman grabbed a net and walked to the starboard side, just behind and below Mike. It would be easier for Mike to drive right alongside the object if he kept it to his side of the boat. They failed to retrieve the object on the first pass in the rough seas, but it gave the men a good look at the object. Something white and orange, about the size of a beer bottle. When Mike came around the second time, he brought the boat within a few feet of it. Sturman scooped it into his fishing net.

"Get a GPS, Mike." They would need a waypoint of the location where they had recovered the object.

"Good eye spotting that thing. What the hell is it?"

Sturman lifted the orange and white object out of the net. It appeared to be made of heavy-duty PVC, with a metal cap. It seemed hollow. "Not sure. There's writing on it, though. 'Property of P-L-A-R-G. Reward if found.' There's a phone number, and some writing in Spanish that I think says the same thing."

"PLARG. The Point Lobos Aquarium Research Group. That's a research institute up in Monterey Bay," Mike said. He pronounced it "plarge."

"A research institute. Well, this probably isn't going to help us much."

Sturman headed to his radio to call in what he'd found. Part of the search protocol. Unless the uncle or his brother had brought this thing onto their fishing boat, it probably was unrelated to their search. He picked up the mouthpiece of his marine radio.

"Three-four-one, Sturman, over."

The radio crackled back. *"Sturman, this is three forty-one. Go ahead."*

"Hey, Montoya. Phan and I have found something."

CHAPTER 16

It was dark at the wreck of the *HMCS Redemption*, as it always was a hundred feet down. But it was peaceful. This ship had always made Sturman think of a church cathedral, and in a way it was.

When he had been a kid growing up in the mountains of Colorado, he had felt the most connected to God when out in the woods. Hunting alone on quiet mornings in the snowy pines and watching the sun rise over distant purple peaks, or sitting atop a bluff near his father's ranch and watching the sun set over red rocks to the west in the summertime, he had somehow felt connected to it all. When he dove down to the silent, otherworldly stage set by the *Redemption*, he sometimes had the same feeling.

Now, as he approached the deck of the huge vessel, he felt a strong urge to enter the hull and explore. He had time, and he wasn't worried about the divers he had brought down with him. Had he even brought down other divers? He couldn't remember, but it didn't seem to matter.

He felt no fear as he swam through the black recesses of the hull. Only a strange calm, despite being alone deep underwater. As he passed through a hatchway, he glimpsed another diver.

Dark hair flowed around her head, but even with help from the bright beam of his dive light he couldn't make out her face in the blackness. Yet there was something familiar about her petite figure, the way she moved gracefully even under the bulk of her scuba gear. He drew closer, trying to see who was behind the dive mask. Just as he was drawing close enough to see her face, he caught a playful look in her eyes, and she spun effortlessly in the water and disappeared through an opening in the ship.

Maria?

Sturman's heart leapt at the thought, although he knew it was impossible. He kicked powerfully and hurtled after her. As he entered the next chamber, he saw that she was waiting on the far side, looking back at him. When he approached, she again darted away, deeper into the ship. He smiled and continued after her.

He followed her for several minutes, her teasing him by staying a short distance in front of him and enticing him to follow. He entered a larger room, perhaps a galley, to find that she was not there. He hovered weightless in the darkness, scanning three openings set into the walls of the room. Which way had she gone? *There.* He saw a thin stream of bubbles rising through an opening to his left.

He entered the next room. She was there, but something was wrong.

She looked at him differently now. She was not floating in a relaxed manner as she prepared to lead the chase. Instead, he noticed that for some reason she was turned toward him with her body positioned over a smaller exit. Her arms were outstretched to either side, hands gripping the sides of the hatchway. As though she was trying to hold on. Suddenly she was pulled violently backward, and a burst of bubbles escaped her mouth as she strained to maintain her grasp.

Heart pounding, he thrust himself into the room and kicked toward her. He could now see her eyes in the dive light. They were wide with horror, pleading. *Help me.* He hurried forward, desperate to reach her, but the thing in the blackness behind her tugged violently at her waist again. This time, she lost her grip and was wrenched backward through the opening, disappearing into darkness.

Sturman fought his way forward, but realized he was hardly moving anymore. A current was pushing seawater into the opening through which she had vanished, driving him away. The water flowing out was very cold, and somehow even darker than the water around him. He struggled against the powerful surge and managed to reach the hatch. As he grasped the rough steel of the ship and strained to pull himself forward, he came face-to-face with the woman. *Maria.*

Her dark eyes bore an expression of terror inside the dive mask, and her brown hair swirled around her head in the icy current. Her hands were outstretched toward him.

As he extended his free hand to save her from the invisible thing drawing her away, her regulator erupted from her mouth, and even in the heavy press of the water he was able to hear her muffled scream. Her body was torn away from him, wrenched into the blackness and out of the glow of his light.

Sturman cried out in fear and pulled himself forward, but then his fingers slipped off the edge of the opening and the powerful current sent him tumbling backward, away from her. His dive light went out and he began to spin in the blackness, helpless in the grip of the merciless black water.

In the darkness, something fleshy began to touch the side of his face, sliding along his cheek and into his lips. He cried out as the thing ran over his skin, swinging his fists toward the unseen evil.

Sturman bolted upright in his bed, causing Bud to leap backward. The dog wagged his tail warily and looked at his master with a confused expression. Sturman was covered in sweat and breathing hard. *Only another dream.*

He rubbed his face and felt dog slobber on his cheek. Maybe he had accidentally struck Bud while gripped by the nightmare. "Come here, buddy. I'm sorry."

After a moment of coaxing, the dog padded back over to him and let him scratch his ears.

"That's what I get for staying sober, pal. More damn nightmares."

After a cold swim to wash away the dream, Sturman toweled off and fixed himself a pot of black coffee in the boat's cramped galley. He threw on some clothes and sat in the stern, soaking up the morning sun as the warmth returned to his body.

As he sipped the steaming coffee, he studied the orange-and-white object in his hands. There was something alluring about it, as though it represented more than a simple fish marker. Sturman realized that despite having what many would consider a very exciting job, he lived a very routine life. Eat. Dive. Drink. Sleep. Something as small as finding this unique object provided a much-needed distraction.

It was a typical July morning in San Diego. There was a thin marine layer obscuring the sun, but it would burn off in a few hours. Sturman was comfortable in just shorts and a T-shirt even this early in the morning, and the country music playing over the radio was helping him relax.

Yesterday had been a long day. Sturman hadn't pulled *Maria* into her slip until dark. Not surprisingly, they hadn't found any evidence of the missing father and daughter. Sturman had fixed himself a steak before sunset, and then fallen onto his bed and into a heavy slumber.

As the county SAR official in charge of the operation, Sergeant Joe Montoya had let Sturman keep the orange device after a member of the Coast Guard on another vessel identified it as a pop-off tag marine biologists used to study large fish and marine mammals. Apparently, the tag had detached from a tuna or sea lion or some other larger animal, then floated to the surface. It had only been in the search area by coincidence. Finding unrelated detritus on the ocean surface when conducting searches was nothing new. All kinds of junk could be seen floating off Southern California: fast-food packaging, water bottles, plastic bags by the thousands. If they kept every piece of trash they found on SAR missions, the investigators wouldn't know where to start on a case, so the search teams acted as a filter and didn't mention all the miscellaneous manmade debris they found.

The floating tag had a phone number listed on it because apparently it wasn't actually a transmitter—just some sort of recording device. So the researchers who had deployed it had no way of finding it unless someone reported it to them. Probably a less-expensive option than a transmitting tag, especially if you were planning to tag a number of fish. The Spanish writing on it made sense, too, since they were so close to Mexico . . . and because so many in California spoke Spanish as their first language. His Spanish had gotten a little rusty since losing Maria.

Sturman fired up his aging laptop as he sipped the bitter black coffee and typed "PLARG" into the search box on his homepage. Topping the list of results was a website for the Point Lobos Aquarium Research Group. PLARG conducted marine research all over the world, focusing on deep-sea organisms and environments. He browsed through the site, but found no specific information about pop-up tags.

"Hey, Bud, should we call them?"

At the mention of his name, Sturman's dog rose from his bed inside the cabin and climbed the stairs to place his head in Sturman's lap. He scratched behind Bud's short, floppy ears, and the dun-colored dog grunted with pleasure.

"We could use a reward, pal. If we don't start making more money, I'll have to eat you soon."

There were two phone numbers on the orange tag. One had an 831 Monterey County area code, and Sturman could tell that the other was set up for dialing in Mexico. He picked up his cell and dialed the first number. The line rang. He took a deep breath.

"Come on, big money. . . ."

CHAPTER 17

Midnight. She was alone, a hundred feet below the surface, surrounded by intense water pressure and near-absolute blackness. Hovering in the dark waters of the Sea of Cortez, far underneath her boat and totally alone, Valerie Martell was a bit frightened, but completely in control. She had been here before. Many times, in fact.

In her right hand she held an underwater camera. A tiny green LED flashed on the camera, indicating that it was recording. On the other wrist, the pull cord on Val's scuba light tugged gently at her wrist as the light swung freely. For now, the light was off.

With her left hand she reached for a nylon tether that ran up toward the surface. She gave a few strong tugs on the tether to test it again, then ran her hand down it and checked the knot at her waist to make sure it hadn't worked itself loose. The rope tether was secured to a cleat on the stern of her boat.

She hoped it was secured, anyway.

In the cast of the six bright halogen lights mounted to her vessel far above, Val was able to see into the dark water around her. She could make out the outline of her own body, down to her dark scuba fins fluttering below her, now that her eyes were accustomed to the dim surroundings. She could see the white tether running toward the surface, and a fine snow of suspended marine particles drifting by. But mostly, all Val saw was endless blackness in front of her. Behind her. To both sides of her. Below her.

And occasionally, she saw something else.

With increasing frequency, she watched large, pale shapes glide by her where the cone of light couldn't quite reach. They were the animals that she was hoping to see.

Val's regulator hissed as she drew in another long, slow breath. Otherwise, the underwater world was silent. She looked down at her dive computer, connected to her tank by a long rubber hose: ten more minutes, then she would have to surface.

Come on, guys, don't be scared. It's just little old me.

At the edge of her vision, Val saw another pale shape dart past her. Her heart jumped in her chest and she exhaled a burst of air into her regulator. Val felt a little jealous of the crowd of bubbles that escaped past her face on their scramble to the surface. *No,* she reminded herself, *you need to relax. Everything will be fine.*

Several more forms appeared at the edge of her vision. Lighter than the dark water, the animals might be emitting some of their bioluminescence, or maybe they were simply reflecting the light from above. Their outlines were still formless at this distance.

Something brushed against Val's scuba tank.

She had just enough time as she spun to watch the

animal disappear into the blackness. Moments later, another shape began to emerge from the water, maybe thirty feet away. Years of experience had taught Val that it was hard to gauge distance underwater, especially at night.

This one was curious. It was moving much slower, approaching her. And it was a big one.

Val felt a combination of excitement and fear. She slowly raised the camera in her right arm, pointing it toward the approaching creature. Based on its huge size, almost certainly a female. *Perfect. Smile for the camera.*

Val suddenly remembered why she loved this job.

The thick shape gliding toward her was nearly six feet long. As the animal neared, Val began to make out its torpedo shape, complete with wide, triangular fins; large, black eyes; and many arms and tentacles, drawn neatly together and coming to a near perfect point where their tips merged at the end of the streamlined body.

What a beautiful animal, Val thought.

These organisms had fascinated Valerie Martell ever since she had first learned about them in an undergrad zoology course at the University of Florida. Her professor, who had once been a marine biologist and was still an avid fisherman, had conveyed his enthusiasm about the impressive animals when the class had been covering the phylum *Mollusca.* Not his usual dry self that day, he had told stories of the creatures' power and aggression. How they had been reported to have devoured fishermen and sharks, how they could leap far out of the water, how they could change colors and fire jets of ink at their predators.

Val had been instantly hooked.

Thirteen years, three degrees, and two research assignments later, here she was. Over a hundred feet down in the Sea of Cortez, face-to-face with the animals she had sought to understand throughout her academic career. And certainly not for the first time—Val had dived with these creatures on countless occasions. Although she understood them better than perhaps anyone in the world, she knew that like all animals, they were unpredictable. And she was always extremely on guard in their environment, their world.

The large individual approaching Val began to spread its tentacles as it slowed to a stop several feet away. It appeared to be studying her. After a few moments, it began to glide again, moving silently past her, allowing itself a good look at Val with one of its oversized eyes as it swept within an arm's length of her camera.

I must be more alien to her than she is to me, Val thought. *At least I know what she is.*

Seeing her this close, Val guessed this was a mature female. Probably almost a hundred pounds—nearly as big as Val herself. She swung the camera slowly by to record the large specimen, then let go of the tether with her left hand and reached for the modified light attached to her wrist. Time to get to work.

The big female reappeared again moments later, off to Val's left. It *was* the same one, wasn't it? Maybe not—Val figured there must be an entire shoal here. She'd be able to tell if it was the same individual when she reviewed the footage later. Val pointed the dive light in her left hand at her new subject, simultaneously lifting the camera in her right to record the animal, then turned on the light.

In an impossibly fast maneuver that made Val flinch,

the big female spun and vanished into the blackness. Val turned the soft light off, then on again. In succession, Val rhythmically activated the beam. Through the thick green lens filter, very little illumination actually shone into the water. Rather than a bright beam, Val's modified dive light emitted only a faint green glow. She completed another series of muted green flashes, directing the diffuse light toward where the female had vanished.

She reappeared.

Below Val, though still in front of her, her subject again rose. No, this one definitely wasn't the same individual. It was much smaller. Maybe three and a half, four feet long. Probably a male in the same shoal. The smaller animal moved up toward her and did what she had been hoping it would do.

In a gentle burst of soft bioluminescent light, it flashed once at Val.

She smiled awkwardly around her thick rubber mouthpiece, and turned her light on again, then off almost immediately. The alien creature's body glowed again in response.

They were communicating.

Okay, Val thought, *let's see if hundreds of hours studying tape will finally pay off.* With her modified flashlight, Val sent out several brief flashes in slow succession. She paused. Nothing. The small male simply hovered in front of her. Next, Val attempted longer flashes of light, in more rapid succession. Still nothing.

Over the next few minutes, Val continued a series of simple flashes of various intensities, durations, and frequencies. The attempts weren't random patterns, but predetermined sequences she had rehearsed after studying her previous tapes of this species' behavior—her own attempt at mollusk Morse code. After several minutes, the smallish male never responded again. He appeared to lose interest and slowly descended into the darkness below her.

Val cursed into her regulator.

She decided to ad-lib. Pointing her light down toward where the male had disappeared, she emitted an erratic series of flashes. Still nothing . . . no, wait. A distant glow. Then the water all around Val lit up as the shoal responded with bursts of light, revealing a multitude of the creatures nearby. Val's heart leapt at the unexpected spectacle. She felt as though she were surrounded by a swarm of giant fireflies.

Then something rushed toward her.

Before Val could react, the creature closed on her. It shot out its two long tentacles like twin pistons and struck her violently in the chest, knocking the air out of her lungs. As she struggled to inhale, something wrapped around her calf. Then it began to pull downward.

She had somehow provoked an attack.

Val tried in vain to kick at the two or more animals now clinging to her legs. She felt one of her fins get jerked off her foot. Using her camera to fight off the predatory advances of the large individual in front of her, Val didn't realize how quickly she was being pulled down until the tether at her waist grew very taut, cutting into her abdomen.

Valerie Martell was not a woman who panicked. On the contrary, she was more than accustomed to hair-raising situations. She prided herself on her ability to remain level-headed and slip out of each and every potentially dangerous situation unharmed by thinking clearly and objectively, putting her emotions aside. It was time for that sort of thinking.

Although the animals were pulling down on her with incredible force, she was tethered to the boat with a thick nylon rope. The tether should hold. *Just don't panic.*

Suddenly the animals released her and she felt herself drawn upward as the strain left the rope. Val drew a deep breath from her regulator. *That was close.* She had witnessed random instances of aggression in the past, but this hadn't been random. She had somehow triggered it with the light. *I need to watch the footage and figure out what I did.*

A ring of powerful arms wrenched the camera from Val's grasp. She watched helplessly as the latex tubing that attached the camera to her wrist tore free and followed the camera, which was now being assailed by several members of the shoal. It vanished in the darkness below Val as it and the animals clinging to it left the range of the bright surface lights, far above.

Val hovered in the darkness for a minute, straining to see if the camera would float back up. It was time to surface. She hadn't seen it reappear, or any of its abductors. She looked above her to the lights of the boat and kicked toward it.

Finally, a breakthrough in her research, and the bastards steal her camera. Something Val had done tonight had worked. But what? If she'd only been able to recover the footage . . .

She left the bathroom of her hotel room and put on a dry bra and panties. She hadn't even bothered to dry her shoulder-length, dark hair. It was warm in the room, so it didn't matter. And she was feeling an incredible urge to sleep.

Her crew had searched for the camera for hours over the rest of the night, since it should theoretically float. She needed it to figure out what had provoked the shoal. Somehow she had effectively communicated with the animals, but not in the way she had planned. Finally, at dawn, her crew had insisted they give up and head in. Back at her hotel, having eaten and showered, Val was now feeling utterly drained.

She yawned. It was early in the morning in La Paz, Mexico, but she was accustomed to working at night. It was her bedtime now. Safely in her room, the familiar morning fatigue was grappling her willpower into sub-mission.

She padded across the broad, rust-colored tiles on the floor, flopped down on the bed, and buried her head in the cool pillows. They smelled clean, like bleach. The room was dark, thanks to the thick curtains hiding the sliding glass door, and mercifully quiet. The bed felt good. Soft. She began to relax, feeling sleep setting in.

The phone rang, and Val's heart jumped. *Dammit.*

She reached over and grabbed her cell phone off the nightstand, glancing at the display. It was PLARG. She pushed the green answer button.

"Hello, Mark."

"Hola, Val. Buenos dee-az!" Mark's Spanish was shit.

"Cut the crap, Mark. I'm tired. Why are you calling?"

"Tough Monday morning, huh? At least you're in sunny Baja California. I get to spend the day in a cold, windowless lab in cheery Moss Landing. There's even summertime fog outside, if I decide to go look out a window."

"I'm sorry, Mark. I had a really rough night and I was trying to get some sleep. What's going on?"

"Well, I'm sorry to bother you, but this is pretty big. Someone called about one of your tags."

"That's nice. Couldn't you call me later? You know I'm usually asleep this late in the morning."

"Val . . . this is big."

There was a silence. "Okay, Mark. What's so big about this?"

"Drumroll, please . . . it's where he's calling from. This guy isn't in Mexico."

"What?" She sat up on the edge of the bed. "What are you talking about?"

"Apparently, your squid took a trip to San Diego."

PART II
ALLOCATION

CHAPTER 18

"**H**umboldt squid."

"Beg your pardon?"

"That tag came off a Humboldt squid, Mr. Sturman."

"So lady, you're saying this here tag isn't from a fish? It's from a giant squid?"

Sturman heard the woman sigh into the phone. "Not a giant squid. The tag was on a *Dosidicus gigas*, or Humboldt squid. You may have heard of them before. They're also called 'jumbo squid' or 'flying squid.' Down here, they're called *los diablos rojos*—'red devils.'"

Sturman turned the orange and white tag over in his hands. "Yeah, I think I've heard of those before. I've seen a few articles in the paper over the last couple years, talking about them washing up dead around here."

"Right. That's them. We're starting to think that periodic El Niño events bring them north from Mexico."

"So this big tag fell off some little Mexican squid?"

The woman sighed again. "All anyone cares about

are giant squid. Look, Mr. Sturman—can I call you Will?"

"Most people just call me 'Sturman.' It's a Navy thing."

"Right. Anyway, *Dosidicus* are nowhere near as big as giant squid, but they're still quite large. There've been reports from South America of Humboldts growing to twelve feet or more, though I'm fairly certain those reports are exaggerations. I've personally seen mature adults two meters long that weigh as much as I do . . . as big as a very large dog."

"Never heard a woman compare herself to a dog before."

Sturman heard another loud sigh. He looked at Bud. His dog was sitting next to him at the sunny street-side patio of a burger joint, staring at him with sad eyes in an effort to elicit a French fry. Sturman scratched his ears. "Hear that, Bud? These things are bigger than you."

"Excuse me?"

"Nothing. Just talking to my business partner."

"Right . . . so what I was getting at is that the only cephalopods people hear about are giant squid, or their cousins, colossal squid, simply because they're so big. The popular media can generate a lot of interest about animals that are forty feet long and weigh a ton. But the thing is, nobody will ever occupy the same space as a giant squid unless they go thousands of feet underwater in a submersible. Giant squid are too few and too deep.

"The squid that I study are much faster, more graceful, and more aggressive than any giant squid. And probably more intelligent. Plus, they're easier to study, since they actually go into shallower water where we can dive with them."

"Doc, you sure know your squids. So you tagged one of these things, these Humboldt squid, off San Diego? They aren't very common around here, are they?"

"No, they aren't. Actually, that squid was tagged in the Gulf of California. The Sea of Cortez. That's why I'm so glad you called. That's the first *Dosidicus* from my study to move out of the study area."

"Let's get something out of the way here. I don't mind helping you out, but it also says something here about a reward."

"Oh, yeah. Right. The people at PLARG should be able to help you out with that."

"They said to talk to you about the money."

"I'm sure they can help you out. I think the going rate is a hundred dollars for a returned tag. Look, Mr. Sturman, this is really important research. That tag you found proves that these squid are moving north into California. We've had many reports over the last decade of Humboldts moving as far north as western Canada, but we've never been able to track any of the animals from Mexico or anywhere else. Many of us think they're now expanding their range."

"So I guess this is great news for you, then?" Sturman threw a French fry at a seagull. *Only a hundred dollars*.

"It's outstanding news. I'm coming back to California in a few days. . . . Maybe I can head first to San Diego and talk with you about the tag. I'd like to learn about where you found it, and maybe spend a few days in the area looking for the shoal. Do you have your own boat, by any chance?"

"I'm a divemaster. Got a live-aboard thirty-six-foot Wellcraft."

"Really? Would you be interested in taking me out on the water for a few days this week? I'd pay you, of course. The grant covers unexpected research costs."

Sturman sat up in his chair. "Actually, my calendar just opened up for this week. We could probably work something out, Dr. Martell."

"That's great."

"You really willing to spend time out on a boat with a stranger?"

"I've done crazier things, and I don't have time to try and research a better deal. Your boat sounds perfect, anyway. I'd just need to bring a little equipment on board. Oh, and we'd have to go out at night. Would that be a problem?"

"No, like I said, I'm sure we can work something out. So why did you say these squid ventured to my neck of the woods?"

"Squid are just like every other animal, even human beings. We all spread wherever we can, where conditions may be as favorable or more favorable than the place we were before, until we are limited by something. People have spread all over the planet because of our amazing ability to adapt using clothing, shelter, new food sources . . . you get the point. But with other animals, which are evolved for a specific set of conditions, movements into new habitats only can happen when the ecology or environmental conditions of an area change. Whatever limiting factors were present before, such as lack of food sources or temperatures out of an ideal range, must change to become more favorable."

"Sounds like you know a lot about this." Sturman thought of the missing father and daughter. "Dr. Martell, these squid ever attack people?"

"There's some anecdotal evidence that they've attacked fishermen in Baja. I've also had them rough me up a bit, and so have some other divers who have spent a lot of time with them. A guy I know down here even wears a custom-made suit of plastic armor when he dives with Humboldts. But there's never been a recorded case of Humboldt squid killing or seriously hurting anyone. Why?"

"Well, I told you where I found your transmitter."

"Off La Jolla, right?"

"That's right. But I haven't told you what I was doing when I found it."

CHAPTER 19

A white-on-black Jolly Roger flapped over Steve Black's head as he steered his boat west into a stiff onshore breeze. He looked up at his flag and smiled back at the skull and crossbones, gold glinting from one of his teeth. He was happy to have some business this evening, even if it was a black family. Sturman would be jealous. Ever since the economy had floundered, all the dive boat captains had struggled to make ends meet. Later tonight, though, the beers could be on him.

Thankfully, he didn't need to find the dive site marker, staring almost directly into the setting sun as he was. He was headed for his well-kept secret—a hotbed of sea life just off the coast that few divers knew about. Here, the bottom rose up to a forty-foot rock pinnacle, which was home to a miniature forest of giant kelp. Below the surface, the kelp's sturdy strands swayed in the current as they stretched for the light of the surface above, securely anchored to the rock with root-like holdfasts. Steve had learned about the spot from a fishing buddy and could only navigate to it using GPS. Since it wasn't far from shore, he would swing *Black Bart* around and approach the site from an angle to make it harder for the people he brought on board to figure out where it was. One guy had tried to GPS the site when Steve had brought him out here, but that device now rested somewhere on the bottom around the pinnacle, collecting silt.

The sun was just dipping below the horizon, looking impossibly large and distorted as it sank into the Pacific. A bright line of color spread along the ocean to each side, and clouds above the sun harnessed its dying light to form themselves into gigantic masses of pastel-pink coral.

Tourists loved sunsets. And happy tourists meant better tips. Regardless of how this dive went, the Jackson family was enjoying their evening.

Steve looked down to the main deck at his dive group. The family from Las Vegas had stopped pulling on their wet suits to watch the sun, smiling broadly and uttering praises for the amazing show Mother Nature was putting on.

Steve was able to charge these people a bit more for the night dive. Maybe it was the novelty, or maybe because night dives were more dangerous. They probably thought a divemaster had more responsibility at night. He probably did, but he didn't care. He expected divers to use their own heads. He'd gotten jaded to scuba diving after logging thousands of dives—more than half right here in the San Diego area. Now he rarely got excited or scared. All the dives were fairly routine now, even shark dives in open water . . . or octopus encounters like he had planned for tonight. This was just a job now.

But it was one hell of a sunset.

When his GPS indicated that they were nearing the site, Steve eased back on the throttle. He held a rubber band between his teeth as he pulled his shaggy gray hair back with both hands, gathering it into a ponytail. Having hair in his dive mask allowed water to seep in, and strands sometimes got tangled in the mask strap. Ponytail secured, he stood and turned to face his clients.

Showtime.

"Ahoy, mateys! Thar be the treasure we seek," Steve boomed down at his passengers. Tourists loved the ridiculous pirate gimmick, especially the really young divers.

"Captain Curt, lad, help me fetch the anchor." The boy looked at his father for approval. Steve wondered for a moment what it would have been like to have known his own father.

The boy's father smiled. "Go ahead, son."

Good kid, Steve thought. The youngest in the family, a boy of maybe thirteen, Curtis grinned and followed Steve to the bow. Steve had learned long ago that one key to a bigger tip was remembering the names of the kids. He had already forgotten the mother's first name; the dad's name might be Bill. But he was certain the kids' names were Jennifer and Curtis. Jennifer was too old to be amused by his pirate act, but her brother was loving it.

After Steve had dropped anchor, they all headed to the stern for a pre-dive briefing.

"Aye, ladies and gents, here be a real gem of a night dive. Below us be the lair of many an eight-armed octopus. These scallywags are said to gather the treasures of the deep, and ye never know when you'll discover a gold watch or diamond ring in thar clutches!" This was only partially a lie; Steve had found a watch at this site on a dive years ago, which surely had fallen off a careless diver. An octopus had even been next to it, curious about its glint in the beam of the scuba lights.

"Take care to watch yer own jewelry—these beasts will snatch 'em right off of you and make for their caves." The brother and sister smiled at each other as she touched the gold chain around her neck. Steve wasn't surprised they were more eager than scared, since their father claimed each of them already had logged over thirty dives. This was going to be their first night dive, though, so Steve wanted to be sure he built up the anticipation without frightening them.

"Also keep yer eyes out fer the other active denizens of nighttime waters. Ye may spy me mate the leopard shark, and be warned to not touch the spiny lobsters, as they may decide to stick ye!" Steve knew they would never actually get close to any of the wary lobsters.

"Is this safe? I mean, none of these animals are really a threat, right?"

Steve smiled at the children's mother and gave her a wink. "None more dangerous than Captain Black himself. If ye stay with me, no harm will come to ye."

After Steve finished his colorful pre-dive briefing, everyone finished suiting up and checking their air supplies, weight belts, and other scuba equipment. The sun had vanished beneath the waves and the first stars were appearing to the east.

On Steve's instruction, the family entered the water one at a time. Steve would be the last to leave the boat. Seated on the side of his vessel, he watched them all go in until Jennifer finally fell backward and splashed tank-first into the waves. She surfaced a moment later near her family and looked back at Steve as she touched the top of her head with one hand. *I'm okay.* He nodded and looked back to make sure everything was secure on his vessel, then leaned back and rolled off the side of the boat.

Cold water instantly flooded his wet suit at the openings in his face mask and neckline. To him, this was the worst part of night diving off California. As he sank below the surface in the darkening water, he gritted his teeth on his regulator as he waited for the chill water against his torso to warm. By the time he bobbed back up to the surface and gathered the family off *Black Bart*'s stern, he felt relatively comfortable again.

Steve faced the Jackson family on the surface to give an "okay" sign with thumb and forefinger and waited for each person to return it. Nobody could respond verbally, with masks on their faces and regulators secured in their mouths. Everyone returned his gesture; they appeared ready to go under. Steve flipped on his dive light and began to dump the air out of his BCD. As his eyes dipped below the waves and cold water closed in over his head, he caught a final glimpse of his boat.

Underwater, Steve directed his light toward the vessel. He couldn't make out the hull just twenty feet away as the cone of light was swallowed by the gloom. He looked toward the bottom as he slowly sank, and felt the first hints of pressure on his ears.

It was very dark.

CHAPTER 20

Brightness.

Rising along the small seamount from darker, deeper water, the fading illumination from above was still unpleasant, but no longer painfully bright to the eyes in the shoal. Yet now there were other, more intense lights in the distance ahead of it. The lights moved erratically, and when directed toward the animals' powerful eyes, they caused discomfort. The squid nonetheless obeyed their urge to move upward and toward the source, in search of sustenance.

The shoal had found adequate food for several nights now. Safe from predators in the shallower waters and finding abundant prey, its members had remained in the same area, retreating to the depths at night but no longer migrating farther from their birthplace. The quarry in this environment was unfamiliar, but each aggressive attempt at new food sources had been met with success.

Still, the shoal had grown hungrier.

Slower than the nimble, younger members of the shoal, the largest females in particular had struggled to capture enough of the small local fishes to fuel their formidable bodies. Several had together devoured a smaller sibling the previous night, but it was not enough. There was not sufficient food.

Because they were growing.

Already much bigger than the mature adults in other shoals, many of the animals in this gathering nonetheless grew larger with each passing day. But they were also getting slower, hungrier—and more aggressive.

The large females near the front of the shoal did not contemplate these changes, nor plan to attack other members in their group. They simply reacted to their instinctual urges, which at the moment were not driving them to cannibalism. The urges simply pulled them toward the distant lights, followed closely by the other members of the shoal.

With the lights, they sensed something else. Running through and bouncing off the soft bodies of their brothers and sisters around them, a faint vibration coursed through the water just before the first bright light had appeared. The aggressive females had sensed this vibration recently—a distant impact on the surface as something entered the water.

Potential prey.

When they sensed several more vibrations emitted from the surface above, they turned and glided toward the origin. A thousand others followed.

As they drew closer to the lights, the large females began to make out very long, slender shapes silhouetted against the lights. The kelp, running in a series of uneven lines toward the surface, bore many leafy fronds that drifted in the ocean surge. Hesitating at first, the shoal slowly moved toward the unfamiliar underwater forest. The large, one-eyed female curiously extended a tentacle toward a waving frond attached to one of the stalks. The frond moved freely in the water, away from her touch. She eased both tentacles out, closing them around it. The soft suckers on her arms caressed its slick surface, tasting it. The kelp was living, but cold and bitter, and she quickly released it. This was not food.

She began to weave through the inedible vertical obstructions, followed closely by the others. Soon the water became uncomfortably shallow. Yet the lights were now much closer and her curious nature only amplified her hunger. One of the beams shined in her direction, blinding her remaining eye and sending a jolt of pain toward her nerve center. She spun and darted away from the stimulus, her retreat mirrored by nearby members of the shoal.

Their alarm was brief. The painful lights soon were again focused away from the shoal. Once again it moved toward them.

CHAPTER 21

Steve waited patiently for the tentacle to reappear.

The Jackson family was gathered tightly around and above him in the ink-black water, eager to see what their divemaster was trying to show them. The novice divers struggled to stay in place in the light current sweeping across the pinnacle, managing to maintain neutral buoyancy but occasionally bumping against Steve's scuba tank. He never did think black people could swim all that well. Undistracted by the other divers, he continued to wiggle his index finger in front of a dark recess in the reef.

In a brightly illuminated patch of rock under the dive lights, the tip of a tentacle reappeared. Inquisitively, the red-orange appendage slithered out farther from under the rough slab of dark rock and stroked Steve's finger with small, white suckers. The animal finally drew itself out of its hole and flitted along the rock on eight arms. Its body was about the size of a softball, with arms the length of a man's hand. A typical California two-spot octopus.

Steve had always thought octopi were fascinating

animals, and much smarter than many people realized. Normally on night dives, the inquisitive creatures were visible everywhere on this rocky reef, staying in the open unless agitated. Steve wondered why he was having to coax them out tonight.

He wriggled his fingers again, and the curious animal wrapped its arms around his hand, enveloping his gloved fingers with its smooth, muscular body. Steve looked over his shoulder toward the family, directly into Jennifer's mask. Even in the dim illumination of their dive lights, he could see her delighted expression. He extended his arm toward her, offering the octopus, but she drew her hand away, shaking her head. Another hand appeared from the right side of Steve's field of view. *Curtis.* Her brother was apparently a little bolder. Steve held the animal next to the boy's hand, and after a few moments it gently pulled itself over to the boy's wrist and latched on to its new perch, flattening its soft body.

Suddenly the octopus grew redder in color and released the boy's arm, disappearing back into its hole in a swirl of shell fragments. *Jumpy little guy.* Steve directed his light away from the octopus, along the surface of the rocky pinnacle. He drew in a lungful of air to increase his buoyancy and began lifting off the bottom. Time to head off in search of more attractions. He knew he could find the Jackson family plenty of lobster down here, and some of the huge local sea stars. He panned the light upward into the open water, and something darted across it.

Something big.

Steve's heart leapt against his ribs. He exhaled a cloud of bubbles and scanned the water. Probably a sea lion or blue shark. It hadn't been a truly massive animal, no bigger than himself. Too small to be a great white or mako. Nothing to worry about.

He swept the light all around, hoping to see the mystery visitor again. As his beam of light hit the dark green kelp fronds off to his left, Steve glimpsed two more pale shapes, which withdrew almost immediately from the powerful beam.

Those weren't sharks. And they certainly didn't move like fish. Harbor seals? If the other divers hadn't noticed these animals yet, they would soon. Steve hoped none of them would panic.

He turned to face the group and waited for the family to assemble near him. He swam over to Mrs. Jackson first, looking into her eyes from a few feet away as he touched his own air gauge directly in front of her mask: *How much air do you have left?*

She glanced at her gauges under her flashlight and then held up one finger, then three. *Thirteen-hundred psi.* Most important to Steve, she looked calm. He proceeded to each family member in turn, checking their air—and their expressions. Nobody seemed anxious.

Steve turned and swam over the reef with measured kicks, staying several feet above its rough surface. This pinnacle was always teeming with life, covered with crevasses for animals to find refuge in. It offered an island of shallower water away from the human disturbance near shore. Along its surface, he noticed a multitude of orange sea stars as large as serving platters, spiny purple urchins in the thousands, and other motionless critters affixed to the rock face. But where were the fish, the octopi, the other more mobile residents? Everything seemed to be hiding. Maybe they were avoiding—

Steve's light revealed a dead man's face, regarding him with empty black eyes from within a dark recess in the reef.

His heart, already racing, lurched again as he swung the light back to reveal the face's features, less than ten feet away. The head swayed gently within the opening in the rock, eyes unblinking and unobstructed by a dive mask. With a thick jaw and flat nose, this was the face of an ancient, drowned prizefighter. This man couldn't be alive, with lidless dark eyes and mottled gray skin. . . .

As recognition dawned on him, Steve released the breath he had been holding into his regulator, sending out a burst of bubbles. *Of course.* It was only a big wolf eel, curled within a crevasse of the reef. He had often thought these eels looked like very old men without noses. Despite block-like heads shaped by muscles in their powerful jaws, from a distance they seemed very human.

Steve turned away from the reef and the beam from his light caught another large shape. Just as the gleam found the animal, it twisted its body and spun gracefully, vanishing into the darkness once again. Near the middle of its form, Steve had distinctly seen a round, dark spot.

An eye.

Few animals had eyes near the center of their bodies. Steve immediately realized what he had seen. He knew a couple divers who had encountered jumbo flying squid before, but he himself had never seen them before. Until tonight.

They were much bigger than he had imagined.

He remembered that the deepwater animals were sensitive to light and directed his beam downward, making it difficult to see more than a few feet into the water in front of him. He indicated to the others to redirect their lights as well. They probably had no idea what a treat they were in for. Steve looked out into the darkness.

And waited.

Moments later, the first of the squid showed itself. It was uncomfortably close when Steve first noticed it—fifteen feet or less. Although a little on edge, he smiled as he got his first good look at a live jumbo squid.

Built like a torpedo, but with its fins at the front instead of the rear, the pale apparition hung almost motionless in the blackness. It peered at Steve with twitching ebony eyes much bigger than his own, fluttering the broad fins as it held its position. One fin appeared to be damaged at the tip, and scars covered its body. The squid's arms and tentacles, drawn seamlessly together, slowly separated and it began to move toward Steve. He saw that it was missing an arm.

He had seen flying squid in pictures before—fishermen liked to brag—but those had probably never been more than three or four feet long. The old warrior he was looking at now was far bigger—maybe eight feet. He began backing away from it until his tank bumped into the other divers.

He could tell the squid was assessing him, its dark, animated eyes rolling in deep sockets. They resembled the expressive eyes of a doe, Steve thought, but had an alien quality to them. Unsure of how he should interact with the large animal, or what it might do, he remained motionless. The squid drew closer and he raised his left arm to maintain distance.

When it was near enough, it reached out and explored Steve's outstretched hand with its tentacles. He could scarcely feel the gentle touch through his neoprene glove. Its body, covered in scars, rotated and he caught a glimpse of the dark beak, nestled in sphincter-like muscle at the axis of its meaty arms. Steve turned to smile at the other divers, but quickly realized that with all their lights aimed downward they wouldn't be able to see his expression anyway. Apparently this squid wasn't much different from an octopus. With one exception.

If this thing wanted to, it could really do a number on him. Steve had no doubt about that.

The animal suddenly pulled back and its entire pale body emitted a shimmer of light. A moment later, a similar incandescence lit the water all around the divers. There were more nearby. A lot more.

Steve Black had logged thousands of dives, but he had never seen anything like this. He figured there had to be hundreds of other squid around him. He should have brought his camera.

Steve recalled something else other divers had said about their encounters with these squid. While the animals hadn't actually harmed anyone, they had showed some aggressive behavior, pulling at one of the divers, forcefully gripping her air hoses and limbs. He better keep a close eye on the Jacksons. He hadn't checked on them for a few minutes, entranced by the strange animal hovering before them.

He turned to face the other divers. Curtis was right

behind him, his sister Jennifer at the boy's side. They were holding on to one another. He raised the light over them to check on their parents.

Mr. Jackson was just behind his kids, looking delighted. And his wife . . .

Steve scanned the water all around. Nothing but blackness.

Shit.

Steve swept the area again with his light, startling a few more squid. Mrs. Jackson was gone. He turned to face her family. They were looking back at him, clearly unaware of her absence. He held his palm up toward them, looking them in the eyes. *Stay put.* The boy nodded. His sister just stared back, wide-eyed.

Steve looked at their father, who was turning his head side to side. Steve saw the recognition dawn in his eyes. He lifted off the bottom and started to swim into the darkness.

Steve grabbed at him in an effort to hold him back. He needed to maintain calm in the group. As he struggled to maintain his grip on the flailing man, one of the children made a break for the surface, kicking toward the boat in a cloud of bubbles. Jackson struck Steve's mask, instantly filling it with seawater. As he struggled to readjust the mask on his face, he felt Jackson slip past him in the water as he went after his wife.

Steve tilted his head back and held the top of the mask in place, then exhaled through his nose to force air inside it. The water drained and his vision restored, he realized he had dropped his dive light. He kicked down a few feet to the bottom and retrieved it, then began to sweep the beam up and around him.

They were everywhere.

In his light, an impossible number of squid revealed themselves, the closest just a few feet from his face. The enormous shoal dispersed explosively and in all directions as soon as the light hit them, as if Steve had detonated a depth charge. He flinched backward and exhaled all his air, sinking down into the rocks. Obviously, these animals were afraid of his light. He shined it above him protectively, hoping that like vampires faced with a crucifix they would keep their distance. He had to regain control of the situation.

Find the kids first.

He had seen one of them ascend a minute ago, but where had the other one gone? He scanned the reef where they had been before the struggle and saw nothing. That *was* where he had been before, wasn't it? In the dark water he had totally lost his bearings. He spun around, searching, and finally saw a dive light a short distance away. He pushed himself off the bottom and kicked toward it.

When Steve neared the light, he saw that it was resting on the rocky reef. There was nobody around. Okay, so the kids must have surfaced.

A powerful urge to head for the boat overcame him. *Don't think,* some part of his brain urged him, *just go.* He fought off the impulse. This family was his responsibility, and he was merely letting his imagination get the best of him now. The Jackson family had predictably panicked when they saw the school of huge squid so close to them. It made sense. If he couldn't find the two kids, he would surface, to make sure they'd made it back to the boat. Then he would come back down for the two parents if necessary. Everyone still had plenty of air left—

Something struck Steve in the back of the head, hard.

Dazed, he turned to face his aggressor, but as he spun something tore at his air hose and wrenched the regulator from his mouth. He jerked the backup regulator free from a clip on his vest and shoved it into his mouth, gulping in air to calm the sudden burning in his lungs. Adrenaline flooded his body and he couldn't get enough air, drawing it in faster than the regulator would release it. Whatever was gripping his hose began dragging him backward.

Helpless against the powerful pull, Steve tumbled over the reef, striking his hip on the rock as he tried to roll over onto his stomach. *The light. They're afraid of the light.* He aimed the beam over his shoulder where he thought the squid must be. A moment later, it released him and he rolled over in the water, no longer sure which way was up. His rear end struck the rocky bottom and he found himself tank-down, like a helpless turtle. He scanned the water above him before he attempted to turn over, and caught a glimpse of three large shapes passing by in the narrow beam of light. *Squid.* These fuckers were actually attacking him.

One of the other divers came into view behind the three enormous squid, and appeared to be following them. Steve shook his head to clear it. The diver—was that Jennifer?—was moving oddly after the squid, though, somehow swimming sideways. No. She wasn't swimming at all.

Oh, Jesus.

They were dragging her.

One of the squid towed the girl's limp body along

with some white ropy thing. As they neared Steve, he got a better view in the dive light, and he felt bile creep into his mouth. It wasn't a rope.

Jennifer looked desperately at him through her fogged mask as she passed, dragged by her own entrails. A fourth squid appeared and wrapped its arms around her elbow. It began to pull her body in the other direction.

Steve watched the macabre tug-of-war for what seemed an eternity, until it ended in a draw as a mass of organs silently erupted from the girl's torso. Her body disappeared into the darkness as two more squid lunged at the drifting sac of entrails.

As Steve rolled onto his knees and began to push off the bottom, something smacked his arm, sending him tumbling forward. He looked down and saw that he had dropped the light, which shone sideways in a crack in the rocks below him. He shoved his arm into the crack and felt his fingers brush the handle of the flashlight. Before he could grasp it, something settled on top of his head, followed by a mass of tentacles that covered the glass on his dive mask.

The squid began groping at his head and hair. He felt his mask pull free of his face and the regulator wrenched from his mouth. He reached blindly for the dive light, taking water in through his nose. A viselike grip closed on his thigh. A tentacle tore at his face, slashing it. Something sharp pierced his left eye, and he screamed into the black water.

The pain grew strangely distant as the burning in his lungs became more powerful. He thrashed violently, struggling to free himself as the mob closed in around him. They kept coming.

After a minute, he couldn't fight the unrelenting urge to breathe any longer. His body commanded him to breathe. He inhaled.

When his lungs filled with seawater, a searing agony tore at his chest.

Before he lost consciousness, he felt something cold and soft worm its way into his open mouth.

CHAPTER 22

"**Y**ou gonna eat that?"

"Excuse me?" Val looked up from her book at the tourist sitting next to her on the plane.

"I was just wondering if you want your pretzels. If you don't, let me know. I'm starving."

The obese man advertised where he'd been with a ridiculous tropical shirt and sunburned face. She offered a weak smile and handed the free snack to him. Maybe it would shut him up for a minute. He'd been talking her ear off since she had sat down.

"Thanks. They never give you enough snacks anymore, right?"

Val grimaced as the enormous man tore open the snack pack and devoured the contents in two mouthfuls. She turned away and gazed across the Pacific Ocean at the horizon. From thirty thousand feet, it was amazing how flat and calm the sea looked. She closed her eyes and leaned back, trying to block out the muffled belches and shoulder bumps from her sunburned seatmate. Maybe if she pretended to sleep, he would finally leave her alone.

Valerie Martell had flown out of La Paz at 10:05 A.M., bound for Los Angeles. Over the past few days, she had performed post-dive maintenance on her research gear and moved it into storage, where it would await her return to Mexico. In two large, overstuffed duffels stowed beneath the plane, she had packed some of her most important equipment. Bringing peculiar scientific equipment onto an airplane wasn't easy in a post-9/11 world, even when flying out of Mexico. This time, though, nobody had yanked her bags and sat her down in a small room for a two-hour interrogation.

The San Diego divemaster she had talked to over the phone, who apparently went only by his last name—she'd have to remember that—had asked if Humboldt squid might be responsible for the missing father and daughter in California. In fact, he had provided some pretty decent evidence that they were somehow involved. She had gotten online afterward and found a series of media articles, which by now had gained some more attention on sites dedicated to the bizarre.

In her head, she ticked off the clues that Humboldt squid may have actually killed those people. *One:* The data logger previously attached to a squid had surfaced nearby, meaning that unless someone had brought it out to sea and dropped it there, a shoal had been more or less at that location recently. *Two:* The survivor of the incident had claimed that he saw something glowing in the water when his brother and niece went missing. Could have been dinoflagellates, but not many animals emitted an obvious bioluminescence. *Three:* A story posted online had quoted the uncle as saying he thought he had seen an enormous octopus on the fish-

ing line, although SeaMonsterCentral.com didn't seem
like a reliable source.

And she kept thinking of another, more personal,
reason.

Four: The aggression she had witnessed the last
time she had dived with Humboldt squid.

On the other hand, she had spent time with these animals on numerous occasions. They normally weren't
aggressive toward people, or any other large animals.
They were better designed to prey on smaller squid and
fish, and while a cooperating group of them was certainly strong enough to overpower a human being in
the water, why would they? It just didn't make sense.

Sitting in seat 14E on the midday flight, far from the
deep, dark water of the Sea of Cortez, Val unexpect-
edly felt the fear she had experienced on her last dive.
Tentacles latching on to her, pulling her downward.
The realization that she could do nothing to prevent
them from succeeding if her tether to the boat didn't
hold. She shuddered and opened her eyes. The man
next to her smiled, pretzel crumbs in his whiskers and
on his orange-and-red tropical shirt.

"You all right, ma'am?"

Val realized she was sweating. "Yeah." She smiled.
"I'm fine. Just a little hot." She adjusted the overhead
air vent until cool air hit her forehead.

She wondered if the press had talked to Will Sturman yet. *No, just Sturman.* Not simply "Will," or even
"Mr. Sturman." Must be ex-military or something.

Whoever he was, she hoped he hadn't gone to the
media. The last thing an unfamiliar marine animal
needed nowadays was a bad reputation. Sharks around
the world had suffered tremendously following decades

of books and movies that had painted them as ruthless killing machines. Unlike many shark species, Humboldt squid reproduced quickly and grew incredibly fast, so they weren't at a high risk of extinction. They might even be thriving. But it wouldn't do them any good if people began to see them as a threat. Historically, animals perceived to threaten humans or their livelihoods had a way of disappearing from the wild.

When the plane landed, she would hook up with Sturman and get on the water as soon as possible, to assess the location where the tag was found, including the water depth, temperature, and distance from shore. She also needed to download the information on the tag, to see where the squid and its shoal had traveled since being marked. The device should have logged depth and water temperature every two hours until it detached due to physical stressors or the death and dismemberment of the squid. If the shoal had been at the same location as the missing fishermen at the time the incident happened, she might be able to determine if the Humboldts had anything to do with the disappearance.

The seat belt pressed against Val's thighs as the plane struck some turbulence. The aircraft rose and dropped erratically for several minutes, and the pilot got on the intercom with the standard warning. Mr. 14D began to dig through the seat back in front of him, and yanked out an airsickness bag.

Val would take a rough ocean to a commercial airline flight any day.

When Val called Sturman on her cell phone after landing, she learned she wasn't going to get picked up at the airport. He didn't offer to give her a ride, but simply told her she could get a cab. Fortunately, being the only passenger in the taxi meant she had enough room for all her gear.

As her taxi pulled into a marina near where Sturman apparently kept his boat, she saw a man in a cowboy hat and sandals lounging in a plastic chair next to the wire fence surrounding the harbor. He looked asleep. A mutt stretched out on the sunny asphalt next to him perked up as the cab neared. When the cab stopped, she got out and slammed the door, but the man didn't budge. His dog padded over to smell her.

"Will Sturman?"

He finally stirred and slid the hat up his forehead, revealing puffy eyes in a weathered face that had probably been very handsome at some point. He looked hungover.

"That's me. You must be Dr. Martell." He stood up and shook her hand as he studied her face. He continued to stare at her for a long time, as though he recognized her from somewhere. She felt her face flush but held his gaze.

"I just go by Val. Are you all right?"

"I'm staring. Sorry." He shook his head and glanced away. "You just remind me of someone I once knew."

"Can you help me unload this stuff?"

"Sure thing."

Val couldn't help but notice the muscles in his tanned arms as he lifted her heavy duffels out of the trunk of the cab. He had a large tattoo on each shoulder, and wore the straw cowboy hat well. It suited him somehow.

"You hungry, Doc? Because Bud and I are starving. There's a fish taco place a few minutes from here."

"Actually, I'm starving. That sounds great. Let's get this equipment stowed first, though. This gear isn't cheap."

At a table outside the taco stand, as they finished eating fresh mahi-mahi tacos, Val let out a belch, making Sturman choke on his lemonade.

"Sorry. I've spent too much time out with sailors."

"Best damn fish tacos anywhere, right?" The tacos were cooked perfectly, the fish charred but still very moist, the cabbage crisp, the cilantro fresh and aromatic.

"They're not bad, but you need to remember I've spent a lot of time in Baja. If you're ever down there, I'll take you to an even better taco stand."

"You askin' me on a date?" Sturman looked at her with the hint of a smile on his face.

"Oh, so you do have a sense of humor." He apparently wasn't intimidated by her looks, like so many others. She decided to get down to work in order to change the subject. "You asked me over the phone if Humboldt squid ever attack people."

"I did. You told me stories about squid fishermen in Mexico vanishing after falling into the water."

"Yes, but those are only tales. Unconfirmed reports. These squid generally hunt smaller animals: anchovies, lanternfish, miniature squid. There's not much proof that they hunt larger prey. But I was obviously intrigued by where the tag was found. Can you go over it again?"

For the next several minutes, Sturman explained the search for the missing father and daughter, the story the uncle had given, how he and another guy had found the data logger. When he was finished, Val remained quiet for a minute. Sturman leaned back in his chair and pulled his hat down lower over his eyes.

"There's something I didn't tell you over the phone, Will. I recently had a pretty rough experience with these animals . . . you might even call it an attack. So it's certainly *possible* these squid would come after people. Humboldts are highly intelligent and curious. They might give human beings a try if they ran into them underwater and were hungry enough. But even if they did attack those people, they aren't large enough to do a ton of damage or consume the corpses. The bodies would have eventually surfaced when the squid were done with them. You haven't heard about any bodies recovered at sea, have you?"

The waitress came by the table and took their plates away. Val thanked her. Sturman waited for her to walk off before replying.

"No. Haven't heard about any bodies. Pretty awful way to go, huh? Getting killed by a squid. They'd latch on to you with their tentacles, then dig that parrot beak into you."

"Like I said, their physiology isn't really designed to subdue and consume larger prey. They primarily use their arms to capture smaller animals, then to deliver the prey to their beaks. I just can't imagine them suddenly changing their behavior to attack human beings, not to mention being able to consume them."

"Then why are you here? Why not just have me mail you that transmitter?"

Val nodded and thought for a moment. "Like I said before, it's *possible* that these were Humboldt squid attacks. These animals are large enough to overpower a person, especially since they hunt in large shoals using cooperative efforts and complex communication. It just seems highly unlikely that they'd go after someone."

"Stranger things have happened."

"True. One thing I've learned as a scientist is to never rule anything out. It's hard to say with confidence how Humboldt squid will interact with people, since they rarely ever encounter us. I'm one of the few people who have ever been in the water with them. But from my experience, they're more curious than anything else."

"So you're saying these things have never really had many chances to eat us? That if they did, they just might give us a try?"

"Something like that. Imagine if you went back in time and placed human beings in front of smaller, predatory dinosaurs. Who knows what the dinosaurs would do? They might attack the unfamiliar, slightly larger animals, or their instincts might instead tell them to flee. It would all depend on how aggressive or hungry the dinosaurs were, and what past experience had taught them. These squid are like dinosaurs, in a sense. Although they aren't removed from human interaction in a temporal sense—by a gap in time—they are removed in a spatial sense. Except for on the deck of a fishing boat, Humboldt squid and human beings never really occupy the same space."

"There must be times when people and squid are

swimming in the same place at the same time, though, right? Mexico has plenty of tourists."

"Not many times. How many people go swimming over the very deep ocean, in the middle of the night, when Humboldt squid are active? Especially in those areas of Mexico with low populations, where these squid thrive?"

"What about those stories of missing Mexican fishermen?" Sturman smiled. "Seems they were unfortunate enough to occupy the same space, at the same time, as some squid. And these folks who went missing here fell off their boat while fishing."

"Those attacks on Mexican fishermen are just legends. If Humboldts have ever actually killed a fisherman, it was probably because he created a feeding frenzy of sorts as he lured them in, and then fell directly into it. The point is we don't ever really occupy the same space as Humboldt squid on any regular basis. That said, from what we know, these squid are beginning to occupy shallower and shallower water. They also appear to be moving north, closer to large centers of human population in the United States."

"So why are they here now? Why not fifty years ago?"

"There are a lot of theories as to why Humboldts may be showing up regularly off California. Some of my colleagues think this migration is merely cyclical, and that they've done this in the past when currents and water temperatures drove them north. Others, myself included, think this is unprecedented, due to the absence of predators and competition, in addition to favorable environmental conditions and acidification due to CO_2 increases in the ocean."

"Beg your pardon?"

"Sorry. Let me explain. Populations of sharks, whales, and billfish that feed on or compete with Humboldt squid for food have been decimated by fishing fleets in the North Pacific over the past several decades. Combine that fact with the effects of climate change, such as changing water temperatures and deepwater current directions, and you make it possible for Humboldt squid to permanently immigrate into new habitats."

"That makes sense."

"Also, the natural deepwater environment of Humboldt squid has always been low in oxygen, which is one reason they rise to shallower water at night to feed and recover. There's more oxygen in shallow water, and less carbon dioxide, which is toxic to squid in the same way it's harmful to people. But increasing atmospheric carbon dioxide appears to be leading to higher levels of the gas in shallower waters. Besides acidifying the water and destroying the shells of marine organisms, this increase of carbon dioxide in the water will probably force Humboldt squid to spend much more time closer to the surface to absorb enough oxygen to survive."

"So your Humboldt squid are now residents of the state of California?"

"They are. And they may be here to stay."

CHAPTER 23

A small wave rushed up the beach and licked the toddler's toes with foam, then slid back down the sand into the sea as another wave churned over it. The girl, dressed in a red sun hat and matching one-piece swimsuit, giggled as the waves reached her feet.

Her mother watched her from a folding beach chair, close enough to grab her if a bigger wave rolled in. Susan Weld had taken a break from her romance novel to watch her daughter enjoy the sand and water. Her husband was snoring loudly under a baseball cap, having fallen asleep immediately once his wife had quit reading.

They had brought Lucy to the beach before, but every time she seemed to be as excited as the first time. Her parents, on the other hand, weren't big fans of the beach or ocean. What was so great about getting sandy and sunburned, while letting a bunch of strangers look at your less-flattering body parts? Susan had grown restless after an hour of sitting by the surf and repeatedly burying her daughter's legs in the wet sand. She sighed. Lucy would probably end up being a marine biologist someday, or a pro volleyball player.

"Tom . . . Tom, wake up, honey."

"Huh? What? Is Lucy okay?" Tom Weld's hat fell off his wide face as he jerked upright.

"Lucy's fine. I need to run to the bathroom. Will you watch her for a few minutes?"

"Yeah, sure." Tom put the hat back on his head and sat up. "Can you grab me a water, Suze?"

"Sure. Honey, she's getting too close to the water. Maybe you should move her."

"I got it under control." Tom looked at his daughter. "Don't I, sweetie? Tell Mommy Dad's got it covered!"

Susan rolled her eyes and rose from her chair. She walked across the broad expanse of gray sand, angling around a group of young men playing volleyball, toward the public restrooms. She wouldn't be gone long. Public bathrooms were disgusting, especially at the beach.

After sanitizing her hands with watermelon-scented hand gel, Susan headed to a junk-food vendor down the beach and stuffed down a waffle cone dripping vanilla ice cream. She made sure to stay hidden from her husband as she ate. Tom would give her his critical look if he knew she was having sweets, and then she'd get defensive about her weight. With the ice cream on her chin wiped off, she tossed the dirty napkin in a garbage can and picked up the two bottled waters she had purchased, scaring a seagull off the raised planter next to her.

As she headed back toward the water, Susan watched a huge banner passing by in the sky, towed by a comparatively tiny plane flying parallel to the coastline.

The beach advertising, Southern California style, not surprisingly showcased another new energy drink. The sky above the plane was an unbroken blue, the air was warm, and the wind was light. Susan was enjoying the beach today despite herself. They would need to go soon, though. They'd been here three hours already, and even with SPF 45 on, Lucy might start to burn.

Weaving through a throng of sun worshippers in board shorts and low-rise bikinis splayed out on their beach towels, she began to wonder if she was headed the right way. Where were Tom and Lucy? She raised her hand to shade her eyes and scanned the beach for her daughter's bright red outfit. There, just off to the right. She was playing with something in the surf.

In the surf.

My baby is in the water.

Looking past Lucy at the ocean, a sick feeling hit Susan's stomach as she saw a wave, much larger than the rest, just about to break over her daughter. She dropped the bottled waters and started running.

"Tom!"

Her husband jerked upright in his chair. He looked toward his daughter and lurched awkwardly up out of his chair, falling sideways into the sand. The wave rose higher and began to break behind Lucy.

He wasn't going to get there in time.

"Help! Somebody!" Susan ran toward her daughter. She was too far away.

As the wave crested and broke, a skinny black teenager splashed over and grabbed Lucy, lifting her above it. The wave crashed against his thighs, but the kid managed to hold Lucy safely over the water.

Susan's husband reached the boy first. He handed

the toddler back to her father, who hugged his daughter against his chest as he thanked the boy. Tom looked toward his wife as she jogged up. She glared at him momentarily, then turned to the boy.

"Thank you, thank you, thank you!" Susan hugged the teenager impulsively, then suddenly felt embarrassed and stepped back to look over her daughter. Lucy was smiling, oblivious to what had almost happened.

"She can't swim yet. She's only sixteen months old. If you hadn't come along . . ."

"No worries, lady. I got a couple kid sisters. I know how it is." The teenager smiled and then ran off to join his friends and resume a game of catch, as though he saved kids from drowning all the time.

Susan looked at her husband, who met her eyes for a moment before looking down at his feet. "I'm sorry, Suze. I was watching her the whole time, I just closed my eyes for a second—"

"Save it, Tom. I'm tired of your excuses. You can stay up all night creating complicated software programs, but you can't stay awake for five minutes to prevent your only daughter from drowning. And this isn't the first time. We've been through this before, and . . . Tom? Tom, are you listening to me?"

He was staring down at his daughter, his face turning pale. Susan followed his gaze and saw that he was looking at the dark object still in Lucy's hands. It must have been what she was playing with in the water. Whatever it was, she was now putting it into her mouth. It was V-shaped, and looked sort of like . . .

Tom swatted the object out of his daughter's hands just as she was putting it between her lips, and it fell into the sand. Small white nubs of bone gleamed through an opening in the black neoprene. Lucy started crying.

"Tom, what the hell is that?"

"I think it's part of someone's hand."

The diver's body was in a severe state of rigor mortis.

Curled into a semi-fetal position, the corpse's arms were frozen in front of it, outstretched defensively, and one of its stiffened legs was suspended well off the sand.

Sergeant Joe Montoya and a deputy stood looking at the body from a short distance away, not wanting to approach it until they were sure there were no tracks or other obvious evidence in the sand. A wave washed up and splashed over the mutilated body, causing it to sink slightly into the beach. If anyone had approached the corpse, their tracks had been washed away. Joe looked up and down the coast. Besides a small group now drawn to the police presence, there was nobody else nearby.

"Thank God it isn't the weekend yet, or someone would have definitely come across this by now," Joe said. The body was a good distance from where a family had found the remains of a human hand—maybe half a mile away, where some low bluffs backed the beach at a less-popular stretch of sand.

"Both the hands are intact on this one, sir." Deputy Dave Smithfield's voice wavered.

Joe was reasonably sure this was the first mangled corpse the rookie had seen on the job. "Good eye, kid. But the hand was from an African American kid. This corpse appears to be Caucasian. It looks like we've got more than one corpse to ID."

"The sharks really got into this one."

"Remember to breathe, son. Through your mouth." Joe swept the scene with his eyes a final time. "I think we're safe to approach now. Let's go get a better look, but be careful where you step. And remember, Smithfield, keep your eyes open for evidence."

"Yes, sir."

Joe stepped closer to the body, which was turned away from him, toward the water. There was something overly familiar about the matted grey hair of the corpse, which was encased in a black wet suit and bore a single fin on one foot. Joe had a bad feeling. He knew that Steve Black and a group diving with him had all been reported missing a few days ago, their boat found anchored many miles from the coast. He didn't care for Steve, but the guy was Sturman's friend.

On the left wrist was a dive watch, and strapped to one leg a titanium dive knife. The wet suit was torn in multiple places, exposing torn flesh.

"He must have died recently, sir. Probably this morning. He's still in rigor mortis."

"I know what you may have learned about rigor mortis, Smithfield, but they obviously didn't teach you about it in drowning victims. When a body remains immersed in colder water, rigor can remain advanced for much longer. This guy might have died two or three days ago."

"Most of the flesh on his upper arm's gone. Looks like it's been eaten."

The humerus bone of one of the corpse's arms was completely exposed, the muscles and skin gone. In fact, Joe thought it looked like something had tried to eat parts of the body. Without warning, Deputy Smithfield grabbed the stiffened corpse by the shoulder and rolled it onto its back.

"Dammit, kid! You know we're not supposed to disturb the scene until we get pictures and a CSI on scene."

"I'm sorry. I just thought that with the waves around him, moving the sand, it didn't matter. . . ."

Montoya exhaled loudly. "Just step back."

"Yes, sir."

The corpse, which appeared to be an older man, stretched its limbs desperately toward the sky. A mess of long, wet grey hair covered the pale face of the corpse. Joe had to know if this was Steve. Besides, the rookie had a point—the surf had moved this body around a lot before they found it. Joe put on latex gloves and carefully swept the hair away from the corpse's face to reveal small, pale crabs, which scuttled out of empty eye sockets through the tangled strands of hair.

"Christ."

"What's the matter, sir?"

"I think I might know this guy."

It would take dental records or prints to ID the body, but Joe was fairly sure he was looking at what was left of Steve Black. His nose and eyes were missing, replaced by dark recesses. Probably the work of hungry crabs. Some of the flesh on his face had been torn away as well, torn lips revealing a ghastly grin of yellowed teeth. One of the front teeth was capped in gold.

Deputy Smithfield turned away and took a few steps, then stood looking off toward the sea, breathing deeply.

"Hey kid, you all right?"

"Yeah." He took a deep breath. "Just not used to this, I guess."

"You will be. Keep an eye on the body, and make sure nobody approaches. I need to call Will Sturman."

"Who's that?" The rookie was still looking away.

"Friend of mine. A local divemaster. He knows all the divers around here, including the one who went missing this week. I hope to hell this unfortunate bastard isn't who I think he is."

CHAPTER 24

"**T**his where you found the tag?"

"Give or take a few hundred feet."

Standing at the helm of his boat, Sturman had shifted into idle. As he and Mike Phan gave Val a minute to think, he realized he was staring at the marine biologist's trim figure while she faced away from him. He suddenly felt guilty and looked away. Mike continued to stare.

"Little pervert," Sturman whispered.

"What? She's hot."

Just as Sturman had expected, Mike had made no effort to hide the fact that he was checking Val out when they first met this morning. Sturman couldn't really blame the guy, even if he was married.

Val turned to face them. "Did you say something, Mike?"

"Nothing important." He grinned at Sturman.

"So you guys didn't see anything else unusual when you found it? Nothing else floating, maybe dead fish or something?"

Sturman sat down in the captain's chair. "Just the tag, Doc."

"Please, call me Val. I'm not a college professor." She looked a little irritated. She'd already asked him to call her by her first same several times, but he found it amusing how she reacted when he didn't.

"Sure thing, Doc. And I'll pretend you aren't still calling me Will."

The biologist put her hands on her hips. "But that's your name."

Sturman squinted at her. "There's nothing wrong with my last name."

"Look, call me whatever you want . . . Sturman. How deep is it here?"

Sturman glanced at his depth finder. "Ninety-seven feet."

"That's awfully shallow for Humboldts. But I'm sure the tag drifted some distance after popping off."

When Val turned around a moment later, Sturman noticed her catch Mike staring at her deeply tanned legs. She ignored the leer and reached down to scratch Bud's ears. Sturman's big mutt had followed her around the boat ever since she'd boarded that morning.

Sturman grunted. "He likes you."

"I can see that." Val smiled as the dog groaned with pleasure. "I love dogs. I've never been able to have my own, though, as much as I have to move around." Val stepped over the dog and sat down in the shade of the cabin near the two men. She was wearing short shorts and a tight tank top, making it hard for Sturman to concentrate. He realized he hadn't slept with a woman in several months.

"It bothers me how close these squid are to shore,

especially in an area that's got so much human activity," Val said. "I'm still finding this hard to believe, but we've got to consider the possibility that the shoal may have been involved with the disappearance of those fishermen."

"And she's smart, too." Mike winked at Val. "So what are you thinking, Dr. Martell? The squid killed them, right? I mean, what are the odds these squid just happened to be in the same place at the same time as those fishermen—a million to one?"

Sturman regretted allowing Mike to join them on the boat today. Mike had asked to join them when he heard Sturman was following up on the tag they'd found. It never hurt to have another capable set of hands on deck, but Sturman hadn't counted on the little bastard hitting on the biologist.

"I hear what you're saying, Mike, but as a scientist I try not to jump to conclusions. Remember, we're talking about an animal that has never been known to attack people."

"Maybe your textbooks don't say anything about it, but I'll bet I could find you some Mexican fishermen who would disagree."

"Really? I'd like to talk to them."

Mike blushed. "Come on, though. I've watched shows about Humboldt squid. Mexican fishermen have a lot of stories about being killed by them when they fall in the water. *Los diablos rojos,* they call them. It means 'red devils.' "

"I know what it means."

Sturman tilted his hat back and shook his head at Mike. Mike met his gaze for a moment, then looked away.

"Mike's got a point," Sturman said. "This seems an unlikely coincidence, based on the data from our tag."

Mike glanced at Sturman and stuck his chest out. Sturman laughed and looked away as Val continued, seemingly oblivious to their antics.

"But what you're seeing on TV *are* just stories, Mike. Those shows don't produce a whole lot of facts."

"Go on, Phan. Tell us what else you know." Sturman grinned at Mike from underneath his hat.

"Shut up, Sturman."

"Be nice, boys. So here's the deal. That tag definitely dropped off of one of my squid from Baja. And when I downloaded it while on our way out here, I found some pretty surprising information. Here, let me show you guys." Val picked up her laptop and navigated to a file, then turned the screen toward the men. Sturman leaned forward to look at the display, some sort of text-only file with a set of the numbers highlighted to call their attention to them:

203	1800	54	14.7
203	2000	40	16.2
203	2200	37	17.3
204	0000	44	15.4
204	0200	44	15.6
204	0400	52	15.1
204	0600	185	5.0
204	0800	211	4.6
204	1000	209	4.8
204	1200	218	4.7
204	1400	204	4.8
204	1600	197	4.8
204	1800	43	21.2
204	2000	12	17.1

204	2200	32	17.0
205	0000	36	16.8
205	0200	40	16.9
205	0400	47	15.0
205	0600	112	9.5
205	0800	103	9.4
205	1000	136	6.9
205	1200	164	5.4

"The left hand column represents the ordinal date . . . the sequential day of the year. I've scrolled down to the end of the dataset, right before the tag popped off on day two hundred and five. We're lucky it popped off when it did—right after the people went missing. We're interested in day two hundred and four since July twenty-second is the two hundred and fourth day of the calendar year . . . the day those people went missing."

Sturman and Mike exchanged a glance.

"The second column is the time. These tags record depth and water temp every two hours, which are shown in the last two columns." Val sat quietly for a minute as she allowed the men to look over the data.

"Just looks like a bunch of numbers to me," Sturman said.

"Let me explain." Val pointed to a number on the monitor. "Take a look at twenty-hundred hours on day two hundred and four. That's eight p.m., right around twilight, on the day of interest."

"The tag was only twelve feet deep right then," Mike said.

"Twelve *meters*, actually. And the water temp is in Celsius. . . . Scientists never use Fahrenheit. But twelve meters is less than forty feet from the surface, which is shallower than these squid normally venture. And almost all of the recorded tag depths that evening are well within the range of a fishing line. Besides, this probably wasn't the shallowest squid in the shoal."

"So you think those fishermen came across a school of these squid, and maybe snagged a few on their lines?" Mike smiled. "Then what? Overwhelmed by guilt from eating so much calamari, they decided to jump in and sacrifice themselves?"

Val laughed. "That's a stretch. But these data clearly indicate that this individual squid was awfully shallow that evening, and there's something else. This shoal has been trending toward shallower average depths each day. Take a look at this." Val turned the laptop back toward herself and pulled up a new screen, which she showed to the men. "You can see that this shoal is moving into increasingly shallow water, probably because they're staying so close to shore. I've never seen this before."

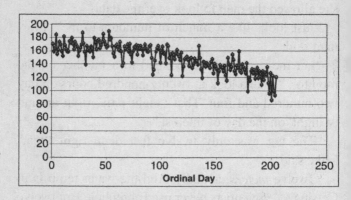

"It looks like they're going deeper," Sturman said.

"Sorry. I should have reoriented the graph with the

surface at the top. If you look at the Y-axis, you'll see that the average depth is actually decreasing. The squid are getting shallower."

Sturman tried to think of something intelligent to say. Before he could, Mike spoke. "Your graph shows that they're still staying over a hundred meters down every day, though. Right? Isn't that too deep for people to worry about?"

"True, but this graph only depicts *average* daily depth. When you consider that at midday these animals are down very deep, normally over a thousand feet, that means they must be in very shallow water at night to generate these averages. I've looked over most of the data, and some recordings indicate that sometimes this shoal is right at the surface."

"I'm no scientist, but it seems to me your squid are the reason those fishermen are missing," Mike said. "I think the real question here is what we do about these squid."

Sturman laughed. "We? Who's *we*, Mike? You and your superhero office buddies?"

Mike opened his mouth, but Val intervened. "I know it seems easy to draw conclusions here, guys, but we simply don't have enough evidence to point the finger yet."

"How much proof do we need?" Mike's expression grew somber. "Hey, Doctor, I've got three kids, and we spend a lot of time at the beach. Do I need to worry about a school of enormous squid tearing my kids to pieces when they go swimming?"

"I wouldn't worry about your family," Val said. "Even on the off chance that this shoal did actually kill those people, it would be the first confirmed case—

ever—of Humboldts killing anyone. This would be considered a very isolated incident. Honestly, whatever you might have heard, these animals are not a threat."

Sturman said, "How can you be sure these things haven't killed other people?"

"Why would I have any reason to believe they have? Surely we'd have heard about it by now if this shoal had attacked other people. These types of bizarre stories always make the news. Why? Have either of you heard about any other strange disappearances lately? Any possible shark attacks, maybe?"

"I haven't," Mike said. "What about you, cowboy?"

Sturman thought about Steve Black for a moment. He'd been missing for days. Nobody at The Lighthouse had seen or heard from him. "No. Nothing."

"Well, then—"

"Wait a minute," Sturman said. "Montoya did say some immigrant left out in the ocean got all torn up a few weeks ago by a shark or something. Said that a bunch of other illegals might have gone missing that night."

"Really? Well, that kind of makes me wonder. But, gentlemen, for now let's simply assume that this shoal may still be in the area, and may have been involved with the disappearance of two people . . . and *possibly* more. This is an incredible case study though, whether or not the shoal has killed anyone. The fact that they're in such shallow water, and so far north of their original range, *and* still apparently surviving, is reason enough to try and track them down. The individual squid I tagged here wasn't the only one in the shoal that was marked. If this male is still with the same shoal he was with when I tagged him last year in Baja, then two more squid in this group have tags on them that may drop off soon. I really need to locate those tags."

"Can't we track them using the tags?"

"Good question, Sturman." She frowned slightly when saying his last name. "Unfortunately, these tags aren't designed to transmit in any way. They're a less-expensive version we use to tag a lot of squid at once. These tags simply gather data every two hours, then float to the surface when they eventually work free. In fact, the only way to retrieve one is to have someone else find the tag and call us. The way you did."

It was silent on the boat for a moment as everyone was lost in thought.

Sturman said, "Well, if you think there's any possibility your squid killed these people, we need to talk to Montoya."

"Montoya?"

"Sergeant Joe Montoya, with the county sheriff's office."

"I'd rather wait until we have more proof. There isn't much of a point in scaring people unless we're convinced of the shoal's involvement. Besides, the odds of another attack are practically nil. Unless a person goes out intentionally looking for them, at night, using bright lights . . ." Val smiled at Sturman.

"Which you apparently want to do."

Val's smile grew wider. "Yes. That's something I was most definitely hoping we could do."

Mike sighed. "Shit. My wife will never let me out at night."

* * *

As they headed back in to shore, Val joined Sturman up in the flying bridge while Mike stood below them, alone in the stern, staring off into the distance. Sturman knew how much Mike liked to be out on a boat.

"Sorry about Mike. He's a good guy, really. I wouldn't have brought him today if I'd known he was gonna act like this . . . you know, flirting and all." Sturman knew that standing down near the rumble of the engine, Mike wouldn't be able to hear their conversation.

"Relax. He seems harmless. About what I was saying before . . . would you consider taking the next week or two off from your dive operation, to bring me out to study this shoal? Your boat meets my needs, and I don't want to spend time looking for another vessel. But I'll warn you . . . you'd need to be nocturnal for a while. We'd almost always have to go out at night, but all you'd really have to do is drive the boat. I'd be the one in the water . . . and I'd pay you well, of course."

"Well, I could definitely use the money."

"I'm not always bad company. And you won't be bored."

"What you got in mind, Doc?" Sturman was happy to see her flush.

"In all seriousness, Sturman, would your wife mind if you planned to spend a lot of time on your boat at night with a woman?"

He followed her gaze until he was looking down at his left hand and the thick gold band on his finger, scratched and scarred from years of wear.

"You saw my ring."

"Well, you haven't talked about her yet, but I don't want to get you in trouble."

"You won't. I'm not married anymore."

"Oh? Well, then why do you still wear the ring?"

"I don't like to talk about it."

Val nodded. "Okay. Let's just talk business then. This research is my life, and I'd love to use your boat if there won't be any complications from your personal life."

"You've got nothing to worry about, Doc."

Val offered a price, more than Sturman had expected, and he accepted.

"Then we've got a deal."

For the next several minutes, they sat in silence until Mike joined them on the flying bridge.

"What are you kids talking about?"

"She's hoping to go swimmin' with these suckers. Right?" Sturman smiled and looked over at Val. "She's more nuts than I am."

"That's a bad idea, Doctor." Mike's eyes were wide.

"Don't worry, boys. I appreciate your concern, but I've done this a few times."

"I'm not worried." Sturman tipped his hat at Val. "I'll be driving the boat."

"Speaking of, I'll need to make a few temporary modifications to your boat. We'll need to rent some outdoor stage lighting, and rig it to shine down over the sides into the water. Would that be all right?"

"As long as we don't damage her." Sturman rubbed the dash gently. "So is this what you do down in Baja? Swim every night with big-ass squid?"

"Pretty much. I know it sounds crazy. My current research is devoted to understanding Humboldt squid communication. Think of a shoal of Humboldt squid like a huge pack of wolves . . . or, better yet, an ant colony. The shoal needs to communicate to survive, to coordinate their efforts as they hunt, travel, or evade predators."

"Makes sense. I guess they can't talk."

"Actually, they can, in a way. But they use visual cues. For one thing, they change the colors and patterns of their skin, using cells called chromatophores, just like octopi do. But what's the problem with using different colors to communicate when you're a thousand feet underwater?"

Mike beat Sturman to the punch. "It's dark . . . so they can't see each other."

"Exactly. So Humboldt squid use bioluminescent signals to talk to each other. They have these tiny organs, called photophores, inside their skin, which can be used to emit light. . . . Have you ever seen pictures of deepwater fish, like lanternfish, which have glowing lures built into their bodies?"

"Yeah. They use them to catch smaller fish for dinner."

"Well, these squid have similar capabilities. But Humboldts use their photophores in a more complicated fashion, and emit rapid pulses of light in complex patterns. I'm trying to figure out what those different patterns mean."

"How do you figure out what they're saying?"

"Well, I haven't yet. But I think I'm getting closer. I try to observe them in their environment and film a lot of footage underwater, and then I spend time in the lab . . . a *lot* of time . . . reviewing the glow patterns and the behaviors I observe during and after the light emissions."

"Are they really that smart, Doctor?" Mike asked. "I mean, do they say anything to each other besides 'Who's hungry?' and 'Let's eat'?"

Val said, "They say a lot more than that, but we're not sure how extensive their communication is."

"How do the tags come into this?" Sturman asked.

"What do you mean?"

"Well, how do you use these floating tags to figure that out?"

"Oh, the tags are a secondary part of my research. Even though I'm most interested in cephalopod communication, there's so little known about Humboldt squid that it's beneficial to track even the most general of their habits, like where they spend their time each day. That's what the tags are for."

"Aren't you ever worried about the risks? You said these things get pretty big." Mike always did this, Sturman thought—act like an enthralled child, unable to quit asking questions.

"They do get big, but no, I'm never really worried. I was worried on my first ten or so dives, a long time ago, but after hundreds of dives with these squid, I've only had a few scary encounters. They're usually just curious about what I am."

"So tell us—what was the biggest one you've ever seen?" Mike asked.

"Men are so obsessed with size." Val sighed. "Certainly over a hundred pounds, maybe seven feet long."

"Longer than Sturman is tall, but only a hundred pounds?"

"They don't have to carry around a lot of internal fluids, like we do, and they lack a skeleton. Seawater in the mantle adds volume and gives them shape, so underwater they look a lot heavier than they really are. The biggest one I've actually weighed and dissected was ninety-two pounds. Like I told Sturman, though, there are reports of these squid reaching twice that size off the coast of South America."

"That's what I call a big squid."

"I'd like to head down to Peru someday and find out for myself."

"Sturman's right. You really are crazier than him. You wear armor or something when you dive with these things? Like the chain mail used for shark diving?"

"No, I don't, but some dive operations down in Baja have a sort of plastic armor they wear when they dive with Humboldts. Here's the thing . . . these squid don't have huge mouthfuls of teeth like sharks do, so there's no real risk of getting a limb taken off. But I always tether myself to the boat, because the real danger with these guys is getting dragged down into very deep water if they grab hold of you. That can happen fast if they get overexcited."

Sturman said, "So is that what you're going to do here over the next few weeks? Study how they talk to one another?"

"Not exactly. I may look at that, too, since my research is centered on that. But I'm really just interested in their basic biology here—what they're eating, where they're spending their time, how healthy they are. That sort of thing. Coastal California was never really their habitat until the last decade or so. Even then, usually only for brief periods, which have often ended with the shoals dying and washing up on shore."

"I've read a few articles about dying squid washing up on the beach here," Mike said. "And also up in Monterey, and even as far north as Washington state. Never seen one myself, though."

"They're definitely expanding their range. Up in

Monterey, we've actually been keeping a video log of the deepwater inhabitants of Monterey Canyon for decades. Our video footage has shown that Humboldts have now become permanent residents off the coast there."

"So how are we gonna find these guys?"

"What do you mean 'we'? For some reason you keep using that word." Sturman looked at Mike from under his cowboy hat.

"I could maybe come along—couldn't I? I could help you out, buddy. I know my way around a boat."

"Your wife will never let you. You know that."

"She's not my boss."

Val said, "I've got to be honest with you guys. It's going to be a little like a needle in a haystack, and we may spend weeks just looking for them. It can be pretty dull.

"There are probably a few other tags in the shoal, but like I was saying, they don't actually transmit. So we can't simply track them. The good news is that if we find any squid at all, it's very likely our group. There aren't a lot of different shoals up here, like there are down by La Paz. I thought we could start by doing what we do in Mexico. We'll start this weekend, if that's all right, by heading to likely locations, near the continental shelf off the coast where there's deeper water. We'll try to lure them to us with bright lights and glowing fishing lures."

"And what do we do when we find them?" Sturman asked.

"Ever landed a squid before, cowboy?"

CHAPTER 25

Sturman got the call that night.

It was a warm Friday evening, and he'd just finished washing dishes after eating a relaxed dinner of runny fried eggs and crisp bacon on his boat when he realized his cell phone had been off. He pulled up the voice mail and listened to the message from Joe, and knew even before he'd called him back what he was going to hear. Until then, he'd even been going very light on the beer, and had been thinking about the feisty biologist he'd spent the day with. But now only one thought went through his mind.

Steve Black was dead.

After calling Joe back and hearing more of the details, Sturman had gone to the coroner to help Joe identify the body. Apparently Steve had washed up on the beach yesterday, mutilated almost beyond recognition. A diving accident—that was what the sheriff's department was calling this now. They were also looking into a possible shark attack or potential foul play. An entire family that Steve had taken on a dive excursion had gone missing with him.

Sturman knew it was Steve because of the tattoos. Despite Joe's recommendation, he had looked at the face of the corpse, but that hadn't been Steve's face. Just a wrecked crater of flesh that fish and crabs had hollowed out. After that, Sturman had needed a drink. That was last night.

"Hey, hon, how about another smoke?"

Jill stopped wiping down the bar and headed over to Sturman. He had been drinking beer at The Lighthouse since its doors opened at 10:30. In reality, he'd been drinking since about ten o'clock the night before, but had passed out somewhere—he couldn't remember where—in the wee hours before resuming his binge in the morning.

She walked over to him and pulled a pack of lights out from under the bar, handing it to him along with an ashtray. Sturman lit a cigarette and took a deep pull.

"Are you gonna be all right, Will? You've had a lot of beer, and it's only lunchtime." When he didn't respond, Jill continued. "Look, I know you're upset about Steve. I am too. But you should be with friends and family right now."

"Steve was my family, Jill."

"I know, I'm sorry. I'm just saying—"

"Thanks for the cigarette, but save the advice. Gimme another."

Jill shook her head and walked down the bar to refill Sturman's glass. "All right, but this is the last one." She set the beer down in front of him. "Let me know if you want to talk. Okay?"

Sturman took the beer and got up, staggering a little as he rose. He walked slowly toward the bar's quiet pool tables. Nobody was playing right now. The few other regulars were sitting at a booth at the far side of the bar, laughing over a game of cards. Sturman put his hand on one of the pool tables, feeling the faded red velvet surface.

He and Steve had spent a lot of time at these tables.

Sturman heard Jill talking to someone, and turned to see Joe Montoya entering the bar. Joe had never liked Steve, but Sturman couldn't blame him. Steve had certainly had his faults. One of the biggest was that he could be a racist old bastard. That obviously had never sat well with his other friend, whose family was from Mexico.

Joe looked up as he finished talking to Jill and saw Sturman at the pool tables. He clenched his jaw and headed toward his friend.

"Hey, pal. After I didn't see you at your boat, I figured you'd be down here."

"Hey, Montoya."

"Buy you a beer?"

"You may have to. Jill cut me off."

"Shit. You're pretty drunk, aren't you? How you holdin' up?"

"I'm all right." Sturman smiled weakly. "Steve spent a lot of time here. Even more than I did, amigo."

"Yeah. He liked his drink."

"Let me get you a beer."

"I can't, pal. I'm on duty. I just thought I'd stop in to see how you're doing."

Sturman looked away. "I can't even remember what he really looked like, Joe. All I see is his dead face."

"Give it time. You'll remember again."

Joe put a hand on his shoulder and squeezed—a rare gesture of affection from the all-business cop. Sturman felt his throat knot and swallowed it back. He tilted back his glass and gulped down the full glass of beer. He turned and hurled the glass against the wall. When it hit the bricks, it exploded with a loud crack, sending broken glass back at them. Sturman took off his cowboy hat, bits of glass now on the brim, and rubbed his head.

Joe stood motionless, but Sturman couldn't blame him. What was he supposed to say? The men hadn't spoken for a few minutes when Jill walked over and cleaned up the mess without saying a word. Finally, Sturman spoke.

"Find out what happened, Joe. Just find out what happened."

When he staggered out of the bar, he didn't care if they knew he was only headed to another.

CHAPTER 26

Sturman drank heavily all weekend. He never took his boat out at all, and didn't return any of the biologist's persistent phone calls.

When he had gone to The Lighthouse on Saturday morning, still mostly drunk from the night before, he hadn't planned to spend the entire day boozing, but under the circumstances he had lost all self-control and had again gotten blind drunk. Somebody had helped him home Saturday night after he had nearly gotten into a fight with a husky biker in a black leather jacket. He'd vomited at some point, and only remembered being in some sort of alley, near some Dumpsters. That, and some black-and-white posters peeling off the brick outer walls that advertised a band called "Aphota."

He awoke still reeling on Sunday morning. He thought of making himself a screwdriver to quickly fall back into the numbness of the night before. Instead, he poured himself a tall glass of orange juice. Then he called Val to explain what was going on. Her equipment hadn't arrived as scheduled from La Paz, so there was nothing they could have done over the weekend. Lucky for him—Steve dead or not, he needed the money.

With his binge winding down, he thought about going fishing, but fishing without Steve wouldn't feel right. The thought made him feel even hollower. Tonight he needed to head out with Dr. Martell and try to find the shoal, though, and knew he had to clean himself up. He lit a cigarette and resolved not to drink any more today. He didn't want her to see him this way. He was hosing off his boat when Joe Montoya walked up.

"Hey, Sturman."

"Montoya." He lowered the hose.

"How are you doing?"

"Seen better days, but I'm holding up. Thanks for stopping by yesterday."

"No worries. Let me know if Elena and I can do anything, okay?"

"Sure. What's up?"

"I just left the coroner's office. They finished their preliminary report this morning."

Sturman took a drag off his cigarette, nodded, and set the hose down. He stepped into his boat and grabbed a towel, which he used to dry the sweat and water off his face and the gray-tinged stubble on his head. "Come on in, Montoya."

Joe boarded the boat and sat down across from him in the stern. Joe looked at him for a minute without saying anything, and Sturman put his stained hat on, pulling the brim down low over his eyes. Joe reached out and Sturman handed him the cigarette. Joe took a deep, long pull and handed it back. Somewhere nearby reggae music drifted toward them from another boat.

"Just spit it out, Montoya. What did they find out?"

"You sure you want to hear this, Will?"

Sturman gave an almost imperceptible nod.

"They don't think it's a shark attack anymore. It looks like Steve drowned."

"Drowned? What about his injuries?"

"I had assumed it was all just from sharks, crabs— you know as well as I do what happens to a body left in the ocean for more than a few hours."

Sturman nodded and stood up. He walked over to the side of the boat and looked out at the harbor. A white sailboat was heading out to sea. It was a calm, sunny day. In his mind's eye, he saw Steve's face again.

"The coroner wasn't certain about the cause of the damage, and some of it was inflicted postmortem. . . ." Joe sighed loudly. "But most of the wounds on his body were inflicted while he was still alive."

"What are you talking about?"

"The damage to his face, his arms . . . some of it wasn't from marine scavengers. It happened before he died. The coroner wasn't able to attribute the cause yet, but she suspects some sort of animal."

Sturman felt his blood chill. He turned and stood before Joe before he spoke again.

"What kind of animal?"

"Kathy—the coroner—doesn't know yet. But she said she's never seen anything like it before. The body had a lot of symmetrical, round tears in the skin, and so did the wet suit, and something sharp and serrated was responsible for the damage to the flesh. But she's positive it wasn't a knife, and definitely not a propeller. She said the cuts aren't clean enough."

"What are you saying? Did something try to *eat* him?"

Joe shifted in his seat, adjusting his gun belt. "She thinks so. I wish I could tell you he didn't suffer, Sturman, but—"

"That's enough."

"Sturman, the coroner doesn't specialize in these types of injuries, so it may be some time before they can tell us anything else. They don't want to rush to conclusions."

"What about those other divers? You find them yet?"

"Nothing yet. Just that kid's hand . . ."

"Right." Sturman sat down again and rubbed the side of his boat with a calloused hand. "You have a marine biologist looking into this? Someone who knows sharks and such?"

"They're looking to contact someone now. A doctor at the university who specializes in shark attacks."

"I might know somebody else who can help."

CHAPTER 27

Six all-weather stage lights with broad aluminum domes, clamped to the railings surrounding *Maria,* illuminated the dark water around the vessel as it drifted on the nighttime ocean. Small bugs darting in and out of the harsh cones of white light stood out against the black background, like miniscule starfighters battling for the freedom to incinerate themselves on the hot bulbs. Dr. Valerie Martell's universe had shrunk to the small, overlapping patches of light, because it was impossible to see beyond the glaring brightness near the boat.

Val figured the bugs had probably been stowaways when they headed out, since flying insects rarely ventured this far from the coast. She sat next to Sturman as he steered the boat on a slow course, parallel to the shore as they headed up the continental shelf. It was just the two of them, since his friend Mike Phan couldn't make it. Every few minutes, Sturman scanned the depth finder for signs of the shoal. They rarely talked.

She studied his profile in the shadow cast by the Western hat, dark under the glow of the stage lights rigged to the boat. It was hard to read this man. When she had spent time with him last week, she had thought he was an awfully quiet person. And he always wore the same hard expression. He was a potential asshole. Although his demeanor was the same tonight, he must be hurting after just losing his friend. She decided to try striking up a conversation again, to get his mind off things.

After he wouldn't divulge much about his own past, she told him about her upbringing in Florida, how she had gotten her undergrad there and then gone on to earn her PhD at UC Berkeley.

She asked, "Where did you go to school?"

"I didn't."

"Oh." She looked away for a few moments. "We really don't have a whole lot in common, do we?"

"Nope. Doc, I need to talk to you about something important." Sturman wasn't looking at her, instead gazing off into the darkness over the sea.

She sat forward. "Oh? What's on your mind?" The breeze brushed a lock of her hair loose and she blew it out of her eyes.

"What would it look like if a Humboldt squid attacked a man? What kind of injuries do they inflict?"

"Is this about your friend?"

Sturman looked at her. "The coroner identified drowning as the cause of death, but she hasn't figured out what happened to Steve before he died. Something really laid into him while he was still alive."

Val thought for a moment. "What kind of injuries were on the body?"

Sturman briefly described the damage to Steve Black's body, the circular tears and serrated cuts the coroner had seen. He also told her about the damage he had seen himself, to his friend's face.

"Are you sure you're okay talking about this?"

Sturman looked away, as if checking their heading. There was a hollow, sunken look on his face exaggerated by the deep shadows under his hat. He nodded.

"Well, I've never seen Humboldt squid attack anything larger than a tuna, so it's hard to say. But the wounds you're describing could possibly be from a Humboldt squid. *Dosidicus* have thousands of suckers lined with small teeth, so they can grip prey. And their beaks are serrated, like miniature saw blades. When they bite into larger fish, they can remove large chunks of . . . I'm sorry. I'm so used to getting carried away with this subject. It's just that Humboldt squid have been the focus of my life for so long."

"I just want to figure out what happened to Steve." Sturman rose and stepped over to the side of the boat, leaning on it with both arms as he looked down into the black water. "I'm kind of wondering if your shoal killed him."

"As much as I don't want to admit it, you've got me starting to worry, too. This doesn't sound good for the shoal either. If these animals were involved, you can't take it personally—"

The depth finder emitted a loud series of beeps. Sturman spun to the helm and leaned down over the display.

"We've got something directly under the boat."

Val's heart jumped as she sprang from her seat, even though she knew the device wasn't actually picking up Humboldt squid.

"What does it look like?"

"A large school . . . probably made up of smaller fish. So the squid aren't detectable on sonar?

"Right. Their soft bodies don't reflect sound waves effectively. But they pursue sardines, anchovies, and other small fish that are detectable. Sturman, can you cut the engine?"

He put the boat into idle and turned off the key. It was suddenly very quiet in the darkness around the boat, with just the sound of small waves lapping against the hull. After a moment, the backup generator used to power the lights kicked on in the stern. The depth finder beeped again as the heavy boat continued to drift slowly forward in the artificial light.

"They're about a hundred feet down. This school extends pretty far, and it looks like whatever's in it is probably pretty tiny. A few larger readings occasionally, though."

"Sounds like a school of baitfish. Those bigger readings are probably swordfish or tuna. Let's see if we can catch anything."

Quickly, Sturman and Val lowered fishing lines into the water. Val counted off fourteen seconds as the line spooled out, knowing from practice that this would be roughly a hundred feet of line. Each line was rigged with a massive glowing jig surrounded by treble hooks, with a steel leader and eighty-pound test line. They placed the first two poles in rod holders, then dropped two more lines into the water and began to jig them vigorously.

"Think the squid might be here, too?" Sturman asked.

"I don't know. Hopefully we'll find out soon."

"You got that GPS transmitter ready?"

Val picked up the object next to her, which looked like a karaoke microphone with an orange bulb on top, from which protruded a short antenna. Inside was a GPS transmitter designed to allow satellite tracking of both cartographic location and depth. The plan was to tag a member of the shoal, then track the shoal's movements based on the signal from the transmitter, to determine if it might be posing a threat. She set the device back down to focus on her fishing pole.

"I turned it on earlier, and the seal looks good. We just need somewhere to put it now."

If they ever landed a squid, they would affix the transmitter to the squid's fin and then get the animal back into the water as fast as they could to maximize its chances of survival.

They both stood holding the fishing rods, waiting. In the quiet night, Val could feel excitement and anticipation building inside her, although she knew their chances were slim. After a few minutes, Sturman broke the silence.

"So why are these things attracted to light, anyway? Aren't they more comfortable in the dark?"

"Their eyes are actually very sensitive to light, but when the water is lit up at night it's their powerful eyes that allow us to attract them. The lights shine off of small fish, plankton, and other smaller sea life, which draws the shoal up to the surface. Humboldts can detect this light from—"

Val's pole bent downward in a violent arc. She jerked back on the line and began to reel. "I've got something! Whatever's on here, it's big."

"You got it? Can you handle it?"

"Just reel in the other lines. I don't want to get everything tangled."

Val began to regret her decision not to accept his help as she fought the adversary on the other end of the line, but she stubbornly reeled as her arms and shoulders ached and then began to burn.

After fifteen minutes, before Val's lure became visible near the surface, Sturman stepped over to help her after he had secured the other poles. He stood over her, gaff in hand. Val noticed as she leaned back to pull on the line that the expression under the hat had changed. Sturman's narrow eyes and flared nostrils said one thing: aggression. He probably wanted to kill one of these squid, or all of them, and she couldn't really blame him. She knew that nothing these animals ever did was personal, they were just trying to survive. But she knew how it felt to lose someone you cared for.

When the thrashing silver animal reached the surface, she was almost relieved it wasn't actually a member of the shoal.

"Tuna," Sturman said as she fought the fish to the side of the boat. He sounded as disappointed as she felt.

"Yeah." Val grunted as the big fish tugged on the line. "Albacore."

"Good thing I've got a license." Sturman leaned toward the surface of the water with the gaff.

"Sturman, these tuna stocks are suffering. Do you really need it?"

He looked at the tuna as it rested beside the boat,

protesting with an occasional thrash of its weakening tail. After a moment, Sturman withdrew the gaff and pushed it up under the gunwale. With a long fillet knife, he severed the line in one quick motion. The tuna disappeared into the dark water in a final flash of silvery scales.

Sturman sat down and looked at Val.

"I guess you're right, Doc. I probably shouldn't be keeping those big fish. It's almost more surprising to catch one of these tuna than to catch one of your squid, and they don't even belong here. I don't see many sizeable fish around the coast anymore."

"Which is why people shouldn't be fishing for them right now. The governments of the world have always been too lenient with their catch limits, especially for commercial fisheries. So it's not just happening here. Stocks of big fish have plummeted all over the world in the past several decades, mostly due to overfishing. In fact, that may be one reason this shoal is managing to survive here—these squid don't have much competition, and there are few predators around to hunt them."

Sturman glanced at his watch. "Well, what do you think?"

"It's probably past three o'clock in the morning, right?"

"Three-thirty."

"We might as well call it a night. I just wish we had a better way to find these guys."

"This works for you in Baja?"

"Yeah, but down there, there are millions more squid. The odds are a lot better there. This was only our first attempt."

"You sure there's no way to track these bastards using the tags already on the squid?"

"I'm not even sure there are other tags in this shoal, but even if there are, there isn't any way to track them. Unless . . ."

"What?"

"Well, it's a long shot. While we can't actually track these tags, I might be able to *predict* where the shoal is headed."

"You've got my attention."

"If I can acquire recent surface water temperature maps of the ocean off Southern California, and maybe some accurate bathymetry charts, I might be able to somehow map out where the squid have been by correlating the chart data to the data from the tag we already have . . . and maybe figure out where they might be now."

"How long will that take?"

"Depends on how long it takes to get maps. But I might be able to put something together tomorrow before we head out again."

"I meant to talk to you about that. Steve's funeral is Wednesday morning. I won't be able to make it out tomorrow night."

Val remembered again what Sturman was going through and felt a sudden urge to hug him despite hardly knowing him, but resisted the temptation. His demeanor made it clear he didn't want sympathy. This man had clearly spent some time building walls around himself, long before he'd lost his friend.

"Don't worry about this job, Sturman. It can wait

for a few days." She smiled. "In this job, I've always got something to do."

"I appreciate it, Doc. About my friend Steve . . . do you think maybe you can talk to the coroner? Maybe you can help."

"Absolutely. Just get me the phone number."

CHAPTER 28

The funeral had been a tough one, even for Sturman. There was a motley group in attendance, which wasn't surprising considering the company Steve Black had kept. The old pirate had never married, so his family was made up mostly of members of his motorcycle club, plus a few other dive captains and an assortment of bar buddies. Despite the odd collection of friends, it was obvious how deeply Steve's death had affected the people who knew him.

After the preacher had said the final words, everyone had headed off to The Lighthouse. Where else? Sturman knew Steve would have wanted a lively wake in his second home, and the unashamed drunk would have rolled over in his grave if alcohol hadn't been involved. Everyone's spirits had changed after the service had ended, many people beginning to smile through their tears.

Sturman had been drinking a few in memory of his old friend, but not as much as he usually did—he didn't want to make a scene. He was standing next to the pool tables at The Lighthouse with Steve's younger brother, listening to the others gathered there tell stories about the friend they'd lost. The old man had led a pretty colorful life.

"Want another shot at the title?" Sturman grinned at Cody Black. He'd just beaten him at eight ball for the third time.

"You're gettin' cocky, brother. Time for you to go down."

"Rack 'em."

Cody, a shorter, bearded version of Steve, gathered the billiard balls into the triangular rack and carefully lifted it away. As Sturman leaned forward to break, Cody muttered a curse under his breath.

"Who brought the goddamn Mexican in here?"

Sturman slammed the cue stick forward and broke the tight formation with a loud crack, then stood and turned to see what Cody was talking about as two balls dropped. Near the door stood Joe Montoya, looking around the room. He noticed Sturman and headed his way.

"It's that cop, isn't it?"

"Easy, Cody. That cop is my friend. We were in the service together."

Cody glowered, but he kept his mouth shut as Joe neared. Sturman pulled his hat brim down and wondered why Joe would show up at Steve's wake. Joe already knew every damn member of Steve's family was a bigot.

"Hey, Montoya. What's up?"

"I'm very sorry to come here. I realize this is bad timing, but can we talk for a minute, Sturman?"

"Cody, why don't you play with Hank? I'm gonna go talk to him for a minute."

Sturman and Joe slid into a booth on the far side of the bar. Sturman signaled Jill for two beers, then studied his friend's face.

"This must be important, Montoya." Sturman grinned. "You know how much this crowd likes folks with brown skin . . . and how they adore the law."

Joe smiled. "I hear you. But this is important. Listen—your biologist friend came in to the coroner's. She saw Steve, and we showed her the body of that immigrant I told you about . . . the one who died in the ocean a few weeks ago when trying to cross over."

Sturman stopped raising the glass of beer to his lips and set the beer down. His expression tightened. "And?"

"She thinks they both showed signs of being attacked by those squid. She said it's hard for her to tell, since she hasn't examined human bodies before, but she said the injuries look consistent with the biology of a Humboldt squid. Also, the shark expert who came in wrote off any shark species as a possible cause of death."

Sturman sat quietly for a moment. "Anyone else know about this?"

"Not yet."

"You going to tell anyone?"

"No. Not now. I'm not sure yet how we want to handle such a bizarre situation."

"Goddammit, Montoya. There are people right in this room who make their living scuba diving. Many of them go out at night."

"I know, Sturman. Tell them not to go diving right now . . . but you should probably make something up. I doubt they'll believe you if you tell them the truth anyway."

"When you going to tell the press—make an announcement?"

"Once my boss has a chance to look this over. We don't want to cause an unnecessary panic. These were isolated incidents, after all."

"You'd be comfortable with another 'isolated incident'?"

"That's not fair. This isn't my call anyway."

"So after the sheriff's office announces this, then what?"

"I don't know. We'll probably make some recommendations to prevent it from happening again. Which brings me to my next point. You and Dr. Martell are going to be heading out again after—"

"Hey, you! You, *vato*!"

Two bigger bikers were heading toward the booth. The shorter one, in the front, wore a black leather vest that showed off a tapestry of tattoos running down muscular arms. He was weaving as he walked. Sturman had met him before, maybe while drinking with Steve, but couldn't remember his name.

"Yeah, you, boy. What the fuck you doin' here? Steve don't want no wetbacks at his wake."

Joe watched them come. "Back off, guys. I'm a cop. I'm not here for trouble."

"You ain't a cop in here, wetback. You got two seconds to get the fuck out or I'm gonna rip your head off."

"Sturman, I better go. We can talk about this more later." Joe stood and raised his hands. "Easy, boys, I'm leaving."

"Who you calling *boy*?"

Joe stopped walking toward the door and turned back to the biker. Having spent years with him in the Navy, Sturman wasn't surprised.

"You—*boy*," Joe said. "I said I was leaving, *boy*."

The muscular biker lunged at Joe. Joe ducked underneath the sucker punch that came flying at the side of his head. The momentum carried them both over, and an instant later they were heaped on the floor, with Joe on the bottom.

The second, taller biker moved toward the two men on the floor. As he rushed past the booth, Sturman kicked his leg out, tripping him. The man stumbled and crashed into the next booth, but didn't go down. When he turned to face his attacker, Sturman was already on his feet. Before the biker could cock his arm all the way back, Sturman's fist slammed into the man's cheek with a loud smack. That was all it took. The biker crumpled to the floor unconscious, toppling a bar stool on the way down. By now, everybody in the bar was looking over at the commotion.

Sturman moved to help Joe with the shorter biker, who had straddled him on the floor and started raining punches down. Before Sturman could get there, Joe bucked with his hips and managed to roll on top of the biker. Joe head-butted his opponent in the face and the man rolled to his stomach, covering his face with his hands. Joe forced a forearm around the man's neck and latched into a rear choke. Ten seconds later, the man went limp and Joe dumped him to the floor.

As Sturman reached down to help Joe up, he saw that other bikers were headed their way now, including Cody.

"We better get the fuck outta here, amigo. These guys are dangerous, and they're not in the best mood."

"You don't have to tell me twice."

Sturman and Joe sat on a bench a half-mile from The Lighthouse. Joe finished cleaning up his bloody nose while Sturman enjoyed the cool breeze as he came down from the adrenaline high. They had scuffled with a few more of the bikers' friends in the parking lot. Sturman had a big cut on his lip, but couldn't figure out how it had gotten there.

"Thanks for getting us out of there, Sturman. I owe you one."

"You already owed me one."

"I mean it. Those guys meant business."

"Just like the bars in Thailand, huh?"

"Yeah. Those were the days, weren't they?"

"It's been a while since I've been in a good scrap. You gonna get some backup and go arrest those bastards?"

"Nah. Those guys are pricks, but they've had a rough enough day, and you just embarrassed them in front of Steve's friends. I can let it slide. Hey, man, I'm sorry to ruin that for you. Steve's wake."

"It's all right. Never liked most of Steve's friends, anyway."

"Maria wouldn't want you hanging out with that bunch."

Sturman set his jaw and glared at Joe. "Don't talk about her now."

"You gotta talk about her sometime, Will. And for

Christ's sake, don't fucking tell me I can't talk about my own sister."

The men sat quietly, listening to the sounds of the waterfront at night: muffled music and voices from nearby bars; a cool, steady breeze ruffling the palms overhead; distant traffic on the freeway. The blaring sound of a semi-trailer truck using its jake brakes reminded Sturman of the night he had lost his wife.

CHAPTER 29

"**J**esus, Sturman. What happened to your face?"

He smiled at Val from the stern of his boat, wincing slightly as the scabbed-over cut on his lower lip opened again. Val had just come down the dock and was standing beside *Maria.* The sun had just set.

"Fell off my bike."

Val shook her head. "Men. Really—what happened?"

"Steve's wake."

"What? You mean you got in a fight at your friend's funeral?"

Sturman touched his lip. "At his wake. In a bar. And I didn't start it."

"My God. You didn't start it. Well, you smell like alcohol. Have you been drinking today?"

"Who are you, my mother?"

"No. I'm a paying customer. And I'm not about to go out on the water at night with a drunk captain."

Sturman was silent for a moment. "I haven't had a drink since last night."

"You must have had a lot. You smell like a bar. Are you really okay to drive the boat?"

"Of course I am. This isn't the first time I've had a lot to drink the night before work." Sturman turned and went inside the cabin. The air filled with a loud rumble as he fired up the boat. He returned with a lit cigarette in his mouth.

She frowned. "I didn't know you smoked."

"Usually only when I'm drinking." He blew smoke in her direction. "Or being nagged."

"So pretty often then. Nasty habit."

"Nobody's perfect. Well, you ever gonna hop on board, Doc? Sun's goin' down."

Val stood looking at him, hands on her hips. Why was this man so difficult? "So you don't want to talk about anything, you drink too much, and you smoke. Typical sailor." Val threw her daypack at Sturman, harder than she needed to. He caught it as it slammed into his chest.

"Easy. I'm the one who got in a fight."

"Just drive the boat."

Val felt her father's temper rising inside her. Sturman actually reminded her a bit of her father—tall, quiet, tough. And a drinker. After untying the boat from the dock cleats, she climbed on board and stood facing away from Sturman. She heard an unfamiliar sound behind her. He was laughing.

"You feeling lucky, Doc?"

"You think this is funny? If you don't want to tell me—"

"Whoa. You sure are a feisty one." He grinned. "All I wanted to know was if you thought we'd catch something tonight. I'm feelin' lucky."

Val smiled. "Third time's a charm, right?" Sturman

knew how to piss her off, but she was excited about their chances tonight, too.

As Sturman steered the boat slowly out of the harbor into a light wind, Val studied his face again. He had a fresh growth of dark stubble on his jaw, and his lip was split near the middle. She knew he probably hadn't seen a doctor, but realized it was futile to try and get this man to do anything he didn't want to. And she was feeling edgy because she knew they needed to have another uncomfortable talk, which would probably ruin his mood. Might as well get it out of the way.

"I talked to the coroner, Sturman."

His smile faded. "Montoya told me last night."

"So he told you everything?"

Sturman turned the helm slightly to avoid a large buoy at the mouth of the harbor. "I guess."

"The injuries were consistent with what I'd expect from a Humboldt squid."

"You sure?"

"Well, obviously I can't be certain. In fact, some of the damage, such as the child's severed hand that was also found, seemed excessive for the smaller beak of a Humboldt squid. These animals generally can't bite through larger bones. But my best guess is that the circular tears on the skin of both your friend and the John Doe immigrant were made by the arms and tentacles of a Humboldt. Their suckers leave a pretty distinct mark."

"Yeah. Okay."

"I'm sorry, Will. I hope your friend didn't suffer much."

Sturman clenched his jaw, then forced a smile. "Let's go sink a hook into one of the bastards."

Val thought of asking Sturman again to not take this personally, but she could tell that now was not the time. As *Maria* cleared the buoys at the mouth of the harbor, he forced down the throttles and the twin engines roared. The boat rose to meet the oncoming swells as it fought its way toward the fading light to the west.

This time, she knew they had found the shoal.

They were four miles off the beach at La Jolla, and had spent several hours motoring in the darkness before getting a promising reading.

Val was positive the massive school of fish on the depth finder was being pursued by Humboldt squid because when she and Sturman had reeled in their lines a minute ago, lifeless hunks of tentacled flesh were still wrapped around one of the glowing lures. Sturman's dog, Bud, had whined at the unfamiliar smell and was acting restless.

Val had successfully led them to the shoal, based on its previous location, its trend toward shallower waters, and a slight northerly drift from the currents. Now that they'd finally located the animals, they had a new problem. The shoal was attacking the hooked individuals and consuming them before she and Sturman could get them to the surface.

"Sturman, we need to reel them in faster. I need an intact animal if we want to get a transmitter out there."

"We've got enough here for calamari."

"Funny."

"Doc, I hate to break it to you, but we aren't going to get these big guys in any faster." Sturman's face was still dripping with sweat from the effort to land the last Humboldt.

"Well, we need to try. Don't worry about breaking the line or freeing the hooks like you do with a fish. The next time one hits, just reel as fast as you can."

Sturman looked at her darkly and spat over the side of the boat. "Right."

"Sturman—your dog!"

Bud had jumped up onto the side of the boat and was looking down into the water. Sturman shouted at him to come down, but the mutt was focused on the dark water, his ears laid back and his tail high in the air. A sudden swell hit the side of the boat, tipping it violently to the side. Bud scrabbled on the side but lost his footing. As his front paws began to slide off the side of the boat, Sturman grabbed a handful of hair and loose skin at the back of the dog's neck and jerked him back into the boat.

"Dammit, Bud!" Sturman's expression momentarily changed to one Val hadn't seen on his face before. The look was gone an instant later as he pushed Bud's face away from his and stopped the dog from licking his chin. "Thanks, Doc. I don't want to lose another friend to these sons of bitches."

"I don't want you to, either. Even though I've had good luck diving with these animals, when they're in a feeding frenzy they might attack anything."

"Well, they ain't gettin' my dog." Sturman clipped a

short leash onto Bud's collar and tied the other end to the ladder. "You want the other lines back in?"

"No. I think the two lures still down there should do the trick, and I don't want to tangle the—"

The fishing rod leaning out over the port side bent deeply. Sturman freed the pole from its holder and pulled back on it. His tank top stretched as he jammed the butt of the pole against his stomach, and the hammerhead shark tattoo on his shoulder rippled under the strain of his shoulder muscles. "Start the timer, Doc."

Sturman fought to land the animal. He slammed his hip into the gunwale as his quarry made a run or was seized by other members of the shoal. Val stood next to him with a large net, ready to scoop the catch from the water when it reached the boat. Minutes passed, and Val began to pace on the boat behind him.

"There! I can see it," she said. "It's not alone. Keep reeling. Almost here . . ."

The hooked squid, larger than Sturman's dog, was now visible ten feet below the surface, emitting angry pulses of light as it fought the lure. Around it other shapes darted in and out as members of the shoal snatched at its flesh.

A burst of water splashed into Sturman's face as the creature reached the surface and jetted water out of its siphons. Val leaned forward to net it.

"Sturman, the net's not big enough!"

Val looked down at the large squid. It had to be five or six feet long, nearly a hundred pounds. In the harsh white lights, Val could see it had been badly damaged—but it was still alive.

Sturman grunted as the squid tried to make another run. "Grab the gaff."

"No. I need it alive."

"You got a better idea? I don't know how long he's gonna be here."

Despite his obvious strength, he looked exhausted from the fight. She watched as a smaller Humboldt darted up and latched on to the mantle of the hooked squid. Val raised the net over her head and smashed the aluminum frame into the body of the attacking squid. It released its grip and disappeared into the black water.

Val turned and looked around the boat. *Come on, Val. Think.* She rushed into the cabin and searched for a means of landing the squid, but found nothing. She hurried back to Sturman, who was now bent toward the water, his elbows jammed against the top of the gun-wale.

"Sturman, can you bring her around to the transom? Maybe we can slide her onto it when a wave hits."

He grunted and began working his way to the stern. Val grabbed the transmitter and a coil of rope that was cleated to the side of the boat. She tied a quick loop in the loose end and pulled the rope through the loop to form a makeshift lasso. As a heavy swell rocked into the boat, Sturman pulled hard on the line, and the squid slid up with the water rushing over the transom.

Val leaned forward and slid the loop over the broad fins on the squid's mantle, then jerked the line tight. "Drop the pole! I need your help!"

A minute later they had managed to drag the thrashing animal into the stern using the coil of rope. Bud was barking nonstop at the unwelcome visitor. Out of the water, its soft body looked weak and flaccid sprawled across the bottom of the boat, which was now covered in foamy seawater. Despite obvious injuries from the other squid, it was still struggling to survive. Its arms writhed and coiled in desperation. A jet of ink spurted from its tubular body, coating their feet in dark fluid.

Sturman, still breathing hard, grimaced. "Bastard's staining up my boat!"

Bud went quiet and strained against his leash to smell the animal. It lashed out and seized Bud's head with twin tentacles, dragging the yelping mutt toward its wriggling arms. Sturman stepped forward and slammed his heel onto the squid's smooth body. The stomp sounded like a water balloon exploding against the ground. Sturman stomped again and it released his dog.

"Goddammit, we need it alive!"

"My dog comes first, Doc. Thing's already gone, anyway."

"Well, it is now, isn't it?" Val sat down. She knew Sturman was right. The Humboldt had been badly damaged by the other squid. It was pointless to waste the transmitter on it.

"How about that? I can still see my footprint on it."

On the squid's soft mantle, a glowing footprint was visible where the sole of Sturman's sandal had struck it. They watched as the glowing print slowly faded to match the reddish hue of the body.

"That's just the photophores reacting to the impact."

"Pretty cool."

"This one is too badly damaged. We need to try again."

"What we need is another plan. We need to get them out of the water faster."

Ten minutes later they finished securing the fishing tackle. The squid they had landed lay motionless in the bottom of the boat. Its angry crimson coloration had slowly faded away, until it was simply a large, almost formless slab of pale flesh, marked by large cuts and tears. Sturman squatted down and ran his broad hand over the smooth, lifeless body.

"It isn't as slimy as I thought it would be. Feels like a giant uncooked chicken breast."

"Be careful. I think she's dead, but she might have a final spasm before she goes."

Sturman ignored her advice. "You keep saying 'she.' Is this a female?"

"Probably. That's a very large Humboldt. The males are usually smaller." She sighed. "Well, it's not a total loss. I can dissect this one in the lab. My God, she *is* one of the bigger ones I've ever seen out of the water."

"She's one big girl. Is this a really old one, then?"

"It's probably quite old for a Humboldt, but that's not saying much. These animals only live for a few years. All cephalopods grow incredibly fast."

Sturman's hands moved to the tentacles. He separated one from the arms, stretched it out and ran his palm along the surface. "Its suckers feel like little knives."

"They have over a thousand of them. Each one is lined with serrated teeth to grip the slick sides of fish."

Val headed into the cabin as Sturman continued to

examine the animal. When she returned a few minutes later he was still looking at it.

"So what now, Doc? Any more ideas?" Sturman stood and turned to face her as she pulled up the back zipper on her wet suit. He shook his head. "No way."

"Yes."

"Hell no."

"I'm getting into the water."

CHAPTER 30

"**Y**ou're not really going in with those things, Doc?"

"Please don't be so dramatic. I dive with Humboldt squid all the time." Val began connecting her BC vest and regulator to an air tank in the stern. Dawn was still hours away, but she knew the squid could soon start their descent to deeper water.

"Maybe so. But not these ones. Hell, you saw what this one just tried to do to my dog!" Sturman kicked the side of the squid heaped in the stern of his boat. "You saw what they did to Steve Black."

"Don't worry. We'll make sure I'm tethered to the boat, and I'll surface immediately if I'm worried by their behavior. They're normally afraid of unfamiliar objects, like a person in scuba gear. I'll be lucky to get near one."

"Steve was *in* scuba gear."

Val paused. "True. But we're still not absolutely positive he was attacked by Humboldt squid. And even if he was, it must have been under incredibly rare circumstances."

Sturman shook his head. "You're fucking serious, aren't you?"

"We need to attach the transmitter to a healthy squid, or else there will be no reliable way to follow this shoal and find out if it might be a threat." She fixed Sturman with a hard stare. "You have any better ideas?"

"I don't know. I just don't understand how tracking them now is going to help us figure out what they've already done. Give me a minute to think."

"I can get a better idea what their habits are and we can warn the local authorities if they move too close to shore. Look, we can't risk the shoal getting away. They're here now." Val slid a neoprene hood tightly over her head and adjusted it around her face. Unlike most of her dives with *Dosidicus*, before which she usually felt excited, this time she felt a hint of fear. She couldn't let Sturman know. Without his cooperation, she couldn't make this dive.

"Let me do it, then."

"Don't be ridiculous." Val smiled, and was grateful for the neoprene covering much of her face. Considering how dangerous Sturman saw the situation as being, it was brave of him to offer to go in her place. "I have much more experience with these animals than you do. If they do get agitated, I can read their behavior. Besides, this is your boat. It makes more sense to have you topside."

Sturman looked her up and down, making her feel self-conscious in the unflattering full-body wet suit and hood.

"That's a good look on you, Doc."

"Let's be serious, Sturman. I know you're worried,

but I don't want to joke around now. I know these animals better than almost anyone in the world. Despite how crazy this must seem to you, I'm not suicidal."

Sturman looked her in the eyes. "How do you plan to get this"—he picked up the transmitter and shook it—"hooked to a squid, underwater, while it's alive and doesn't want to be bothered?"

Val smiled. "I've got an idea."

Val paused on the transom of Sturman's boat, holding on to the vessel to brace herself in the gentle nighttime swells. She had donned full scuba gear. The lines had been reeled in. The transmitter was prepped in the boat. In her hand she held a capture net. Sturman knew the plan, and was waiting behind her with nylon ropes coiled in each hand.

Everything was ready. It was time to get in the water. But she hesitated. The generator hummed loudly, steadily, in her ears.

Val cursed herself for her apprehension. *You're letting your imagination get to you—just like a child.*

"You all right, Doc?" Sturman yelled over the generator.

She looked at the cool, black water below the transom, focusing below the reach of the rented lights, where she knew the bottom was almost a thousand feet down, then back into the well-lit cabin of the boat. Bud stood leashed nearby, watching her and wagging his tail. "Yeah. Just give me a minute."

"You don't have to do this. We can try to catch a healthy one on the fishing lines."

On some level, Val knew Sturman was right. But

this hesitation was irrational, even if these squid had possibly killed a few people during a feeding frenzy. She knew these animals. They simply didn't kill people.

Sturman's concern had her feeling a bit panicked, even though she had dived with the animals many times under similar conditions. She shivered as a cold breeze hit her neck, water dripping down her exposed skin from the wet dive mask she had already defogged and dipped into the ocean.

Logic dictated that this would be like any other dive with Humboldt squid. As long as she was tethered, she would be fine. She looked back again, this time at the lights shining down into the water along the sides of the boat, bugs darting underneath them in a thick swarm. *The shoal probably looks something like that under the water,* she thought. Sturman and Bud looked at her, waiting. They appeared almost comical, sharing similar expressions. She laughed out loud to relieve the tension.

"Why are you laughing?"

Now or never, Val. "Just watch the lines, Sturman. I'll be back soon."

Val turned and lifted the regulator up to her mouth. She drew a long breath, listened to the comforting hiss of air flowing freely through the hose. She bit down on the rubber mouthpiece and forced away the terrible thoughts trying to creep into the back of her mind. Time to focus on the task at hand.

She placed her hand over her mask and regulator to hold them in place, raised one leg up, and stepped out over the open ocean.

* * *

As she entered the water, it became very quiet as the sound of the generator faded to a low buzz. Cold water flowed past her face with a rush of small bubbles as her momentum carried her down from the surface. She could hear faint clicks and hums from marine organisms now, and very distant boat motors, because of water's ability to transmit sound much farther than air.

The white hull of the boat stood out dramatically, brightly illuminated by the lights shining into the water, but underneath there was nothing but a black void. She clicked on her flashlight and looked down into the blackness underneath her swim fins, but the beam was swallowed up by the darkness almost before it left the bulb. The shoal was still a few hundred feet down, and she needed to lure them closer. To have enough air to go deep safely, she would have to hurry. She checked her air supply one last time and felt for the reassurance of the tether at her waist. She raised the air release valve on her BC, dumping out the remaining air trapped inside. A moment later she could feel the pressure start to build around her as she sank into the void.

She sank feetfirst. There was no need to waste energy. The lead weights in her vest would do the work for her. The best thing to do was utilize the negative buoyancy provided by the weights and simply control her descent, offering occasional upward kicks and releasing small amounts of air from the scuba tank into her vest, where the air could expand and prevent her from sinking too fast.

Val looked at her dive computer and watched as the depth gauge slowly counted past twenty feet, thirty

feet, forty feet. She scanned the black abyss below her
with the light, but still saw nothing but a fine soup of
particulate matter. Every few feet, she pinched her
nose and blew, equalizing the pressure in her ears to
match the mounting force of the water around her sinuses.

When she passed a hundred feet, she depressed the
fill valve on her BC for several seconds, transferring
more air into it. After thirty seconds of fine-tuning, the
added air in the vest stopped her descent. Hovering in
the darkness, she took a deep breath and shut off her
dive light.

Slowly, her eyes began to adjust. The bright lights
shining down from above provided the only illumination, just enough that she could make out the outline of
her hand two feet from her eyes. She felt the fine fila-
ments of the net snag her gear as she moved it out away
from her body. She would need to compensate Sturman for ruining his fishing net. They had cut the netting free from its handle and wide aluminum ring, and
secured it instead to the end of a long, nylon nautical
rope in such a way that when the rope was pulled taut,
the net would cinch closed. Val had been able to capture Humboldt squid in Mexico using a similar net
fashioned by her crew there. If she was able to lure a
squid into the net, she intended to close the webbing
around it, then tug on the rope as a signal to Sturman to
haul in the catch.

Here goes nothing.

Val reached into the folds of the netting and pulled a
black drawstring pouch off a glowing neon fishing
lure, hooks removed, that was zip-tied to the inside of
the net. They had used Sturman's protective sunglasses

pouch to serve as the makeshift cover because the lure inside was a powerful attractant. In the blackness of the deep, its exposed greenish fluorescent glow actually hurt her eyes for a moment.

If it was this bright to her, she knew her friends wouldn't have a hard time finding it. It was just a question of time.

Val focused on her breathing, making as few movements as possible to maintain her position underwater. By relaxing, she knew she could maximize her air supply and the resulting bottom time.

After a few minutes, she looked at her dive computer. Then back into the blackness around her, turning in slow circles and trying to watch in every direction.

Time dragged on as she alternately watched for approaching life and kept an eye on her gauges. After eight minutes, she began to wonder if her presence near the light was keeping the animals from approaching, but knew her plan wouldn't work if she wasn't holding on to the net, at the ready. It was possible that the shoal was already here, simply staying far enough away from her as to remain unseen as they assessed her. But something needed to happen soon. She moved the net up and down again in quick jerks, trying to imagine what it would look like when they were jigging the lures at the ends of fishing lines. The glowing lure in her net danced erratically up and down in the darkness, like a wounded fish.

Then she saw something.

It had only been a momentary change in the blackness, but she was certain something large had passed by her, vaguely illuminated by the glow of the lure. She moved the lure more rapidly, careful to keep the net open.

She felt a slight pressure wave as something displaced the water near her.

Val began to turn her head to see what had caused the disturbance, then flinched at a sudden movement near the net. A Humboldt rushed out of the darkness and splayed its arms in the green glow in front of the net, like a huge flower quickly opening its petals. It fired its two coiled tentacles toward the lure. The lure moved violently backward as they struck it, but the squid didn't hold on. An instant later it vanished into the blackness.

Val's heart pounded in her rib cage. She willed herself to keep moving the bait. A soft touch brushed down her calf, but when she looked down, there was nothing there. Only her imagination? She thought of the torn flesh on the corpse in the morgue, the missing face. *Stop scaring yourself, Val. You've been here before.*

The shoal descended on her in a mad rush. Val wasn't sure how many animals suddenly appeared—four, maybe five. A smaller squid in the group went straight for the lure, but before Val could react the animal had grasped it and was pulling it away, causing the open area of the net Val had created to collapse and tangle. The squid stubbornly refused to release the lure, emitting flashing bursts of bioluminescent light in its frustration. Val knew this was her chance. She kicked toward the squirming mollusk, trying to close the net around it. Just as she managed to drag the net over its flashing mantle, she felt a powerful clenching around her thigh, and an instant later she was being dragged downward.

Waiting on the boat, Sturman lit a cigarette to calm his anxiety. Worry was not an emotion he had felt for a long time.

Val had been gone for more than ten minutes, but he hadn't seen any signs from her yet. He took off his hat and tossed it into the open cabin doors behind him, wiping the sweat off his brow with a thick forearm. Bud wagged his tail and Sturman scratched his ears.

He looked at the two ropes running into the water, each tied to a different cleat, and reminded himself which was tied to Val and which was connected to the net. She would tighten the rope on his left when she had a squid in the net, signaling him to hoist it up; the rope cleated off on his right was her lifeline.

As Sturman took his second pull off the cigarette, savoring the burn of the smoke entering his lungs, the line on the right suddenly drew taut. *Val's line.*

Sturman flicked his cigarette into the sea and grabbed the rope. As his hands closed around it, he swore as he felt an incredible weight at the other end and the vibrations of an obvious struggle. He considered pulling Val in, pausing as he remembered her request not to worry about her tether unless she was likely out of air. He glanced at his watch—she probably still had ten more minutes. *This is crazy.*

The line remained tight for a full minute. He decided not to wait any longer. Let her be pissed—he wasn't going to let her die down there while he stood idly on the boat picking his nose. He would have to pull her up very slowly, to prevent giving her decompression sickness, so he should probably start the process.

As Sturman braced his feet to begin hoisting her to the surface, the tension instantly left the rope. He slowly drew on the braided nylon, water dripping through his fingers as he passed the now slack line over his palms. He pulled in the line until it ran straight down into the water again, semi-taut, and concentrated on feeling for movement. It was still. *Shit.*

To his left, Sturman caught movement out of the corner of his eye and looked over to see a floating coil of the second rope begin to go under. Something was pulling it down into the water. The second line grew taut, then shuddered off a spray of water as it was jerked tight. He had to make a decision.

He couldn't pull Val rapidly to the surface—it would kill her. He had only one choice.

Dropping her tether, he grabbed the other rope near the cleat and pulled on it with both hands. Something heavy was thrashing aggressively on the other end. He pushed his knees against the gunwale, took a deep breath and, hand over hand, began to haul in the line. The loose rope began to quickly gather into a messy coil at his feet.

A few times during his struggle to bring in the capture net, Sturman was stopped momentarily by powerful downward jerks as the weight on the end of the line seemed to increase dramatically. Once he watched helplessly as the rope spooled out several feet, and grimaced as the flesh on his palms tore under the friction.

Heaving and cursing, his back muscles aching, he continued to retrieve the now-bloodied line. Then he finally saw something nearing the surface.

The lure.

With three more long pulls, the net appeared, tangled around a squirming animal. In a single powerful heave, Sturman swung the heavy catch up out of the water, dropping the sopping mess onto the floor of the boat. He yelled at Bud to stay put.

Inside the net was a squid. It wasn't nearly as big as the other one they had brought aboard, but it seemed a lot more upset. Grabbing the transmitter and its attachment device, he knelt in the pool of cold water around the squid and hastened to remove the tangled netting wrapped around its body.

Tagging the squid was easier than he had anticipated. Beginner's luck, maybe. The squid, though powerful when underwater, flapped helplessly and squirted ink-stained water on the floor of his boat. Sturman aligned the transmitter against the animal's body on the inside of one of its broad fins, just as Val had demonstrated for him on the dead squid, then pierced the fin with the sharp steel point of the attachment device, which looked kind of like a flare gun. After clipping the orange transmitter to the animal, he cinched it tightly against the squid's body with two plastic loops running out from the transmitter's barbs, tugged on it twice to make sure it was secure, then grabbed the squid around its smooth fins and, careful to avoid the beak and tentacles on its business end, lifted it off the floor and stepped to the side of the boat.

The squid fired a final defiant burst of inky water all over Sturman's legs as he threw it overboard. There was a loud splash as it entered the water, and then it was gone.

Sturman turned and looked at the other line. It had grown very slack, several broad loops floating on the surface and drifting into the side of the boat. Sturman looked at his bleeding hands, then desperately down into the water.

And waited.

CHAPTER 31

Never before had Val been happier to be out of the water.

She had spent the last fifteen minutes waiting at her safety stop, just twenty feet below the surface. They had been some of the most frightening minutes of her life. As she lingered in the darkness under the curved, white hull of the boat, kicking awkwardly with one fin, she had fought the incredible urge to sprint to the surface and scramble out of the water. The shoal had robbed her of her other fin, but thankfully had left her alone once she had separated herself from the glowing lure.

As she waited for the nitrogen to leave her body, she had focused on her breathing, and simply counted the seconds until she could surface safely. Then she had rushed topside and heaved herself onto the boat's transom. Now she sat in the stern, shivering, her gear heaped in a puddle of seawater at her feet.

"Are you cold?" Sturman appeared from the cabin and wrapped a thick towel around Val's shoulders.

"Yeah. Thanks. So you got it tagged the way I told you?"

"Bet your ass I did." He sat down next to her. "Glad you're all right, Doc."

"So am I. I told you I'd be fine."

"What the hell happened down there?"

Val explained how the shoal had seized her just as she had first attempted to net the small male squid, and how only the tether had prevented them from pulling her deeper. "These squid were more aggressive than I'm used to, maybe because they're not getting enough to eat. But as soon as they distinguished me from the lure, they seemed to lose interest in me."

"How hard was it to get his ass into the net?"

"I don't really remember, to tell you the truth. He just seemed to work his way inside it, and I pulled on the rope."

"Let's find out if that was worth it."

"Good idea. Can you grab my laptop?"

Sturman returned with Val's computer, and opened it awkwardly with his crudely bandaged hands.

"Jesus, Sturman! What happened to your hands?"

"Rope burns. I shoulda worn gloves."

"Are you okay? You're bleeding a lot."

"I'll be all right."

Sturman navigated on the laptop for her as she toweled off and explained how to open the correct program.

"The research branch of the aquarium I work for has a website researchers can use to track the movements of all our tagged marine animals. Every fifteen minutes, we should get a new location from the tag."

Sturman zoomed in on a map of their general location on the water, locating several dots that represented readouts since they had turned on the transmitter. "So does this mean it's working?"

"We need to wait and see if the transmitter takes a new reading now that's it's on the squid." Val paused. "Thanks for trusting me. I'm sure it was hard for you to let me go down there."

"You kidding? For a while there I didn't think you'd come back."

"Really?"

"Yeah. Really. But I figured I was gonna make a killing when I sold off your state-of-the-art equipment."

"Asshole. Hey, check it out." Val pointed at the new dot on the screen, clustered near the others. "It looks like it's working. He's still pretty much below us."

"Now what?"

"Now? Let's get the hell out of here and go find a late-night diner. I'm starving."

CHAPTER 32

The first thing Sturman noticed as he entered the lab was the odor. Although it looked very sterile, it smelled like a fish market in all its blood-and-scales-and-fins-and-guts glory, mixed with other smells that brought him back to his tenth-grade biology class—alcohol and formaldehyde.

"Damn, Doc. How do you work in this stink?"

Val looked up from the side of a stainless-steel examination table. "I guess it does smell pretty bad in here, doesn't it? I suppose you get used to it pretty fast if you want to be a marine biologist. Come on in."

Walking past metal shelves covered in assorted jars of pickled, giant-eyed fish, marine worms, and other oddities, Sturman took off his cowboy hat and joined Val beside the examination table. She had her dark brown hair pulled back in a neat ponytail and was bent over the table looking through protective plastic lab glasses at a large squid carcass. Based on the size and injuries, Sturman could tell this was the squid that had died on his boat.

They were inside the marine laboratory at the Weston Research Institute, where Val had been granted access to examine the squid. She knew a top researcher, a Swede, at the institute, and had agreed to let him and one of his grad students retain the carcass when she was finished. He also studied Humboldt and other squid species, but focused more on identifying and tracking shoals using a novel technique of sonar imaging.

Sturman pointed at her glasses. "You worried it's gonna squirt on you?" Running his hand over the stubble on his head, he turned to look around the room. "What are all these things?"

"The specimens? You name it. This lab has organisms from every animal phylum, collected on various projects around the world. It's pretty cool, but I think the lab keeps them here more for ambience than anything else."

"Yeah. It's really got a homey feel to it. You catch any of these critters?"

"No. I've never worked for Weston. I hope you don't mind that I started working on this girl without you. You want to record for me as I start cutting?"

Sturman returned to the table. "Sure. This clipboard here?"

Over the unpleasant smells in the lab, he could now smell Val's perfume as he stood next to her—an arousing blend of florals and tropical spices. He felt a charge of electricity run through his chest as her hip brushed against his own, but she seemed unaware as she leaned down to peer at the dead squid. He tried to focus on the examination table, realizing he was looking down her shirt at a gold necklace resting in the dark line formed by her cleavage. Sturman cleared his throat and forced himself to look instead at the data sheet on the clipboard.

Val had already filled out a few sections: her name, the capture date and location, and a few other details. He read one filled-out section aloud. "Female . . . length, one-point-seven-four meters . . . weight, thirty-nine-point-eight kilograms . . ."

"She's a big girl, all right. And heavy."

"How did you manage to weigh her, and get her up on the table here?"

"That student I mentioned who gets to examine her later helped me. You should've seen his face when one of her tentacles snagged his belt loop. He thought she was grabbing on to him."

Sturman looked down at the lifeless mass of flesh on the cold steel table. Val had stretched it out to its full length. It had flattened out even more than when on his boat, the seawater now drained out of its cavities, and much of the color had left its skin. The animal was now a mottled mix of pale pinks and oranges, resembling a giant, wet balloon that had lost most of its air.

"It's hard to believe that this sorry-looking thing is so powerful underwater."

"I know. But you've got to remember, Humboldt squid don't have a skeleton, like we do. They do have a hardened remnant of a shell inside their body—the gladius—but really they use the water itself as their skeleton, to support their body and provide volume to the body cavity. This is pretty much what we'd look like if someone pulled out our skeletons."

"Huh. Don't know if I'd look like this. So what *are* we looking at here, anyway, Doc?"

"Oh yeah, I probably should give you the guided tour. Let's start at the top." Val walked over to the pointed end of the squid. "The squid travels in this direction, even though its eyes are on the other side. When alive, she would have turned her body around to hunt or defend herself."

Val slid her latex-gloved fingers under the meaty, flattened sides of the squid. "These here are her fins. A squid bends and flaps its fins like wings or rudders, to steer and make smaller movements. This whole thing here"—Val ran her hands slowly down the long, tubular main body—"is the mantle. Ever ordered a calamari steak?"

"Good stuff."

"Well, now you know where it comes from. On Humboldts, the mantle is ideal for cutting into steaks. It's basically just a smooth, muscular tube with a fairly uniform thickness."

"That seems a lot thicker than the steaks I've eaten."

"Well, this is a much bigger girl than the squid that normally go to market. Anyway, if we looked at this tissue under a microscope, you'd see the chromatophores that let it change color for camouflage. And inside the mantle are the organs."

"Yum." Sturman licked his lips. He looked at the gashes and marred flesh around tears on the body. "It looks like her shoal found her tasty as well."

"She's pretty banged up, isn't she? Her sisters were hard on her. Anyway, moving down here, you can't miss her big, beautiful black eyes, but harder to see is the siphon." Val searched the soft, wet carcass using the fingers of both hands, and quickly found a thick extension of the flesh next to eyes as large and dark as those of a cow. "Underwater, this feature looks more conical, like a party hat. The siphon is where she gets her propulsion. She expands her body to draw in water, then squeezes that muscular mantle and forces water out the hole at the end of the funnel—just like a jet engine."

"I don't know about water, but I do know she can fire ink outta that thing."

Val smiled. "Right. When she's in a flight mode, she produces ink that also is emitted from the funnel . . . along with all of her waste."

"Hmm. I better clean my boat again. She has ten arms, right?"

"Actually, she has eight arms, like an octopus, but unlike octopi, squid also have two longer tentacles used to capture prey." Val ran her hands down the longer appendages extending a foot farther down the table than the arms. "These two tentacles, or 'whips,' are really quite amazing."

"They look like leaves." The tubular appendages each ended in a structure shaped like a large tree leaf.

"They do, don't they? A squid can fire them out quite far from its body to latch on to a fish or other prey with the suckers. The arms"—Val picked up the end of one of the arms, which Sturman thought looked like short, thick snakes—"are then used to subdue the prey and draw it into the beak."

He felt the ends of the tentacles. "Wow. They're pretty sharp."

"Each one contains hundreds of small teeth to hold on to slippery prey." Val grunted as she lifted several of the shorter, sucker-lined arms up to reveal a small circle at their juncture. "And here's the beak, or radula."

"That black thing in the middle of the circle?"

"Yeah. It's pretty tough to see, because it's nested in a ring of muscle. When we cut the beak out, I'm guessing it will be about the size of an orange."

"Damn. That big?"

"Bigger than it looks here. She can swivel it in all directions to tear off bite-sized pieces. A squid beak looks an awful lot like a parrot's beak, except shorter."

Val spent the next several minutes measuring the arms, tentacles, and other exterior dimensions on the squid, while Sturman recorded the data. "Well, what do you say we go inside?"

"Inside her? As long as it doesn't smell any worse."

Val smiled. "I think the lab smells worse than this girl. She's still pretty fresh." Val picked up a scalpel and carefully ran it along the length of the mantle, making an incision. She set the scalpel down and spent the next few minutes carefully separating the flesh at the opening, then used both hands to spread the mantle out into a few square yards of thick flesh. Inside the exposed cavity were several distinct organs, but mostly it just looked like a colorless, unidentifiable mess to Sturman.

"Looks like she was about ready to have kids. See her ovaries here?" Val lifted a pale, fleshy gob near the top of the mantle. "They're loaded with eggs, but probably haven't been fertilized yet. This also confirms that she's female."

Val pointed out the gills, three different hearts, digestive organs, and other parts that all looked relatively indistinguishable to Sturman. Then she touched a small, darker organ with her index finger.

"Guess what this is? I'll give you a hint: it's responsible for the mess on your boat."

"Ink gland?"

"Right. We call them 'ink sacs,' but same difference. And this concludes your first tour of a Humboldt squid. I hope you've enjoyed the ride."

"So what are you hoping to learn here?"

"Well, I don't see anything unusual so far, but I'll examine the contents of her digestive tract, take some tissue samples to study under a microscope, and look for parasites. See if I can find anything. You want to stick around?"

"I've gotta work on the boat some before we head out again. Have fun without me."

Val brushed her bangs away from her dark eyes with her forearm, which hadn't been coated in squid juice. "I'll try. Want to get dinner later?"

Sturman thought of Maria. "Uh . . . can't tonight. Gotta meet Montoya."

"Oh. Well, he can come over here if he'd like to see our culprit. Then we can all grab a bite."

"Well, I told him I'd meet him at this place, and—"

"All right, fine. Some other time. I'll just call you when I figure out more here."

Sturman nodded. "See you later, then."

"Fine," she said dismissively, and turned back to the squid.

He picked up his hat and walked out of the room.

CHAPTER 33

Black water.

Even to the most sensitive eyes in the shoal, seeing had become somewhat difficult once the sun had gone down. But hunting only a few hundred feet beneath the surface allowed its members to take advantage of the dim light cast by distant stars and a waxing moon suspended far away in the night sky.

Cruising at this great depth, the shoal was nonetheless much shallower than it had been during the day. Since it had moved farther away from the coast days ago, it had spent most of its time in deeper and cooler water each day.

The shoal had made its way to the more comfortable ocean depths farther from the coast because many of its members were not getting enough sustenance in the warmer near-shore environment. For the past week, the Humboldt squid had drifted north in cool, nutrient-rich waters that flowed freely over an abyssal trench far below. Their initial drive to migrate north had again taken over after food had become limited in the shallower coastal waters.

The only time the shoal had fed well in recent days was when it had encountered another shoal of smaller, less-mature members of its own kind. The other group had been feeding on small fish in deeper water, and had created a frenzy of activity. In the frenzy, the larger shoal had joined the others to feed on the sardines.

And on many less-fortunate members of the younger shoal.

Now ready to feed again, the shoal moved through the darkness, hidden from most predators and invisible to most prey. The individuals in the shoal moved with purpose, but with little thought. Instinct drove them to keep moving until they located what they needed for survival. Now they again needed food.

A faint, familiar pulse from something far away traveled through the shoal. *Splashing.*

The one-eyed female, near the front of the shoal, changed course slightly to begin closing the distance on the source of the activity. The splashes might have been made only by a large seabird, on which one or two members of the shoal might feed. But it could be something else—something bigger.

The sonic pulses from the splashing grew louder and more insistent, but now the large female had become aware that the sound was mixed with a deep drone. This was not the threatening, low pitch emitted by the predatory whales that could easily kill many in the shoal, but it was an unwelcome noise. Loud, less familiar. Even so, the urge to feed, coupled with an innate curiosity, drove her forward.

As she rose steadily and surged vigorously toward the potential prey, she was the first to see the activity in the water with her remaining eye.

A bright flash of color.

The nerves inside her surged to life, sending chemical signals through her body. Her eye widened. Her muscles tensed. Her pulse, produced by three hearts, quickened.

More went on in her body than normal predatory reactions, though. A deep aggression swelled in her, stronger and bolder than it should have been. Her mind focused not on caution, defense, learning.

Only on killing.

When she began to pass underneath the large, white shape on the surface emitting artificial vibrations and less-familiar whitish lights, little thought was given to any risk. Not every member of the shoal was as bold as the massive female, but her scarred sister and several others followed her.

There was no fear in the focused throng of predators. Only hunger. The detachment of squid left the shoal and single-mindedly rushed to the surface, toward the bright collection of large objects flashing above them in the moonlight.

Lindsay held the lead.

The knowledge that she was maintaining a faster pace than the other swimmers, compounded with the energy provided by a recent second wind, boosted her spirits and drove her forward, the other women stroking rhythmically behind her through the dark ocean swells.

Using long, measured strokes, Lindsay continued her steady pace toward the light of the charter boat ahead. The lead boat was keeping a course steady to the northeast. Lindsay couldn't actually see the stern light, since her vision was limited to her left side, where she caught a glimpse of the moonlight reflecting off the surface of the ocean each time she raised her head to take a breath. But she could also usually see one of the two escort kayaks gliding nearby. The paddlers, wearing bright headlamps, *could* see the lead boat up ahead, and helped herd the swimmers into a straight path.

It didn't matter that Lindsay's visibility was minimal; it was too dark to see much anyway, and fog obscured the lights of the distant mainland.

Even though the few light sources around her didn't provide much illumination, Lindsay was grateful for them. What had been the hardest for her to overcome tonight was the feeling of blindness that she dealt with every time her face was under the water, which accounted for most of the time on the swim. She could never get truly comfortable with the sensory deprivation inherent to long night swims. Years of training had at least built up her self-confidence and mental focus enough to make a swim like this manageable.

This wasn't her first night swim, although it was her first all-night, open-water swim, a super-endurance test of twenty-one miles from Catalina Island to San Pedro, near Los Angeles. They had left Catalina Island at 11:54 P.M. with air temps in the mid-sixties and the water pushing seventy degrees. She and three other women had been swimming in the San Pedro Channel for roughly five hours, which meant the finish line was still about ten miles away.

Only the best open-water swimmers in the world attempted the all-night crossing, from a small beach in

Doctor's Cove on Catalina to the mainland. Virtually everyone crazy enough to attempt it did it at night, because of calmer seas, lighter winds, and less boat traffic. Only about a hundred and fifty swimmers had ever successfully completed the challenge.

Lindsay and the other swimmers were some of the world's most elite open-water competitors. To even consider a swim of this nature, every one of them had been swimming in endurance-oriented, long-distance swims for years. All of them had at least one swim of over fifteen miles under her belt, and all had been swimming more than that many miles every week in the months before the race. None wore wet suits tonight, because it would rule out their acceptance into the official record books. Instead, each wore a brightly colored one-piece swimsuit that offered virtually no added buoyancy. Hers was neon green; the others had on shades of neon orange, pink, and yellow. The bright, distinct colors made it easier for escort boats to keep track of the women.

Lindsay knew the two older, more experienced German swimmers behind her had previously swum the English Channel, and were well prepared for this. But not Julie. Lindsay's friend and longtime training partner was also swimming behind her—possibly too far behind her. Lindsay and Julie, both in their late twenties, didn't know the older women well. The four had agreed to join for the swim after meeting over the Internet; on a daunting swim of this distance in nighttime conditions, every added swimmer provided a boost of comfort to the others. The more contestants, however, the more complicated the efforts of the team involved. More swimmers meant a greater likelihood of separation as each set a different pace, just as Julie was now beginning to demonstrate.

A separation of the swimmers was unacceptable for safety reasons. All the women had agreed to try to stay together, and that if one of them lagged too far behind, she would concede the channel swim, allowing the charter boat to head back and pick her up. Even though they were competing with one another to some degree, this was supposed to be more about simple accomplishment. But as competitors, none of the women would give less than full effort tonight.

Lindsay had really started to worry about Julie, who was now trailing somewhere behind the other women. She could slow her pace and see if Julie could catch up, but that would mean allowing the Germans to pass her. And she didn't want to give up a great time simply because her friend couldn't keep up. Julie was her friend, but this wasn't her problem. She was going to finish this. To finish strong. She felt sure of herself, her abilities. She still had plenty of energy. The escorts on the two kayaks, including Lindsay's husband, would have to make the tough decision to pull Julie if she couldn't go on.

Although concerned about her friend, Lindsay was elated by a recurring thought. *My first channel race, and I'm leading more than halfway through it.* She forced the image of winning out of her head. She still had a long way to go. It really didn't matter if she had the "lead" now or at the end, anyway. This wasn't a race in any sense except for a best-effort time. The ever-changing conditions of the channel—not the swimmers' efforts—would truly dictate their final times. Lindsay was hoping for a swim under nine hours, but she realized it might take longer than twelve. She was on pace right now for a nine-and-a-half-hour swim.

Lindsay fought off the thoughts of how nice it would be to walk out of the water in San Pedro and collapse on the sand in the mid-morning sun—not to mention the satisfaction she would eventually experience from a warm bed and a hot plate of pasta. All the swimmers had eaten tonight were liquid energy shakes served in plastic bottles. Each time she treaded water with the other women and waited for the escorts to toss her next liquid meal to her, she felt like a dolphin at a marine theme park.

As Lindsay felt a large, rolling swell begin to lift her gently, she thought she saw something far below her. Some sort of dull glow. She turned her face out of the water to take a breath, then looked down into the black water through swim goggles as she exhaled. Nothing. Maybe she was starting to see things. The thought worried her.

She had to finish the swim. She couldn't remember the last time anything had been so important.

The first time the shoal had encountered this unusual form of prey, its members had been hesitant. These animals were not a familiar food source, and were larger than the creatures they normally targeted.

But this prey had proven to be slow, awkward, harmless—and an excellent source of nourishment. Even though they were larger than most members of the shoal, they presented no threat and were vastly outnumbered.

The huge, one-eyed female accelerated toward the

nearest prey, a long, flailing creature exhibiting an exciting green color. She rushed upward until several feet below the surface and then spun in the water, directing her tentacles toward the front of the animal above.

Then she attacked. Just before her tentacles closed around the bright green animal's body, she saw its eyes widen as it flinched backward in an effort to escape.

"Come on, Julie! You gotta pick up the pace a bit."

Bob Brunner paddled slowly and smoothly alongside his wife's friend, hoping she could somehow find the energy to catch up with the other swimmers. They were probably sixty yards behind the other swimmers now, but he didn't feel it was time to cut Julie off yet. There was minimal risk of separation from the others in these calm conditions, and she had trained so hard for tonight.

Bob certainly wasn't going to judge Julie. How any of these women could swim even this far was a mystery to him. He was an active guy, who kayaked, surfed, and went running, but after an hour or so of activity he'd rather plop down in a lawn chair with a microbrew.

"Julie, I'm headed up front for a few minutes. Okay?" His yelling at her didn't seem to be helping. He might as well paddle forward for a minute and see how his wife was doing. Maybe getting left alone would motivate Julie more.

He steered his sixteen-foot kayak through the calm darkness toward the lead swimmers and realized how tired he had become simply paddling a kayak. He looked at his watch. *4:47*. Dawn would be arriving soon.

As he passed widely around the German swimmers, he began to make out the lighter spot on the surface that was his wife, just ahead. As soon as he could see the white splashes from his wife's strokes in the beam of the headlamp, his eyes widened. The splashes were much too big. Something was wrong.

"Lindsay! Is everything all right?"

Bob heard a loud splash as a crescent of water sprayed high into the air, catching the beam of his headlamp. The jet of water reminded him of a water fountain. But it was too difficult to see his wife in the dark water, which quickly absorbed the light cast by the small LEDs. He grunted as he drove his paddle into the water and sped toward his wife. He glanced down to make sure his radio was still around his neck, in case he had to call the charter boat. As he looked up again to make sure he wouldn't run into Lindsay, fear and confusion poured into his veins.

His wife was gone.

The German swimmers were fast approaching, and even though Bob was dimly aware his kayak was in their path, he floated in place, staring down into the dark water where his wife had been and trying to control his heart.

To his right, there was a loud splash, and he heard his wife scream.

CHAPTER 34

"**M**orning, sunshine."

"Hey, Sturman," Val muttered sleepily into her cell phone. She was sprawled out on her stomach in a mess of bedsheets on the hotel room's firm mattress. "What time is it anyway? Don't you know I sleep in on Saturdays?"

Sturman grunted. "It's about six. I know you haven't gotten much sleep yet, but I just got a disturbing phone call. We need to talk."

Val yawned and rubbed her eyes. She had only been asleep for a few hours. Sturman never called her early in the morning, and had become more understanding as he realized that even on nights when they didn't head out on the ocean, she stayed up very late out of habit. "Let me call you back in a minute."

"All right. But hurry."

After a trip to the bathroom, starting coffee, and putting on some clothes, she sat on the flower-print comforter at the edge of the bed and dialed Sturman's phone from her cell. "Okay. I think I can pay attention now. So what's going on?"

"Joe Montoya called me this morning. The sheriff's office picked up emergency transmissions from a charter boat up near Los Angeles that was helping some swimmers cross over from Catalina Island."

"Swimmers? Crossing the channel? That's over twenty miles, isn't it?"

"Yeah. But pros do it every year. Anyway, these were no beginners." Sturman paused. "They didn't make it, though. One of them is apparently dead."

"That's horrible. Don't tell me he was attacked—"

"She."

Val stopped breathing. She suddenly understood the early phone call.

"We don't need a transmitter, Doc. I'm pretty sure I know where the shoal went."

"Did Montoya respond to the scene? Out in the channel?"

"No. He's San Diego County. But he knows a few of the sheriffs up that way, and called one of them a few minutes before he called me. Witnesses said the swimmer was dragged under, at night. She completely disappeared, never resurfaced. Some guy in a kayak, who was there to provide support for his wife, actually had to watch her die."

"My God."

"Yeah. But the good news is he got a real good look at her attackers. And they weren't sharks."

"You're telling me he saw a Humboldt squid attacking her?"

"He saw what sounds like several Humboldts *kill* her. There's more, Doc. He beat the shit out of one of the bastards with his oar, and must have a pretty decent swing. He killed it."

Val walked over to the window and spread the drapes, looking down over the huge Southern California interstate running past her hotel, just beginning to experience heavy traffic in the gray dawn. It was hard to take all this in, especially before having coffee. She moved to the steaming pot and tore open a packet of powdered cream.

"Did they recover the dead squid?"

"I guess so. The charter boat captain got back to them too late to help the one lady, but he managed to get the other swimmers on board and gaff the body of the dying squid. That's one reason Montoya called me. He wants you to look at this thing right away." He sighed. "Look, Doc, I think it's time we accept what's going on here."

"What's that supposed to mean?"

"I mean these squid are obviously still killing people, and the smartest thing we can do right now is figure out a way to stop them, not study them."

"So you want to kill all of them. Is that it?"

"Damn right I do."

"And how do you plan to do that? Have a lot of fishing buddies we can call? Maybe we can set up a big competition this weekend—"

"Goddammit! I don't give a shit how we do it, but it needs to be done. Before anyone else dies. For Christ's sake, these things are headed to the most crowded coastline in the state."

"We still can't even be sure this is the same shoal that . . . wait a minute. Of course. Sturman, how far away did this happen from San Diego?"

"A long way. Why?"

"Where?"

"The Catalina Channel. Or the San Pedro Channel, whatever it's called—between Catalina Island and the mainland. A hundred miles or so north of here, maybe a hundred and fifty."

"Right."

"Hang on. How fast can these squid travel?"

She knew Sturman had caught on. "Not a hundred and fifty miles in a single day. I'm firing up my computer now to check the transmitter's location, but we just attached it, what, thirty hours ago? There's no way the individual we tagged traveled that far north in one night. On the other hand, the shoal that killed Steve Black and the other divers could easily have traveled that far by now, since they went missing over a week ago."

"We tagged the wrong shoal, didn't we?"

"Maybe. We might have been out chasing the wrong animals. Or maybe there's more than one dangerous shoal. Either way, we're clearly dealing with more than one group here."

While the computer warmed up for a few minutes, Sturman suggested that they head north to rendezvous later with Joe Montoya. "He can provide us access to see the squid carcass."

"That's a good place to start. Okay . . . here it comes."

Val had opened the mapping software on her laptop. After what seemed like forever, she downloaded the most recent reading from the satellite tag and plotted it on a map of Southern California.

"Well?" Sturman sounded impatient.

"Just like I thought. The transmitter is maybe a little farther north than where we tagged that guy, but it's

still near San Diego." Val swore and set down the laptop before walking back over to the window. She had
never been faced with anything like this. Her research
was no longer the primary objective. "This still doesn't
seem possible."

"What? That a shoal of Humboldt squid appears to
have acquired a taste for humans? Look, why don't you
ride with Montoya up to Los Angeles? They're putting
the squid on ice at a police station in Long Beach until
they can figure out what to do with it."

"Okay. That sounds like a good idea. But what about
you? Aren't you coming?"

"I figure I can't do much to help. Besides, what
good is my boat down here if the squid are headed to
Hollywood?"

Val shook her head and smiled. "You don't mind
bringing your boat up to Los Angeles, then? Spending
some time up there? We might need to go even farther
north, if the squid continue up the coast."

"I figured you'd ask eventually, which is why I'm offering. I need to get outta town for a few days, and I
want to find these bastards."

"When will I meet Montoya?"

"I'll have him come by your hotel. Might as well
check out in the next hour, if you can."

"Right. I guess all my equipment's on your boat. So
I guess that's it. Wow. Crazy week, huh?"

"I reckon it was. See you in L.A."

CHAPTER 35

The midday sun shone bright and full on the sparkling ocean as Sturman piloted *Maria* northward. He had been chugging along the California coastline toward the crowded metropolis that was L.A.-Orange County for several hours. He knew he was off the coast of Camp Pendleton now because of the lack of visible infrastructure or vehicles on the distant shoreline. The seas were light, and the air and water were both pleasantly warm. The height of the California summer.

Despite it being a Saturday in early August, boat traffic had remained very light near the coast. The stretch between San Diego and L.A. rarely saw heavy nautical activity, other than cargo freighters or military vessels. Until he hit the cross-traffic headed out of Los Angeles to Catalina Island and distant Pacific ports, he shouldn't see many ships.

Two dolphins appeared off the starboard side and began pacing his boat, matching her fifteen-knot clip. Sturman smiled at the sleek, playful pair. They were clearly enjoying his company as much as he enjoyed theirs. He could tell that one was actually looking at him as it turned on its side for several moments to direct a small eye up out of the water. He'd seen whales do the same thing. It was as if they were looking a man in the face and wondering what he was up to. Bud also had noticed the dolphins and barked when one cleared the water.

"Pretty cool, huh, pal?" Sturman scratched his dog's ears.

It was good to see dolphins. Hell, it was good to see any natural marine life doing well anymore. Every year it seemed there were fewer marine mammals and sport fish off the coast.

One of the inquisitive dolphins, still smiling its perpetual smile, gracefully rolled over a few times in the water and hurtled toward the bow of the boat with a few powerful thrusts of its tail flukes. The other dolphin followed. It seemed the duo was going to try its luck riding the wave of water created by the forward-moving hull, but Sturman figured they wouldn't have much luck with a boat as small as his. He stood in the flying bridge and leaned out over the water to try and catch a glimpse of the animals' activities. The salt air and sunshine and scenery brought a powerful memory flooding back. Maria. Hawaii. Their honeymoon. They had watched three dolphins playing as their dive boat returned from a two-tank trip.

Sturman's smile faded and he withdrew back into the boat. It had been a few days since he'd had a drink. Hell, he had a long way to go. He might as well enjoy himself.

As he rose to locate a bottle of rum, his cell phone

rang. He decided to ignore it and head for the bottle, but as it continued to ring he cursed and turned back toward the phone on the dash.

"Sturman here."

"Hi, it's Val."

"Hey, Doc."

"Are you all right? You sound funny."

"I'm fine. Just a little tired, that's all."

"Anyway, I just got finished looking at the Humboldt carcass. It was amazing. The thing was huge." She talked fast and loud, like a tomboy who had just caught her first frog.

"How huge?"

"Biggest one I've ever seen. Fifty-four kilograms. Over two meters long, and thick. And she wasn't too badly damaged."

"So what's that—over a hundred pounds, anyway?"

"About one-twenty."

He whistled. "That is big. Learn anything?"

"So on the last squid we dissected, I didn't see anything unusual, other than its diet. It had been eating fish not commonly found in the Baja diet, like several rockfish species and what appeared to be the remains of a surprisingly large Pacific hake. But this one . . ."

"What?"

"There was something else I've never seen. When I opened her up, I saw that she had some sort of parasitic flatworms all over the organs. I mean, these guys were affixed to the digestive tract, the liver, the gills, and even seemed to be clustered around some other organs."

"Shit. That's pretty disgusting. Won't those things kill the squid?"

"Maybe they would eventually. Actually, Humboldt squid often have parasitic infections from tapeworms and other marine creatures. Never to this extent, generally. This level of parasitism is usually fatal. And here's the other interesting thing—I've never seen this type of marine worm before."

"I thought your specialty was squid, and all them other mollusks. You an expert on worms, too?"

"No. But I've taken a lot of courses on marine life, and I've come across most of the known Humboldt squid parasites when dissecting them. This trematode was something I've never seen. It's probably a known species of worm, but I don't think it's ever been observed in *Dosidicus*."

"And that's really exciting for some reason, then?"

"Well, besides a whole paper on the novel parasitic relationship, if it is a new one, this parasitism might have several implications regarding the recent attacks."

"You've got my attention."

"Well, in many cases, parasites don't just feed off hosts. They also *alter* them."

"What do you mean, 'alter'?"

Val thought for a moment. "Take rabies, for example. You may not think of the rabies virus as a parasite, but its interaction with a mammal host is classic parasitism. And as you probably know, when an animal gets rabies, its behavior is significantly altered. Rabid animals become highly aggressive and more likely to bite. Since the virus spreads from the saliva of infected animals into the blood of healthy animals, the aggressive behavior is essentially the rabies' way of ensuring its own survival. It causes the aggression *intentionally* to facilitate its own reproduction."

"You're saying the rabies virus consciously knows to do that? Come on."

"Not exactly. It's safer to say rabies evolved with its mammal hosts in such a way that those viruses that caused aggression were more likely to spread than other rabies viruses. This allowed the viruses that caused the altered behavior to more effectively reproduce and pass on their genetic material."

"I'll be damned. You think that's happening here?"

"I don't know. I took samples of the worms and the infested tissues, but it will take a lot more research. What I *can* tell you is that I've read several scientific papers on snails, which are also mollusks, that have grown significantly larger and shown altered behavior when infested by parasitic flukes. I can further tell you I've never seen a Humboldt squid this big, and I've seen a lot of Humboldt squid. The heightened aggression this shoal appears to be exhibiting could potentially be the result of parasitic effects to each affected squid's nervous system."

"Rabid squid. Now I've heard it all." He stroked Bud's head, trying to imagine him with rabies.

"The crazy thing is that it may not even be the flatworms themselves that are causing the changes. Parasites can introduce other, smaller parasites, like when a mosquito delivers malaria to a human host. These smaller parasites can easily invade tissues and organs, or the larger parasites themselves may have direct effects on those organs. I could go on and on about this weird stuff. Anyway, you see what I'm saying? An unfamiliar parasite in these squid could have all sorts of implications."

"So how come you've never seen these worms in a Humboldt squid before?"

"I don't know. My guess is that this marine flatworm species resides in cooler North Pacific waters, and normally infests fish or animals other than Humboldt squid. Remember, this species of squid does not typically inhabit waters this far north or this shallow—at least not in recent times. The squid have probably encountered this parasite or something similar in the past, but may have gradually separated over evolutionary time as the squid headed south and the parasite preferred habitat farther north. Now the squid may be encountering it again as they migrate north and rise into shallower waters through the upwelling effect off the California coast. But like I said, I really don't know."

He heard Val sigh, and watched a small flock of brown pelicans float past him as they too headed north. The huge birds reminded him of a tight formation of naval fighter planes. He said, "Nature does some pretty amazing things."

"I'm totally speculating here, Sturman. There's just so little known about *Dosidicus gigas*. I'm one of a handful of scientists in the world who really know much about them."

"I'm not letting you back on my boat if you start foaming at the mouth."

She laughed. "Isn't this fascinating stuff? Sometimes I just love my job. Are you having fun yet, cowboy?"

"Yeah, I guess I am. You're sure as hell not boring."

"Enough on my end. We can talk more when you get here. How's your trip going?"

"Probably halfway there now. I'll be in Long Beach before dinner."

"Well, be safe, and we'll see you when you get here."

"Montoya still with you?"

"Yeah. He stepped out to grab us some lunch. See you soon."

"Wait a sec, Doc. Just wondering something. If you're right about these squid, and about some parasites making them bigger and meaner—you're not planning to dive again with them, right? Last time you went down with normal, healthy squid, and even that was a little too exciting for this old boy."

"I probably won't get in the water again. Don't worry. I'm not stupid. We'll be cautious. Okay?"

"I know you're familiar with these squid and all, and you've dived with them a lot. I'm not saying you don't know what you're doing. . . . Look, I just want you to remember that if what you're saying is true, these squid are more dangerous than you're used to."

"I appreciate your concern, Sturman. I mean it. Don't worry." She paused. "And I'm afraid to say you're right."

"Right about what?"

"We are dealing with some very dangerous animals."

CHAPTER 36

The three diners had just finished an expensive seafood meal on the outdoor patio of the restaurant—crunchy breaded crab cakes drizzled in a citrus-cream sauce, followed by freshly caught halibut grilled over hardwood charcoal. As they finished the late dinner, the summer light had slowly faded and now only a sliver of yellow afterglow lit the horizon over Alamitos Bay.

Joe had been carefully observing his two companions at the table throughout the meal without really meaning to. It was a habit among cops. Despite some obvious tension, he could tell the biologist was growing on Sturman.

The restaurant they'd found in the Long Beach marina had impressed him. The city had changed a lot over the years, with some parts retaining Southern California charm while others had become more dangerous with gang activity and crime. This was one of the better parts of town, though, and sitting on the bistro's terrace overlooking the marina, it was easy to forget they were very near South Central Los Angeles.

Now they were sipping rich gourmet coffee and enjoying a moment of pause in the still summer evening. Earlier they'd finished a second bottle of wine, and were all in relatively high spirits. None of them could really afford the meal and the wine, but they'd all said what the hell.

"So, Sturman, I hear that you got into a fair amount of trouble in the Navy." Val smiled at him playfully.

Sturman frowned at Joe. "Montoya's telling stories about me again, huh?"

"Nothing but the truth, pal."

"I was younger then. Made some poor choices."

"Hell, you haven't changed. Won't take orders from anybody."

"Let's get back to business. Montoya, when you hit the head earlier, Doc here told me she had some theory she wanted to share about the night those immigrants died, and how it may have set the stage for the other attacks."

Val nodded. "Yes, I do. But first, how come I haven't read anything about that event yet? Why wasn't it in the news, Joe?"

Joe's eyes narrowed. "Why do you think? Because nobody cares about a bunch of wetbacks, except for their families back home. And their families had no intention of getting in touch with American law enforcement. They weren't expecting to hear from those guys for a while anyway."

"That's horrible. But why haven't *you* notified the press?"

"The incident is still under investigation."

Sturman spoke up. "Doc, you were telling me that

those men were probably the first these squid ever killed."

"They probably weren't the first actual group of people ever killed by Humboldt squid, despite what the official record books say. But for now we have to assume the immigrants were the first group attacked by *this* shoal. And it makes perfect sense. They were out over very deep water, at night, away from motorized traffic, and according to the authorities they were carrying waterproof flashlights. They might as well have been a group of Baja squid fishermen trying to *attract* the squid to them at the surface."

"So they lured the squid to themselves?"

"Absolutely. These squid didn't just happen upon any of these victims. They had to be in the same general area to detect them. But think about it. The immigrants, the father and daughter fishing, the scuba divers—they all had some sort of glowing lures or artificial lights that attracted the squid to them. Even the woman swimming over from Catalina Island had on a bright, flashy suit, and her crew was using artificial lights."

"Huh." Sturman leaned back in his chair. "You think they got a taste for people when they attacked those first folks—the immigrants?"

"My opinion? Yeah, I think so. These squid are much smarter than people give them credit for. I wouldn't be surprised at all if some of what we're seeing is simply learned behavior."

Joe nodded. "The same way tigers or bears will continue to attack and eat people after they've done it once, and realize how easy we are to kill?"

"Exactly."

Joe thought for a moment as he sipped his coffee. "Tomorrow morning, I'll contact L.A. and Orange County law enforcement, see if I can't get them to issue a press release about the shoal and maybe make some recommendations for people to avoid diving at night. But I gotta be honest, Val. Even though a lot of people have already died here, it doesn't seem like that many people are even remotely at risk. How many people scuba dive at night, anyway, or try to swim to Catalina Island in the dark?"

"I still think it would be irresponsible of us to not get the word out."

"Point taken."

"If nothing else, we can try to prevent people from taking unnecessary risks until we figure out more. But I do have one other concern besides swimmers with bright lights."

Joe set his mug down and studied her. Like his sister once had, the woman always seemed to be thinking. "What's that?"

"Well, anyone that knows much about squid, including the biologists who study them, assumes that they only use their large eyes to visually seek out prey. But think about it—what would be a more effective way to seek out prey in water that's totally dark?"

"Sound?"

"Right. Sonar. Just like a submarine, or a whale or dolphin. I've been trying to include sounds as well as lights when I dive with Humboldts in Baja, and I've recently discovered that they appear to react to some sounds—particularly very long-wave, deep sounds that travel a long way underwater."

"So you're saying squid can hear?"

"I'm not sure if I'd call it hearing, but yes, they can process sound with organs in their bodies. My concern is that in addition to visual cues like lights, this shoal could now be associating certain sounds with food."

"You mean people splashing around on the surface?"

She nodded. "Perhaps. And maybe even the sound of boat motors."

Sturman took his hat off and rubbed the rough stubble on his head. "Christ. What are you saying, Doc? Boaters are ringing dinner bells when they start their motors?"

"I think the best thing we can do for now is simply try to keep track of this shoal and where it's headed. That way we can try to update law enforcement. And we need to keep the public informed."

Sturman leaned forward. "In the meantime, we shouldn't just be tracking them. We need to talk about how we can eliminate the threat."

"You're still hung up on that?" Val shook her head. "It's a ridiculous idea, and it won't work."

"Well, it's better than doing nothing."

"We aren't doing nothing. We'll try to keep tabs on the shoal's location, so we can alert local authorities of a possible threat."

Sturman snorted. "Okay, so we follow your eco-friendly advice and just try to find them. We still heading out at night, then?"

"I don't think there's any need for that at the moment. And it's probably safer going out in the daytime. Joe, we may end up staying out for a week or more, possibly migrating along the coast with the shoal. Assuming Sturman is okay with that."

"Fine by me."

"As we go, we can relay our information back to Joe. And we need to keep in mind that other shoals in the area could also be afflicted with these parasites."

Joe leaned forward and rested his elbows on the table, his face lit by the flicker of the candlelight. "So now you think there's more than one dangerous group of these squid? How many individuals are in each shoal?"

"Each shoal is usually made up of hundreds, or even thousands, of individuals. But I have no idea if there's more than one *dangerous* shoal. Just that there are multiple shoals in the area."

"Shit. Sounds like the start of some biblical plague."

"Don't be so dramatic, Joe. They're just doing what nature built them to do. And also perhaps what this parasite is making them do. I have to admit, I've never seen this body size or level of aggression in a shoal of Humboldt squid."

Joe felt his face get hot. "I don't know, Val. You may see these animals as some natural part of the environment, but I just see them as a threat. And whatever's going on here, it doesn't seem natural to me." Joe touched the cross around his neck. "I've seen some pretty horrible things in my life, being a cop, but when I try to picture what these people were thinking in their last moments . . . If these squid aren't evil, then I don't know what is."

Sturman tipped his hat. "Amen, brother."

"Well, guys, ask yourself this: why are these squid even here, off California? They weren't here even a decade ago."

"I don't know," Joe said. "You said it's because of

lack of competition from larger fish, a changing environment, that sort of thing."

"And who's responsible for that?"

Joe snorted. "You think this is *our* fault, Val? That's a stretch."

"Is it?"

The table went silent. Joe calmed himself by listening to the heavy traffic driving by on the street behind the restaurant as he watched a busboy clean empty bottles and dirty dishes off a vacant table.

Sturman said, "Well, kids, we can agree on one thing. How this happened isn't the most important thing right now, is it?"

"I guess it isn't," Val said.

Joe grunted. "No. But we'll need to employ an old cop tactic to figure out what the hell is going on."

Val looked at him warily. "Which is . . . ?"

"Time to bring them in for questioning."

PART III
RETRIBUTION

CHAPTER 37

Although the threat was obscured by darkness, they knew it was there.

Through the dense seawater, even their sensitive eyes could detect almost nothing but absolute blackness. It was too deep. All the sunlight had been fully absorbed in the layers of water above them. But they could sense the silent, hulking figure nearby, perhaps through smell, perhaps through the vibrations that emanated off its surface through the water. The size and shape they perceived indicated a known threat, based on instincts bred deep into their being. But there was something wrong with this creature.

Hovering in the deep a short distance from the enormous animal, the shoal's fear was gradually replaced by curiosity. A detachment of large squid maneuvered away from the others to approach the leviathan, which rested, unmoving, on the fine, smooth sediments of the level ocean floor. While the great creature's rows of conical teeth may once have been a threat, they were no longer. The many tons of flesh cloaking the jaws and impressive body had begun to decay, and white ribs rose gleaming from the beast's sides, serving as visible beacons in the black water as the squid neared.

As the one-eyed female drew closer, she detected movement on the whale carcass. A group of squirming, wormlike beasts twisted and bored their limbless bodies into the flesh as they fed. Some of the more zealous eagerly wriggled themselves through the rotting flesh and vanished into the body of the dead whale. Though they were small enough to be prey, she kept her distance from the unfamiliar creatures. Her natural fear of the great whale, regardless of its death, was enough to prevent her from approaching any closer.

The shoal had thrived in recent weeks. Drifting along a steady current in the broad undersea channel, they had risen each night to take advantage of the abundance of sea life gathered there to utilize the free flow of nutrients. Despite these successful hunting efforts, however, the shoal was beginning to behave erratically.

Although she was not capable of assessing her own actions, the one-eyed female felt a dim confusion. At the moment, hovering above the bottom of the ocean near the whale fall, she and the other squid began a slow progression back toward shallower waters. Though the shoal thrived in deep water, they had no reason to be this far down, this close to the ocean floor, and would not find food here.

She eyed her scarred sister, who moved alongside her, and her tentacles twitched impulsively outward. She retracted them. Her sister was nearly as large as herself, and posed too much of a threat.

The members of the shoal normally sought out smaller, weaker individuals of their own kind when food was scarce, but recently they had attacked one another seemingly without reason. Many of the smallest members of the enormous group had already been eaten or mortally wounded in the past few weeks. Cannibalism was becoming impossible.

The shoal was beginning to lose its natural rhythms and drives, replaced by an ever-increasing state of unfocused aggression that pervaded its collective being.

And beneath its members' streamlined exteriors, clusters of tiny worms, much smaller than those on the whale carcass, coiled and looped their segments around swollen organs, disrupting the normal functions of each squid as they too fed.

CHAPTER 38

Sturman and Val had been at sea almost continually for four straight days. Although they could wash off sweat and grime with a dip in the ocean or quick shower, their skin constantly had a skiff of fine, itchy salt on the surface, which nagged quietly at them. The freshwater on the boat was not for bathing, since the tanks were not large enough to allow for very long trips and the shower was crammed with gear anyway. They had brought some extra water, but extra fuel containers also took up a share of the boat's space and weight limits.

Val was amused by Bud's toilet habits. Sturman had long ago taught the dog to relieve himself in a makeshift wooden litter box stowed inside the cabin. He would sometimes set the box in the stern to let the dog do his deed, then he would fling the goods overboard. One day, Val asked him if he had ever been caught in rough seas and bad weather, unable to even move the box and its contents to the stern. He had grunted and nodded in the shade of his hat.

Despite their days of effort, they had not located the

shoal. With their one tagged squid in a different shoal still located somewhere far to the south, nearer to San Diego, the only way to find the shoal of interest was once again to utilize a needle-in-a-haystack approach. Starting just south of where the swimmer had been killed by the shoal, Sturman and Val had motored northward in the San Pedro Channel for countless hours each day, using a sweeping, zigzag search pattern. They utilized broad-beam sonar with an alert set to go off if a large school or object was detected between five hundred and fifteen hundred feet, where Val suspected the shoal would spend the daytime.

Each evening they followed the same routine. They shut the sonar down just before dark and sped to the nearest mooring, at Gull Harbor on Catalina Island, to tie off for the night. They slept separately, he on the cushioned bench in the galley, she in the private berth in the bow, and then departed immediately at dawn to resume where they had left off the day before.

Val was becoming frustrated. Although she had expected this to be difficult, she hadn't realized just what a tall order it was to try and locate a specific shoal in an area almost totally devoid of Humboldt squid. In Baja, it had always been easy to locate the animals. There, she was interested in any shoal they could attract, and there were so many millions of squid that locating an unspecific group on any given night was almost a guarantee. She now realized that quickly locating the first shoal with Sturman must have been beginner's luck.

Despite the lack of hygiene and her frustration at the tedious task, Val found she was enjoying herself. While *Maria* plied the blue water, all they had to do was stay on course and snack on sweet or salty junk food. Though

Sturman was frustratingly uncommunicative, she found herself increasingly curious about him. She pried into his past with little luck. He could clam up with the best of them. And just when she was beginning to feel affection for him, he would revert to the jerk she had first met.

She had just ended a cell phone call in the quieter cabin of the boat as she made her way up the steps to the stiff breeze and sunshine on the stern deck. The door swung against her shoulder, and she slammed it irritably behind her. "Goddammit!"

"What'd Montoya say?" Sturman stood in the flying bridge, wearing his sweat-stained cowboy hat and an unbuttoned short-sleeved shirt that flapped in the wind. Val climbed the wooden ladder and fell into the padded bench seat next to him. She scratched Bud's stubby ears. The short-haired mutt was resting in his usual spot, under Sturman's feet. She was impressed at how far the man went to accommodate his dog, not only having thought up the litter box but also seeming always happy to lift the big dog up to join them in the flying bridge when they were motoring for long hours.

"The idiots want to try and catch the shoal."

"You don't say." Sturman smiled and pulled off his hat to run a calloused hand over his head. "The whole shoal?"

"The whole shoal." She and Sturman both laughed. "I guess the conference call went on for hours. Quite a few people joined in—probably because of the novelty of this situation. Some of the big-time law enforcement officials and a few local politicians wanted to take a more reactive approach than just releasing some warning information, because of the high number of deaths.

They're now putting the suspected death toll at between eleven and thirty, depending on how many immigrants died a month ago."

"That many?"

"Yeah. It sounds like a lot, doesn't it?"

Sturman nodded.

"Anyway, Joe said he tried to convey my opinion
that it was a waste of time to try and catch the shoal,
and that as long as people didn't put themselves in
unique situations that might lead to an encounter, there
was no cause for alarm. But I'm not so sure he tried
that hard."

"What do you mean?"

"I know Joe is your friend, but after our talk the
other night I suspect he didn't feel compelled to plead
my case."

Sturman set his jaw and turned away. She had
learned that the man had a temper, and a strong loyalty
to the few people in his life whom he was close to. His
eyes narrowed and he began to open his mouth, but she
cut him off.

"I don't mean that. Sorry. I'm sure Joe did his best.
But with this story all over the news now, these big
shots obviously feel they need to put on some sort of
show for the taxpayers."

There were a few minutes of silence. Val thought
about what would happen next as she scanned the
sparkling water and listened to the drone of the twin
engines.

Sturman turned and looked at her, his eyes crin-
kling. "So how the hell they gonna capture these things
if we can't even find them?"

She smiled. "Good question. I don't plan to help

them, so I have no idea. Joe said something about hiring commercial fishermen, and trying to net them like they're just a bunch of tiny market squid. It will never work."

"Then why you getting your panties in a bunch?"

She smiled again. He was right. The shoal would probably move on, and might even die before anyone could find them. Its members seemed to be fully mature and now sick with parasites, and fast-growing Humboldt squid only had a lifespan of a few years.

"I don't know. I guess I was hoping that somehow I'd get more of a chance to study them."

"They're like squid in the sea."

"What?"

"You know, the expression—like fish in the sea? There will be other shoals. You said it yourself—there are more than enough in Baja."

"Yeah, but not like this one. This is an incredibly unique situation, and could allow me to help predict if this might happen again, and how it happens. And—"

"Doc, there you go analyzing everything again. I hear what you're saying. If you want, we can keep trying to find these things on our own. But it doesn't look like we'll get cooperation from anyone else."

Val sighed and shook her head. She tugged at her ponytail and looked off toward the mainland. "I just thought these meetings would actually generate some help for us. Make my job easier, not harder."

Sturman grinned at her and shook his head. "I've got another favorite expression for you."

"Better than 'fish in the sea'?"

"Yeah, smart aleck. One of my favorites. 'You can't change the wind. But you can adjust your sails.' "

CHAPTER 39

That night, Val decided to take Sturman's advice to adjust her sails. It was a calm, beautiful evening as they headed south toward Catalina Island. A perfect time to open three sheets to the wind.

Sturman didn't need much prodding to join her. When she commented that she just wished they could have a beer, he muttered that he kept some medicinal booze on the boat. Seeing her face light up, he went below and came back with a mostly full plastic bottle of light rum, along with two clear plastic glasses.

"I've even got limes." He smiled and sat down across from her in the flying bridge.

Val smiled back. It occurred to her that he hadn't taken a drink in the five days they'd been out. "Christ, Sturman. You have anything to mix it with? Or a chaser, at least?"

"I thought you were a sailor, Doc. Drink like one."

As Sturman poured the drinks, Val moved to the console and turned on the radio. "So you've gotta tell me something, cowboy. How does a guy like you end up in Southern California on a boat?"

"Oh. You mean this?" Sturman touched the brim of his hat. "I'm originally from Colorado. Grew up on a ranch. Worked it with my dad and brother, hunting, fishing, riding."

"And . . . ?" She said it lightly.

"I liked it well enough. But ever since I was a kid, I dreamed about the ocean. Read the books, watched the shows, you know? *Moby-Dick, Twenty Thousand Leagues Under the Sea,* Jacques Cousteau . . . even *Flipper* reruns."

She smiled. "Who doesn't love *Flipper*?"

"There was something more exciting about the distant ocean than the mountains around the ranch. First time I actually saw it was when I joined the Navy. Here, look at this." Sturman set his cup down and pulled up his sleeve to expose the hammerhead shark tattoo on his left shoulder. "Got it as an ensign. Was on the damage control team, *USS Eisenhower*."

"Nice. My turn, cowboy."

Val stood and turned away from him, lifting the back of her shirt to expose the small of her back, and over one hip the top half of her own tattoo—a small blue octopus. "Spring break, Cancún. My sophomore year in college."

"I can't see it so well. Maybe if you pulled your shorts down a bit lower . . ."

She pulled her shirt back down and smiled. "Sorry, cowboy."

Sturman continued adding rum to their cups as the sun melted into the sea. They talked mostly about her career path, but she managed to coax out a few of the Navy stories Joe had mentioned. He shut the boat down a few miles off Gull Harbor to let them drift lightly on the ocean and enjoy the calm evening.

She curled up on a padded bench in the flying bridge and pulled the rubber band out of her ponytail, shaking her hair loose. Sturman sat across from her, his legs outstretched and feet crossed on the seat next to her. He leaned back and closed his eyes.

"You never told me about your ring."

"Beg your pardon?" He opened one eye and frowned.

"Your ring." She pointed at the weathered gold band on his left hand. "You said you were married before?"

He sat up, moving his feet down to the floor. "Yeah. Once. A long time ago."

"So why do you still wear the ring?"

"I don't know." Sturman gulped the remaining rum in his cup and reached for the bottle.

"I'm sorry. I know you said you don't like to talk about it. We can talk about something else."

Sturman sighed. "No. It's all right. I haven't talked about it in years." He looked at the last color of the setting sun. "She died four years ago."

"I'm sorry."

"So am I."

"Tell me about her."

Sturman sipped at the rum and was silent for a while. "Maria. I named the boat after her. She was Joe's sister."

"Joe Montoya?" Val leaned toward him.

Sturman nodded. "We met through him, after he and I finished our time in the Navy." He smiled. "Montoya came after me when he found out we'd been dating behind his back."

Sturman remained quiet for a minute. The last color left the western sky. "She died before I really knew how much I should have appreciated her." He emptied his cup and poured some more.

"What happened?"

"Car accident. One day she drove to work. That was it. She never came home." He was silent again. "It was Joe who called me. A tractor-trailer hit her Toyota." He swallowed hard.

"It must have been very hard for you, Will." She placed a hand on his knee. "How long were you married?"

"Six years. They were good years. We hadn't quite gotten around to having kids. It wasn't perfect, and we fought sometimes. But I realize how good it really was when I look back." He forced a smile. "Don't think I didn't notice you call me by my first name."

Val set her cup down and moved slowly toward him. She gently slid a leg up onto the seat next to him, then the other, straddling him. His eyes never left hers. In them she saw longing, and pain.

She lifted his cowboy hat off and, cupping his jaw in her hands, she bent down and kissed him. As she pressed his warm lips against her own, he suddenly reached out and pulled her waist deep into his chest. Easing down onto his lap, she felt him growing hard against her. He kissed her back with a furious intensity.

Without warning, he pushed her forcefully off his lap and stood up, staggering.

She was breathing heavily, and her skin felt flushed. "I'm sorry, Will. I didn't mean to . . ."

"I can't do this." His knuckles turned white as he gripped the rails.

"I understand. But at some point you've got to let her go." As soon as she said it, she wished she hadn't.

Sturman turned away, toward the fading light rippling on the ocean. "I'm going swimming."

He shed his shirt, stepped to the edge of the bridge, and dived off. He didn't come up for a long time.

CHAPTER 40

"**W**e can still keep trying."

Val stood on the dock, looking down at Sturman. He remained in the stern of his boat. His arms were crossed, his face unreadable. It was just after dawn on a summer Saturday. The marina harbor was beginning to bustle with activity.

"To find the shoal, I mean. Not to—"

"I know what you mean."

"Just because the government has its own plans doesn't mean we can't keep doing our own thing. Come on, Will. You don't strike me as a man who cares what the hell other people want him to do, anyway." She smiled at him. He didn't smile back.

She still sensed the same anger in him, but something had changed in him—his eyes were distant. He wasn't looking at her, but *through* her. He turned away from her to scratch his dog's ears. She knew he was struggling with what to say.

"I think we should just let Montoya and the others handle this," he finally said. "It's their responsibility."

She hadn't wanted to leave the boat, but Sturman

had made up his mind at first light and headed straight across the channel for the coast. He had dumped her and her gear at the crowded dock in Newport Beach, the closest major harbor on the mainland. The halogen lights, now off in the morning sun, remained attached to his boat, because both realized they were too bulky to simply leave on the dock with her.

"Are you sure? You won't reconsider? I mean, what are you planning to do now?"

"I figured I'd take a few days off. Head back over to Catalina, maybe visit a few other Channel Islands while I'm in the neighborhood."

"And after that?"

Sturman looked up at her. He spoke in a low voice. "Why you askin' so many questions? What does it matter to you?"

"Don't act that way. Look, I know last night was uncomfortable, but we can—"

"I know what you're doing. You're wasting your time."

"Don't give me that bullshit look, Sturman. You're not going to stare me down like I'm some goddamn ensign in the Navy. I thought we were doing all right. I'm sorry for what I said." She paused, then shook her head. "You know what? I'm not sorry. You need to get over it, and get on with your life. Stop wallowing in grief and drowning your sorrows in alcohol. If you did, you might find that there are people who care about you, you big slob."

A man with a fishing pole walked up and stopped next to Val.

"Can I help you?" She glared at the man.

"I just need to get past you, if that's okay . . . ?"

"Nobody's stopping you." She made no effort to step aside as the man squeezed around her on the dock. She continued facing Sturman, hands on her hips, waiting for a response. There was none.

"So that's it. Okay. Well, good luck, Sturman. Maybe someday I'll see you again."

He said, "I'll ship the lights to you in Monterey when I have the chance."

"I hope one day you're happy again."

Sturman nodded almost imperceptibly. "Good luck. With . . . everything."

She watched him start the engine, unfasten the nylon ropes from the dock cleats, and slowly make his way out of the harbor. Even though he had made sure a taxi van was coming to pick up her and her gear, she felt utterly abandoned. The powerful emotion puzzled her.

She watched as he headed around a bend into the main channel of the harbor. Bud ran to the back of the boat and looked back at her, whining and barking. Underneath the dun-colored dog, the name of the boat burned itself into Val's memory.

Maria.

Sturman never looked back, and then he was gone.

CHAPTER 41

When Bobby Flynt walked out of the yacht's stateroom, zipping up his fly, that's when the drugs really began to kick in.

He wasn't sure if it had been a good idea to mix blow and Ecstasy, but at the moment he didn't care. The electronic dance music blasting down from above-deck pulsed through him. He could actually *feel* the music. He smiled at the thought, utterly euphoric. He loved his life.

The twenty-two-year-old had become an overnight success in Hollywood after starring in a summer blockbuster two years ago. He had played the lead, a vampire who led a group of youthful, impossibly attractive vampires against an army of demons sent from hell to claim what remained of their souls. Teenage girls around the world loved it, and worshipped Bobby and his classic good looks and dark hair. Before that, he'd just been a nobody from Ohio who'd been fighting to land acting roles as he shared a one-bedroom apartment in Los Angeles and worked regular hours cohosting a children's television show.

But that was two years ago. He slid his fingers along the polished cherrywood paneling in the yacht's main dining room as he strolled toward the stern, indulging in its rich feel. This boat was *his*. So was a sick pad back in Palos Verdes. *And the girls*. He didn't technically own them, but he sure got to use them. Man, he'd only just met the blond girl he'd banged in his stateroom. She was from Germany or something. He'd been too messed up to care, but she had a sexy accent and big tits.

Flynt opened the door to the rear of the cabin and stepped up into a wave of stimuli that overwhelmed his Ecstasy-fueled senses. The pulsing bass pounded through his body, mixed with the smell of salt, the feel of cool night air on his skin, the laughter of the partiers. And a light show was erupting from glowing jewelry hanging off thirty or forty groupies, all rich SoCal kids and wannabe actors.

An hour ago, the cheap glowing necklaces and bracelets had simply been a fun gimmick to add to the yacht party, but now they were almost magical as he watched them move rhythmically back and forth on the dancers' swinging wrists and swaying bodies, leaving behind glowing trails of green, orange, and purple that were temporarily burned into his retina. The stern was packed with people.

Flynt's seventy-five-foot toy, named after his first big film, was drifting off the calm southern coast of Catalina Island. His captain knew better than to moor the yacht in Avalon Harbor—Flynt's parties got very noisy, and he preferred to avoid unwanted attention from both the law and nosy rich people with yachts of their own, who always tried to drop by on their dinghies to join the party.

Flynt could easily make out the big island's silhouette despite only a sliver of a moon in the night sky. They were adrift about a half-mile from shore. The dark bulk of Catalina's mountainous flanks stood out against the brighter sky, which glowed artificially from the lights of shore that were muted by the humid air.

"Fernando, gin and tonic!" Flynt had to shout to be heard over the pounding music, but this was how he liked it.

After his bartender mixed the drink, he took a sip and then slowly moved through the crowd toward the upper deck, delighted by the sensations on his skin as he brushed his arms against the other bodies crowding the boat. He was especially pleased when some of the naughtier girls ran their hands through his thick hair or touched him suggestively as he passed. Already he felt himself becoming aroused again. He'd have to pick another girl soon to christen another part of the boat. So far he'd done it in all but one of the staterooms and most of the common areas.

He made his way up to the top of the yacht, where the captain stood in the darkness in front of a lit helm, sipping a cup of coffee.

"*Hola*, Leonard!"

"Good evening, Mr. Flynt. Enjoying the party?"

"You know it, man. There's just one thing missing."

"What's that, sir?"

"We gotta have the hull lights, Lenny!"

"Of course, sir."

The captain reached to the dimly lit dashboard and

found the proper switch. Immediately, the water around the sides of the boat lit up. Whenever Bobby could see into the clear water under the boat, he felt like he was flying instead of floating.

"*Gracias, capitán*! Now our underwater friends can join us."

He wandered over to the top railing, looking down as the first visitors began to flash silver as they darted through the brightly lit water.

The shoal first felt distant vibrations.

As they hung silently in the blackness a hundred feet down, the deep, low sounds pulsed regularly, quickly, through the squids' bodies in waves. Instinct told them this was not a known threat. Instead, the vibrations were somewhat familiar, similar to other sounds that they now associated with food.

One by one, members of the huge shoal gradually turned to follow the enormous assemblage of mollusks, some of which had immediately turned to seek out the source of the vibrations. Even though the shoal had diminished in size, with many of the smaller individuals having been consumed by their own, several hundred feet separated the lead individuals from those trailing at the end of the underwater armada.

Moving their torpedo-like bodies with perfect efficiency through the dark ocean depths, the squid soon began to sense yellowish lights ahead, shining deep into the water from near the source of the vibrations.

Yet as the shoal neared, the one-eyed female banked around the bright lights, which shone with a painful, unnatural intensity. Circling the underwater lights, she saw many smaller prey fishes darting within the cones of light. A large, inert object floated at the center of the white lights.

Frustrated, she remained with the rest of the shoal as it kept its distance, seeking a way to approach the prey gathered around this source of sound and light.

Captain Leonard Dawkins regarded the young owner of the yacht he skippered. Bobby Flynt sat alone on the top of his toy, legs dangling through the railing. His employer was clearly high, as usual, watching the multitude of small creatures that had gathered in the lights embedded in the hull. Often when Dawkins turned on the lights, the actor would take a break from his party to simply get lost in all the aquatic life that was attracted to the vessel. At these times the captain could see how sad and lonely the kid really was. Dawkins knew Bobby had no idea that his captain was looking at him now, his pale blue eyes transfixed as they were on the water below.

Captain Dawkins had often wondered what it was like to own a grand vessel like this, to have so many people who called themselves your friends simply because you showed them a good time, to have beautiful young women throw themselves at your feet. He saw this all the time. He'd been a professional captain on many Hollywood yachts over the years. It paid pretty well to be a captain for hire in Southern California, and beat having a desk job.

Dawkins shook his head and looked away from the young actor. Bobby wasn't a bad kid—he didn't appear to have a mean bone in his body—but the captain knew how this would turn out. No matter how much money, fame, and sex these guys got, he had seen them all become unhappy. Yes, he wanted a yacht of his own someday—a real boat, not just a little twenty-two-foot fishing boat like he had now—so he could travel the world with his wife. Maybe his two daughters could join them for a leg of the trip, if they had careers then that would allow it. True happiness didn't come from bedding a lot of women who cared nothing for you, or from six- or seven-figure paychecks. If he ever needed proof, all he had to do was look at people like Bobby.

"Mr. Flynt, may I ask what you're doing?" The young man had stood and was leaning over the railing, staring intently into the water below.

"The fish are gone. I need to find them!" he shouted back at the captain over the loud music. The actor was taking off his shoes, one at a time. He grinned at the captain.

Dawkins glanced down into the ocean. Flynt was right—he no longer noticed any fish in the hull lights. But his employer was his foremost concern.

"Sir?"

"It's a beautiful evening, anyway, Captain! I thought I might go for a swim. Maybe I can find the fish."

"Sir, we're over a kilometer from shore, and—"

"Lenny, stop worrying so much. Look how amazingly calm it is. I want to be in the water now!"

Dawkins watched as Bobby downed the rest of his drink, then stripped down to his boxer shorts and stepped over the railing, a leg at a time. He paused, holding on to the railing behind his knees, to shout down into the party below in the stern.

"Anyone want to get in the pool with me?"

A few girls shouted incoherently back over the music; then Dawkins watched Bobby dive with surprising grace off the upper deck into the water below. A single small fish darted off in the clear water as his body broke the surface.

Dawkins didn't like having his passengers swim in open water, especially at night, because of the unknown risks at sea and the very real chance that one of the intoxicated swimmers might drown, or get accidentally left behind if they got too far from the boat. He knew it was senseless to try and stop the other revelers that were now shedding clothes on the bottom deck, though. He needed this job, and as sickening as it was, young Master Flynt was in charge here.

As Dawkins counted the splashes of other people entering the ocean, a statuesque brunette climbed to the top deck and walked past him. She smiled as she pulled her sundress over her head to reveal a beaded necklace dangling between firm breasts against her taut abdomen. Wearing only yellow thong panties, she jumped feetfirst off the top of the yacht with a scream, nearly landing on the swimmers below. After a few minutes, more than a dozen partiers had entered the water to join their host, as the other fifteen or twenty passengers looked on, laughing. Dawkins couldn't be sure exactly how many had gone in now. Despite the chaotic situation, at least Dawkins was able to see the swimmers in the bright hull lights.

The tall brunette swam over to Flynt, and they coupled and kissed, oblivious to the others around them. Dawkins thought sadly that she looked a lot like his oldest daughter, and wondered if she too was chasing movie stars when he wasn't around. She did have her own place, after all, and—

"Lenny!" Bobby was shouting up at him.

"Sir? Are you all right?"

Bobby laughed as the brunette clinging to him kissed his face and neck hungrily. "It's a little too bright down here, Lenny! Think we can get some privacy?"

"Sir?"

"The lights, captain. Turn off the lights!"

"But sir—"

"You don't want everybody gawking at these poor, exposed women, do you?"

Several men on the boat yelled in opposition to Flynt's request as the nude women in the water screamed and giggled. The captain shook his head and reached down to the dashboard switch. He paused, then pressed it down. Around the yacht, the water went dark.

Despite the pulse of the deafening music, Dawkins could still hear the shouts and screams of the partiers. And in the dark water next to the boat, at least he could see the eerie, moving glow of the chemically lit jewelry some of the guests were wearing.

He'd leave the lights off just for a few minutes. He didn't want to upset Flynt, who was as spoiled as any young celebrity with sudden money and fame, but he didn't want to risk anyone getting hurt, either. Yes, it was an unusually calm night. These situations had a way of luring one into a false sense of security, however. The captain knew very well that accidents happened when intoxicated people went swimming. No matter what the petulant brat wanted, he wasn't going to compromise everyone's safety. His hand hovered over the switch for the hull lights, then withdrew.

Just a few minutes. Then he'd turn the lights back on and make everyone get back on board.

With the bright lights gone, the shoal closed toward the prey in the water.

As it had encircled the boat, most of the smaller fish had left the bright lights and gathered into a tight ball several fathoms underneath the floating hulk—still too close to the lights for the shoal to approach—in a defensive formation. Now, with the lights extinguished, the squid hurried in to snatch up the small fish swarming in confusion as they were attacked from every direction. A few of the fish darted for the surface, from where now came an irresistible glow.

The one-eyed female felt deep vibrations emanating from the large object ripple through her soft body, mixed with fainter vibrations from the splashing of the smaller living things around it on the surface. The shoal had consumed the swirling ball of fish under the object in an instant. Now, as the eyes of a thousand of its members quickly adjusted to the darkness, it surged upward toward the larger prey. The ravenous female avoided the nondescript bulk of the larger object to focus on the irresistible glowing lights emitting from the beings moving on the surface around it.

This time the squid did not hesitate to attack. They were no longer unsure of these strange creatures—they posed little threat and provided ample sustenance. The huge, scarred female was the first to seize one of the quarry. She easily dragged it below the surface, joined by several smaller members of the shoal.

The other squid rushed up to meet the warm, blood-rich prey in the dark water, seizing each thrashing individual in many sets of arms and tentacles and dragging them into the deep.

The one-eyed female moved in to clasp one of the creatures, with two of her brothers closing the distance with her. As her companions seized the kicking legs of the creature and began to pull it under the surface, she moved toward its head to find purchase on the body. The animal turned to face her underwater. The large female paused as her black eye met those of her prey. It did not struggle, but reached an appendage slowly toward her, extending what appeared to be a set of smaller tentacles. The massive female hovered motionless next to the submerged prey as it now began to touch her own flesh, gently running its own small appendages along her body. The eyes of the creature widened and its white teeth showed in a small arc.

Aggression overwhelmed her curious impulses. Her body turned a deep purplish color. Joining her brethren, she hurtled into the being before her, enveloping its head in her arms and pulling her body down tightly against it so her beak could find flesh.

The writhing mass of predators and prey drifted ever more gracefully downward in slow ballroom spirals as the prey ceased to struggle. Farther and farther from the surface, their courtship took them deep into the blackness as the shoal fed.

The excited screams of the swimmers gradually died down.

It was a relief. For a few minutes, the drunken group in the water below had really made a ruckus that Captain Dawkins had been able to hear even over the loud music blaring through the yacht's speaker system. In that sort of chaos, people might get hurt. Now the dance music was all he could hear.

He reached for the switch on the dash. He hesitated, knowing all too well that he was probably going to see an embarrassing scene in the water next to the yacht. If it was quiet, the horny young men in the water were almost certainly clinging to the mostly naked women in the water with them, kissing and groping and more.

Dawkins pondered his job security a moment longer, then swore. He couldn't leave the lights off any longer. He had already been irresponsible to allow Flynt to have his way this long. If the young actor was upset, he'd deal with him tomorrow when he was sober. The kid was usually apologetic on the morning after, if he'd gone too far.

Dawkins fully expected to see one of several possible scenes when the lights again pierced the dark water. One involved pairs of lovers clinging to the sides of the boat; another was composed of a full-on orgy in the water next to it. Less likely, but also quite possible, they would just be treading water and talking quietly. Yet as the bright hull lights revealed the ocean along the sides of the yacht, he was totally unprepared for what he saw.

Dawkins jumped to his feet and stared at the clearly lit water around the boat.

They were all gone.

Surely this was some sort of trick. The captain hurried to the railing and followed it down the length of the yacht to the tip of the bow, then back down the far side, scanning the clear blue water from near the vessel to as far out as his eyes could see in the dark night. Nothing.

Except there *was* something—some sort of dark cloud in the water, slowly dissipating as he watched. Blood? A moment later, the dark spot was gone. Maybe he was seeing things.

Dawkins stopped near the staircase leading to the stern and stood motionless for several moments, unsure of what to do. They couldn't all be gone. It wasn't possible. It had only been a few minutes. The lights had only been off for a few minutes. The boat hadn't even drifted. Dawkins squinted past the reach of the lights at the darkened sea surface. Even in this almost moonless night, however, he knew he should be able to see the group on the surface if they were within a few hundred yards. It was some sort of trick. He shook his head, then rushed down the staircase to the stern.

"Fernando, turn off the music! Now, goddammit!"

The handsome Latino bartender looked at him with a puzzled expression, then wiped his hands dry on his vest and turned a knob on the wall behind him. The music died. After a few seconds, the loud chatter around the men died down as well.

"What's up, man? Get the tunes back on!" A stocky young man with spiked blond hair, mixed drink in hand, was looking at Dawkins.

"You, son. What the hell is going on here? Where did they go?"

"Where did who go?" The kid was in a drunken stupor, looking as though he might pass out on his feet. A large tattoo covered one of his pectoral muscles and one shoulder.

"The swimmers, you idiot!" Dawkins grabbed the

man roughly by the shoulders, pulling his face close. "Your friends in the water! This isn't funny. Are they hiding somewhere?" They must have reboarded. They were playing some sort of game, with the captain the sole victim of their joke.

"Who you callin' an idiot, grandpa?"

Dawkins shoved him aside and raced inside the yacht. He stormed through each room, smashing in one locked door to find a couple having sex, but there were only a few others belowdecks. He knew this boat well. There was no hidden location where more than a few people could conceal themselves. He returned to the helm on the upper deck, huffing as he felt the extra pounds he'd put on over the past few years. He reached into the storage cabinets underneath the dash, withdrew a spotlight, and plugged it into the console.

Breathing hard, he swept the beam of light across the surface of the ocean. As his search began to come full-circle back to the starboard side, he felt sick to his stomach. Nobody. Nothing. Bobby and the other kids were no longer there. They weren't anywhere.

They were simply gone.

CHAPTER 42

Valerie Martell accepted the bearded yacht captain's hand as he helped her board his vessel. She jumped lightly from the gunwale of the law enforcement boat down onto the transom. It was a beautiful, sunny morning just off Catalina Island, with gentle seas and a cool westerly breeze.

The middle-aged captain looked weary and discouraged, which didn't surprise Val. Joe had told her the man had lost an estimated sixteen passengers last night when the missing group had gone swimming in the open ocean. Joe jumped down onto the transom after Val, followed by a Los Angeles County deputy sheriff named Bailey and one of his crime technicians, and the police boat pulled away from the yacht to idle on the waves nearby.

Joe had called Val on her cell early in the morning to tell her about the missing kids. She'd spent the previous night at a hotel in Costa Mesa, south of Los Angeles, where she'd stayed up late trying to decide if she should head back to Mexico.

Because so many of the yacht's passengers had gone

missing—and, according to witnesses, in very rapid fashion, apparently in a matter of minutes—Joe had followed a hunch that they might be dealing with another incident related to the shoal. He had called Val and asked her to come along.

"Captain, I'm Valerie Martell."

The captain took his hat off to shake her hand, resting it on the pressed white shirt covering his full belly. "Pleased to make your acquaintance, ma'am. Leonard Dawkins. I'm the captain of *Night Flight*. Are you a police officer?"

"I'm a marine scientist."

He frowned. "Why are you here?"

"She's helping us with an ongoing investigation." Joe stepped up to shake his hand. "I'm Joe Montoya, a sergeant with the San Diego County sheriff. Can we go sit somewhere to talk? We'll want to interview each of the passengers in turn, but we'd like to start by talking to you."

"San Diego County? But I would think that—"

"I know it may seem unusual to have the two of us here with the local authorities. We'll explain in a bit."

"I understand. Fernando, can you please bring our guests some coffee? We'll be in the dining room."

After Deputy Bailey and his technician had introduced themselves to Captain Dawkins, he led them all to a beautifully crafted dining area belowdecks, complete with hand-carved cherrywood trim and paneling. The passengers sleeping or sitting bleary-eyed in the room were escorted out, and the group sat down at the solid cherrywood table. After the police officers took out notebooks and a tape recorder, the L.A. deputy, who sported an old-time pencil-thin mustache and a crew cut, started in on a basic series of questions about the previous night's events, all directed at the captain: "Full name?" "Are you the regular captain of this vessel?" "What were you all doing here last night?" "Who was on board when you left shore?"

After determining the basic scenario of the previous night, the sheriff's deputy asked tougher questions. He asked the captain to explain his relationship with the missing yacht owner, to detail the situation at hand. The captain's story was brief, and rather puzzling, Val had to admit. It didn't seem possible for every one of those kids to go missing as fast as he claimed they had, in calm seas. Off the top of her head, she couldn't really think of any plausible explanation for the disappearance of so many.

"Have you searched for them in the daylight today?" the deputy asked.

"No. I did as your dispatcher instructed, and remained here. We're at approximately the same location as we were last night. You have vessels out searching for them, though, don't you? The water isn't that cold, and if we find them soon enough . . ."

"Of course, captain. The Coast Guard has two boats in the area right now, and officers in Avalon have been dispatched to search the coastline. We'll let you know as soon as we learn anything."

"I know what I've told you may seem impossible, but ask the others—they'll tell you the same. Many of them were drinking heavily . . . or otherwise not in their right minds. These kids today, you know how they are. But Fernando was sober. He's my first mate and handles bartending and other duties. He'll corroborate my story."

"We'll be sure to get his statement, Captain. Now, was this a usual practice? To allow your passengers to swim in the open ocean at night?"

"Of course not." The captain's face turned red. "You have to understand the vessel's owner, Bobby Flynt. He's a young actor. You've probably heard of him? He did that big vampire film that came out last year. Well, he often wants to do things that I disagree with, but as my employer . . ."

"Go on."

Val felt the tension as the lawmen stared at the heavyset captain, waiting for more. She felt a sudden urge to leave. "Excuse me, gentlemen. Is there a head nearby, Captain?"

"Sure. The second door on the right."

"Thank you."

Val walked off, grateful to leave the others to the interrogation. She wasn't sure how she was going to help in this process. The poor old skipper was already having the worst day of his life.

Even for a yacht, the washroom was enormous, with fixtures much nicer than Val had in her bathroom at home in Monterey. After washing her hands, she shut off the decorative chrome faucet and dried her hands. As she opened the door to leave, she thought she heard a muffled sob. She paused in the doorway for a moment, listening to the men talking in the dining room. *There.* She heard it again, behind her. She turned back into the bathroom and slowly pulled aside the striped shower curtain.

Hiding behind the curtain in the large tub was a beautiful, deeply tanned young woman, almost completely naked. She was curled into a fetal position, her head turned to the wall away from Val. Long, damp hair covered her face.

"Miss? Are you okay?"

The woman shuddered and pulled her arms tighter around her folded legs. Val reached down and touched the woman's hair lightly. Without warning, she let out a terrible scream and swung her fist awkwardly at Val's hand. Val jumped backward and stumbled against the toilet.

An instant later, Joe burst through the doorway. Val noticed that his hand rested on the pistol at his belt. The L.A. deputy sheriff's head appeared over his shoulder. Both men took on concerned expressions when they saw the girl in the tub.

After wrapping a towel around the young woman and offering her much gentle coaxing, Joe and the others managed to persuade her to leave the tub and join the group in the main cabin. The girl was handed a warm cup of tea. Then the questions started. As when talking to the captain, they got her name, her profession (unemployed, from the Valley), and her age (twenty), before moving on to the big questions.

"So tell us what happened last night," Bailey said.

She paused, then looked right at Val as she answered. "They took them."

"Who took them?"

"I don't know. These *things*. They pulled them underwater, and they never came back."

She told her story in a quiet, wavering voice. Val suspected the cops from L.A. were simply writing off her strange story as the effects of hallucinogenic drugs. But to Val, whose stomach sank further as the girl's story unfolded, it was all too clear. Despite everything Val thought she had known about Humboldt squid, she quickly became certain that they were dealing with another attack.

Val could tell Joe realized as much from the looks he gave her as the statuesque brunette described what had happened. How when they had gone swimming the previous night, vaguely glowing shapes had suddenly materialized in the water beneath them after the hull lights had gone out. Her story didn't flesh out many details, as she had understandably gone into a full panic upon seeing the faces of the people around her disappear under the waves, one by one, their arms violently thrashing at the water as they went under. Yet Val knew of only one thing that could be responsible.

Apparently, the girl had somehow gone untouched in the frenzy and, finding herself near the transom, lunged back onto the boat and rushed unnoticed past the drunken dancers into the safety of the cabin. They couldn't be certain, because the poor girl couldn't remember anything after the terrifying scene in the water.

When they finished with her, they allowed her to lie down and rest while they spoke with the remaining passengers. By the time they had finished speaking to everyone at the end of the day, only the girl's story offered any clues to the disappearance. All the other kids had been too busy partying.

One thing that everybody sober enough to remember agreed on was that the hull lights had been off only for a few minutes. The group in the water had disappeared very quickly.

Late in the afternoon, Deputy Bailey stood on the top of the yacht with Val. Joe was also there, making some notes in a small pad, but the crime tech and the other passengers were belowdecks.

"I don't know, doctor," the deputy said. "A vague description of some underwater lights sure doesn't single out these squid as the explanation for what we're dealing with here."

"I don't know, either. But have you got a better explanation? The Coast Guard still hasn't found any survivors, have they?"

"No word yet."

"If we could get my scuba gear, maybe I could dive down here, look for evidence—"

"Ma'am, you've already done enough. And nobody's going into the water, especially if our current theory is that a pack of squid is in the area killing people. I'm going to get this boat in to shore now. These people have been through enough." The deputy walked aft, leaving Val and Joe alone.

"Val, how long can you stay here in Southern California?" Joe looked tired.

"Well, I've already been here for over two weeks. I hadn't really set a return date, though."

"I was hoping you might stick around. We might need more help with this."

"I can probably stay for another week, but at some point I need to get back to my research. It's what pays the bills."

"I understand. Any help you can provide would be

appreciated. Hey, Val—what happened with you and Sturman, anyway? He never returned my phone calls, either."

"I don't know, Joe." Val looked toward the emerald-green mountains rising on the south end of the scrubby island, backlit by the late-afternoon sun. "I wish I did."

CHAPTER 43

Sturman focused his drunken gaze on the two matching parrots, willing his eyes to merge them once again into a single bird. It was no use. No matter how hard he tried, the double vision kept winning out and the bird split into a blurred pair standing on the bar. The big red birds cawed and bobbed their heads up and down happily. Sturman was distinctly aware he was being mocked.

"No crackers for you, you little fucker."

Sturman tried to sip his beer, then remembered that his glass had been empty for quite a while and he had already tested the empty pint a few times. He was separated from three other patrons by several vacant bar stools at an open-air bar in Gull Harbor. The collection of facilities, thrown together on the northeast side of a narrow isthmus on the northern end of Catalina, serviced a natural harbor facing the mainland. Palm trees a few hundred yards from the calm, protected waters in the small harbor shaded the bar.

"Hey, buddy, how 'bout another?" Sturman waved

his glass at the bartender, dripping beer onto his fore-arm.

"Sorry, man. I told you I can't serve you anymore. You really should head back to your boat and get some rest."

"I'll get all the rest I need when I'm dead."

The stocky bartender shook his head, then resumed wiping down glasses.

"If you won't pour me a beer, I guess I'll go make myself one."

"Make yourself a beer? Whatever. It's a free island."

Sturman lurched out of his chair as he stood to go, nearly falling. His hand instinctively shot toward the bar as he steadied himself, which sent the big bird squawking away.

Sturman grinned. "Your parrot's an asshole, pal."

The well-to-do patrons nearby stopped talking and looked at him. He tipped his hat to them, but they looked away. He turned back to the bartender and fished in the pockets of his cargo shorts for money. He threw a few crumpled dollars on the bar. Fumbling for a cigarette in his shirt pocket, he lit it unsteadily and walked out of the bar.

Sturman had sailed straight for the north end of Catalina Island after he left Val. He had spent some time halfheartedly bottom-fishing for dinner in an outer bay near the island as he pondered his situation, and miraculously managed to land a stubborn twenty-pound white sea bass on a hunk of frozen market squid. He filleted the slender, silver-blue fish and placed it in his refrigerator, knowing the bass would be delicious when he grilled it. But it did little to cheer him up.

He couldn't get Val's face out of his mind. And when he tried to think of Maria's, it took an effort to conjure up. Angry, frustrated, and feeling guilty, he had reeled in his lines and headed for the largest harbor on the northern half of the island to drown his emotions at the rustic bar. He had been drunk for two days now.

As he made his way down toward the water, he remembered that he had left Bud behind. He turned and nearly tripped over the dog, already standing at his heel.

"Hey, Bud. Nearly forgot you. Let's get something to eat."

Sturman lurched past several groups of tourists near a sand volleyball pit at the upper end of the narrow beach, and they all stared at him. He smiled at them, a tall, rough-looking drunk in a battered cowboy hat and unbuttoned shirt. Everyone averted their eyes and hurried past—except one girl wearing a sundress and carrying her sandals in one hand. She had wavy blond hair, full breasts, and a beer in her hand. She giggled when he leered at her and her friend.

"Hey, ladies, got any plans for dinner?"

Her shorter, plainer friend was not smiling like the blonde was. She spoke first, with a light British accent. "Yes, we do. Terribly sorry. Let's go, Heidi."

"My friend is lying." The pretty blonde smiled at Sturman. She looked at her dark-haired friend. "Some fun, Allison. We are on holiday, are we not?" She turned back to Sturman. "You are a real cowboy, yes?" Her accent was vaguely European.

"Yes, ma'am. I've even got a boat."

She laughed, but her friend continued to look at Sturman suspiciously.

"What are you making for your dinner, cowboy?" the blonde asked.

"I've got some fresh fish. There ain't nothing like grilled sea bass. And there's beer and limes back on my boat." Sturman pushed his hat back from his face and smiled. "Whataya say, gals? Ever had fresh sea bass grilled by a cowboy"—he swung his arm dramatically toward the sky over the island behind them—"at sunset? It's a beautiful evening, isn't it?"

The girls exchanged glances, but before the short one could speak, the blonde stepped toward Sturman and lifted his arm up over her shoulder. She put her own arm around his waist and tilted her rosy face up to his.

She smiled. "Dinner sounds brilliant. But only if you've got beer, Mr. Cowboy."

"That I do, Miss Cowboy. And rum. You like rum?"

"Oh, yes. It's Allison's favorite."

"Here we go again." The brunette shook her head as she and Bud followed the pair. Sturman had planned to swim back to his moored boat with his cigarettes under his hat, but he was happy to pay for a water taxi. Anything for some company on the boat.

Sturman sat up from restless slumber. As his mind caught up to his body, he realized he was in his own bed inside the cabin of his boat. Next to him, poking out of the blanket, was the sleeping face of an unfamiliar blonde.

He had sobered up some as he slept. Now he felt the

dull ache of guilt in his chest and wished he hadn't brought the women on board, despite the fun he'd had with the girl. He'd found out she was Dutch.

He quietly slid on his tan cargo shorts and stepped out of the cabin into the cool night air. The harbor was quiet, save for the soft clanging of sailboat rigging from boats moored nearby and the light snoring of the other European girl. She was curled up in the stern. She'd had fun, too, once Sturman had convinced her to take a few shots of rum. She and Bud had become pals. These girls were all right, but now he wished he were alone.

Sturman looked up at the stars and shivered. Bud padded out of the cabin to join him, nuzzling his head against his master's leg. Sturman reached down to stroke the dog's head. Bud always seemed to know when his master was troubled.

Sturman looked back up at the night sky. He saw Val's face in his mind. Then he tried to picture Maria's. He could barely do it.

Damn.

CHAPTER 44

Determined waves crashed against stubborn steel in the open waters northeast of Catalina Island. A drab, seventy-foot gray vessel plied the rough Pacific swells, fighting her way slowly to the southwest.

A month previously, a storm in the southern hemisphere near Antarctica had sent a legion of waves marching thousands of miles northeast. Those waves now relentlessly overtook seas that had been calm near Southern California the day before. Even here, on the leeward edge of the island, swells crested ten feet above the sea, easily lifting the prow of the *Centaur* before pulling it deep into troughs. The wind did its part to make the passengers on the fishing seiner miserable, driving heavy spray sideways across the deck. A thick layer of marine fog concealed the sun.

No one was more miserable than Joe Montoya. Of that, Val could be fairly certain. She looked outside the cabin of the fishing vessel to the stern, where Joe was leaning over the side of the boat. His face and jet-black hair were drenched from the spray assaulting the port side. The poor guy had been sick for hours now. He had spent most of his time aboard alone in the stern, shivering and pale. They had offered to drop him off back in Gull Harbor until they could retrieve him in a day or so, but he had refused. He had been asked to observe the capture operation, and had set his mind to do so.

Val and Karl Nikkola, a tall, gangly researcher with longish yellow hair, sat huddled in the elevated wheelhouse of the *Centaur*, safely out of the wind and spray. Karl was monitoring what was essentially a very expensive, highly sophisticated Fathometer clamped to a table. Below the Fathometer was a laminated nautical chart depicting the waters of Monterey Bay, where the seiner was based. The device was completely out of place in the cluttered wheelhouse, save for an expensive radar and depth finder bolted down side-by-side on the dash.

After talking to the yacht captain, Joe and Val had returned to the coast and met up with Nikkola, who had once been one of Val's colleagues. His employers at the Weston Research Institute, a renowned marine studies group located in San Diego, had hired the squid-fishing vessel out of Monterey Bay. The boat had steamed down from California's central coast the day before with Karl aboard. Once the vessel arrived, Val and Joe had met the crew and headed back out to sea to catch up to the shoal before it could travel far.

Through the salt-streaked pane of glass facing aft from the wheelhouse, Val watched as Joe leaned away from the gunwale, wiping his mouth. He walked unsteadily across the heaving deck toward the wheelhouse, his hands grabbing at anything available for support. At least instead of a uniform he had worn street clothes—a Windbreaker over a gray sweatshirt, jeans, and tennis shoes, all now soaked.

"Feeling any better?" She handed him a roll of paper towels as he entered the wheelhouse, dripping cold seawater.

"Never been better." He grinned and wiped his mouth. "Always feels better right after you hack. I think I'll probably be at this for a while, though."

"You must be freezing."

"Feels good, actually."

"You and Sturman were in the Navy together. I thought for sure you'd be immune to the high seas."

"We were on an aircraft carrier. Even the open ocean couldn't really move that sucker much, except in a typhoon. I guess I've lost my sea legs, though."

"I guess you have, son. Hah!" The *Centaur*'s captain, a grizzled, squinty man in a heavy cable sweater, sat at the helm, a grin on his bearded face as he spit chewing tobacco into a plastic cup. Besides laughing at everything, he had a bad habit of commenting frequently on Val's conversations with Karl and Joe. He didn't have much to add.

Joe had been handpicked to join the others after his boss had talked to Southern California political officials. They wanted law enforcement to observe this unusual operation, and since Joe had been involved from the first reported squid attacks, he was the best choice. Because Humboldt squid weren't technically native to Southern California waters and were now believed to be actively pursuing human targets, government officials had allowed the Weston Institute to organize the operation to try and capture the shoal. A lot of money had been donated, so the institute heads had jumped at the chance to help.

Val knew they wanted to figure out what was going on as much as she did, and the task provided a great opportunity for exposure and positive PR for the institute. But she wasn't convinced that what they were doing would either be effective or set a good example.

"Karl, do you really think what we're doing here is a good idea? I mean, are we sending the wrong message to everyone? That these animals are the enemy, and we're here to try and to stop them?"

Karl looked up from the monitor of the Fathometer and shrugged. "I do not know, Valerie. Our expedition here gives me a great opportunity to observe the squid in their environment."

"Inside a net is hardly natural."

"Do not be so negative. This is unbelievable! Besides, it sounds like these squid really are becoming quite dangerous. If we capture this group, then you will have a lot more specimens to examine. And enough material for at least two or three papers, *ja*?"

"I prefer to study living squid. It's hard to study the behavior of a squid sprawled out on an examining table."

Captain MacDonald slapped her shoulder. "But the dead ones are easier to eat! Hah!"

"I'm with Captain MacDonald. Let's just round these bastards up for slaughter." Joe was beginning to regain color, and his voice sounded stronger.

Val looked at Joe, then the captain. "At least you two agree on something."

Joe smiled. "I just hope we can find them before this seasickness kills me."

Val shook her head. What was the point? Joe and his pal Captain Ahab were like so many other people who didn't understand biological science. Society tried to humanize every animal, making them all helpless victims or horrible monsters. That way of thinking was good for animals like cuddly-looking polar bears, but bad for cold-blooded fish and faceless, ten-armed oddities that lived deep in the ocean.

She said, "Joe, you already took something for the nausea, right?"

"Yeah, but that was a long time ago. I really didn't think it would be this bad."

"I have some pills stowed in my duffel, if you need them. It's the red bag in the berthing area."

Joe nodded. "Yeah. I better take another pill. Thanks."

"You want me to get them for you?"

Joe waved his hand. "No, I can get them."

As Joe began to lurch unsteadily out of the wheelhouse, Karl looked up at Val. "Valerie, I know you would prefer live specimens. But necropsies may help us figure out why this is happening now, with this shoal—you said it yourself. The squid you already examined was heavily infected with parasites, which were perhaps vectors, and very, very large. With more specimens, you might be able to theorize what is now merely a hypothesis, *ja*?"

Joe paused in the doorway and turned around. "I don't know what the hell you're talking about, Karl, but I have no problem taking out what is a proven threat to people."

"That makes two of us, copper!" The captain slapped Joe on the back as he walked out of the wheelhouse.

Joe yelled back from outside. "Just drive the boat, asshole!"

The captain laughed. "Our copper's feeling a bit spicy again, eh? Maybe the man's getting his sea legs back after all."

Val wondered how long these men and their big egos could suffer being crammed together in the confined space. Karl alone seemed immune to the captain's ribbing, instead focusing on the readout of the Fathometer. He had been glued to the device since about an hour after they had left shore.

Val didn't like to work with other researchers, but Karl wasn't so bad. The self-important Swede had a great work ethic and was friendly enough. Based in Southern California, he was a leader in the use of acoustic backscatter, or ABS, to describe the biological signatures of marine animals. He'd been brought into the growing squid circus once the very rich parents of a young man missing from the actor's yacht had donated a lot of money to the Weston Institute—in exchange for a serious effort to capture and "study" the shoal. Of course, capturing in this case meant killing, but Val sympathized with the parents' motives.

But she still felt a bit guilty for her part in this witch hunt. She had not lost a child to the shoal. Humboldt squid in a way *were* her children. And what a mother she was.

She had told Joe, the police, and everyone else that their best shot at finding the shoal would be through the use of more sophisticated sonar and, more specifically, by hiring Karl and his institute. She had led the vengeful parents right to the researcher—and they could afford to hire his institute. The national media exposure on the Humboldt squid attacks had now become ubiquitous, so Val tried to convince herself that the rich parents could have found Karl on their own. Mother of squid or not, she figured that it would be crazy to miss this opportunity now. And she had a free ticket to join in the effort. So here she was.

If anyone could find the shoal, it would be Karl. His doctoral thesis had been on validating the use of ABS to accurately identify different forms of sea life that were normally difficult or impossible to identify using standard sonar. Most of his work had been done in the deepwater environments farther north in Monterey Bay, where he had worked in the past with the crew they were with now. The rusty fishing seiner they were on— which looked similar to a trawler—was now officially chartered by the institute. It was still rigged for netting tiny market squid, but the group hoped they might use it to net the huge Humboldts.

After years of research, Karl could not only locate soft-bodied animals like squid on the Fathometer, animals that had previously been thought more or less invisible to sonar, but from what Val knew he could even differentiate a shoal of market squid from a shoal of much larger Humboldt squid—which is why she had suggested him for the operation. It was also why she tagged along on the operation—not so much to help out as to learn.

"Karl, it still amazes me that you can really identify Humboldts on this thing. I've never had much luck with sonar."

"*Ja,* it is no problem." Karl's attempts at hip Americanized English didn't always work. He pointed at the device below them. "This baby is calibrated to have a higher sensitivity than typical sonar, so that helps. But it actually happens that squid are great sonar targets."

"I ain't seen a squid yet that'll show himself on sonar, son." The captain of the seiner sent another brown gob of spit into his plastic cup.

"Probably not. But you never use this Fathometer, Captain." Karl didn't look up at the captain as he continued fiddling with his toy. The captain scowled, then looked out the windshield. Sheets of seawater rained against the cabin as the *Centaur* crashed into another large wave.

Val was quite familiar with how Fathometers worked. They sent out rapid pulses of sound, and depended on the different densities of animals or other underwater features in the water column to bounce echoes back to the device emitting the signals. The problem with squid had always been that their bodies were so similar in density to seawater that they didn't reliably show up on sonar.

She said, "Squid don't generally reflect sonic pulses, but a few smaller parts in their bodies do. Right, Karl? I've been trying to catch up on your research."

Karl nodded. "Right. Most of their soft bodies are invisible, *ja*? But as you must know, some parts of these squids are not soft. This makes detection possible. You hear me?"

Val felt as though she were being quizzed by a professor in a first-year marine science course. "The beak, the pen, the braincase, parts of the suckers . . . they're all dense enough to reflect sonar. I know, Karl."

"Excellent. So all I must do was spend some time observing captive squid. I figure out how to fine-tune the Fathometer in a controlled setting, and how to recognize the resulting acoustic signatures of the different animals. You hear me?"

"We both hear you, Karl."

"Then I validate my research in the field, first off Monterey, then down in the Gulf of California, as you know. Holy shit, Valerie, you have a lot of squid down there!"

The captain spit into his cup. "I myself have thought of relocating to Baja, but I don't trust them Mexicans. They'd probably steal my boat. Now my deckhand here, he's a pretty decent fellow, though."

"I don't know about thieves, but Mexico does have a lot of squid." Val was glad Joe had left before the comment from the uncouth captain. "Karl, I was sure that the best luck you'd ever have would be down there with me. But now it looks like the crowded conditions and high rent in Baja have driven our squid to seek accommodations up here."

"Rent? I do not understand what you are saying."

The captain laughed. "Figures. Damn Norwegians."

"I am Swedish, Captain. I have told you before, *ja*?"

The captain had already made one derogatory comment about Scandinavians. The last thing Val needed was these two arguing. "Never mind the rent comment, Karl. I was just making a joke. So what have you learned in your research?"

"Yes. My research. So it turns out *Dosidicus* can move in very dense groups. Sometimes ten or more individuals packed into each cubic meter of water. And they sometimes hunt in very shallow water, though the belief is that they are only deepwater animals."

"Right. We saw that firsthand down in Baja." Val had met up with Karl for a few days when he had come down to Mexico the previous year. Knowing the area well, she had led him to several shoals of Humboldt squid, but hadn't spent much time staring at the Fathometer with him. She preferred to be in the water, doing her own research.

"*Ja.* Also, some of these guys get very large, if my interpretations are correct. I think I have seen many over two meters in length."

"Jesus and Mary, did you say two meters?" The captain slammed his cup down. "Ain't that six or seven feet?"

"Precisely, Captain. You know, Valerie, this species, it worries me. They prey on everything they encounter, it seems, and there is nothing to stop their progress northward. They are now establishing themselves up in British Columbia. Did you know this? I fear they will kill off other marine life in the North Pacific."

Val frowned. She knew exactly what Karl was talking about, and knew his facts were straight. But she didn't see eye to eye with him on the outcomes. "You make them sound villainous. I wouldn't expect that sort of persecution from a scientist."

"Ah, Valerie." He assumed a wounded look. "This is not my emotions talking. I know that human beings probably cause this change, but I am thinking it is really a serious problem. Just like observable increases in jellyfish blooms, coral dying off around the world, the drop in marine arthropods due to increasing carbon levels dissolved in the water. I believe this is going to be a serious issue we will need to deal with someday."

"You have a point. Maybe there will always be plenty of sea life, but the ocean makeup is certainly changing into one most people would find less favorable."

"Bullshit," the captain growled. "God'll sort out what needs sorting. He always has."

Val stared at him, a disheveled mess with a strand of brown spittle clinging to his whiskers. "Brilliant. That sort of thinking allows you to relinquish responsibility for the earth's problems. It's all in God's hands, so we don't need to make any changes to our way of life, right?"

"Exactly!"

She shook her head. Like Karl, she knew all too well the impacts of overfishing, warming seas, and higher carbon dioxide levels in the atmosphere that eventually were absorbed by the ocean and converted to carbonic acid. The captain clearly was an old-school fisherman who didn't care much about squid populations, as long as he kept a steady income. He had already made it clear he was fine with killing the entire shoal. It was, to him, simple compensation. A paycheck.

In the confines of the forecastle, the roiling sea was far more potent than up on deck. Joe leaned his hand against the angular metal frame of a bunk, taking a deep breath and steadying himself, focusing on the feel of the cold steel. Maybe he should have let Val get the pills for him after all.

On the messy bunks he saw an assortment of personal items that belonged to the crew. Joe preferred the tidiness found on a naval vessel, but he smiled at the photos of nude women taped to the walls. That was also something the Navy wouldn't have allowed. He made a mental note not to touch the sheets the crew slept in.

In addition to soiled clothing, toiletry cases, magazines, and other litter on the unmade beds, he saw several bags, but no red duffel. He groaned as he lowered himself to his knees and peered under the bunk to his left. *Thank God.* He reached for the straps of Val's heavy bag and slid it out from the cramped space, resting on its bulk for a moment as he mustered the will to stand. He doubted if taking another seasickness pill at this point would even have any effect, but it was worth a shot.

Just as he was about to stand, his eyes caught a small wooden box crammed far back in the dark recess under the bunk, where it had been concealed by Val's duffel. It wasn't the box itself that caught his attention, but a single word, printed in large capital letters, which stood out over the other text on the crate. He paused. The box was probably being reused for some other purpose—it couldn't still contain its original contents. Could it?

He stretched his arm far back under the bed, trying not to breathe in the sweaty stink of the linens, and caught hold of a rope handle on the box. The small crate proved even heavier than Val's duffel. When he had the box in front of him, he unclasped the lid and stared at the remaining contents.

He shook his head. "That dumb son of a bitch."

* * *

When Joe stormed into the wheelhouse, Val was arguing with the captain, but they stopped when they saw his face—and the yellow stick of dynamite in his hand.

"Captain, you want to tell us what in the hell this is for?" Joe shouted loud enough to cause Karl to jump. The kneeling Swede, who had been fiddling with his instruments, struck the back of his head on the dash and swore.

The captain jumped out of his chair. "That's my property, copper. Give it here!"

"Not until you tell me why it's on board. Do you even have a permit for this?"

"You cops and your laws. A man needs a permit for everything, doesn't he? This is my boat, and I'll bring what I damn well please on her!"

"Not when we're on board, you asshole! For Christ's sake, you've got these stowed under the bunks of your own crew. Do any of them smoke?"

"All right, everybody take a deep breath." Val stepped between the two men. "Captain, Joe's right. We deserve an explanation."

Captain MacDonald glared at Val, but after a moment he took a step back and looked out toward the sea. "I got it in Mexico. Cheap. My cousin's doing some gold mining in Alaska. He'll pay me top dollar for this."

"Nice try. Now—why do you really have it?" Joe leaned out of the wheelhouse and tossed the explosive into the passing waves.

"Damn you and your laws! You owe me for that!"

"We'll see about that. When we head in, I'm taking

that crate with me. If you're smart, you'll just leave it at that."

The captain swore and advanced toward Joe.

Karl bellowed, "Stop!"

They all looked at him.

He said, "I think I may have found them."

CHAPTER 45

The two European women were hardly awake when Sturman politely ushered them off his boat. As they hailed the water taxi cruising by in the morning fog, he explained that he had business to attend to. It wasn't a total lie. He really would be leaving Gull Harbor for the day. Just not by sea.

He guzzled a quart of orange juice with several aspirin and forced down a big bowl of hot oatmeal with cinnamon to settle his stomach. After Sturman packed two peanut butter and jelly sandwiches and some water into a daypack, he and Bud hailed the water taxi for a ride to shore. The thick damp in the air muffled the sound of the approaching boat. The driver asked about the hungover women he had ferried off the boat earlier, but Sturman didn't answer.

Once the taxi reached the dock, Sturman and his dog set out immediately. Sturman knew where they needed to go. Up. He had developed an incredible urge to climb, to go to the highest point he could find. A place he had been to once before.

They followed a rocky trail snaking west out of the

harbor, up the island's steep seaward flank, and ascended through a wet mist that began to dampen Sturman's face and clothes. He huffed his way up the open hillside along a series of switchbacks, the wet air cooling him. The trail alternated through thick chaparral and rocky outcrops, with few taller trees to obscure the view. Not that it mattered. He could see very little of the beauty that spread out from the island, the thick fog blinding him to the rest of the world.

His head still pounded from the night before, but the exertion was therapeutic. It felt good to push himself, to focus on the pain in his legs and chest, to feel his labored breathing. He climbed for a long time. The day brightened as the sun rose high in the sky and fought to burn through the fog. As he picked his way through the Mediterranean landscape along the narrow trail, his dog exploring the steep hillside before him, he kept thinking of the messages on his cell phone. More than anything, he wanted to talk to Val. But his shame wouldn't allow him to return her calls. He needed to sort some things out.

A few hours into the hike, the thick fog finally broke. In the short span of just a few hundred vertical feet, the path carried Sturman and his dog out of it and into full sunlight. At the same time, they crested an exposed hilltop that Sturman had once climbed, years ago, with Maria. It was a rocky knoll surrounded by low chaparral, many shades of green but no trees in sight. This high point wasn't much to look at in itself, but on a clear day the view was unsurpassed. There was silence. Sturman sat against the rocks, Bud at his side.

He looked down on a white quilt of fog spreading to

the eastern horizon. Viewed from a thousand feet above sea level, the thick blanket of clouds disguised any turmoil on the surface of the ocean below. Turmoil that was so often there.

When Sturman and his wife had climbed this peak in the past, while on a weekend excursion to Catalina Island, there had been a long stick jammed vertically into a cairn of rocks piled to mark the summit. A white T-shirt had dangled from the end. They had waved the makeshift flag in victory when they arrived, then made love on the exposed summit before anyone else might arrive to discover them. The rock cairn was still there. But the flag was gone.

Sturman scratched Bud's ears and looked at the blue skies above, the fog bank below, feeling the warm sunlight on his shoulders. Although Maria was gone, sometimes he thought he could feel her. He could feel her now.

"I miss you, babe. I need you."

Then he closed his eyes and bowed his head. Bud nuzzled under his arm and Sturman scratched the dog behind his ears. He smiled. Then he stood up and began the long walk down.

CHAPTER 46

"**W**e found the shoal."

"You found *what*?"

Joe Montoya realized his wife didn't understand the terminology he had picked up over the last few weeks. He shifted the cell phone to his other ear. "The squid, hon. We found the school of monster squid."

"That's great. So are you coming home now? The girls miss you. I miss you." Joe could hear his daughters arguing in the background and smiled, forgetting how seasick he felt for a moment.

"I can't leave yet, Elena. All we've done is find the squid on sonar. They're not even sure it's the right shoal, actually, but I guess it's at least a group of squid. We're going to try and net them soon. With any luck, maybe this whole thing will be over tonight and I can come home." At the moment, Joe missed dry land even more than his family, but he wasn't going to tell his wife that.

Joe leaned against the cold, wet metal gunwale of the *Centaur*, holding the phone tightly to his ear. Apparently he was close enough to either Catalina Island or the mainland for a signal. They had given him yellow rubber bibs and boots to wear, so he wouldn't get any more dirty or wet. He was glad to have the bibs on, since he needed to lean his hip against the low, filthy gunwale of the boat to maintain his balance. He figured the low height—which in some places was only as high as his knees—must be intentional, to allow the fishermen access to netting equipment over the sides or down in the water.

Off to the west, the last traces of sunlight were seeping into the Pacific and the first stars would soon begin to twinkle through the marine haze surrounding Catalina, several miles distant. The sky was finally clearing. They were close enough to the island to see it, a low black silhouette to the south, but in the darkening evening all he could see to the north and east was ocean. The seas were beginning to calm now, yet the boat still rose high out of the water on some of the passing swells.

Joe didn't understand much about the Swedish scientist's research or his fancy Fathometer, and didn't really care how it worked. But he was grateful to have him on board, if their success had come because the guy was as good as Val said. Karl had proven his worth when at seven o'clock that night—it was hard to believe considering the way Joe felt, but it was still just their first day out—the Swede had located a shoal of Humboldt squid, less than four miles from where the yacht passengers had disappeared.

"So we sent down some sort of device to like five hundred feet, and used it to predict the prevailing underwater current," Joe said. "Then we reeled that thing back in and Dr. Martell did some calculations before we started our search in the area where they predicted the shoal to be. Technical stuff. Way over my head."

"And mine. Sounds like you're with some pretty smart people."

"They know their stuff. I was pretty disappointed when I looked at the screen of their depth finder, though. It was just noise. You know how when we've seen fish on a depth finder they look like pretty obvious dark spots? Well, when we found the squid, they looked to me like vomit. Just a bunch of scattered color. Actually, it made me run out and puke again."

"I'm sorry, baby. You really shouldn't be out there."

"I know. Anyway, this Swedish guy seems certain we're looking at Humboldt squid."

All afternoon, the sea had taken advantage of the *Centaur*'s exposed flank as it tracked the shoal, pitching the boat wildly in all directions. Joe had been forced to remain outside to stare at the horizon and try to suppress his sickness. As the sea began to settle over the last few hours on the lee northeast side of the island, Val had come out after a while and given him the details. There was a large shoal, possibly the one they were seeking, eight hundred feet below the surface.

By eight o'clock at night, the shoal began to rise and everyone went into action. Except Joe, who had no role. So he'd called his wife.

"So how will you capture them?" Elena was almost certainly not interested in their methods, but Joe appreciated her efforts to pretend she was.

He laughed. "*I'm* not capturing anything, hon. These fishermen from Monterey Bay are using their net to catch 'em. Apparently Japanese and Kiwi fishermen both use these special jigging boats to catch bigger squid, but there's nothing available like that around here. So we're using a good old-fashioned net."

"But how will they get the squid to go into the net?"

"Using lights. Our plan's pretty simple, really, but apparently nobody has ever tried to catch Humboldt squid like this."

"Like how?"

"We'll use bright lights to lure in the shoal, then try to net as many squid as we can, the same way they gather up those little market squid in Monterey. They send out a skiff to wrap the net around the squid, and then they attach the end of the net to a motor and pull it in with the squid inside. They plan to just keep the squid in the net until they die from too much oxygen or something. I don't understand all the science."

"Market squid are my favorite. Do those fishermen have any on board now? Can you bring us home some calamari?"

He chuckled. "I'll see what I can do."

"So what's your job, baby?"

"I'm just here to observe. The token cop. I feel like hell anyway, so I'll just stay out of their way."

"Is Will with you?"

"No, he . . . he had some things he needed to take care of. It's just me, Dr. Martell, this other squid researcher, and the fishermen. The captain's a real nut job."

"Well, you be safe. When you get back, I'll make you my paella."

The thought of seafood roiled Joe's stomach. "Yeah. That sounds great, baby. Tell the girls I love them. I'll see you soon."

As Joe zipped the phone into a pocket, Val walked out onto the deck.

"Was that your family?" she asked.

"Yeah. My wife. Didn't get to talk to my girls, though."

"You miss them?"

"All the time. Older one's really becoming a woman, which isn't easy on her mother . . . or me. And our fifteen-year-old is really having a hard time being a teenager. They're so different. . . . Why are you looking at me like that?"

"I was just thinking that you seem to be feeling better. You look better, Joe."

"Like hell I do. You're smiling like a car salesman. What do you want?"

"We need you to do us a small favor."

The sea had grown very dark. The dim light of the crescent moon did little to illuminate the ocean, in part because of the thickening marine layer that was trying to reform into a foggy mist off Southern California.

Joe stood unsteadily on deck, looking through the viewfinder of the digital camcorder. The rusty metal of the well-worn seiner contrasted sharply with the smooth surface of the ocean. He leaned out over the side with the camera to get footage of the tiny, barnacle-encrusted skiff tied alongside, which the captain had just lowered from a huge metal boom into the water.

"Soon one of the deckhands will board this skiff to run out the lead end of an enormous purse net." Joe couldn't resist narrating when the camera was rolling.

He had reluctantly agreed to assist the researchers

by documenting the entire netting operation using the small video camera after Val had explained to him that everyone else had jobs to do. The filming was important not only from a scientific standpoint but also from a PR standpoint, since the rare footage could likely be sold for use in nature documentaries. Joe didn't want to do anything other than try to avoid being sick in the stern of the vessel, but at least the job they had assigned him would allow him to stay outside, with fresh air and plenty of room to get sick.

The captain had now fired up the boat's assemblage of glaring halogen lights, intended to attract the squid underneath like moths to a flame. On the brightly lit deck, Joe turned to film the wiry Latino deckhand as he ran around checking the net rigging with the other, bigger fisherman. Joe didn't narrate because he had no idea what the rigging was called. The net and its various yellow floats and lines were stacked in the stern below the boom, near something that looked kind of like a huge spool with a motor. Joe figured when the deckhand was done here it would really be showtime.

Apparently the guy was going to hop into the skiff and, towing the lead end of the gigantic net, trace a circle a few thousand feet in circumference around the squid gathered under the main vessel and its lights. Once the net had been run out, he would return to the *Centaur* to complete the loop. Joe would film the action as the net was deployed, creating an underwater curtain that extended two hundred feet down and then was cinched closed at the bottom like the drawstring on a cloth purse. At that point the fishermen would slowly draw the net in at the top and sides until their catch was condensed in a much smaller space near the vessel. Joe figured that the best footage would come later, when you could actually see the squid.

"Dr. Martell says that the purse seine net we're using is normally deployed to encircle a school of small market squid. The fishermen suck the catch up out of the net using an enormous vacuum." Joe laughed. "I want to see if they have a vacuum that can suck a hundred-pound squid up out of the water." He didn't think it was a good idea for the skinny young deckhand to be in a tiny, unstable boat floating over a net filled with angry squid. When he had expressed his concern to the captain, the man had just laughed.

Joe was a little concerned that the guy had spent too much time at sea, especially since he frequently hummed to himself. He stopped humming now as he approached Joe in the stern of the vessel.

"It's time, copper. Your camera ready?"

"Already rolling." Joe continued filming the captain while they talked. "You're really going to vacuum up these squid after we catch them, huh?"

The captain laughed. "No way we're getting these fuckers on board with a little suction."

"You know I'm filming, right? They'll be editing out cusswords. So how do you plan to get the squid on board?"

"I'll be brailing these fucking devils, which will be interesting if they're still alive." He winked. "Your lady friend tells me if we keep the buggers in the net long enough, they'll die. But whatever these here scientists want to do with the live ones, they'll have to do it in the water. Or kill the lot before I'll bring 'em onto the deck of my vessel."

"What do you mean 'brailing'?"

The captain sighed. "Not a fisherman, eh? We use a smaller net to scoop 'em out of the big net and into the hold."

"Can you really bring the entire shoal on board?"

"We take on fifty tons of market squid on a good night. This group? No problem at all. Now quit asking so many fuckin' questions."

Joe paused the camera and repositioned himself to watch the skiff deployment. The smaller deckhand moved past him toward the smaller boat.

Joe said, "Good luck, pal."

The man turned toward him and nodded.

"You've probably done this a thousand times though, huh?"

The deckhand merely nodded. When the swells died for a moment, he lowered himself over the side of the boat. The lightweight aluminum skiff looked unstable compared to the seiner, but the man didn't appear concerned as Joe watched him through the camera's viewfinder. Val stepped out of the cabin to watch the action. The deckhand pulled the cord of the sixty-horsepower outboard motor until it fired up on the fourth try. The other deckhand, a slow, Eastern European–looking fellow with a shock of brown hair and several days' worth of whiskers, untied the skiff. He sent his smaller pal off with a laugh.

Joe felt sick again as he tried to keep the camera fixed on the tiny boat. It slowly motored away from the safety of the larger vessel, into the darkness, to capture several tons of sea monster.

CHAPTER 47

"Out past the banks and shallows, where all the jiggers meet . . . you'll find the squids a'gathered, fifty fathoms deep.

"Swimmin' in the blackness, the rigs can barely reach . . . yon squids they lie a'waitin,' fifty fathoms deep."

Captain MacDonald spat into the water, ignoring the remnant strand of saliva that clung to his gray beard. He often sang when at sea, usually unaware that he was. It was a habit he'd formed when fishing with his father and uncles in Newfoundland, sometimes for squid. They all sang. Singing kept a man from losing his sanity.

Tomás had set off on the skiff a few minutes ago. A capable lad, and unshakeable. Better than his other deckhand, a big, strong fellow but dumb. And better than these soft researchers getting in the way and filming everything, and the son-of-bitch cop with them. He looked as green as any virgin deckhand after a night of rough seas. Served him right. MacDonald sang toward the cop's back, and the cop turned to film him.

"First one's hooked by Jimmy, and shouts go round

the fleet . . . he's gonna get some supper, from fifty fathoms deep!" MacDonald liked that part. Now how did the rest go? He took off his glasses and wiped salt and mist off the lenses onto his rough sweater.

"Ink splats in your faces! Catch squirms at your feet! Don oilskins if jigging . . . fifty fathoms deep."

MacDonald stood facing the darkness around his vessel, feeling the ocean's rhythms through the deck. She was really beginning to calm, which pleased him. Hauling in a purse net in rough seas was no fun at all. He fished a fresh wad of wintergreen-flavored tobacco out of the tin in his shirt pocket and placed the treat inside his lip.

The captain listened as the skiff motor began to hum louder. Tomás was picking up speed. He would make the half-mile loop in less than five minutes, dragging the lead end of the net, despite the darkness and rough conditions. The captain felt his heart beat faster. He hadn't gone after larger squid since he was a younger man, and never had gathered an entire net-full. Soon he would have a mess of the flying jumbo squid in the hold. Asian markets were paying top dollar for these squid right now, and if he could haul them in with the setup he already had . . . as a cool night breeze on his whiskers gave him goose bumps, he remembered the end of the song his uncle had taught him:

"Good days end a 'laughin.' There's no cause to weep . . . if you land a catch from fifty fathoms deep.

"But beware a slip or stumble, boy. A mistake you're hers to keep.

"You'll find yourself a 'lyin' . . . fifty fathoms deep."

CHAPTER 48

Joe tried to track the skiff towing the seining net as it hurtled through the waves in a wide circle that would end back at the *Centaur*. He couldn't actually make out the small boat in the darkness, especially not through the camera's narrow viewfinder, just the single small light on its bow as it gradually progressed. He wondered how crappy this footage was going to look, especially with the accompanying audio dominated by the obnoxious captain singing loudly behind him.

"Captain, I'm glad you're the only singer on this boat. What's up with your deckhands, anyway? The younger one never even talks."

"Tomás?" The captain smiled grimly. "Aye. For good reason. Missing part of his tongue."

"What?"

"I found him living near the port in Guerrero Negro, when he was fifteen."

"Down in Baja?"

"Aye. He was doing odd jobs for the men loading salt. Big salt mine there, you know? Anyway, his mother . . . let's just say she had quite a few boyfriends working at the mines. One of 'em didn't like the boy talking so much, and tried to cut out his tongue. Only got part of it, though. Kid's mother did nothing."

"Jesus. That's terrible."

"Now the *Centaur*'s his home. Best hand I've ever had."

"Your other deckhand doesn't seem to talk, either. Surely—"

The captain chuckled as he walked away. "Naw. He's just a big, stupid galoot with nothing to say."

Joe smiled and turned back toward the edge of the boat. He couldn't forget about the dynamite, but maybe he could let the captain off with just a warning.

He directed the camera toward the water below him. The waves were much smaller than they had been during the day, and he could see fairly well into the water next to the hull because of the *Centaur*'s bright lighting. Were there any squid gathered underneath them now? The ocean out here was very clear, but all he could see alongside the hull were occasional smaller fish darting past in the boat's lights or hovering in the shadow it cast. He could tell there were some larger fish hovering underneath them, but there was no way to film them because of the angle he was shooting from, and the distance above the water.

Joe looked back up at the horizon, where the skiff was now maybe five hundred feet away and probably two-thirds of the way finished with its route. As he watched the distant, oscillating light, a wave of nausea suddenly washed through his stomach. He was going to retch again. He paused the camera.

He gripped the cold metal edge of the gunwale as his abdomen tightened and he dry-heaved over the side. There was still the smell in his sinuses from his earlier sickness, which didn't help any. As a second convulsion subsided, he opened his tear-filled eyes and for an instant thought he saw a large, pale shape moving in the water into the shadow underneath the boat. He hit the record button on the camera and leaned farther out to see if he could find what he had seen.

To the camera, he said, "I think I just saw something big. Maybe a Humboldt squid. I'm going to lean out for a closer look." Bracing his knees against the side of the boat, Joe stretched out over the water. He still couldn't quite get a good angle to film under the boat. He leaned out farther. An instant later, a rogue wave abruptly lifted the opposite side of the seiner. Joe lost his balance and instinctively grabbed for the side of the boat with both hands. He watched helplessly as the expensive camera dropped into the ocean.

"Fuck!" He held his breath for several seconds, waiting, until he saw the camera bob back up to the surface. Apparently the air trapped inside the waterproof plastic housing made the camcorder buoyant.

"Hey, guys? A little help?" Joe looked over his shoulder. The captain and his big deckhand were nowhere in sight, and Val and the Swedish researcher were inside the wheelhouse. Joe scanned the deck for something to retrieve the camera and saw a long wooden pole with a large hook on the end—maybe an oversized gaff. He dragged it over to the side to find the camera still visible, but now slamming up against the hull.

He could fish the camera back on board if he could snag its shoulder strap, but doing that was harder than it seemed. The camera kept moving in the surging froth, all the while moving steadily aft. Dodging equipment as he stumbled along the side to keep up with the camera, he tried several times to snatch the camera, but missed. The captain yelled at him from up in the wheelhouse, wondering what the hell he was doing, but he ignored him. If he didn't retrieve the camera pretty quick, it was going to vanish into the darkness behind the seiner. He stepped up onto the side, almost to the stern end now, and thrust the pole tip under the water, jerking upward once, twice, three times.

He felt resistance. He had it.

Slowly, he lifted the camera up. As he reached to grab it with a free hand, he heard the squeak of ungreased hinges and turned just in time to see a large, rusty pulley swinging toward him.

Suspended from the towering boom by cables, the heavy pulley struck his shoulder, disrupting his balance and forcing his upper body out over the water. He tried to turn and grab at the pulley, but couldn't reach it.

As if in slow motion, he felt himself falling over the side.

His left shoulder hit the cold water first and he plunged below the surface. In the brightly lit water beside the boat, he thought he saw shifting movement below him that contrasted with the blackness of the deep. He kicked up to the surface and frantically grabbed at the side of the seiner with both hands, not pausing to look down. He realized that he couldn't climb up the featureless metal side of the vessel, which rose five or more feet out of the water. He kicked for the stern, only a few body lengths away, but it was as sheer as the rest of the boat. He heard shouts from up on the deck.

Then something tugged at his right leg.

He looked down and saw something pale moving below him in the dark water. Something big. Suddenly the thing wrapped tightly around his leg and pulled.

Yelling in fear, he kicked at it and clawed at the side of the seiner. The captain's face appeared above him, and a second later a rope landed on Joe's head. Just as he grasped for it, the tugging increased on his leg and he went under. He reached up over his head with his hands and managed to get them around the rope.

He had been a pretty good rope climber back in junior high, beating most of his gym classmates as they raced to the top. He was in worse shape than he'd been all those years ago, but he would have dominated his younger self in this particular rope-climbing competition. He exploded out of the water and, using all his strength, he pulled, kicked, and clambered up the rough metal until he tumbled headfirst onto a stack of netting in the stern of the *Centaur*. Sprawled out on the rigging, Joe looked at his leg, expecting to see the pulpy body of a squid affixed to his calf. But he had come out of the water alone.

"Jesus Christ!" Joe pushed himself to his knees, water pouring off him onto the deck. He rubbed his hand over his wet pant leg, but saw no damage or sign of injury. He felt a hand on his shoulder. It was Val.

"Are you okay—?"

"You damn fool!" the captain yelled. "Almost became a meal for our squid, eh? Looks like I need to be babysitting this head-in-his-ass copper."

Joe crawled off the stacked net, grateful for the hard wooden surface of the deck beneath him. He looked at Val and began to laugh.

"My camera?" she said.

"Shit. Your camera. Sorry, Val." He laughed again.

He wouldn't have thought a few minutes ago that he could actually be happy to be on the rusty old seiner.

"What the hell were you doing, you fool?" Captain MacDonald squinted down at Joe, sopping wet and shivering at his feet.

Joe could hardly stop laughing. "Thanks, Captain."

"You deaf, lad? What the holy Moses happened? Looks like you aren't going to be filming after all, eh?" The captain began to laugh, too.

"And my goddamn cell phone was still in my pocket." They both laughed harder.

"You two think this is funny, but that was an expensive camera." Val crossed her arms.

"Too bad, ain't it, losing that camera? Would have made some nice video." The captain spit tobacco onto the deck. "Tomás knows how to handle a skiff. I'll wager he closes off the net before the shoal sounds, and lands us some squid."

"I guess I owe you a camera," Joe said.

She sighed. "Well, Joe, we can—"

"You owe them a camera, son!" the captain shouted. "Now get the hell away from my net and get out of the way."

There was a whistle, and Joe realized that Tomás was already pulling up to the *Centaur* with the lead end of the net. Val grabbed Joe's shoulder and together they hustled away from the stern, climbing the short, steep staircase to the wheelhouse platform to get out of the way. Karl stepped out of the wheelhouse to join them, and from the raised deck they watched the action unfold.

The bigger deckhand, Ari, hurried down the gunwale to meet Tomás. In a few moments they had secured the lead end of the net to the seiner's machinery. Using a hydraulic power block mounted to the long black boom, the big man began to wind the weighted cable at the bottom of the net through the boom, the machinery groaning under the strain. If there was anything inside the net, as Karl assured Joe there would be, they would soon find out.

"The weighted lead line will now be cinched tight. This will close off the bottom of the net and prevent the escape of what is inside, *ja*?" Karl ran his hands around and under an invisible vase, clinching his fists below it. "They will then stack the net as they draw it in and—how do you say?—*squeeze* our catch in the ocean alongside the seiner. You see?"

"How do you know so much about this, Nikkola?"

"Well, Joe, I am from a family of fishermen. And I have been before on vessels such as this one."

With the net apparently secured and on its way in, Captain MacDonald climbed up to the wheelhouse and shouldered past them. He stepped into the cabin and came back with a dry towel and threw it to Joe. Joe realized he was shivering. After drying his head and neck, he followed the others inside the wheelhouse as the deckhands continued to work.

Joe said, "So what now?"

The captain looked down at Joe's feet and frowned. Joe realized that he was dripping all over the floor.

"Put on some dry clothes, lad, before you drown my boat. I've got a clean sweatshirt under here somewhere. . . ." The captain leaned down to fish through the mess underneath the helm. "What we do now, you say? We wait. Closing a net that size takes time."

"And then?"

"If the squid are in there, we'll let your friends here do what they need to do. Then we'll brail the buggers out of it and fill my hold with profits. Aha! Found the damn thing."

A moment later a smelly, grease-stained sweatshirt landed in Joe's face.

CHAPTER 49

Midnight came and went.

More than a half hour had passed since they started pulling in the seining net. The large volume of water inside the net had now been reduced to a fraction of what it had been before, and most of the net's length was back on board, dripping in huge stacks in the stern between the two deckhands. From the actions of the crew, Val sensed the net was almost completely hauled in.

She and Joe waited together on the starboard side of the seiner, his hair and pants still damp, but the rest of him looking warmer under a dry T-shirt and hooded blue sweatshirt that said "Alaska!" in huge white letters on the front, with a peeling image of mountains and wildlife. It was colder out in the breeze on deck than inside the cabin, but Joe's nausea had returned after his adrenaline had worn off, and he clearly felt better out in the open air. Val told him that she planned to keep an eye on him, in case he dropped something else overboard.

And, like Joe, she couldn't resist seeing what they had inside the net.

The waiting reminded Val of the excitement of catching her first fish when she had been a child in Florida, her imagination at play as she'd wondered what was on the other end of the line. You never knew what you had until you landed it. When she was six, it had been a shimmering sunfish, and her father had been relatively sober. Despite his drinking even when they went fishing together, they'd always had fun and she'd quickly become interested in aquatic life.

She was a long way from that first cane-pole attempt to catch sunfish. There were probably ten or more tons of jumbo flying squid inside their net.

"The captain was right, Joe."

"What do you mean?"

"You do owe us a camera."

"Ha ha."

"Did I tell you Sturman called me back?"

"No . . . when?"

"I just pulled up the message a little while ago. He's still in Gull Harbor, not far from here. He said he wants to help us out. I figured I'd call him in the morning."

Joe smiled. "That's great to hear. Dumb bastard's finally coming to his senses."

"Yeah, he is a dumb bastard, isn't he?" They laughed together. "Still, he's got a few good qualities."

Joe looked over at her. "Been my best friend for a long time. At least he's got great taste in women." He smiled.

"He said he was married to your sister once."

"That he was. Like I said, great taste." Joe cleared

his throat. "So . . . I was-wondering. What are we going to do with these squid when we have them drawn in next to the boat?"

"Yeah . . . well, Humboldt squid have these very high metabolisms, which is one reason they spend the daytime in deep, cold, oxygen-depleted water. Some people call the low-oxygen layer the 'dead zone.' Humboldt squid can slow their systems down to conserve energy, sort of like going into suspended animation or short-term hibernation."

"Okay. I'm following you so far."

Overhead, the power block clanged loudly under the strain of the incoming net cables.

"Well, the idea is that if we keep them in the net near the surface for a few days, without food, theoretically they'll all weaken and die and can then be brought on board."

"I'm a little surprised that you're okay with that. You seem to be a champion for these squid."

She sighed. "Someone needs to be. Look, I don't agree with our methods here. But I've been outvoted. I'm just focused now on the possibility of obtaining live squid for observation or research, even if they don't live long on the surface."

"You're one of those 'the net is half full' kind of people, then?" Joe smiled at her.

"Stick to law enforcement, Joe." The net clanged up on the boom. "I think the net's almost in."

It was difficult to make out the outline of the floating upper edge of the net at first, but as the last several hundred feet of net were drawn in, the *Centaur*'s lights revealed the yellow floats of the corkline on the surface. A confined space no more than about a hundred and fifty feet across now remained inside the shrinking enclosure, with still no sign of any catch inside. The crew had greatly slowed the winch as the volume inside the net decreased, so that the heavy line barely crept through the boom pulleys. The captain walked out of the cabin and hopped down next to them at the gunwale.

After another few minutes and nothing visible in the net, Val was beginning to wonder if they had come up empty when Captain MacDonald spoke quietly.

"There."

"What? Do you see anything?"

"Aye." MacDonald squinted down into the net. "We've got something."

The shoal was agitated.

Drawn in by bright lights, the squid had found some small fish but little food. Now they jostled against one another as though they had been forced into shallow water, something pressing them together.

Those on the outer edges of the shoal instinctively tried to separate from the group to allow more room for the others, but found themselves held back by the rough lines of an almost invisible barrier in the water. Those that sounded in an effort to escape found themselves up against a much more obvious barrier, a thick gathering of the object and heavy obstacles gathered in a tight mass beneath them.

As the space inside the barrier continued to shrink, the painfully bright lights above drew closer. While some of the squid began to make panic-stricken rushes into the rough barrier or lash out at one another, most in the shoal followed their instincts and moved toward the deep, huddled as far from the light as possible.

And waited.

"Is it the shoal?" Joe saw a torpedo-like shape catch the lights from the vessel as it hurtled across the shrinking space inside the net, a fathom or two under the surface. "Was that one of them?"

"Aye. We may have caught the shoal after all. Tomás! Slow it down!"

Joe heard the winch slow to an almost imperceptible crawl. Now that he knew what he was looking for, Joe began to see the shoal. Not just a few squid. All of them.

"That's them, all right. What do you think of them, Joe?" Val looked excited and sad at the same time.

In the black water within the net, the ghostly bodies materialized. The shapes were huge, seemingly lifeless. Most drifted in place, barely visible as they crowded together in a great mass at the bottom of the net, almost out of sight of the surface.

"They look like rows of gigantic sardines in a can."

Val smiled. "I guess they do, crowded inside the net like that."

A few more panicked squid darted frantically above the organized mass, releasing flashes of self-generated bioluminescence, apparently aware that they had been caught. Many of the squid were the size of large tuna, and appeared to have a similar shape as they jetted through the net.

Joe watched as one of the light-emitting creatures propelled itself against the side of the net, then slowly turned and changed shape, its body spreading out dramatically under the waves as its body unfolded from a neat point into a tangled confusion, its arms seeking a means of escape as they grabbed at the webbing along the wall of the net.

"How many are there, Captain?"

MacDonald grunted. "Hard to say yet. We've got a decent catch, though. And if—look at that!"

The captain was pointing at the water toward the center of the net, but movement there had already caught Joe's eye. A lone squid erupted from the water, blasting skyward with tremendous speed to reveal a wet, bruised-looking body hurtling in the lights. It arched through the air, trailing a perfect jet of water, then splashed down into the water thirty feet away with a loud smack.

Joe laughed. "Holy shit! That was awesome!"

"That's why they're called flying squid." Val shook her head. "Remarkable, isn't it?"

"Goddammit, Ari! Back to the net!" The large deckhand had ambled over to see what the commotion was all about, but hustled aft at his captain's orders.

Joe said, "Damn, they're huge."

"These do look bigger than what I'm used to."

The captain didn't seem as interested. Joe noticed that the man was frowning. He figured out why a moment later, when a pair of squid erupted from the water almost simultaneously, leaving the water at about the same spot near the far side of the net. They gradually separated in a broad V as they lofted above the water, then splattered down into the ocean.

Only one landed back inside the net.

"Shit." MacDonald shoved Joe out of the way and

hurried to the net machinery. Joe could hear the motor grow quiet as the captain shut it down, but it was too late.

Another squid rocketed out of the water, almost straight into the air, and while it hung motionless over the net for a split second, several more broke free of the water in all directions.

"The shoal knows it's been corralled. Some are trying to escape." Val smiled broadly.

"Yeah, I can see—"

Thwump. Something struck the *Centaur* just above the waterline, but when Joe looked down it was already gone. He watched as the air became alive with a continuous display of jumbo flying squid erupting from the surface in the artificial light cast by the two vessels. The captain and his deckhands moved to stand beside Joe and Val and watch the show. The squid emerged as singles, pairs, even threesomes. Many were now hurtling through the air to land outside the perimeter of the net, where they immediately vanished into the deep, leaving faint tracers of bioluminescent light. The seemingly coordinated groups of squid blasting out of the ocean trailing ropes of water looked strangely similar to a water show Joe had once witnessed outside a Vegas casino.

Twenty feet away, a hefty projectile launched out of the water, directed at Joe and Val. He grabbed her shoulders and pushed her down just before the animal cleared the gunwale and sailed just over their heads. Water rained down on them as the flying squid finished its balletic flight with a graceless, resounding splatter of soft flesh on the wooden deck. They hurried over to the animal, which was the size of a short adult.

Joe said, "What do we do with it?"

"Just don't touch its business end."

The squid was huge and alien-looking, a flattened oddity of squirming meat, somehow alive. A stream of dark fluid jetted out of the squid and found Joe's feet, covering them in watery ink.

"Nasty fucking things."

"They're just foreign, Joe. There's nothing nasty about them."

Joe stepped back from the squid as it struggled to return to the water, its tentacles writhing and mantle contorting. The big deckhand rushed past Joe and struck the squid near the eyes with a wooden club. He struck again, the swing ending with a smack that sounded like a palm striking skin. Val cried out and stepped toward him. He struck a final time before Val grabbed his wrist.

"Please. There's no need for that."

The big man retreated a few feet. The squid still moved, but barely.

Joe heard another thump against the side of the boat and looked at Val. He sensed that she too realized they couldn't afford to stare at this ill-fated squid when others were still dangerously airborne. They dashed over to Captain MacDonald and the other deckhand, who stood near the boom supporting the net.

"They're escaping, Captain!"

"Aye, is that what they're doing, copper? I sure as shit know they're goddammed escaping!"

"What can we do?"

"We give 'em more room."

Joe watched as the captain and Tomás started to slowly run the net back out. The reason suddenly hit him—they wanted to add volume back to the space confining the shoal, so they wouldn't feel so trapped. The squid continued to escape as they watched, despite their efforts. Joe figured that by the time they had enough net out to calm the shoal, half of its members would be long gone.

The captain cursed, and Joe heard the winch motor quiet. It had stopped peeling out line. Joe followed the captain's gaze upward. At the tip of the sturdy steel boom, the line had coiled where it had tangled on its way out. They probably didn't usually attempt to run the net out backward through the winch.

"Tomás! Free it up!"

The nimble deckhand was already running to the base of the boom. He straddled it and began pulling himself up to the top, where the net had tangled in the rollers.

"Is that safe, Captain?" Val asked.

It was a good question. The end of the boom, besides being fairly high over the hard wooden deck, looked like it might reach out past the stern—over the water. And the blackened metal looked dirty, almost greasy. Joe didn't like the idea of anybody moving out over the squid inside the net, especially after his experience earlier, but MacDonald ignored Val's question.

They all watched as the slender Mexican quickly reached the end of the elevated boom, then crossed his ankles to grip it. He leaned down and began jerking with both hands at the coils caught above the taut line. He was only there for a few moments when Joe saw the squid.

Suspended in the darkness behind Tomás was another of the airborne squid, clearly visible in the lights. It was impossibly high, much higher than any of the other flyers, its trajectory carrying it toward the boom. Joe opened his mouth to shout, but he was too late. He watched as the squid crashed into Tomás's back.

The impact ripped the small man bodily from the boom, sending him tumbling off toward the deck twenty feet below. He jerked in midair, and Joe realized that his foot was hung up in a loop of loose rope, suspending him. The squid fell onto the stern, splatting loudly on the metal as it just missed the water inside the net. For a split second, Joe's eyes met those of the panicked deckhand before his body twisted round once and his ankle came free. He plunged headfirst toward the squid on the stern and struck the edge of the deck with a disgusting thump. His limp body rolled off the boat into the dark water inside the net.

"Tommy!" The big deckhand called out in a thick accent, club still in hand, looking pitifully over the stern as his friend failed to surface. Even after the splash fully dissipated, all that was visible was a crowd of densely packed squid in the water. A squid squirted out of the water and away from the vessel, landing on a float at the edge of the net as it hit the water. MacDonald was hurrying to the far side of the boat.

Joe struggled with a range of emotions as the small man failed to surface. He turned to search for something he could extend to the deckhand and thought of the pole he had used to go after the camera. He realized it had probably floated off with the camera. "Val—see if you can find a pole, anything we can use to fish him out!"

"There was a dive light in the cabin."

"What? No, we need—"

She rushed off without an explanation.

Joe could tell that Tomás was somewhere down in the compacted shoal, near the stern along the starboard side of the vessel, because the neat rows of squid were being disrupted by a disturbance beneath them. Somewhere down there, it appeared he might be struggling to surface. For a moment, Joe thought he saw the man's hand.

"Dammit, Captain! He's going to drown!" Joe turned to look for MacDonald, who was rushing back with a long pole, similar to the one Joe had lost—probably another gaff pole with the hook removed.

"Where is he now?"

"I don't know for sure." Joe pointed to the water. "Somewhere around there, where the squid are agitated."

The captain jammed the end of the ten-foot pole into the water. Joe turned and scanned the deck for something. *Anything*. He saw a life ring hanging above the wheelhouse and ran over to grab it.

He tossed the life ring down into the water, but felt stupid doing it. There was nothing much they could do. Val ran up with the dive light in hand. Karl was with her. She leaned over the edge and shined the bright light down onto the shoal. The squid attempted to move away from the light for a moment, but in the confined space the white beam only seemed to agitate the shoal. Rather than rest in place, they began to churn the water violently where the deckhand had disappeared.

"Dammit, woman! You're making it worse!"

"I can see that, Captain!" She shut the light off. Alongside Joe and the big deckhand, she stared helplessly down at the water.

They watched as the captain cursed and used the pole to fish around for Tomás in the net full of squid. Joe's life preserver bobbed untouched on the surface nearby. It grew quiet. As MacDonald swept the pole around in the net, several more squid propelled themselves into the air and landed on the ocean with loud smacks.

Suddenly the captain tensed. "I've got something."

He pulled up furiously with both hands as the pole jerked downward. He grunted. "Need help!"

Joe and the big deckhand reached to help him, but just as they were about to grasp the pole MacDonald doubled over as an unseen force tore the pole from his grip. Joe grabbed the back of the captain's belt as he almost went over the low gunwale. They watched as the pole disappeared under the surface.

All five stood shoulder-to-shoulder, silent, focused on the water. Tomás had been under for several minutes. There was no sign of him in the throng of squid, which had again assembled in organized fashion inside the net. Another minute passed slowly, the waves bumping indifferently against the hull and rocking the vessel. The big deckhand started to moan.

Most of the shoal still appeared to be confined inside the net. Some of the squid had managed to escape by going airborne, but many had landed back inside the net, while many more had never made the attempt. Joe noticed that the squid gathered in the net below them were gradually beginning to move downward, as though they were settling toward the bottom of their holding cell—or gathering around Tomás's body.

He said, "Christ, are they headed down after him?"

The captain grimaced. No one answered.

CHAPTER 50

Something else was bothering Joe. Captain MacDonald leaned heavily on his hands next to him, his head bowed, still looking over the side of the seiner. Fifteen minutes had passed since Tomás had gone under, and none of them had any illusions about his fate. Ari sat near the boom, still sobbing.

It was as if everything had ceased around them, the universe pausing for a moment to pay its respects to the poor man, whose lifeless body was probably now being consumed, or perhaps simply pressed against the bottom of the squid-filled net, eyes unseeing, lungs full of black seawater. Maybe the bastards would at least ignore the body as they focused on escaping. It was hard for Joe to tell what the squid were doing because he couldn't see most of them.

Joe suddenly realized what was bothering him. "Captain, why aren't they jumping anymore?"

MacDonald didn't answer. Joe was about to repeat the question when he felt the vessel shudder almost imperceptibly. It felt different than when a wave struck a vessel. More sudden.

Val said, "Joe, what was that?" In the bright lights of the boom, she and Karl looked at him, wide-eyed.

"I don't know."

"Maybe if we just open the net and release the squid, they'll leave that man's body here, intact? No research is worth what's happening here."

"I don't know. Captain, what do you want to do?" Joe looked at MacDonald. He was still staring into the water. Joe asked again, gently. "Captain, I'm sorry about Tomás, but we need you to focus on the—"

The *Centaur* shuddered again, more noticeably.

"What the hell was that?" Joe followed the captain's gaze down into the net. He couldn't see the squid, as each last one had descended in the dark water.

"They're sounding." MacDonald spoke softly, almost in a whisper.

"What do you mean?"

There was a burst of activity underwater as hundreds of squid swelled upward toward the surface, a supernatural glow emanating from the black water as many of the animals produced pulses of pale light. A few seconds later, the shoal reversed direction and vanished toward the bottom of the net. The vessel shuddered again, and Joe felt the deck tip to the starboard side as a loud *twang* came from the taut cables running into the boom.

"The bastards are sounding, dammit!" The captain shoved past Joe toward the machinery in the stern.

"What the hell is he talking about, Val?"

"He means they're trying to go deeper. They're working together to try and escape through the bottom of the net!"

"Are they smart enough for that?"

The boat shook again. "I don't know. I just don't know."

Karl looked at her. "Yes, you do, Valerie."

"You can't do it! You're not going anywhere, you sons of bitches!" At the stern, the captain shouted down at the shoal. The squid answered with another rush toward the bottom of the net. Joe stumbled as the boat tilted and spun a few degrees in a rapid jerk. He heard the lines and metal cables sing again, and the towering boom groaned as its steel frame was tested. Joe tried to picture the amount of squid that must be down there, capable of moving what had to be an eighty-ton vessel.

He noticed something bobbing on the surface of the water, alone above the net now that the squid had headed deeper. Tomás. His corpse was floating face-down. Joe heard the big deckhand moan when he saw his friend's body.

"Captain, Tomás's body—"

"No time for him now. He's gone."

"Can you cut the net free?"

"Cut it free?" The captain scowled. "You have any idea how much that net costs?"

Val said, "My God, you're worried about the money? Can't the shoal damage your boat, though? The net isn't worth losing your boat, or our lives."

"Weston can pay you for the net, Captain." Karl spoke quickly. He was breathing fast. "Safety is paramount here—"

"Bastards could never hurt the *Centaur*. She's too

big. Hear me, you bastards? Wear yourselves out! I'm still going to brail you out and have one of you for supper!"

Joe watched as the shoal rose again, swirling to the surface like autumn leaves and bumping against the deckhand's lifeless body as they regrouped for another go at the net. A flash of dim greenish light rippled through the shoal before its members descended in unison. The main cable running from the boom changed angle and hummed as the deck beneath Joe lurched. He looked up at the cable just as there was a loud pinging noise.

He thought he saw something flash on the boom and blinked instinctively. For a brief instant, his mind registered that something was about to strike his face.

Val heard more than saw the small metal part give way on the seiner's boom. There was a piercing whine, which ended a split second later as the shard tore into Joe's head. She watched in horror as his face erupted into a red mist with a sickening, audible crunch, spraying her face with blood. He instantly crumpled against her knees and onto the deck.

"Oh my God! Help me!"

The men rushed over to where Joe had fallen, but instead of kneeling to help Val, they merely stopped and stood motionless. She took hold of his shoulder and turned over his inert body. She gasped and covered her mouth with her palm as Joe's arm fell limply to the deck.

He no longer had a face.

Where Joe's nose and left eye had been was a gaping

hole, the remaining eye white as it rolled back into the socket, twitching slightly. His tongue was visible inside his mouth, where the upper palate and teeth had also caved inward. Broken teeth slid down his tongue.

Val looked up at Karl. He shook his head, then reached down to squeeze her shoulder. Joe kicked her leg and she yelped, recoiling from the touch. She watched his legs jerk and extend on the deck, and then he was still. Karl tried to hug her. Ari had stopped sobbing. He yelled something inarticulate. The deck shuddered again as the shoal made a run.

Joe couldn't actually be gone, could he? Had two men really just died in front of Val in the last few minutes? She felt as though she was watching some sort of sick dark play in which she was merely a spectator.

"He's gone, Valerie. I'm sorry." She realized Karl was still embracing her, trying to turn her away from Joe's body. She knew Karl was right. She looked away from the warm corpse toward the ocean around them.

"My best mate's gone, too." The captain spat into the ocean. "And soon, so will be these goddamn squid."

Val wiped at a tear and watched the man stride toward the front of his vessel, vaguely wondering why he wasn't headed to the net to free it somehow. He climbed the steel stairs to the wheelhouse and disappeared inside.

She looked down to the water and saw the outline of the net near the surface. Tomás's body was now bobbing against the hull of the *Centaur* in the dark waves. She leaned against Karl, watching, uncertain what the captain was planning to free the shoal. The boat lurched again as the squid made a run, and Karl held her shoulders to keep his balance.

"Valerie, we should move from here in case something else gives. Valerie?"

"Right. I'm sorry."

"It is okay. But we need to move—" Karl stopped and stared at something over her shoulder.

She turned to see what he was looking at. The captain had reappeared from the cabin of the vessel and was hurrying toward them. In his thick hand was a stick of dynamite.

Its fuse was already lit.

CHAPTER 51

When Val saw the lit dynamite coming her way, she ducked behind a raised metal box on the deck that opened into the hold. Karl crouched down beside her. The captain strode past them without a glance as he headed for the stern.

"Valerie! Come with me!"

She realized Karl was pulling her along by the elbow. Together they raced toward the front of the vessel, away from the threat. She glanced back and saw the captain yelling at the shoal below, the fuse burning down in his hand.

The fuse was much longer than Val would have expected on a stick of dynamite, with another foot or more still unburned as the sparks inched toward the cylinder of nitroglycerin-based high explosive. The captain was yelling loudly enough for Val and Karl to hear his words.

"Goddamn you, you ungodly bastards! It's you today, not me! And not my vessel! I'm sending you back to hell! You hear me?"

He paused to look at the explosive in his hand, only

about six inches of fuse left now. Val and Karl had paused as well, in the doorway to the wheelhouse, each holding their breath and unable to pull away from the drama unfolding on the well-lit deck below them. The captain said something to himself, this time too quiet to be heard. Then he hurled the dynamite well away from the boat, into the water where the shoal was gathered inside the net.

The shoal was resting.

A visual cue had rippled through the mass of squid, a signal, as millions of photophores in their mantles lit up in a patterned response. After the signal flashed through them, they had gradually ceased moving.

Their attempts to escape confinement required great exertion. And individual sacrifice. Some of them now drifted lifelessly in the dim seawater, having been crushed against the wall of the net by the force of the others.

Yet not all the members of the shoal acted in unison. Within the hovering mass of motionless squid, several agitated individuals continued to flash from within, bumping into their passive brethren as they darted in every direction. Like the others in the shoal, the one-eyed female made no effort to calm the agitated rogues or cease their activity. She simply disregarded them in an effort to retain energy.

One of the rogue squid darted past her. It bore a new injury—a long tear in its left fin, just above the mantle. The obvious wound momentarily triggered an attack response in the one-eyed female. The injured rogue would be easy to overcome, but the impulse faded. Her instincts were clouded by confusion, her motivation to act lacking a clear direction in which to focus her energy. She watched the rogue jet upward through a clump of her gathered siblings, bouncing lightly off their soft bodies as it passed. Another larger female—it was her badly scarred sister—lashed out in response, tearing into the injured rogue's mantle as it passed. It ignored the attack and continued to move toward the top of the shoal.

As the rogue neared the surface, the one-eyed female detected a powerful stimulus in the water. *Light.* A brightly lit object was descending from the ocean surface. The small object bore the signs of possible prey, and the rogue had turned to intercept it.

The object was painfully bright, its light faltering, yet somehow still burning with a fierce intensity. The rogue appeared immune to the damaging light. It snatched the thing up and darted away from a pursuing squid also seeking to claim it.

Intent on keeping the prize to itself, the rogue propelled its body horizontally through the dark water, but it quickly encountered the rough net wall. The one-eyed female watched as the squid changed direction and jetted sidewise, parallel to the inside of the net and away from her. It neared the massive, smooth structure on the surface that had been generating the deep sonic pulses. There the structure loomed alongside the net wall.

Although the large female retained a faint impulse to avoid the huge object as a possible threat, the rogue did not. It instead moved closer to it to escape its pursuer, but its rival flicked a tentacle out and briefly caught hold of the prize.

The rogue squid sent a burst of water through its siphons, hurtling itself against the net wall and colliding with the smooth surface. Just as it made contact, the light clutched in its arms winked out.

The captain had backed away from the gunwale, waiting for the detonation. Karl tugged at Val, and together they backed into the safety of the wheelhouse.

She peeked through the aft window and watched Ari move through the shadows on the deck, stumbling over Joe's lifeless body. He stopped at the side of the seiner, leaning against the gunwale and looking toward the water where the dynamite had disappeared. Val knew there was a risk to him standing that close to the side, but the captain said nothing to him.

She opened her mouth to yell at him, but Karl pulled on her again and she ducked below the window and crawled toward the hatchway that led into the boat's berthing area. As she and Karl scrambled around a corner into the first inner doorway, a small room on the portside that contained two stacked bunks covered in boxes, a deafening explosion thundered through their bodies.

Pain erupted in Val's ears as the shock wave passed through the steel vessel.

CHAPTER 52

Sturman woke with a start, out of a dream. He had heard something. He lay in the darkness, straining to hear anything—if someone had boarded his vessel, perhaps—but he heard nothing. He looked down at the floor and saw Bud asleep there. They were alone on *Maria*. He must have been dreaming.

He sat up and looked at the clock. One in the morning. Why the hell had he woken? He rolled onto his side, away from the clock, and tried to focus on the gentle motion of the waves rocking the boat. Instead, his mind went directly to Valerie Martell.

He knew what he needed to do now, but he also knew he needed to be patient. He had called her earlier to explain how he felt, to apologize if he could. He would offer to help them out when he heard back from her, if she was still in the area. He had made dinner and whistled afterward as he washed the dishes, feeling better than he had in a long time. Sleep had been impossible at first. He had tried reading, but in his excitement it had taken him more than an hour to finally drift out of consciousness. Now he was wide awake again.

He left the cabin to relieve himself in the cool night air and looked out over the calm, starlit waters of the harbor. He returned to his bunk and gave Bud a pat on the head before pulling his blankets up over him. As he began to drift off again, he thought he heard something again. Was he hearing things? No, there it was again— his cell phone this time. Was something wrong with his father? Nobody called this late unless it was an emergency.

He jumped out of his bunk inside the darkened cabin and hurried through the door to the galley. Where was the damn phone? As it rang the fourth and final time, he found it on the portside bench in the main cabin and grabbed it, looking at the glowing screen. Val.

His heart leapt as he flipped open the phone. "Val, I've been thinking about you. Is everything all right?"

"Will, I hope you're close. We're in trouble."

"Karl, there's no time to argue. Put on the gear."

"But Valerie—"

"Dammit, Karl, you don't have a choice. You know I'm right. Sturman or someone else might find us out here, but this ship is going down. This is our best chance." She had given Sturman their coordinates over the phone, but she didn't know if he was close enough to reach them in time. He was coming from Gull Harbor, no more than ten miles away, but by the time he got the boat running, out of the harbor, and across the dark channel . . .

"If we just put on life jackets, we can stay on the surface—"

"Karl! Listen to me. I *know* these animals. We'll be safer near the structure of the boat than on the surface out in open water. The longer we can stay with the boat, the better our chances."

"But when the boat sinks—"

"When it sinks, we'll have to fend for ourselves on the surface. At least with scuba gear on we won't drown if the ship pulls us down with her."

After the explosion, Val and Karl had stumbled out into the smoke on deck to find that the dynamite had somehow exploded directly against the *Centaur*'s hull. What was left of Ari had been sprayed in a crimson mess across the area where he had stood moments before, just above where the dynamite had detonated. The captain had been nowhere in sight.

In spite of the death around her, what bothered Val the most was the steady sound of rushing water. The gaping hole in the side of the seiner had gradually become visible as the smoke cleared. It extended from below the waterline to as high up as the starboard gunwale.

"Valerie, if we can get to the skiff, we will be safe there."

She looked out toward the small boat, its gray hull barely visible in the darkness a hundred yards or so from the seiner as it drifted away toward the mainland. The cleat to which it had been tied had been destroyed in the explosion, but the skiff had somehow survived, propelled across the waves away from the larger boat. In the moments of panic as they had searched for the captain, it had floated too far away to risk swimming to retrieve it.

"How the hell are you going to get to the skiff, Karl? It's even farther away than before."

"I do not know."

"If you want to swim out to it, be my guest. I'll wait for you here."

"But you know I cannot swim. That is not funny."

"You don't need to be able to swim to use scuba gear, dammit! This is your only choice. You're a fucking marine scientist, for Christ's sake! You can go into the goddamn ocean!"

Val took a deep breath. The air still smelled slightly of sulfur.

Karl picked up a dive mask and turned it over in his hands. "How will we protect ourselves?"

"The squid shouldn't be able to seriously injure us, as long as they can't drag us into deeper water and we stay near the wreckage. We'll hold on to anything floating if they try to pull us down. And we can try to keep them at a distance with our dive lights." She wondered if their lights would be bright enough to actually deter the shoal.

"They will still bite us, *ja*?"

"Maybe. But they aren't like sharks. The damage they can inflict with their beaks is limited. The real threat is that they could overwhelm us and drown us. If we hurry up instead of talking about it, we might actually survive." She took another deep breath and tried to stay calm. She touched the arm of the gangly scientist, and in her most soothing voice said, "Karl, I'm scared, too, but you have to trust me, okay? This is what we need to do."

He breathed out and nodded. "*Ja*. Okay, Valerie."

"Let's get moving, then."

Karl sat and forced his arms into a scuba vest to which she had already affixed a heavy tank and regulator. She continued talking to him as he prepared to go under.

"So why can't you swim, big guy? Never been in water too deep for you to stand?" She forced a laugh and stood on her tiptoes as he stood up next to her. He didn't laugh, but at least he was moving.

"My father was a fisherman. Where we are from, it is considered bad luck for a fisherman to learn to swim. If you do not trust in your boat, she will sink, so you prove your faith by not learning to swim."

"Are you kidding me?" Val shook her head. "How could you become a scientist if you grew up so superstitious, with—"

She felt water on her feet. The first waves were now washing over the main deck and had begun pouring down into the seiner's hold, sounding like a small waterfall as they rushed into the empty chamber. The *Centaur* would go down soon. If they could just manage to stay on it for ten more minutes . . .

Fins in hand, they moved up the steps toward the elevated wheelhouse, the highest point on the boat, and stopped just outside it. They watched quietly as the water rose to the top step and began to flood inside. The sound of water running to fill the hull had now stopped. Val stepped into the confined space of the wheelhouse, but Karl hesitated below her on the wheelhouse steps, water up to his knees, his eyes wide.

"We will at least tether ourselves to the boat, *ja?*"

"We can't, Karl. We'd go down with it." She reached for his hand. "Come on. We'll stay in here as long as we can. Once she starts to go down, just get away as fast as possible and make for the surface. Maybe we can swim to the skiff."

There was a loud bursting noise as the relentless seawater forced a pocket of air out of the bowels of the vessel. It wouldn't be long now.

Prey. The splashes and movement could mean there was food entering the water.

The one-eyed female, closer to the surface than most in the shoal, moved through the water beside her badly scarred sister. They had retreated from the harsh glare as the massive object began to sink. Now, as its blinding lights suddenly disappeared, they returned to its hulking form. And the possible prey within.

As they hovered near the object, the one-eyed female detected a faint sound in the water. It was distant, only detectable for an instant in the blackness. Then it appeared again, and became stronger, and the deep vibrations gradually increased, pulsing through the water and into her soft body. The sounds vibrating against and through her now had become familiar. Like the leviathan slowly sinking before them, she now identified this new sound with many things. *Food. Confinement. Stress. Danger.* The explosion in the water had killed or maimed many in her shoal, some of which were consumed by other squid. Yet the sinking object in the water before them seemed to pose no immediate threat. It remained inert. And inside it, she could detect prey.

Her natural instincts had dulled. Confused, she had become more aggressive, sensing but not comprehending that something was wrong. Within her and other members of the shoal, parasites wormed past nerve fibers and around organs, interfering with the natural impulses and rhythms that drove their hosts. The shoal was weakening, its efforts to capture prey less successful, its attacks less coordinated. Its members had eaten little over the past two nights, and had become increasingly cannibalistic to feed their relentless metabolisms.

She was hungry. Now free from confinement, she was motivated by a single purpose.

To feed.

Her shoal had become uncharacteristically scattered. Once a tight collective of a thousand members gathered far below the surface, it was now composed of small groups and individuals spaced widely in the black water around the submerged object. Alongside her scarred sister, trailing several others also circling the object, the one-eyed female moved slowly, struggling to keep up. She sensed conflicting signals pass through her body. That something was wrong inside her, her focus uncertain. Several smaller members of her group had noticed this, and had become aggressive toward her already, sensing her weakness. They were all hungry. Always hungry.

Two squid moved toward her and followed her closely, watching. But they kept their distance from her and her equally imposing sister.

As she propelled herself in a slow circle near the lower fringe of the others moving around her, she was unaware that her own parasitic infestation was very advanced. Her organs were heavily impacted now. But she was still alive. Like all living things, she would not yield willingly to her death. And to survive, she needed to feed.

As she turned her broad fins to redirect her body, her black, bulbous eye caught a sudden change in the water column. A variance in the dark water. Her fins stopped fluttering. Her mantle stopped pumping seawater. There, ahead of her, she saw it again. A small, moving light within the massive object.

Light . . . and life.

CHAPTER 53

Maria raced surely over the dark swells to intercept the sinking seiner. At twenty-five knots, she was quickly closing the distance. Sturman scanned the darkness from her flying bridge, a cigarette burning between his teeth, ashes whirling down against his shirt and into the night wind. The sea had calmed considerably from earlier in the day, but was still far from flat. He could see almost nothing ahead of him, even with a spotlight trained on the small waves off the bow.

Under the circumstances, he had made the dangerous decision to go full throttle. Although there was some risk of a collision out here at night, running aground was an impossibility. It was thousands of feet deep here.

He tossed the cigarette over the side and tried to call Val. No answer. As he drove farther into the dark channel, he fought to push aside distracting thoughts. Thoughts about Joe, and the guilt that came with what Val had told him. Thoughts about Maria. Now they were both gone. But right now Val needed him.

Bud sat beside Sturman, his head thrust out over the

side, nose sniffing the cool night air rushing past the bridge, short ears laid back. Sturman looked at his watch. Val had called him twenty minutes ago. The GPS on his dash indicated that he had just over a mile to his destination—at least to the coordinates Val had hurriedly given him. Could the seiner still be afloat, after so much time had passed? Maybe another vessel had been out night fishing and had already come to her aid. Val had put out a mayday on the VHF before calling his phone, but she didn't know if anyone had received it.

As he tried for a second time to raise the Coast Guard on his own radio, *Maria* crashed furiously into a trough, sending spray down the sides of the hull. If there was a response on the radio, he couldn't hear it over the wind and the roar of the straining engine.

As the "distance to next" figure on his marine GPS passed under a thousand feet, he pulled back on the throttle, slowing to ten knots. With his spotlight, he scanned the swells and troughs off the bow. If he had arrived too late, there might be nothing but floating debris. Hell, out here, in the dark, he'd be lucky to find anything if the vessel had gone under. He tried Val on the phone but again got only her voice mail.

Sturman swore and struck the helm with his fist, then snatched his hat off his head and threw it onto the dash. Bud licked at his arm. Sturman was sweating despite the cool air on his face.

The GPS beeped to indicate that he was nearing his destination. *307 feet. 292 feet.* He slowed the boat to five knots, sweeping the darkness left and right with the spotlight. He reached the coordinates and slowly passed the location where the vessel had been. Nothing. He felt sick to his stomach.

The boat should have moved some to the east, which would mean it would be past the coordinates Val had given him. He veered left and covered a few hundred feet, then turned ninety degrees and steered back toward his original heading. He motored past the GPS coordinates again and continued southeast for a minute. Nothing. *Wait.* Off the starboard—something white. He spun the helm. Floating junk. A water bottle, some other trash. A life preserver. *There.* He saw a boat bobbing on the waves, and held the spotlight on it.

It was only a small fishing skiff, obviously the seiner's. He approached and saw that it was empty. He began to pass it, but something told him to bring it with him. He ran *Maria* alongside the skiff, striking its hull with a loud thud, and quickly tied it to a cleat on the stern before resuming the search, skiff in tow.

Thirty seconds later, as he continued to move in an eastward search line, he looked back to his right and caught something in the beam of his searchlight. A hundred or so feet away, pointing up out of the water, were part of a large boom and the smooth, grey edge of a bow. He had passed the seiner in the darkness. He spun the helm to starboard and eased back on the throttle as he approached.

"Val!"

He eased back further on the gas to lessen the engine noise, but there was no response. *Think, Will.*

Sturman idled near the sinking seiner, scanning the water for survivors or objects that could damage the boat's propeller. A collection of yellow floats crowded together near the vessel, marking the top of a massive fishing net. Something red in the beam of light caught his eye. A dive flag. *They went under. Of course.* They had to be underwater, inside the vessel, where they would be safe from the shoal. But for how long?

Somehow the seiner was still on the surface. There had to be a pocket of air trapped in the forward hull that was preventing it from sinking, but it wouldn't be long before the rest went under. A rivet or hatch or seam on the old boat would give, and then it would be a matter of seconds. Val and the others had to be hiding in or near the hull, where they could find some protection from the shoal. Sturman remembered the six large lights mounted to the outside of his boat, still in place from the nighttime excursions with Val. Although they had used the lights to attract the shoal before, she had explained once that the squid wouldn't want to get too close to the blinding beams. Maybe the lamps would scare off the shoal now, if it was close to the surface.

He flipped the lights on. The surrounding ocean went from black to deep blue in the patch of artificial daylight. In it, more flotsam appeared on the surface. Sturman's gaze paused on an object bobbing in the swells near the sinking boat. A body, floating face-down. Sturman's heart lurched, but when he trained the light on the inert figure he saw that it was not Val. This was an older person, probably a man, with a mess of wet, graying hair moving in the surge.

He nosed *Maria* slowly toward the body, avoiding the masses of netting just below the surface. As Sturman neared, he saw several large, submerged shapes around the floating figure retreat as the lights reached them. Squid. A dark cloud in the water around the corpse gradually became bloodred as the light touched it. Bone showed on the man's limbs, where flesh had already been devoured. Sturman spat into the water.

"You sons of bitches."

He turned the helm away with a mixture of revulsion and anger and fear. There was nothing to be done. This man was already dead.

He needed to find Val.

CHAPTER 54

As Val paused to draw in air in the darkness she heard the unmistakable drone of a large motor. Another boat was nearby.

The subdued beams of what had to be very bright lights above began to appear a short distance away and fought their way down through thirty feet of dark water as the vessel approached the submerged seiner where Val and Karl hid. *Will.* It had to be his boat, with so many lights directed down into the water. Her heart pounded as she felt the tonic of excitement, hope, and something else. He had found them.

She thought of making a rush for the surface. But there were too many squid just outside the safety of the vessel, and Karl was a poor swimmer. They had only been under for a few minutes, entering the water once there was nowhere left to stand on the *Centaur*, but already the shoal had pursued them. She looked at the whites of Karl's eyes as he churned through the air in his tank in a fast pant. She couldn't blame him for being terrified. Unlike him, she had spent many hours underwater near Humboldt squid, but even she was frightened by the aggressive behavior this shoal displayed.

At the edge of her visibility, two more pale shapes loomed into view, pausing ten feet from the submerged cabin opening where they huddled inside like two hermit crabs that would become an easy meal outside the steel shell in which they hid. Her light found a black, lidless eye resting in one of the smooth bodies, just above a nest of unfurled tentacles. As the light hit the pair of squid—or were there more than that?—their bodies blossomed into an angry red color and they disappeared in a swirl of tiny particles.

My God, they're enormous.

These were the biggest Humboldt squid Val had ever seen, longer than Karl was tall, mantles the size of punching bags, skin the color of human flesh and blood.

She swore to herself. There would be more of them, just outside the range of their lights. A lot more. She used to joke with the Mexican crews that Humboldt squid were like cockroaches—for every one you could see, there were at least a hundred more nearby.

She had worked with these animals for years, and now her instincts told her they needed to stay within the safety of the seiner as long as possible. Something about the shoal made her certain they were confused, desperately hungry, or simply angry, as though aware of their capture and who was responsible. *Nonsense, Val.* Leaving the safety of the sinking vessel might be suicide, but she knew they couldn't simply stay inside the structure. It was going down, and probably very soon. Sturman had arrived, and his boat would offer safety. They had to try for the surface eventually.

Val turned to Karl and looked into his panic-stricken

eyes. He exhaled a huge cloud of bubbles, then another an instant later, then another. He was breathing much too fast, hyperventilating. She needed to get him out of there before he ran out of air. He grabbed Val's arm and squeezed, pointing to the illumination from Sturman's boat. He motioned for them to move toward it. She held her palm out to him, indicating that he should stay put, then slowly moved out of the dark recess in the boat for a better look. She flinched as a dull boom sounded, air under intense pressure erupting from somewhere below, inside the boat. A wave of bubbles rushed past Val as she leaned out of the cabin.

Suddenly Karl grabbed her shoulder and pushed past her, kicking her head with his fins as he surged out of the seiner toward the lights. Apparently they were going to make a rush for it now. *Fuck it, why not?*

She began to follow Karl out of the wheelhouse, but he turned back toward her as abruptly as he had left. She raised her light to try and read his expression. In the beam of light, something pink appeared on his shoulder.

He turned his head toward it and tried to swat it away. As he tilted his body forward to kick back to the seiner, several more fast-moving shapes emerged from the blackness. Their color shifted from pink to red as they closed around him with astonishing speed.

She tried to frighten off the attacking squid with her light, but they hid behind their quarry. All she could do was shine her light on Karl from a body-length away and watch as more squid closed on him, some scattering when the light found them, sending them retreating into the darkness, but others taking their place. She felt anger suppressing her fear and finned out of the cabin toward her friend.

Something brushed her arm, then slowly curled itself around her elbow, testing. As she recoiled, she imagined small teeth from hundreds of tentacles cutting into her neoprene wet suit. She twisted her body and shined the light over her shoulder, and the feeling disappeared. She saw nothing behind her but minute particles swimming in the beam.

Then something wrapped itself around Val's thigh, almost gently, and followed with a powerful squeeze. She reached down and felt the rounded firmness of a Humboldt squid's muscular tentacle twisted around her leg. As she began to direct her dive light toward her attacker, another squid propelled itself against her shoulder, breaking the airtight seal on her mask. Water flooded inside, blinding her. Unable to clear her mask of water, she tried to shine the light where she thought the animal's eyes might be.

Then they started to bite her.

She wasn't sure how many there were, but they pulled her away from the structure, toward the open water, and she knew they were increasing their advantage as they overpowered her and she struggled clumsily to move back to where she could grab hold of the boat again. Val glanced at Karl one last time. He was too far away to make out his face anymore. She watched as the powerful arms of one of the massive squid clinging to Karl's back—each of the arms thicker than her own—encircled him, its eyes shielded from her lights by his body. She could only watch helplessly as the beast took her struggling friend down into the blackness. His light was soon swallowed up by the abyss below her.

The soft bodies of the squid pressed eagerly against her, their hunger unmistakable.

CHAPTER 55

Sturman tore open the wooden lid of a gear compartment mounted in the stern of his boat, against the rear of the cabin. Beneath the chipped white-painted lid were his wet suit, BC, mask, and other dive gear. He dropped each piece of equipment onto the deck at his feet, then flipped open another large compartment. Tossing out dirty towels, canvas tarps, and fishing gear, he finally found what he was looking for at the bottom of the bin. From beneath a box of fishing lures came the metallic gleam of small, shiny rings. Grunting, he heaved the oily, heavy garment out onto the deck and dropped it next to the other gear.

He took a deep breath. "Who do you think you are, Sturman? A knight in shining armor?"

Val and the other researcher had not surfaced. They had to know he had arrived, so if they were alive, the shoal, or something else, was preventing them. If Val couldn't come to him, he would go to her instead.

With no time to don a wet suit under the shark suit, Sturman immediately began to slide on the heavy chain-mail garment. The two-piece protective suit, made up of thousands of tiny stainless-steel links of the sort found in butcher's gloves, was designed for diving with smaller sharks. It wouldn't protect a man from the crushing pressure of a great white's maw, but it was adequate against blues, reef sharks, even small makos. Sturman had acquired it from Steve Black years ago as a means to pay off a large debt, and he'd used it a handful of times when diving in open water with schooling sharks. A blue shark had once taken a bite at his upper arm on a winter dive with Steve, and the suit had done its job. He had gotten a nasty bruise, but nothing more.

As Sturman yanked the suit on, he watched the angled hull of the seiner on the water next to him, the tip of the bow now barely above the surface. It was going to sink before he could even get in the water. The lights on his vessel might help ward off the shoal, but unless Val appeared at the surface very soon, she and whoever was with her were about to ride the dying vessel down to Davy Jones's locker. He needed more time. If only he could stop the boat from sinking, even slow it, he'd—

Sturman looked at the seining skiff he had towed over, drifting a few yards away, and at the heaps of drifting net in the water and its mass of cables and ropes tangled on the surface, all kept from sinking by the yellow floats through which the ropes were threaded. How strong were those cables? Would they hold? No, it didn't matter. They were too lengthy and unworkable. He glanced at the last few visible points of the submerged seiner. Part of the boom protruded from the surface. It had to be strong enough. But how could he fasten it to his vessel?

The anchor chain. It just might hold long enough for him to find her. But would it even work? And his own boat—

He ran his hand along the worn wood of *Maria's* cabin door, knowing it would be for the last time.

Val had remained relatively calm, focused mostly on the blackness where Karl had disappeared, until she felt the first sharp teeth tearing through her wet suit. Instincts took over, and she panicked.

Kicking, reaching, squirming, willing herself toward the dark cabin doorway behind her, she continued to lose ground as the animals clung ever tighter against her body. Even in the relative weightlessness underwater, she could feel their bulk pressing into her, pulling her down. Ten feet from the doorway, she somehow reached the vertical side of the sinking boat and clawed at its surface, dimly aware that one of her nails broke off as she managed to grip a groove in the rusty metal. She turned her back toward the boat and forced her attackers against the rough metal, and felt them release her. She turned and finned along the vessel until she saw some sort of hatchway, maybe the opening to the hold. She bumped and clanged through, into the black water inside the *Centaur*.

For a moment, she would risk drowning inside the boat. She needed another plan.

In the cast of the lights, she studied the hundreds of silhouettes in the water above her, each the size of a blue shark, moving past as they were disturbed by the stimulus. She looked at her depth gauge. She was fifty feet below the surface. Her air wouldn't last long here. She began to feel pain on her left leg and with her hand found a gaping tear in the neoprene on the back of her thigh. Warm blood seeped past her fingers into the cold water. It felt like a lot of blood. Her time was running out.

She would have to leave the safety of the sinking seiner. But how?

The groans of the dying vessel rose in volume and frequency, and Val saw a cloud of bubbles rise past her face in the shifting beam of her dive light. She felt the *Centaur* begin to push down into the top of her head. If she didn't leave it soon, it would drag her to her death when it gasped the final pocket of air trapped in its steel lungs and began its long journey into the abyss.

But how to get out of the sinking ship? With Sturman's boat now above her somewhere, she needed to find it and get on board as fast as possible. If she swam upward against the hull it might provide cover long enough for her to locate the bright lights beaming down from *Maria*. Once she was close to the lights, the lit water itself might provide some measure of protection.

It was time to decide now. Karl was gone. She could try for the surface, knowing it was probably hopeless. Or she could give up and die inside the doomed vessel.

She was gathering herself to move again out of the darkened hatchway when she felt dull vibrations run through the hull. It had come into contact with something on the surface. Then the seiner slowly began to change its position in the water. From its vertical orientation in the water, prow at the surface, it somehow started to slowly right itself in the depths. The lights on the surface grew brighter—or closer? As though pivoting around something up above, the vessel continued a slow-motion swivel for a few minutes until it was nearly upright.

Impossibly, the boat protecting her had somehow stopped sinking.

CHAPTER 56

Sturman rolled off his boat and into the cold water, sinking like a stone as his armor sought the bottom. With no air in his BC and lacking the buoyancy of a wet suit, the heavy shark suit dragged his body under faster than he had ever descended. He wasn't worried about going too deep, because around his waist was a tether that secured him to the skiff.

He plummeted down toward the seiner, which hung from its boom below him. In the bright glow cast by the lights on board *Maria*, he could see the boat's raised cabin and part of the deck through the tangled threat of netting near the surface, but everything faded into black around the sides of the vessel. In the fringes of the light he could also see other things. Moving things, living things, close to his size and clearly at bay only because of the brightness.

As he pushed aside a mass of netting, he realized it offered some degree of protection. The squid moved closer now as he fell farther from the light, drifting shapes several yards away in the water, but they seemed hesitant to approach the netting. Black spots marking their watchful eyes were visible near the mid-points of their tapered bodies, which appeared darkish grey as the dim water absorbed their true reddish color.

Dense water rushed past his face for another few seconds as he avoided the net, the seawater becoming noticeably colder as he moved deeper through a thermocline. The vessel loomed closer, a few large squid darting along its surface, and then he was there.

He slammed into the surface of the seiner with a rasp as the hard chain-mail links at his knees and elbows scraped against the rough metal hull. He released air into his BC vest to achieve some measure of buoyancy as he pulled himself over the deck of the vessel. He had no idea how long *Maria* could keep the enormous boat from sinking, or whether the anchor chain might give.

He kicked along the tilted deck of the vessel toward the raised wheelhouse at the fore end. As he passed a hole in the deck, a blinding beam of light caught a cloud of bubbles as they whooshed past his face. The beam was redirected and he squinted at the dim outline of a diver holding the light. He shined his own dive light toward the diver's face.

Val.

Sturman's heart swelled. Her dark hair flowed around her head, and her eyes met his. She squinted against the brightness of his beam and raised a hand to shield her eyes, and he turned the light away as he grabbed her hand. After nobody else appeared, he understood that she was alone.

The tether at his waist began to tighten. He had allowed nearly all seventy-five feet of the tether to trail him down, wanting to make sure there was enough line to reach Val, and it had been just enough. Until now. He was literally at the end of his rope.

He gestured with his thumb toward the surface. She nodded, but didn't move. She was looking past him, hesitating. Sturman had spent enough time in the mute diving world to recognize what people were thinking based on their expressions. She didn't want to leave the seiner, even though it was sinking. A loud crack resounded from above, and the vessel shuddered.

He jerked another "thumbs-up" in front of her mask. She nodded and slowly emerged from the safety of the hatchway. Sturman squeezed her hand tighter and looked around. He could see the shoal huddled in the darker water, hundreds of squid still darting past at the fringes of the bright light. He added air to his BC and began to kick upward along the length of the boom, dragging Val with him at first until she committed to their ascent and began to rise faster than him, unburdened by the shark suit. He paused, hearing the rumble of a motor—another vessel had to be approaching.

Then the first one attacked.

The squid slammed into Sturman's side. He managed to keep hold of Val's hand, but dropped his dive light with the impact. He pulled her down in front of him and wrapped his armored body around her as more squid joined in the assault. Then they were sinking, as their attackers maneuvered them toward the deep, away from the bright lights above. He forced himself to ignore the squeezing and pulling as the lights faded in intensity and other squid moved in.

A fast-moving one appeared in front of them, filling Sturman's field of view, and hurled its body into Val. He grabbed the mantle of the animal and pushed his thumb into one of its large eyes. The badly scarred creature maintained its grip for several seconds as he crushed the black orb deep into its socket. It finally relented and shot away in a cloud of ink. He could hear the eerie sound of their beaks scratching across the steel armor encasing his sides and legs. There was another booming crack from above. *Maria* would go under soon. The lights would short out, and without them . . .

His heavy armor would not allow him to make an emergency ascent. But Val had a chance to escape before the shoal fully closed on them.

Sturman pulled her body against him in the increasing darkness and reached for her waist. In the fading glow of *Maria*'s lights, he looked into her eyes for an instant and wondered if she knew what he felt for her as he searched her belly for the clip on her weight belt. The plastic clip popped open under his fingers.

As the heavy belt slithered off her body and sank past her fins, he pushed her outstretched hands away as she reached for him, terror in her eyes. She accelerated away from him, unable to fight the powerful lift created by the air in her vest and lungs and wet suit. She was still looking down at him when her silhouette shrank into the bright lights above, and then Sturman was alone in the gloom. He reached for his dive knife. *Let them come, then.*

He felt the press of the closing shoal and swung the blade at his attackers, the tether around his waist tightening as the squid enveloped his body and dragged him deeper.

CHAPTER 57

Val watched Sturman disappear below her, helplessness overtaking her fear as she accelerated up toward the surface. Then the terror returned as she felt something touch her head and slowly wrap around her shoulders. She screamed into her regulator and thrashed her arms at the unseen attacker, but her hands met only folds and piles of rough narrow strands. *The seining net.* She had risen into it, and now it was preventing her from surfacing.

Even with the lights from above closer now, Val couldn't see exactly what was happening. Her view was obstructed by the dark mass of the net intermixed with the blinding glare of the lights. She knew that she was close to the surface because the lights were brighter and she could hear the waves above and feel the swells moving the seawater around her. The shoal should be upon her now, but it was not.

It was the net. Although it kept her from surfacing, clumped around her upper body and scuba tank, it appeared to be protecting her as well. Maybe it was the light, but more likely they were unable to detect her in the net or were unwilling to enter its confining folds.

She thought of Sturman, down there in the blackness with the shoal upon him, but pushed the image from her mind. She couldn't help him unless she could get to the surface and find a way to help from there. At least he had a tether. With enough air and the shark suit protecting him, there was a chance.

She forced herself to calm down and carefully sorted through the folds of netting around her, trying to push it past her so she could maneuver around it and surface. She was close to *Maria*. She could board the vessel from the stern.

As she felt her way through the netting in the darkness, she sensed a gradual change in the fistfuls of loose strands. They were growing tighter. Moments later, they began to tow her away from the lights on the boat above. Away from the surface.

The seiner was finally going down, and taking her with it.

Unable to resist the pull of eighty tons of steel, Val fought the hundreds of strands pressing against her head and shoulders as the *Centaur* began the long descent to the bottom of the ocean.

CHAPTER 58

The one-eyed female darted between two of her sisters for a better grip on the immobilized prey. She powered her way through the smooth, wriggling bodies of the other squid and again found purchase on the creature's body. Wrapping her sinuous arms tightly around it, her beak again met the pliable yet dense outer shell. She scraped against the rough surface, which gleamed in the light like the scales of fish, and sensed the soft flesh underneath.

Around her the shoal was now busily feeding on itself as wounded members pulled away from the struggling prey, which still fought furiously but was gradually slowing. Yielding. The female sensed a growing weakness.

Another large squid jostled against her and she lost her grip on the prey. As she sought another opening, she watched a vulnerable member of her shoal pulse through the water past her, already wounded by the silvery creature. Her heavily scarred sister darted out of the darkness and attacked the wounded animal, wrapping her arms around its middle. The one-eyed female's focus shifted back to the prey. Although the injured in her shoal would make an easier meal, she had become focused on this alien thing.

She would feed on it. This armored thing that would not be brought down, that was somehow suspended from above.

Her aggression spiked and she closed on the prey again. She fired her whips and their tiny teeth tore at a fin on one of her sisters. The other female quickly yielded and darted away from her.

For an instant the one-eyed female saw the thing's gleaming armor part under the tugging of her hungry brothers and sisters, exposing a pale, smooth surface beneath. She oriented her tentacles toward the prey and hurtled forward, forcing her arms into the opening before the outer armor could close over it.

This time her beak found what it was seeking.

She sensed a renewed energy in the creature as her massive beak dug eagerly into warm flesh and blood. The rough edges of her maw scraped alongside the prey's protective bone but continued to dig into the writhing flesh. The taste of blood excited her.

Abruptly she felt something sharp pierce the side of her body, punctuated by the slam of a hard appendage into her organs. The prey was resisting. She only squeezed tighter, burrowing furiously into her assailant's side, as the sharp pain again exploded against her body. The thing struck her again. And again.

Her tentacles loosened, her well-developed but impaired brain less focused on feeding. The sharp object struck her a final time, opening a wide gash in her side. Her eye twisted in its socket and she watched a nest of foreign worms drift out of her body into the black water, wriggling wildly as they found themselves in open water.

One of her sisters rushed in to attack the prey, crashing against her own body, and she finally lost her grip. Something was wrong. As she felt herself rapidly weaken, her urges began to focus on her own survival. Instinct told her to move down. *Darkness. The deep.* That was where she would be safe.

Directing her mantle away from the surface, she tried to force a jet of water out of her siphon. As her mantle squeezed to pressurize the water inside it for propulsion, most of it spurted out of the gaping holes in her body in a cloud of damaged flesh. Her body spun away at an angle, spiraling away from the mob of squid attacking the armored creature.

The prey was forgotten. There was only safety. Safety, and survival.

She tried to swim toward the deep, away from her frenzied siblings and the bright lights, but her body would not respond. Awkwardly, she managed to jet herself sideways, but her body turned again, sending her upward. Each pulse of water she tried to emit from her siphon somehow sent her in the wrong direction.

In the dark water, the female began to notice several members of her shoal hovering nearby. Among them was her badly scarred sister. They were looking at her as she spun aimlessly in the open water. Watching.

Waiting.

She was emitting another pulse of water when the first one struck.

The smaller squid seized the top of her mantle, well away from the dangers of her tentacles and beak. Normally she would have flung off this weaker member of the shoal and devoured it, but she was powerless. The squid ripped at her body, tearing into her. For a moment, her scarred sister hovered close to them as they struggled. Assessing. Then her body bloomed bright red, and she, too, attacked.

The one-eyed female felt her sister's arms wrap around one of her fins. She tried to dig her tentacles into her, into any of the attackers, but her body was failing as her life fluids poured out of her damaged organs. With her remaining eye she watched a smaller sister use her beak and wrenching arms to tear through one of her tentacles before darting off with its prize.

Then the shoal engulfed her.

CHAPTER 59

The seining net pressed down against Val's head, forcing her deeper as it trailed the sinking vessel. Fighting panic, Val grabbed handfuls of the mesh and tried to push it aside, seeking an opening where she could maneuver around the gathered folds and make her way to the surface through open water. She could see almost nothing in the weak beam of the dive light.

Several meters below the surface, Val found the opening she was looking for. But her tank was caught in several strands of the netting, and she had no knife to cut them. There was only one option left. She tore off her BC vest and slid free of the entangled scuba tank, spitting the regulator out of her mouth and kicking through the net. Moments later she broke the surface.

The huge lights shining down from *Maria* forced her to squint as she looked around. Sturman's boat was fifty feet away, farther away than she had imagined— and there was another problem. The boat was listing, the reason obvious to Val in an instant. Sturman had somehow attached his boat to the *Centaur* to prevent it from sinking to the bottom. He had bought time to save her.

Near *Maria* was the skiff from the seiner. Sturman's dog stood with his paws on the edge of it as he barked at two men in a third, unfamiliar boat, this one much closer to her. She kicked hard for the new vessel, which appeared to be a recreational fishing boat. She splashed past the floating red dive flag she had deployed when she and Karl had gone down and reached the side of the boat. She stretched her arms up to two men leaning over the side. They looked at her in disbelief, but reached down anyway.

"Help me! Hurry!"

The two men grabbed her forearms, but before they could haul her out of the water she felt something grasp one of her legs. She cried out as the men tried to haul her out, the weight of something very heavy now clinging to her legs. She saw their eyes widen. One of the men released her wrist and turned away. He reappeared at the side a second later and swung an oar over her head. She heard a loud slap, and the squid released her. Val felt the men's hands slide under her armpits and then the three of them spilled over the gunwale in a drenched heap on the deck of the fishing boat.

Val tried to speak but only managed a loud cough. The men fired questions at her, but she needed a second to process the situation.

"Christ! What the hell was that thing?"

"It's okay, lady. You're safe now."

"We got your SOS. What the hell's going on here, miss? Were you underwater this whole time?"

"Is that your boat? It's sinking."

"Jesus, what happened to your leg?"

She had been rescued by two middle-aged guys in a private fishing boat. They smelled like beer. Several rods rigged for tuna jutted out of holders in the stern. Exhausted, she tried to stand, but her left leg gave and she slipped on the wet wood. She decided to stay on her knees until she could adjust to being out of the water.

She yelled "Will!" and the men quit talking. She coughed, gagging up seawater. After a moment, she caught her breath. "Someone's still down there."

"You're bleeding, lady. I'm going to find the first aid kit."

Val looked at the bloody seawater pooling underneath her on the deck as one of the men ducked into the cabin of the boat. She remembered now that the shoal had attacked her earlier, before she had seen Sturman, and she realized that this was her own blood. As she stared at it, she felt itching in her elbows, a sign that she was going to suffer the effects of the bends from surfacing too quickly. She drew in a deep breath, fighting the faintness creeping over her, and grabbed the hand of the heavyset man still sitting with her on the wet deck.

"Forget about me, please! I'm all right. Listen. There's a man still down there!"

"Down there? Are there more of those squid down there?"

"Yes."

"How were *you* even down there? You don't even have scuba gear on."

"He does, though. Listen to me, dammit. We have to hurry!" She grabbed his arms and shook them, as much to rouse him as keep herself from losing consciousness. "Don't you understand? They're going to *kill* him!"

"What more do you want us to do, lady?"

She heard a loud crack and looked over at *Maria*. The stern of Sturman's boat, the last part of her still above water, was now sliding under. Somehow he had affixed the massive seiner to his own boat so effectively that apparently they would go down together. The lights mounted on *Maria* winked out as she succumbed to the pull of the *Centaur*, and darkness fell over them.

Her mind raced as the other man returned and tore open the boat's first aid kit. When she had last seen Sturman, just as he had released her, his face had disappeared in a swarm of squid. They had covered his body, his face, as the heavy shark suit dragged him down. But he couldn't have sunk farther, because he was tethered to the surface. Tethered to *Maria* . . .

She looked over at the darkened boat, very low and angled steeply in the water. She stopped breathing. His tether, rather than save him, would now drag him to his death.

Sturman's dog suddenly barked from the skiff, twenty feet away, and Val looked over at the small boat. Its stern was much too low in the water. *Of course*. Sturman knew his own boat might go down. His lifeline was attached to the skiff, then—not *Maria*.

"Listen to me! We need to pull alongside that skiff right away. My friend is tethered to it."

The portly man nodded and moved toward the helm. She looked around the boat. There were fishing rods, a gaff and a hand net tucked in the side, a few beer cans, and several ropes coiled on the deck, each running up to a cleat on the gunwale.

"Are there any flares on this boat?"

"What?"

"Any flares? Or waterproof dive lights? Dammit!" She didn't know why she was even asking about the lights. She had no scuba gear and was in no shape to dive down again. She would probably pass out before she could even help him.

The skinny guy wrapped a bandage around her bleeding thigh, right over the neoprene, as his friend put their boat in gear and nosed it toward the skiff. The big man tied the skiff to their boat, then leapt into it. Sturman's dog wagged his tail warily at the stranger, then saw Val and bounded onto the unfamiliar fishing boat and rushed to lick her face.

"We need to pull in the rope running off this boat," she said. "My friend is connected to that line." She stood, and a wave of weakness flooded through her. She again felt as though she might pass out. She blew out a deep breath and fought it, shaking her head, dimly aware Bud was still licking her.

"How much does your friend weigh, lady?" The heavyset man grunted, leaning over to pull in the line. "I can't pull this rope in. There's no way—there's too much weight on the other end. The entire skiff's about to freakin' sink—shit!" The man suddenly fell backward in the skiff, clutching his hand.

The line running down from the skiff had suddenly grown even more taut. It skidded along the edge of the small vessel with an audible twang.

"Will." She whispered his name. She knew it might

already be too late. He had been down deep for some time, but she didn't know how long. He couldn't have much air left. But whether he was alive or not, they had to bring him up.

Val rose unsteadily, took a deep breath, and stepped onto the skiff. She rested her hand on its outboard motor to steady herself, fighting the overwhelming desire to simply crumple and pass out. Then it hit her. They could use simple physics. She looked around for a sturdy fulcrum, and spied the transom of the men's fishing boat. It just might work.

She took another deep breath, braced her feet, and jerked the starter cord on the skiff.

CHAPTER 60

The deep water around Sturman went completely black. So that was it, then. *Maria* had finally gone under.

He knew that his boat wasn't going to keep the much larger vessel from sinking for long, and that she had been doomed as soon as he had affixed her anchor chain to the exposed boom of the seiner. All he could hope for now was that Val had made it safely to the skiff. She would take care of Bud.

The darkness disappeared for an instant as the shoal lit up, its members displaying an internal bioluminescence brought on by their agitation. In the flash of weak greenish light, Sturman saw sets of black eyes, symmetrical rows of suckers, a gnashing beak near his face. Then it was black again.

Even if he couldn't see them anymore, he knew their intentions from the insistent squeezing, scraping, clawing, dragging. Though he was badly bruised from the attack, the shark suit had kept him relatively safe. Only one of the huge beasts had found a way through it in the darkness, parting his chain mail to dig into his side.

Before he could fight it off with his knife, it had done considerable damage to his rib cage. He could feel warm blood seeping out through the wound.

The pressure on Sturman's arm and shoulder surged as the throng of squid pulled downward in unison, and excruciating pain wracked his body. The shoal had already pulled him to the tether's limits, gradually forcing the loop of rope around his waist to rise up his torso and almost to his neck, nearly strangling him. He had managed to free his neck by wrapping the tether around his wrist several times in a momentary slack of the line, but with the tension back on the line now there was no longer any way to free his hand. Not that it mattered. If he lost the tether, he was finished. He would be dragged down a few hundred feet in a matter of minutes without it.

The tension rose again, unrelenting and fast, and he screamed soundlessly into the black water as he felt his shoulder pop out of its socket. Blood mixed with the cold seawater in his mouth. He had bitten into his lips or tongue.

He might have let go of the rope at that moment, if he had been able. But his adrenaline steered him through the pain as his limp left arm stretched out above him, bearing the mass of what felt like a thousand pounds of squid suffocating him in the darkness.

His free right hand was still cramped from clutching the dive knife. He had lost the small weapon when his hand began to curl itself awkwardly into a cramp, and then quit working, no longer able to grip. He knew the titanium blade had found its mark many times, but there were simply too many of them. He used his right hand now to shield his mask and mouthpiece as the squid felt their way along his body, seeking an opening where they could feed.

He felt a huge volume of water swirl past him and he knew that *Maria* was headed past him on her way down. Over the whispery sounds of the squid's chitinous teeth and beaks rasping on his steel armor, he heard loud but muffled pops and groans as his boat succumbed to the sea and moved past him, fading into the depths below.

Good-bye, Maria.

The line grew tighter once more, his torn shoulder ligaments and muscles screaming. He wasn't sure if the squid were pulling him down so much as the line from the boat was pulling him in the opposite direction, but quickly the line became impossibly tight and his wrist twisted and stretched, adding to his agony. He was being torn apart under the weight of the shoal. He thought his arm might actually come off, could tear free of his body, as the line grew even more taut, the mass of squid clinging to him seeming to pull away in unison. He heard more than felt the bones in his wrist crack.

An unexpected calm washed through his body. He felt his muscles relax. He stopped struggling, his fear replaced by acceptance.

As he gradually felt his mind separate from his body, from the pain and fear, he wondered vaguely if what he was experiencing was the same sensation gazelles and other animals knew when they were in the jaws of a predator. When they had no hope of escape. He had read that prey animals sometimes simply died in those situations, before actually receiving a mortal wound.

A memory:

Hiking, in Colorado, with his father. He is twelve. They have come across a rare scene. They sit beneath a ponderosa pine, hidden by a low scrub of oak brush. They are silently watching a coyote kill a fawn. The fawn is simply lying there, panting, not resisting. There had been a brief chase and struggle, but now it almost looks as though the coyote is cradling its prey on the ground, the warm fawn comfortable, yielding to death.

A moment passes. The coyote looks down at the fawn and digs its teeth in, shaking the animal by its belly. It disembowels the silent fawn, and begins to eat it.

No.

He would die now. But that was not how he would die.

He let go of his mask and clawed along one of the squid with taut fingers, feeling for its eyes. He dug a thick thumb into the firm orb of an eye socket, and thought he felt the squid release him. Another took its place. He seized one of its arms in his hand and twisted, wrenching at it, seeking its eyes also.

The tether pulled at him again, jerking, and he had the sensation of moving upward. Or was he moving at all? Losing consciousness, he reacted slowly as a squid wrenched the dive mask from his face, cold water rushing into his nostrils. Another tentacle tore the regulator away from his mouth, and the shoal dissipated momentarily in the resulting cloud of bubbles. He fumbled for the regulator with his free hand, but it was pointless. They were now pressing against his face, his head. The air hose was gone. His lungs began to burn.

He held his breath as long as he could, exhaling slowly, feeling his arm stretching grotesquely even farther from his body as the shoal refused to relinquish their meal. He grabbed at another squid in the darkness, but his middle finger ended up in its beak and he sensed it being gnawed off. Another of the animals found its way through the chain mail, and there was a separate sharp pain on his lower back as it tore into him. He pushed at the soft bodies ineffectively with his free hand. It didn't matter now.

His mind wandered, and he fought to focus on a final prayer. He thought of his father. His boyhood home. Maria. Val.

The urge to inhale became overwhelming. In the last seconds of delirium, the dark world seemed to grow suddenly very bright. His eyes widened in the reassuring brightness.

He inhaled.

As the cold water entered his lungs, he coughed, then inhaled again. He arched his back at the sudden, overwhelming burning in his chest, and his body went into shock. He had the calming sensation that suddenly the shoal released him, and that he was alone.

But just as he lost consciousness, he was not.

He saw Maria's face. Then he knew nothing more.

PART IV
EXTINCTION

CHAPTER 61

Val walked out the glass front doors of the mortuary, wiping her eyes. The pain and grief of saying good-bye had been accompanied by guilt. She was still alive.

Visiting him one last time in the mortuary wasn't what she wanted. The funeral would be held in two days, back in San Diego, but she needed to say good-bye alone. She couldn't do it in front of others, least of all at a memorial.

"Are you gonna be all right, Dr. Martell?" His friend, Mike Phan, was already standing outside the building, hands in the pockets of his slacks. He had left his family for a few days to come up to Long Beach and help out with the complications of sorting through the chaos. Mike had also helped law enforcement retrieve the bodies of the dead men while Val was treated in the hospital for a mild case of decompression sickness and the tissue damage inflicted by the shoal. They had searched long and hard and found the badly muti-lated corpses of the captain and Tomás, but they still hadn't found Karl Nikkola's body. Val knew they probably never would. His oceangoing family would at least be happy to know he died at sea.

She and Mike stood on the grass outside the brick building. The mortuary's landscaped entrance featured a lush lawn and flowering vines creeping up a small, gurgling fountain.

After a deep breath, she smiled at him. "Yeah. I'm all right. How are you?"

"I'm okay. I really want to get back to my family, though. Losing someone makes you realize what you've got."

Mike didn't look okay. He looked tired, as she was. The poor guy had probably been awake for most of the past forty-eight hours. He had been selfless and thoughtful to come help out with the search activities and still comfort and keep Val involved. She had only met him once before.

"Go home, Mike. You've done your friend a great service. Really. You've done so much already."

"I feel bad about not going with you."

"It's fine. I'll call you back in San Diego."

Val kissed him on the cheek and then walked down the steps to the parking lot, not looking back. Mike didn't say anything else.

Bud was waiting for her in the rental car. The short-haired mutt whined and licked her face as she got in the driver's seat and started the blue compact. It was a beautiful, sunny day, the Pacific alive with smooth, even sets of waves rolling in from the far side of the world. She drove down the coast, looking out at the ocean stretching to the horizon. Bud hung his head out the window, now blissfully unaware of all that had happened even though he had experienced it. *Oh, to be a dog.*

This wasn't the ocean's fault. She was surprised that she felt angry looking at it. She wanted to be angry with the shoal, with nature—with *something*. But as a scientist, she couldn't. She knew that Humboldt squid, like sharks or African lions, were no more evil than cold viruses or hurricanes. They were merely filling their roles. They just *were*.

She would move beyond this.

She thought of her specimens back in the lab. There was still much to learn from this situation. By understanding why everything about this shoal had been so atypical of Humboldt squid, perhaps she could avert deaths in the future. If the marine worms infesting the shoal did indeed represent a new species, maybe she'd name it after him. She smiled. Who'd want a parasitic marine worm named after them, though, besides her? Maybe Karl. She smiled and wiped away a tear as another wave of emotion passed over her. Yes. She could name the new species of worm after him instead.

When she reached her destination, she parked in front of the huge, modern-looking hospital and smiled. She normally hated hospitals, but not today. She clipped a leash onto Bud's collar and they headed inside, where she lied to the elderly receptionist that he was her service dog and hurried past before the woman could respond.

When she entered the hospital room he was asleep. She smiled at the new cowboy hat Mike had hung next to the bed.

Sturman was asleep. He looked peaceful, and surprisingly well. He was healing. His face only had a few stitches, but his neck was swollen and badly bruised. Apparently his arm had been broken in six places. He had a dislocated shoulder, a punctured lung, one missing finger, and a host of other minor injuries. Sturman had also gotten a minor case of the bends. Thankfully, he had been mostly unconscious since they had dragged him out of the water, clinically dead, two nights ago. By some miracle, her CPR had brought him back on the deck of the fishing boat. Once onshore, he had spent the first ten hours in a decompression chamber, attended by a doctor.

She looked at the bandages on his shoulder and felt a little guilty. It had been a real tug-of-war once they had employed the power of the skiff's outboard motor. But they hadn't really had a choice. They knew he was almost out of air, and the shoal was simply too strong for her and the two fishermen to pull him to the surface. So they manipulated the rope over the transom of the fishing boat and then used the skiff to start a slow, steady pull, with Sturman's tether bending ninety degrees as it ran over the curved edge of the transom. The whole time Val had prayed the rope wouldn't snap from the friction. But it had worked.

When Val had reached into the water to grasp Sturman's limp body as it appeared just a few feet below the surface, he had been dead, his lungs full of water. He had drowned. But he was still alive now. The doctors had said it was only because of her persistence at chest compressions and breathing air back into his lungs.

So many things had somehow worked out. If the

other boat hadn't arrived when it did, if the tether hadn't held, if her CPR hadn't been successful . . .

But he was alive.

She slid a chair next to the bed and sat down. His eyes opened.

"I think the guy you're looking for is in the next room." His voice was a hoarse whisper. He would have trouble speaking for several days, since his inflamed lungs had been full of seawater. He coughed a little, wincing.

"Hi there, sleepyhead." She smiled and put a warm hand on his stubbly head. "You're kind of cute without your cowboy hat."

He managed a weak smile. "Your squid thought so, too. Like a bunch of groupies."

Val laughed. "How are you feeling, cowboy?"

"I'm alive."

She smiled and moved to sit on the bed next to him. She squeezed his good hand. "I'm glad."

"Did you see Joe?"

Val swallowed, nodding. "Yes. I said good-bye to him. Mike said the funeral is going to be a closed casket, with a memorial, but I don't want to be some stranger around all his friends and family. I said good-bye from both of us, just in case you can't make it."

"Bullshit. I'll be there. You should come, too." Sturman coughed, then spoke in a whisper. "He would have wanted you there."

"Let me think about it. Will . . . he'd be happy to know that you're alive. Remember that. Live for him."

Sturman reached his good arm up and touched her face. "I owe you my life, Val."

"No more than I owe you mine."

"I mean it."

"Thank the shoal. If it hadn't shown you some mercy, you wouldn't be here now."

Val remembered how the weight at the end of Sturman's line had suddenly disappeared, just when the tug-of-war was threatening to tear the man apart. For some reason, the shoal had released him. She still couldn't understand why the squid would have let him go.

"Only thing I remember is seeing a face—your face—as I lost consciousness. Funny . . ." He looked away and swallowed hard. "I remember thinking at the time it was Maria."

Val gently squeezed his hand. "Maybe it was."

CHAPTER 62

In late September, the squid began to wash up on the beaches north of Los Angeles, after most of the tourists had left for the season.

Sturman woke Val one morning in their motel room by softly shaking the Sunday paper in front of her. She rubbed the sleep from her eyes, squinting at the newsprint in her face. She read the headline:

'Sea monsters' wash up
On Santa Barbara beaches

The shoal had more or less disappeared after their last dramatic encounter and Sturman's time in the hospital. There hadn't been any more attacks on people, and the Weston Institute had been unable to locate the shoal when a new set of researchers headed back out after their ordeal with a Fathometer like Karl's.

In the rented motel room, Val and Sturman made love and then threw some clothing and gear into a few duffels and went shopping. They bought two large plastic coolers, a few boxes of garbage bags, several bags of ice, and some tarps, and headed north to Santa Barbara in a rented SUV. They spent most of the day cruising up the Southern California Bight from San Diego in the light weekend traffic. The early-fall weather was warm and pleasant, an onshore breeze blowing through the windows of the vehicle.

Val had stayed with Sturman and his dog in the San Diego motel for the past month, tending to his wounds. With three of them in the small unit, the conditions were cramped. None of them minded, though—least of all Bud, who seemed especially fond of his new friend.

She had expected that such close-quarters interaction might result in some friction, but the time they had spent on his boat in the weeks before had apparently paid off. And Sturman made his feelings for her clear. She couldn't remember being so happy.

He had been pretty useless since he left the hospital, unable to work and struggling with the cast on his arm and shoulder sling. It didn't really matter anyway, though, since he had lost both his home and business when *Maria* went down.

Val took care of him each night and morning, helping with chores and his bathing. She had spent most of the daylight hours in the lab examining the Humboldt specimens or working on her new paper—a case study detailing the shoal's parasitic hosts. Her schedule and his lack of one had left Sturman a lot of time to think. He went for walks. He said he thought a lot about Joe. He didn't drink, and he had almost completely given up smoking.

True to his word, he hadn't missed Joe's funeral, and

Val had joined him. He had already visited his friend's grave regularly as he healed, and visited his family often. Val could tell that his guilt was slowly subsiding. His other guilt seemed to subside as well. He had even told her he knew Maria and Joe would both be happy for them.

They reached the beach described in the newspaper just before sunset. The breeze smelled of seaweed and rotting fish, and there were several groups of curious observers who had probably also seen the article about the dying squid. Val realized they should have left Bud in the car as they approached the largest squid on the beach and the dog rushed up to investigate, ignoring Sturman's shouts. The huge squid helplessly flopped its fins on the sand just above the surf line. Sturman yelled at Bud again, just before he could lick the dying animal's mantle, and he sat down a few feet away and looked at it.

"Dumb bastard never learns," he said.

"They say a dog takes after its owner. . . ." She smiled at him.

They stopped next to Bud, and Val set down the large cooler she had been carrying. Perhaps the squid was harmless now, but after what they'd been through, they weren't taking any chances.

"Look at this old fighter. I almost feel sorry for her." Sturman poked at the huge, flattened squid with the toe of his shoe. The badly scarred animal, which was missing an arm and the tip of one fin, didn't seem to feel the touch. It was clearly dying.

Val figured the massive specimen, maybe eight feet long, had to be a female. "Yeah, I know what you mean. They look so pathetic out of the water, don't they?"

Sturman pointed at the other squid drying out on the sand, which were spread over hundreds of yards down the beach. Gulls screamed as they fought over the rotting flesh. "You think these are all from our shoal, Doc?"

"I don't know. But they're incredibly large for Humboldt squid, aren't they?"

"Beats me. I guess I've never seen a small one." He grinned.

"By their size, I'd say they certainly could be from the shoal we encountered."

Val snapped a photo of the reddish animal at her feet. Its eye rolled slowly in the socket, its arms turning slightly on the wet sand as a wave rolled up the beach high enough to wet the doomed animal's flesh. Its arms tensed and reached toward her convulsively. She felt an unexpected twinge of fear, and fought the urge to step back.

Sturman put his hand on her shoulder. "It's okay, Val. This one's pretty damn big, but it isn't going to hurt you."

"Right." She took a deep breath. "Once we get a few back to the lab, I'll see if they're infested with the same parasite as the others. We'll probably never know for sure if this is the same group, though."

"It doesn't really matter, does it?"

"No. I guess not." Val patted the cooler. "Well, it was pointless bringing this."

"I won't say I told you so." He began to unfold a tarp on the sand. "Maybe we can drag her back on this."

"You think she'll keep until we can get her on ice?"

"Probably. So it's female, huh? I still have no idea how you can tell if they're boys or girls."

"Takes practice. Give me a hand, cowboy."

"She's not even dead yet."

"Close enough."

Sturman lifted his left arm and moved it around a bit. It was healing nicely. "Yeah, I think my arm's workable." He knelt by her. "Hey, Val . . . why do you think they're dying now?"

"Might be the parasites, but it's probably just old age. Humboldt squid don't live long after maturity, you know. Mere months."

"Candles in the wind, huh?"

"You could say that. It's their time now."

"If they don't live that long, maybe they're not as big a threat as everyone thinks."

Val realized that he, like everyone else, probably didn't grasp where the oceans were headed. "There will be more, Will. A lot more."

"More than there should be?"

Val shrugged. "How many should there be? There are certainly fewer sharks and whales than there were before people came along. And more Humboldt squid."

He looked away from her toward the distorted orange sun setting over the water. She followed his gaze, neither of them speaking as they got lost in the moment.

Despite the vastness of the ocean, and its seeming ability to shrug off the destructive actions of mankind, it was changing. Val looked out at the sea, where four powerboats belched exhaust as they cruised noisily down the coastline. She looked at an oil platform several miles offshore, solidly built on top of the seabed. She looked at the trash amassed at the high-tide line just above them—water bottles, cigarette butts, Styrofoam bits. She could do her part, and that was all.

She looked back at the man in the cowboy hat.

"Let's get to work, partner."

EPILOGUE

Many fathoms below the turmoil on the surface of the ocean, it was calm. Silence dominated.

A storm had just moved in from across the Pacific, and where air met sea the waves slammed mightily against one another as they fought to establish order. Their efforts would eventually yield a rhythmic series of swells from the chaotic input of energy, but only after a fierce battle. Farther down the water column, the energy of the storm steadily dissipated, until in the dim light a few hundred feet below the surface, there was no indication that there was any storm at all. There, the pelagic world was tranquil, quiet. Seemingly empty.

But in the sluggish, steady current of the ocean's cool womb, it was not empty. There was life.

There, they drifted.

To most creatures, even those designed to live and hunt in the open ocean, they were invisible. For not only were they miniscule, they were also transparent, with bodies composed almost entirely of the water that surrounded them. Only when they rarely happened upon shallower waters to be struck by direct sunlight could even their gossamer outer skins and solid structures be detected.

For now, they were small. They had come into being and dispersed across the open ocean only recently. Their primitive nervous systems, larger structures, and deadly stinging cells would not fully develop for some time. For now, they were just beginning to attempt the aimless, rhythmic pulsations that pushed them blindly through the water in no apparent direction, as they lacked the ability to see. Most of them would not survive.

But others would.

They were countless in number, millions upon millions.

Billions.

They had survived almost since the dawn of time, but would soon thrive in a way their kind never had, with few predators and less competition than in any point in history. But they would not relish this victory. They could not process any thoughts without a true brain. They simply existed.

So they would grow, slowly, as they fed on passing food. They would mature. The ocean currents would gather them in their indifference into a massive horde. They would drift into prey.

They would immobilize it.

And then, on their living prey, they would feed.

ACKNOWLEDGMENTS

Publishing a novel, from the idea phase until it hits the shelves, is not possible without the efforts and advice of many. The author's gratitude goes out to the following wonderful people:

To my wife, April, thank you for your endless patience and for putting up with me during my mental absences.

To my brother, Matt, thank you for your creativity and keen eye for detail.

To KT, thank you for making me believe in my work.

To my mom, thank you for your support and faith.

To cousins Terry and John, thank you for the legal advice.

To my editor, Gary Goldstein, thank you for bringing in all the right people and swinging for the fence—and for enjoying the manuscript in the first place.

To the copyeditors, cover artists, sales staff, and all the professionals at Kensington Books involved in this process, thank you for making my dream a reality and giving this book a supreme shot at success.

And to my agent, Jim Donovan, thank you for taking a chance on a new author and showing him the publishing ropes.